Sheila Adams was born
University. She has two
Stockport with her husbanc

Set in Hull, this light-hearted, sexy crime novel is the third
book in the 'Rachel Hodges' series, featuring the
adventures of Rach, a calamity-prone private detective
and her fiancé, police inspector, Steve Rose.

Previous books in the series:
'Red Stiletto'
'Black Velvet'

Also by Sheila Adams:
'Deadly Deception', a Young Adult science fiction mystery.

Acknowledgements

I wish to thank Dave, Jenni and David once again for their constant encouragement, help with editing and for their belief in me as an author.

I should also like to thank the 'Hornsea Pottery Collectors' and Research Society' members for allowing me to use the society's name in this book.

GREEN SILK

Sheila Adams

BB

First published in 2018 by Bredbury Books
Stockport, Cheshire

Printed and bound in Great Britain by Deanprint Ltd,
Stockport, Cheshire

Typesetting by Dave Uttley.
Cover design by Sheila Adams and Dave Uttley
Cover photo by Lesley Lomas

ISBN 978-0-9564183-3-3

www.bredburybooks.co.uk

For Dave, Jenni and David with much love

I was eighteen when my world fell apart.
Then I discovered it had never even been my world.

CHAPTER 1

I woke in a hospital bed, with no idea what had happened or how I'd got there. I felt a sharp pain as I tried to sit up and realised that my ribs were tightly bandaged. Carefully I moved my arms and legs, wiggled my toes and fingers. I was hurt but not too badly.

Gradually it came back to me. I remembered sitting in the back of Dad's car listening to music on Emma's iPod, gazing out of the side window, dreaming of a scary but exciting future. I can't have heard the initial impact, but when the headphones dislodged I was aware of loud crunching noises, then a massive jolt, and that was all.

If I'd been looking towards the windscreen, would I have seen it coming? Would I have been conscious of their hands meeting, clinging to each other for comfort? Their eyes wide with horror as they realised the consequences of Dad's actions? I'll never know.

In the days that followed, I woke every day to the guilt of knowing that if I hadn't insisted on leaving the cosy enclosed world of the farm to study at university, then they would've still been alive. Dad may have been the one who lost concentration, but I had been ultimately responsible, and I hated myself for it. The police said it was lucky that the road had been quiet at that time of the day; that no-one else had been hurt.

As I lay in the hospital bed, I had never felt more utterly

1

alone. Mam and Dad had been my world. I thought there'd once been mention of a couple of distant relatives, but as far as I can remember, I'd never met any. The farm is five miles from the nearest small village, itself isolated in the depths of Lincolnshire. I have friends, of course, but because of the isolation, I rarely see them outside school. That was why I was so determined to leave home, despite all the opposition from Mam and Dad.

They brought me up in a tiny cocoon, highly protective, determined to shield me from the outside world and all its problems, its evil. I can hear them now. I can't shut them out, however much I try.

But I loved books and music. No-one could understand where my ear for music came from. Mam and Dad never listened to any. We had no TV, no stereo, only a radio, constantly tuned to the local channel. As I grew older, I asked for a radio of my own for my birthday, but that wish was never granted. Books, though. I had plenty of books and I immersed myself in their world.

Turning seventeen, I asked for driving lessons, saying I'd work to pay for them when given the usual answer that money was tight. But all I got was, they needed me on the farm, and it was too far into the village to get to a Saturday job, even if there was any work going. And the overriding objection - what was the point in driving lessons when I would never be able to buy a car? It was a vicious circle. Without transport, no job. Without a job, no transport.

My best friend from school is Emma. She lives in Boston, so I hardly used to see her outside school, but she learned to drive in her mam's car and I swear if she'd had the time to come out to the farm before starting her job in a baker's shop, she would've given me a lift. But Boston is fifteen miles away. It's a small, fairly sleepy market town, I know that now. But back then, it was the equivalent of a bustling metropolis for me.

I loved my parents, of course I did, but as I grew older I felt more at odds with them, more eager to fly the nest. I might never have done it. Maybe I would have stayed on the farm until they

died of old age and only then discovered the truth, but I was
saved by my teacher, Mrs Charlesworth.

But I'm getting ahead of myself. I want you to hear the few
important details of my life that I remember, to give you the best
chance possible to help me. So I'll start with my earliest
memories. The first thing I can be sure of, was feeding the geese
with Mam, and crying because they nipped me on the leg.

I paused for a minute, trying to imagine how I would feel if I
were Kate. I'd been brought up in a loving family and although I
didn't see as much of them since I'd moved in with Steve, I was
still close to my parents and sister and knew they were always
there for me.

I found it hard to imagine the loneliness. How did this Kate
cope without TV, always out of the loop when school friends
gathered to discuss the latest programmes? And no going round
to spend time with her mates, listening to music and gossiping? I
couldn't imagine not living in a city, browsing the shops, seeing
the latest films at the cinema. It would've driven me crazy.

- - - - - - - - - - - - - - - - - - - -

'How's it going, Rach?' Steve had asked the previous
evening when he got in from Hull Central police station in
Queens Gardens. He'd only just been back at work a week and
already he was working late, even if it was just an hour. Despite
being shot in the shoulder in Amsterdam a few months
previously, when he was caught up in one of my escapades, he'd
been itching to get back.

'I've been curled up with a book most of the day, to be
honest. There doesn't seem to be any need for a private detective
in Hull at the moment.'

'That's just where you're wrong. As it happens, I have a case
for you.'

'You have? You never give me cases. What's it about?'

'How far do you think you can get in the world without

having a birth certificate?'

'I'm not sure. Everything's on computer these days. I reckon you only need it to get a passport, and you can get a replacement, if you lose it.'

'That's just the thing. This girl, she can't do that. As far as the world's concerned, she doesn't exist. Geoff in Road Traffic gave me the details. About six weeks ago, while I was on sick leave, a car went off the road and hit a concrete bridge support on the A63 coming into Hull. The driver and front passenger were killed outright, but the girl in the back seat, their daughter, she survived and was lucky not to be badly hurt - just broken ribs and concussion. Amazingly, there was no other vehicle involved. The car had no mechanical failure, and the driver died of his injuries in the crash, not a heart attack or anything that could have caused him to lose control.'

'And...'

'Well, obviously I wondered why Geoff was bringing it to an inspector in Serious Crimes. He seemed to think he should run it by me in case it was suicide and murder, as the bloke could have driven into the concrete pillar on purpose. I thought things were bleak enough for the girl without that possibility hanging over her, and nothing would be gained by prosecuting a dead man, so told him to put it down as accidental. The bloke could have just nodded off or got distracted, after all.'

'That was kind of you.'

'Yeah, well, I'm like that, and it would have meant a pile of paperwork for nothing. Anyway, to cut a long story short, the girl, Kate, came round in hospital and confirmed the couple were her parents, but it turned out there was no record of her birth. We did a routine check before we let it go, in case she'd been abducted or was an illegal worker or slave or whatever. We have to be so careful these days. Her school confirmed everything, so that satisfied us she wasn't in the car against her will.'

'Fair enough, but where do I come in?'

'Well, this Kate's just sat her 'A' levels and one of her

4

teachers is willing to take her under her wing until she gets her results and goes to university. Lovely lady, Mrs Charlesworth. Her children have left home and she's happy to look after Kate and have her in the holidays until she gets a life of her own. Social Services have sorted out a temporary National Insurance number for her, but as she's eighteen, they seem reluctant to get involved otherwise. However, she'll need to prove who she is to sort out her dad's farm.'

'Farm? She's not from Hull, then?'

'No. her parents were driving her up from Lincolnshire to look round the university. Anyway, I told Kate you might be able to help her. I feel so sorry for her, Rach. She's lost her parents, been injured herself, and then finds out she can't prove who she is.'

'Poor kid. Of course I don't mind helping. Has anyone tried looking in the registration records for name variations or on the dates just before or after her birthday?'

'We haven't got anyone to spare at the moment, and I was kind of hoping you would do that. What I have got is some notes that Kate's written, to try and make some sense of who she is, and to give to anyone who might be able to help her. I brought it home on this memory stick, hoping you might be able to read it before you got in touch with her. I wouldn't ask normally, as I doubt she has money to pay your fees, but …'

'I know what you're going to say, "… with the insurance reward on the stolen paintings". Yes, I can afford to work for free for quite a while.' A year or more, to be honest, I thought to myself. My last big case had been very lucrative indeed.

'Well it sounded like an interesting job, and one where even you can't get into trouble for once.'

Steve never stopped fretting about my work as a private detective. You'd think that, as a police inspector himself, my record for solving cases connected to 'real' police work would make him thrilled with my career choice. But he wasn't. Somehow, the memories of his fiancée being abducted by a serial killer, and more recently being shot at by armed smugglers, couldn't be wiped out by the success I'd had in solving the cases. It wasn't as if I set out to tackle major crimes. Most of my cases were of the humdrum, trivial variety. But Steve was right about one thing. For all my best intentions, I did keep getting sucked into trouble.

'No need to give it the hard sell. I'll do it. Now tea's ready. Shall we?'

We ate one of my hastily assembled meals. Ready-made chicken pie, peas and broccoli cooked from the freezer, with a handful of quickly-peeled and boiled potatoes. Steve's accepted I'm not cut out to prepare beautiful meals from scratch. He's just happy to eat something filling that's reasonably healthy. If he wants something more elaborate, we eat out.

After we'd finished, he came up close behind me as I was washing up. He reached round and cupped my breasts. I splashed him with suds and he retaliated and wet the front of my blouse. Gran might disapprove of my living with Steve, but she wouldn't want me to catch a cold from wearing wet clothes, so I had no choice. I let Steve unfasten the buttons and remove my blouse.

It was quite a bit later when I insisted Steve finish the washing-up and make a cup of tea before we watched the news and went to bed. I honestly don't know where the evenings go when Steve's at home…

CHAPTER 2

The next morning, free from distractions and with a cup of tea by my side, I settled in front of my laptop and read. The initial part was heart-breaking to read, and I had to fortify myself with chocolate biscuits and more tea before carrying on.

I haven't many memories of the time before I started school. We never took holidays, even when I was older, and rarely went out in the car, except to Boston for clothes, food and other essentials. But I didn't know any other life I suppose, and I was certainly happy on the farm, trailing after Mam, watching her cook, and sitting on her knee as she read me stories. I can't remember being scolded, except when I got near the tractor or baling machine - and that was just to make sure I didn't get hurt.

Mam and Dad never seemed to argue. He'd come in, hot and tired from working, and she'd put her arms round him and give him a kiss. He'd ruffle my hair, give me a hug and ask me what I'd been doing, and I'd ask him for a story, and after he'd washed, he'd sit down with a cup of strong tea and read, while Mam finished cooking the tea.

I did well at school. Mam had taught me to read and write before I started. There were no children to play with after school. Our farm was down a track off the narrow lane that ran along the side of a 'drain', one of the many dykes criss-crossing the flat landscape to drain water from the rich farming land. As I grew, I asked if I could have a brother or sister, but Mam just smiled and said she was too old.

Other children were always talking about what they'd seen on television, and naturally I wanted to know why we didn't have a TV, but Dad just said we didn't need one. Every now and again he'd come in with books, and when I had my head in a book, I forgot about television. We never seemed to have much money, or at least Dad never had much to spend. I think he picked up the books from a charity shop in Louth when he went to the auction there. I brought home plenty from the school library. There was a bus from the primary school that went along all the lanes, picking up and dropping off the few children from the farms at the end of the tracks. I had to get up really early to catch it, but it meant I didn't have too far to walk with my haul of books.

When we had to write about our family, I made my piece longer by writing about the animals on the farm. I never met any aunties or uncles or cousins, and if I was ever told anything about any distant family, I can't remember. That's why, when I learnt Mam and Dad were dead, I felt I had no-one left in the world.

Every September I invented some holiday we'd been on, conjured up out of stories I'd read about holidays at the seaside. Mam hated the seaside and that's why we never went. Dad had explained to me once that it brought back terrible memories for her, and I shouldn't ever mention going, so I didn't. I loved Mam and wouldn't do anything to upset her.

When I got to secondary school, Dad ran me to the bus stop on the main road every day and I walked home from there after school, as he was too busy to come out and Mam didn't drive. It was a long way but I got used to it. When it rained, an umbrella wasn't much use as the wind could blow the rain sideways, but even so, I stuck to my promise to Dad. I never got a lift from one of the solitary cars or vans that passed. I knew Dad wouldn't punish me if I broke my word to him. He just looked at me with such disappointment if I did anything wrong, and that sense of letting him down stopped me from breaking his rules. I loved my dad as much as Mam, and would never hurt him.

There came a day when Mam and Dad were finally persuaded by Mrs Charlesworth, my form teacher, that I needed *a computer for school work. She managed to get me one cheap, someone else's second-hand model. We had no internet connection out at the farm, but at least I was able to write essays and take them in on a USB stick to print out. I'm not sure Mam and Dad really understood about the internet, that you could look up so many things and learn far more than from television, but I only got to use it in my lunch break until I got into the sixth form and stayed after school sometimes. Mrs Charlesworth would run me back home. I could tell Mam and Dad weren't happy about it, but I didn't know why and they didn't say anything.*

It was Mrs Charlesworth who finally talked them into letting me go to university. I was good at all subjects, but particularly at Maths, English, Music and the one I enjoyed the most, German. I was told I had an ear for languages. I loved music, and Mam promised me a guitar if I stayed at home and worked on the farm, but I had other ideas. At seventeen, I wanted to leave the narrow confines of my home, and that desire was finally stronger than that of not wanting to hurt my parents. It took months of wearing them down, and I'd hear them talking in whispers after I went to bed but eventually, when I'd accepted a conditional offer to study German, they agreed to take me to an open day at Hull so we could see what it would be like.

The day started badly. You'd have thought they were taking me to the airport to fly to Australia, rather than seventy or so miles just to look at a university. Mam was crying in the kitchen when I got up, and Dad was quiet. I remember now that they both hugged me before we got in the car, and I thought that was strange, but Emma had lent me her old iPod so I could listen to it on the journey, and before long I'd shut out the world and forgotten about Mam and Dad's behaviour. When I look back, it seems cruel of me, but even usually obedient teenagers like me can be selfish.

Then came the crash. When I was well enough to go home, Mrs Charlesworth came for me and let me stay with her and her husband. She said I could call her by her first name, Grace, but she's still my teacher and I find it hard. We drove over to the farm. One of the neighbouring farmers has taken over the animals and a few of the neighbours are helping as best they can to keep the farm going, but it's obvious it will have to go up for sale. After getting through the horrendous double funeral I immersed myself again in studying for my 'A' levels. People don't expect me to do well, but I don't want to let Mam and Dad down by going to pieces, and in any case it's the only way I know of blanking out that last day, and the guilt I've felt ever since - that it was somehow my fault that they died, because they hadn't wanted to go to Hull.

The police investigated the crash, but could find nothing wrong with the car or the road conditions, and there was no evidence of any other vehicle being involved. They worked out somehow that Dad hadn't been driving too fast, and there were no skid marks, no sign that he'd braked sharply at the end. So the coroner ruled that Mam and Dad's deaths had been the result of a tragic accident, with Dad temporarily distracted, perhaps by a wasp flying into the car, or a bright reflection, and that there was no other explanation for the crash. On the way out of court, I overheard the police sergeant tell Mrs Charlesworth that it had been 'almost as if Mr Willis had turned the wheel and driven off the road on purpose', but she dismissed that idea, telling him how much my parents had loved me.

It's been devastating to learn that there's nothing to confirm I am who I think I am; that I don't have a birth certificate to say I am Katherine Willis. But I've settled into my new life with the Charlesworths, I'm about to take my 'A' levels and am determined to get the grades needed to go to Hull University. I didn't apply to any other universities, as I want to stay within a reasonable distance of the farm, Mr and Mrs Charlesworth, and places I know well.

I'm very lucky that they won't accept any money for my meals or for looking after me. Their children left home several years ago, and I think they enjoy having someone else around the house again. After my 'A' levels, I plan to help on another farm for a bit of cash to support myself over the summer. With a student loan I reckon I can manage until things are sorted, survive financially by borrowing like every other student in the country, and that Grace and Jack, as they would like me to call them, will make a home for me in the holidays as long as I need them to. I'm not used to spending money on myself anyway. The difficulty is, I can't sell the farm unless I can prove who I am, so it's going to be hard to move on.

Social Services have issued me with a birth certificate to enable me to go to university, just as if I was a 'foundling', an abandoned baby who was never identified. My date of birth is given as 29th March 1998, which is the date I was brought up to celebrate as my birthday, my name was given as Katherine Willis, my parents as 'unknown' and Boston as place of birth as that's where the social security office is. That really hurt. Mam and Dad were my parents. They weren't unknown.

I know I can make a future for myself, but I want to know my past. I need to know who I really am. Maybe it's just a mistake in registering my birth, but I keep feeling as if it's more than that. I've read stories of children abandoned in carrier bags, and how they never gave up hope, but ultimately many of them never found out who they were. I don't want to end up like them.

After I'd finished reading, I knew I had to speak to Kate. She'd put her mobile number at the end, so I texted her and asked if there was a convenient time I could ring her, possibly at lunchtime, as I wanted to get started as soon as possible. I didn't want to duplicate anything she might have done since she wrote her notes. I went out for a walk along the marina. It was a warm, sunny day and I felt incredibly lucky to have my own supportive family close at hand.

When I rang just after twelve thirty, I introduced myself as a friend of the police inspector who'd looked into the accident and told her how sorry I was that her parents had died. Then I mentioned that I was a private detective and that Steve, or Inspector Rose, to give him his proper title, had passed her memory stick to me. I asked if she'd done anything since she'd given it to the police in Hull.

'Once I was out of hospital, the Charlesworths helped me arrange my parents' funerals, then I concentrated on my 'A' level exams. After they were over, I knew I had to do something about the farm. I searched the house from top to bottom looking for a will. When I couldn't find one, I contacted Dad's bank to see if he'd had a safety deposit box, but drew a blank.'

'Next, I went to the solicitor Dad had used in a boundary dispute. He told me that because there were no wills, I would have to apply for probate and a grant of representation to access my parents' bank accounts. But to do that, I need proof of identity. Obviously, I don't have a driving licence or passport, never mind the birth certificate.'

'Oh, that's a pain, Kate.'

'I know. Stupidly I hoped maybe someone had slipped up at the police station, so I applied for a copy birth certificate. When there was no record of a Kate Willis, Katherine or even Catherine with a C born on 29th March 1998, I was stunned. I tried again for the 30th just in case Dad had gone the following day and there'd been an error recording it, but still without success. I don't know what to do. I can't keep going back with different dates. I also wondered if my name had been recorded incorrectly, but I don't see how I could ask for a record of everyone born on that day.'

I made a few notes, making sure I got her birthday right, before asking, 'Have you done anything else?'

'I've not had much time because I've been working since my exams. I thought of The Salvation Army, but their website says they only search for 'known living relatives, for whom a birth certificate exists.'

'Mmm.., that's true, unfortunately', I confirmed. 'They can't even search adoption records, and they definitely don't help with searches for estate or other legal purposes.'

'I don't know whether you'll be able to do any more than the solicitor, but he quoted an astronomical amount to look into it, and said it might take months or even years, even if he does get anywhere. I don't want to take up too much of your time, and I don't have much money to spare...' Her voice petered out. She was near to tears.

'Look, I don't want you to worry about the cost. It won't be much, and I have contacts a local solicitor doesn't. Let's say fifty pounds, and you only pay if I find something. Can you manage that?' I felt she wouldn't have accepted if I'd said I'd do it for free, but even if I did find something, and I really hoped I did, then I just wouldn't send her a bill. If she insisted, because she inherited the farm, then it might be different, but I didn't want to take anything she couldn't afford.

'That would be great, Miss Hodges.'

'Call me Rachel, and don't forget, I can't promise anything, but I'll try my best, and you can always go back to the solicitor if I fail. Now you'd better give me your parents' full names and birthdays, the address of the farm, and anything else you think I might find useful. You can email me to save time.' I gave her my email address.

'Thanks. I'll email you a copy of Mam and Dad's birth and marriage certificates, and the letter from Dad's solicitor, in case you need to speak to him. That's got our address on it too.'

'Great. We might need to trace details of your mum and dad before they married, so their addresses at the time may come in handy.' I did wonder how come Kate's birth certificate wasn't kept with those of her parents, but decided not to mention that to Kate.

'Thanks so much, Rachel. I can't tell you how much it means to me that you're even willing to try to look. I can email you a copy of Mam's address book too. There's not much in it, I'm afraid, mainly local people, but there are some names I don't recognise. I think Mam spoke once about having a sister who lived up North, and maybe some cousins. I tried ringing but the number's been disconnected, so I wrote, but the letter came back, with 'gone away' written on it. I didn't know what else to do. It meant a lot when the policeman said you'd help me.

13

Everyone here has been so kind, telling me not to worry, but it's there in the background. I just need to know who I am.'

'Well, if anything else comes to mind, please contact me. Otherwise I'll be in touch as soon as I have any news.'

I typed up my notes and put them with the printout of Kate's notes from the memory stick into a new folder marked "KATE WILLIS".

CHAPTER 3

The next morning, after Steve had gone to work, I turned my attention to the email that had arrived from Kate.

Poor Kate. I'd be devastated if I was her. It was bad enough to lose her mum and dad like that. I was determined to find out if she really was Kate Willis. I wondered where to start. Obviously she'd tried to get hold of a copy birth certificate and had drawn a blank. If it was me, what would I have done next? Rung Pete, of course. Pete had helped me out on so many cases where I needed to track down information about people. He was an IT whizz-kid, and I hoped he'd be able to help me out on this case too.

An old school friend, Pete had left Hull to go to Oxford University, only to return with his own IT company, and the funds to buy a mansion. No-one quite knew how he had made his money. He'd loved to flirt with me in the past and I'd been sorely tempted by his interest several times when Steve was working long hours and I was lonely, but I'd pulled back, even if it was at the last minute on one occasion, and Pete had finally got the message.

Steve had proposed in Amsterdam, in a jokey, off-hand sort of way, but when we got home he'd surprised me by taking me out for lunch one day and then to a jeweller's, where he didn't go down on bended knee, but did ask me to pick an engagement ring. We hadn't yet named the day, which would really disappoint Gran when she found out, but I was happy for us to take our time. I was determined not to be one of those women whose relationships with policemen flounder because of 'the job'. The reluctance to talk about work, the camaraderie with workmates, male and female, and the time spent apart, often all combine to toll the death knell in a police officer's marriage, but not for us. Steve seemed to have recognised that I was sticking with my job, because I was good at it, and I enjoyed it, and also because my hours were also long and unpredictable sometimes, so I wasn't sitting at home like other partners, getting bored or depressed, or both.

I felt sorry for Kate and although my bank balance was much healthier than usual, I wanted to be busy, not hanging around waiting for Steve all the time and getting resentful when he's working late, so I dialled Pete's number, but got his voicemail. I left a message asking him to ring back as soon as possible and turned my attention to the scanned copy of Kate's mum's address book.

It didn't take long for frustration to set in. There were very few names and addresses. Mostly the entries were just first names and phone numbers. I tried them all. Some were unobtainable. Presumably the phone numbers were no longer active. A couple belonged to people who only exchanged Christmas cards with the Willis family. I questioned them about their memories of Kate's birth, but the general consensus of opinion was that the family had kept themselves to themselves.

I searched the electoral roll, and found one couple with the same surname for the same address as in the address book, so I got their new number from directory inquiries. I rang but had to leave a message.

The Willis family's farm was so isolated that I had difficulty seeing from the postcodes in the address book which homes might be near the farm, and which were in nearby villages, so I logged on to Google maps and put in the postcodes. If anything, the map only emphasised the isolation.

Time dragged by. In desperation, I started to mess about on social media, but when I decided I needed a cuppa, I looked at the clock and was horrified by how much time I'd wasted. I tidied up my notes. With so little headway made, I was forced to realise how much I rely on Pete.

I gave up, gave the bathroom a clean and hung up the

washing that had just finished. I had plans for the afternoon, so after eating a quick sandwich, I headed out. I had to make good on a promise to my mum - to call in on Gran while Mum and Dad were on holiday in Scotland.

Gran's bungalow is more properly known around here as a 'pre-fab'. Thousands were erected just after World War 2, many of them in Hull, because so many homes, particularly near the docks, were destroyed by bombing. They were pre-fabricated - hence the name - from slabs of reinforced concrete and pebble-dashed on the outside. They were highly desirable at the time, having the luxury of an inside toilet, and gardens. Although only intended as a short-lived solution, designed to last for ten to fifteen years, there are still a good number around the country being used as homes today.

I'd hardly set foot in Gran's pre-fab when she started on about the X Factor audition programme coming up that Saturday. I wasn't surprised. That was the reason Mum had talked Dad into a short break in Edinburgh. Dad had said Scotland would either be full of midges, rain or both - you can tell he's not a big fan - but Mum insisted she needed to be well away from the neighbours until the fuss died down.

Gran had dragged Mum and me to Leeds earlier in the year, where she'd been rejected by The X Factor, and had badly sprained her ankle. That wasn't the bad news. The worst of it, according to Mum, and I had to agree with her somewhat, was that Gran had still made such an impression with her 'erotic' dancing before she fell, that the tape of her singing a Tina Turner song, dressed in a strappy red satin top and a short velvet skirt with black fishnet stockings, would be going out to millions of homes that coming Saturday.

'Of course I'm going to watch it, Gran, and you know Mum will when she gets back. She's set it to record.'

'Well, I don't understand why she had to go away at this time of the year. I was hoping she'd throw a big party for me with all our friends and neighbours. As it is, I'll have to go down to the community centre tomorrow, check their TV's working, and arrange for a bit of food for my guests. I can't fit many in this bungalow, and I'd been hoping your mam would do the food.'

'You'll have more fun there, Gran. You always say that Mum's too reserved to throw a proper party.'

'Maybe so, but I do think she could have come along to support me.'

That was the last thing Mum wanted. She was so terrified of what the neighbours would say, that she had literally left the country. Sometimes I wondered if she'd had been adopted by Gran, as they were nothing like each other.

'Have you got any other news, Gran?' I asked, changing the subject.

'Not really, but look at my hand.'

The back of her right hand was all scraped and badly bruised. 'What did you do that on, Gran?'

'Pushing advertising leaflets through the doors all over the estate. I'm going to get up a campaign. Letterboxes are lethal these days. Did you know there're stiff brushes in most of them that take the skin off your hand?'

'To keep the draughts out?'

'That's not all they keep out. I don't know how the poor postmen cope. If I do it again I'll wear a pair of your dad's thick gardening gloves.'

'Who roped you into delivering leaflets, or have you got a job?'

Gran looked at me as if I was crazy. 'Publicity, our Rachel. Don't you know anything about personalities? You've got to publicise yourself. I had Wilf print them up on his computer. I told you I was having guests at the community centre. You will be coming, won't you?'

You have to hand it to Gran. She lives life to the full, and no mistake. 'Of course I will, Gran, as long as nothing crops up in connection with work.' Mentally I crossed my fingers, hoping something would get me out of it. 'But what a great idea, about the leaflets. Now, shall we have a cup of tea, and then if you've anything you want doing while your hand's hurting, I can get stuck in?'

Gran was soon distracted, hunting for the swiss roll she'd bought specially for my visit, and then she saw my diamond ring, and there was no stopping her wedding fever. No housework got done, but I left Gran's at five, more exhausted than if I'd spring-cleaned the entire bungalow.

I threw together a quick casserole and slung it in the oven, knowing Steve would be working late to make up for having physio on his shoulder half the afternoon. He arrived shortly after I'd finished watching 'Bake-Off'.

Needless to say, I don't watch it because of any love of cookery, but for the human interest. I don't like other reality shows, apart from 'The Choir' with Gareth Malone, as he's so impossibly nice, and I like the music. Whenever it's on, I find myself thinking I should join a choir, because it looks so much fun, but I don't think my nerves could stand being on stage performing, and I doubt if I could commit to a regular weekly practice session. Alright, I admit I can't read music either... so I suspect no choir would have me.

Anyway, Bake-Off's fun because my friend Sarah and I have got into the habit of texting each other to comment on who we like or dislike, and who's likely to leave the tent. We'd just vented our mutual displeasure that the pretentious one who grew all his own ingredients hadn't been sent home, when the door opened.

'How did the physio go today, love?'

'Good. It's less painful now and she was pleased I've almost recovered full movement in the joint.'

'And work?'

'A pile of paperwork and also, I got dragged into a meeting with the organisers of Hull Fair to address parking and safety issues. Graham Watts always makes sure he's away in October so he avoids being tainted with the rise in crime around the time of the fair. This year it's the turn of Serious Crimes to step in and lend a hand while he's away. I ask you…' he groaned.

'That sounds a pain.'

'Yeah. Anybody would think they don't know what 'serious' means. Why can't some other department get involved? I mean, Hull Fair - it's been the same every year since the year dot. You'd think they could just use last year's plans, with the odd tweak to take account of any changes to traffic regulations or road layouts.'

'You should be grateful you didn't get called in again this year for the pre-planning meeting of The Freedom Festival. That's a much bigger event with lots of venues.'

'At least that's worth the extra hassle.'

'Yeah, remember the torch-lit procession with giant puppets and the Viking longboat with fire coming from the dragon's head at the front? The bands were great too.' Steve and I had even managed to get to a gig.

'You do know that when I dived in that canal in Amsterdam to save you, getting shot at for my efforts, it was just so I could be off sick and avoid these meetings?'

'Ha! Ha!'

'I must admit Hull's got a lot more going for it than most people think. When I first arrived from Leeds, I thought it was just a flat sprawling city with not much to recommend it apart from cheap accommodation, but I've changed my mind. Despite being bombed to bits, there's still a lot of history, and the people are the sort who'll do anything for you. I really hope Hull, European City of Culture 2017 is a success. You all deserve it.'

'Thank you. According to the video, there'll be something happening every day of the year - live music, plays, ballet, exhibitions, you name it. The spruced up city centre and the area around the marina make me really proud to come from Hull. The whole town's got a buzz about it. Dad says he can't believe the turnaround. Only last year, Hull was supposedly the second worst place in the UK to live and now, in 2016, we're eighth in the "Rough Guide" list of top ten cities in the world to visit!'

'I didn't know that, but I'm not really surprised. It's very quirky, like you. You've got all those hidden corners like the old town with its cobbled streets.'

'Are you saying I'm lumpy?'

'As if I'd dare. Anyway, what did your gran have to say today? I can always do with a good laugh.'

'I had to give her a reality check. She told me she was going to volunteer to have her photo taken naked and painted blue. She was really disappointed when I told her that the 'Sea of Hull' photograph was a one-off event the other week and they weren't doing it again.'

'She's crackers, your gran. Fancy imagining anyone would want to see an old, skinny, wrinkly gran in that photo.'

'You can't have looked closely when it was in the paper, Steve. There were loads of old people in among the three thousand odd who took part.'

CHAPTER 4

The next morning I ate breakfast and checked my phone. I'd turned it off the previous evening, not wanting to be disturbed. There were a couple of missed calls and a text from Pete, saying he was back in circulation, and I could call when it suited me, so I did.

A deep, rich voice answered. 'Hello. Peter Shannon here. Can I help you?'

'I hope so. It's Rach and I'm on a case that's right up your street.'

'Hiya, Rach. How's things? And what's this case? I hope it's not going to end up with me on the run from a dangerous criminal again?'

I wasn't the only one being pursued by the bad guys on my last case. Pete had got involved as well. I felt a pang of guilt, then pushed on. 'Not at all. You're safe this time. A young woman, still a girl really, has hired me to find out who she really is.'

'Sounds intriguing. As long as it doesn't involve unofficial channels, I'm your man. Tell me more.'

I filled Pete in on Kate's story and asked him what he could do. He said there were several things he could do which would only require access to vast official databases, and plenty of processing power, both of which he had. Firstly, he could check on girls with births registered in the couple of weeks either side of her birthday, in case Mr Willis had put the registration date down as the date of birth, or, less likely, the registration date had been the one they remembered as Kate's birthday.

I told him all the scant information in the address book, along with everything I'd gleaned, which wasn't much. I said I was still working on it, but asked if he had any suggestions that might help me? He said he should be able to get somewhere, though he'd be looking for people not in the book, such as any living relatives of Kate's mother, because if they could shed some light on the missing birth record, then that would be the quickest way to solve the matter. He explained it was a bit like researching family history.

I gave Pete the information on Kate's parents' birth certificates. 'She'd said she'd found them in an unlocked drawer, which to my mind only made it all the stranger that Kate's certificate was missing.' I also gave him Kate's supposed birth date of 29th March 1998, the address of the farm and details of the crash, promising to scan and email him copies.

'Next, I can look into all girls born on Kate's supposed birthday in the Lincolnshire area. You did say the family had lived there for as long as Kate could remember?'

'That's right.'

'So I'll be able to compare the records with those in the following census records and see if any were no longer recorded as living with their parents.'

'What will that show, Pete?'

'Well, it would show if a child had moved away from its birth parents. Say for example, if a couple with a lot of children gave their child to a childless couple to be brought up.'

'So you think she might have been adopted?'

'I think that's a strong possibility, Rach. More so than the date or name being recorded incorrectly. Of course, there's always the possibility of human error, but I think it highly unlikely, if not impossible, that a mistake of that magnitude would have been made in the last twenty years, even in the backwaters of Lincolnshire. Has Kate checked out adoption records yet?'

'No. She's just sat her 'A' levels and I think, even if she knew where to start, she couldn't cope with anything else for the time being. It's crossed my mind, of course, but I wanted to rule out an error in the birth records first if I could.'

'OK, Rach. You could also speak to the pathologist and ask if her mother's body showed whether she'd given birth. You might strike lucky and be able to charm the information out of him or her.'

'That's a thought. Thanks, Pete. I'll get on to it before I do anything else, and then I'll get back to you. If Helen Willis didn't have a child, then I can look into adoption records.'

'Adoption records aren't always that easy to get hold of, and if other family members know more, or you can find out the original birth name of a child who might have been adopted, then I'm sure it would help. You can make a start anyway.'

'You're a star.'

'You had your chance, Rach', he joked. 'I'll get back to you soon. Bye.'

So I had another task to carry out before I could get started on the inquiries I had in mind. I made myself a cup of tea, broke open a packet of my favourite quadruple chocolate chip biscuits, and got working. I love chocolate. I swear it helps me think better, but maybe that's just a justification to all those who say it's bad for you. I'm very lucky in being able to eat reasonable amounts of pretty much everything I like without piling on the pounds, because I went through childhood as skinny as a rake. Imagine Twiggy in the sixties but with an unruly mass of long hair, and that's me.

The pathologist was tied up when I called, but I was told I could ring back in half an hour, so I did a bit of googling to get hospital phone numbers, and then I rang back.

My charm didn't need to work on the pathologist. He said he remembered the crash, and although he wasn't allowed to give me information from the post-mortem results, he felt it wouldn't hurt to tell me that, as Helen Willis had long since gone through the menopause, her womb had shrunk to a size where it was difficult to determine whether she had ever given birth, and it had not been considered relevant to the findings of the post-mortem on a woman in her late fifties to look further. I thanked him for his help, and had a brainwave.

I rang Kate, and updated her. 'I know it must be hard for you, but we have to determine whether your mother actually did give birth to you, and I'd like you to contact your family doctor and ask him to check her medical records. The doctor won't give that information to me, I'm afraid.'

'That's okay. Obviously I'd like my mother to be my real mother, if you know what I mean, but I can't pretend it hasn't crossed my mind over the last few weeks that I might be adopted. I've never been there myself, but I know which doctor Mam went to. I'll ring up just before surgery and see if I can find out. I'll get back to you as soon as I can, though I might not be able to get the information straightaway.'

I'd finally had a call back from the couple whose address I'd traced through the electoral roll, but they couldn't tell me anything. They didn't move to the area until after Kate started school, and they weren't close to Helen and Tony Willis, just farming contacts.

As soon as possible I was going to drive over the Humber Bridge to Lincolnshire to take a look around and get a feel for where Kate grew up, maybe ask around the neighbouring farms to see if anyone remembered anything unusual around the time of Kate's birth.

But first I planned to contact all the maternity hospitals in the area and see if I could find anyone who might have worked there around the time of Kate's birth, and arrange a visit or two. Helen might have had a home birth, of course, but you never know what information you can find when you start digging. Maybe a woman died in childbirth, there was no-one else to bring up the child, and relatives brought up the baby. There were many possibilities.

The nearest maternity unit to Kate's home was at the Pilgrim Hospital in Boston. The lady I spoke to was very helpful. She told me they had no records of Helen Willis, but gave me the number of a midwife nearer to the Willis family's farm. She did divulge that although these days, with a large migrant population in the area, an average of three babies are born every day at the hospital, the computer was showing that on that particular day, 29th March 1998, only one baby boy was born at the unit.

I also wanted to find out if there was any sort of village community centre. I might be able to find one of those ladies who knows everybody's business. I made the other calls I'd planned. Over an hour later it was almost time for lunch and I'd done as much as I could to sort out my trip, but in order to see the midwife while I was there, I'd had to pick a day early the following week.

I had to accept that I was going to have to put Kate's case on hold, difficult though that was. There weren't going to be any quick or easy answers. I suppose she would have found them herself if there had been.

On Saturday Steve watched some cycling and snooker on TV and I buried myself in a book most of the day. Gran rang to have a good old moan because she'd been dropped at last minute from the X Factor show and was cancelling her party. I felt sorry for her but I admit I was secretly relieved that Steve and I didn't have to turn up to support her. Instead, we watched one of the 'Hunger Games' DVDs we'd had since Christmas and not got round to watching.

We managed a short drive to the coast on Sunday afternoon after I'd insisted Steve needed a bit of a fresh air. It rained, but we had fun playing air hockey, ten pin bowling and messing about on the slot machines.

Shortly after lunch on Monday I got a cryptic call from Mum. They were back from Scotland, and did I want to pop round, and if so, could I please park round the back. When I got there the blinds were drawn.

'What's going on, Mum?'

'I don't want anyone to know we're back in case the dust hasn't settled from Saturday.'

'Oh, I shouldn't worry about that.'

'But I do, Rachel, you know I do.'

'Well, you needn't worry ever again. Gran's gutted but she was dropped from the show. They sent her some flowers with a note saying said they were sorry to make changes at last minute, but one of the other people who'd auditioned was being featured instead, due to the film quality. When she watched the programme, she realised they'd put in a lad who'd been seen with a famous celebrity and had head-butted a photographer, getting himself on the front pages just last week. She says she's taking it up with her MP, but I think you've got away with it now.'

'Oh, Rachel! You don't know how happy that makes me. Now let's have a cuppa, and I'll tell you all about our break in Edinburgh.' It seemed like Mum had had a great time. She and Dad had walked miles, seen the sights and done far more shopping than Dad thought necessary. He took her to the coast to escape the shops and they'd driven up to St Andrews, where Mum had enjoyed poking around in the charity shops and imagining Prince William and Kate having sat at the same café table as her and Dad. Knowing Mum, she probably expected to see them, having just popped back up there to meet up with friends. The weather had been lovely and they'd not seen any of the dreaded midges that everyone had talked about.

She had an extra bit of news for me. On the way back they'd called to see an old school friend of Mum's in Scarborough, called Laura. 'You like all those pre-Raphaelite paintings, don't you?'

'Yes, you know I think they're fantastic. Apart from the reward, they were the best bit about my last case.'

'Well, when you're next in Scarborough, you must go.'

'Go where?'

'The church on the top of the South Cliff. What was it called? It'll come back to me in a minute. My memory's getting worse the older I get. Anyway, Laura took us to see it and it's full of pre-Raphaelite treasures. The designer of the church got William

Morris to decorate it. There are stained glass windows by Burne-Jones, and... I forget the names of the others, and there's a pulpit with panels painted by Rossetti.'

'Wow! And so near to us. Why didn't we know about it before?'

'Haven't a clue, Rachel. Maybe they want to keep it a secret to stop vandals. You wouldn't believe how gorgeous it is inside. It's hard to believe we've been going to Scarborough and driving past the end of the road all these years and never knew anything about it.'

'We'll go, next time we're up that way. By the way, I nearly forgot to mention, I've got a new case. It's a bit out of the ordinary.' I only just had time to tell Mum about Kate Willis before Dad got in. I kept it confidential with no names, but I had to tell her. I don't get many interesting cases that I can share with her. I talked to Dad for a bit about football and was on my way out when Mum shouted, 'St Martin-on-the-Hill, that's the name of the church. I've just found the leaflet.'

CHAPTER 5

On Tuesday morning, I'd eaten by eight and dressed in smart trousers and a shirt, rather than jeans and a t-shirt, ready for my trip to Lincolnshire. I'd remembered to ask Steve to change a fiver so I could pay the toll to cross the bridge without holding people up, and I was soon on my way, heading south past Barton-upon-Humber, then swinging south-east past Humberside airport on the A18, avoiding Immingham and Grimsby with their docks, eventually joining the A16 heading to Louth. I stopped for a coffee and a scone, and rang Pete, leaving a message to tell him that the pathologist had been unable to confirm if Helen Willis had given birth or not, due to her age.

Continuing south on the A16, I drove to Spilsby, where the local midwife was based. It was a small village with a few shops around a market square, and a supermarket, other shops and a large Chinese restaurant strung out on the Horncastle road. Sister Turner lived at the edge of Spilsby, and thankfully it seemed there hadn't been any emergencies, because she was there to greet me, as arranged. She was a friendly older lady, not wearing a uniform but dressed neatly if casually.

She invited me in and asked me to call her Mary. Then she offered me a cup of tea, and I showed her the file from Kate to support my unofficial request for information. When I'd told her of Kate's situation, she'd been willing to meet me, even though, understandably, she wouldn't give out details on the phone.

'I feel really sorry for the lass. I can't see any harm in telling you what I know, particularly as I'm retiring next month, although officially I shouldn't without some sort of authority from the Health Service.'

'Thanks. It's kind of you.'

'Helen Willis was a sad case. She'd already had two miscarriages when I became the senior midwife for the area, and I was in charge when she lost the third. They were desperate for a baby and adoption wasn't a likely option due to their age, so they wanted to try again, despite my misgivings. I wanted to refer her to the hospital in Boston but she was adamant she wouldn't go. A couple of years later, her fourth pregnancy seemed to have taken, and they were over the moon when I saw Helen at a six month check. Due to her earlier problems, I tried to persuade her against a home birth, but she was convinced all her problems were behind her.'

'But they weren't?' I prompted as Mary Turner paused, deep in thought.

'I couldn't have done anything differently, I'm afraid. Tony Willis called me in the middle of the night about a week or so later. Helen had lost the baby by the time I arrived. She was devastated. They both were. The baby was deformed. It was a wonder it had survived as long as it had, and the doctor and I counselled her against trying again. Miscarriages have always been nature's way of avoiding gross abnormalities, and I feared another pregnancy could be dangerous for her as well. She must have been about forty-two when she had that fourth miscarriage. I was secretly glad when she didn't come to my clinic again.'

'Did you see her afterwards?'

'I called round a couple of times as I was worried about her, but then she told me she'd rather I didn't call any more, and I haven't seen her for years. Their farm is only ten miles or so from here, but they never came into Spilsby as far as I knew, and when you get out there, you'll understand why I would never be passing. Where did this girl Kate start school?'

'Spilsby Primary School, but she came in on the bus on her own, I believe, and I don't think her mother ever came to Spilsby. You're sure Helen couldn't have given birth somewhere else?'

'No, I can't be sure of that. I would have thought it extremely unlikely, but I can't rule it out.'

'I've just got one last question then, please.'

'Yes?'

'Would there have been the remotest chance that Helen Willis would have been given an unwanted baby? Say a teenager who got into trouble, or an abandoned baby?'

'No way. That sort of thing might have happened in my predecessor's day, but even as long ago as twenty years, it just wouldn't happen. Doctor Stanhope wouldn't have involved himself in anything underhand, and I certainly wouldn't.'

'Sorry if I offended you, but I had to ask. I'm just trying to rule things out.'

'That's alright. I can understand that. But the most likely answer to Kate's parenthood is that she must have been adopted and Helen and Tony Willis never told her. Hasn't she checked the records yet?'

'Not yet. But it's only just come up as an option. Thanks ever so much for your help, Mary.'

'Well, I hope Kate gets the answers she wants. Goodbye.'

I retraced my route into Spilsby, stopping to buy a sandwich and visit the loo at the supermarket. Then I left on the Boston road. After a couple of miles, I turned left onto one of the narrow unclassified roads that criss-cross the fens, following and crossing the drains. The land was flat and you could see great distances, but there were very few houses, and I was on one of the larger roads. I understood a little of Kate's isolation, even before I turned off onto a tiny track leading almost a mile to their farm. I hadn't passed a single car in a quarter of an hour.

Kate had marked the location on a map, scanned it and sent it to me but that didn't really prepare me for the silence and the biting wind which swept across the fields with barely an odd straggly tree, no other buildings, no hills or even the gentlest of rises to stop it. The people who lived in this area led isolated lives. Despite the wide open spaces, it was hidden away from the world. It looked and felt like a world that harboured secrets.

There was no 'for sale' sign, and I wondered if I'd got the wrong place, but then I realised the farm couldn't be sold until the estate was settled, which could be months, years even. I got out and peeped through the farmhouse window. Everything seemed tidy and in good order, if a bit shabby. I was glad for Kate's sake that no-one had broken in and made a mess. There was really nothing for me to learn there, but I wanted to get a feel for the place where Kate had grown up and lived until she was eighteen. The house didn't seem so bad, even if it was pretty basic. An ancient rusting tractor stood in the yard. The barn was draughty with an assortment of unidentifiable tools and other objects piled in corners.

Then I turned my back on the farm to return to the car, and the isolation hit me again. There wasn't a single other building in sight, but it was more than that. True, I was looking at it from the viewpoint of a girl brought up in a city, but I'd visited a school-friend who lived on a farm near Ellerby, on the road from Hull to the coast, and it just didn't have the same feeling at all. Although her parents' farm was also surrounded by fields, I hadn't felt cut off from civilisation there. I got in the car and drove away, searching for the nearest farm.

I drove for a couple of miles, taking turns at random until I found a house. A young woman answered the door. New to the area, she couldn't help at all. They'd bought the house after the previous owner died, she told me. I cast the net wider, driving up and down tracks, and would have got lost if it were not for my trusty ordnance survey map. How do the vast majority of folks with just a sat-nav cope when they're not sure of the postcode for the house they're looking for, or when, like here, the postcode covered a large area, I wondered, for the umpteenth time? Like a dinosaur, I was holding out against relying totally on sat-nav.

After about half an hour, I found a farm with signs of life, and was welcomed in for a cup of tea. Mrs Giles was obviously pleased to have company.

'What a terrible business. I've known the Willis family for

years, although they kept to themselves pretty much, and I don't think they got many visitors, but as you can see, we're hardly close neighbours.'

I didn't want to tell everyone Kate's business, so was deliberately vague about the details, but said Kate was having trouble establishing her exact birthday, that her birth certificate was missing, and she needed a copy to start settling the estate.

'Oh, I wondered why the farm hadn't gone up for sale. Let me think... I remember seeing Helen when she was pregnant with Kate. It must have been in autumn 1997, because my Paul got engaged and we asked Helen and Tony over. It was a hard winter, and the next time I remember seeing her was the following summer, pushing the pram, and she showed me the baby. So proud and happy, she was. I remember it well. Kate must have been two or three months old by then. I wondered at first how Helen would cope. She'd already had her fortieth birthday, I'm sure of that. But Kate was the apple of their eye, and Helen was no stranger to hard work.'

'So that would place Kate's birthday sometime in the spring. She was told it was 29th March 1998, but there doesn't seem to be a record of her birth on that day. You don't remember hearing the exact date mentioned, I don't suppose?'

'No, I can't say I did. I'm sorry I'm not much help. What about the midwife?'

I didn't want to get sucked into revealing more, so pretended that's where I was headed next. 'I've just one final question. Would Helen have belonged to any local groups, such as the Women's Institute, knitting circles or the like?'

As expected, the answer was, 'No, she kept to herself. The farm, the house and looking after Tony and Kate were enough for her.'

I said my goodbyes and left. It was almost time to call at Mrs Charlesworth's house and meet Kate before I headed home. But I had a quarter of an hour to spare before Kate finished work, so I tried one last thing. Back in Spilsby I called at the church, only to establish, as suspected, that the Willis family had never attended church and the vicar could add nothing to my few scraps of knowledge about Kate's birth.

Grace Charlesworth answered the door. 'Thanks so much for doing this for Kate. Even if you don't get anywhere, it means such a lot to her. It's given her a focus instead of fretting over what happened.' She showed me into a back room, brought us tea and cake, and then left us alone.

Kate looked almost like a younger version of me - slim, with long hair, dressed in jeans and a t-shirt, but she seemed a little shy and vulnerable for an eighteen-year old, so we were probably like chalk and cheese. I told her everything I'd managed to achieve that day and she was so grateful.

'Actually I feel a bit awkward because it doesn't seem like I've got anywhere, but I'm hoping I will, Kate.'

'Well I've got a bit of news. I'm sorry it's taken me so long to get back to you, but the doctor insisted I take in copies of the solicitor's letter and my parents' birth certificates before he was prepared to give out information. It's hard for me to get my head around, but I'll have to accept it. It's looking like Mam wasn't my real mother. Her doctor has no record of her giving birth and, get this, he didn't even know I existed!'

'That's strange.'

'Apparently I've never been registered at the doctors and have no NHS number. He said that my mam had had four miscarriages, but there are no live births recorded, and he doubted if she would have been able to get pregnant again. He said that if she had miraculously given birth, then it was somewhere else entirely.'

'Did your mother take you to a different doctor, then?'

'I was rarely ill, and if I was, Mam never took me to the doctors. She kept me off school when there were vaccinations. I remember being glad I didn't have "the needle" like my classmates, but of course I didn't ask why. It's all a bit mysterious, and it makes me wonder if that's why my parents were dead set against my getting a job. The doctor said I wouldn't normally have been able to get a National Insurance number without an NHS number. Also that apparently means Mam can't have even claimed Child Benefit for me. No wonder there was never much money.'

'That does seem odd.'

'That's what I thought. I asked him how Mam managed to put my name down for school, but apparently, although you have to show a birth certificate these days, it wasn't always like that. He said that, as recently as 2000 or thereabouts, not all primary schools asked for birth certificates when children started school, particularly those in remote rural areas like ours. Mothers just completed a form.'

'Well I do know that after information's been entered into a computer, no-one queries it, so presumably when you moved to secondary school, your records went with you. I know it's a shock, Kate, but try not to worry. I'll see if Pete's come up with anything yet.'

'Pete? Who's he? Does he work for you?'

'No. Sorry, I should have said. Pete's an old friend of mine who runs a computer firm. He helps me out sometimes with computer searches.'

'I'm afraid I'm not sure if I can pay your friend Pete as well.'

'Forget it. He's a friend and it's nothing to him to have his computers run some extra searches.'

'Well, if you're sure about the money… Actually I've something else to tell you. Mrs Charlesworth has organised a DNA test for me. I'd been thinking about it for a while. She sorted it all out for me yesterday. Sorry I didn't ring to tell you but I thought I'd be seeing you today and I won't have the result for a couple of days. It would have taken five days or more, but Mrs Charlesworth said I shouldn't wait and insisted on paying the extra for a quick result. I feel awful taking her money, but it would have been hard having to wait any longer once I'd decided. I've asked the pathologist if he'll compare my DNA with Mam and Dad's and he agreed. It might be expensive, but it'll be worth it to rule out the slightest chance that Mam did find a way of giving birth to me, or if I'm Dad's by someone else, or

35

related in some other way. I need to know who I'm not, even if I still don't know who I am.'

'I think it's a great idea, if you're sure you can afford it.'

'It's fine. I've got a bit of cash coming in now I'm helping out on my neighbour's farm until the 'A' Level results come out and I know if I've got into university.'

'Oh, when are the results out?'

'Next Thursday.'

'Oh, gosh! I'd lost track of time. Do please let me know how you get on, but I'm sure you'll have done well. It sounds like you' really worked hard.'

CHAPTER 6

It was a slow, boring journey back to Hull. I kept thinking about Kate and wishing I was getting somewhere. Not for the first time, I was pinning my hopes on Pete's computer searches to move the case forward.

I stopped at the Sainsbury's just on the north side of the bridge and parked behind a car with a sign in the back window - '*Marshall & Denver. Brother and Sister on Board'*. I wondered who in their right mind would give children those names and worse still, advertise the fact. At least Kate's parents hadn't saddled her with such a stupid name, although it might have made the investigation easier.

I'd left a message for Pete to call me so I could fill him in on my visit to Kate and wasn't surprised that I'd only got as far as buttering a slice of toast the next morning when the phone rang. True to form, it was Pete. Unless he's working away, he's usually quick off the mark to reply.

'Hi Rach. I'm calling with an update on your unknown girl. Have you got time for me to run through it?'

'Yes, sure. I've not really got started yet this morning. I'll just grab a pen.'

'Don't worry, I'm emailing you the details right now in case any new information comes to light in the future. There's a full list of all girls born in the likely time frame in a hundred mile radius. I played safe and went for four weeks either side of 29th March 1998. There were sixty-eight. Sadly none of them was called Kate Willis, even allowing for a variation or misspelling of the first name, so I think we can safely eliminate the possibility that Mr Willis registered her date of birth incorrectly.'

'Well, it might not be good news, but it's a big step forward. Thanks very much, Pete. You've done a lot in such a short time. It would have taken me ages.'

'It's not hard for me, Rach. I'm glad to help. There's more. I also checked the census records to see which of those sixty-eight baby girls were no longer living at the address where they were born. The next census was 2001, and I came up with nine. Of those, two had died before their third birthday. I've sent you a list of the other seven. One of those could have ended up as Kate Willis, but none was called any variation of Kate, Katherine or anything similar, and none had the exact birthday of 29th March. I haven't looked at the 2011 census yet, because I felt Kate would have remembered getting new parents, if she was older than three at the time, but I could do that to rule it out, if you wanted.'

'There's no need for that, Pete. When I went to Lincolnshire yesterday I spoke to a neighbour, who saw Mrs Willis with Kate when she was a couple of months old, so she must have been one of those seven if she was born locally. That's one of the things I was ringing to tell you about. If she did move to live with the Willis family, officially or unofficially, she was young enough to have her first name changed.'

'Do you want me to look further into those girls, Rach?'

'Possibly, but not for the moment, thanks. I also discovered Helen Willis had four miscarriages and was unlikely to conceive again, but I need to rule out the possibility that she gave birth somewhere else before we go any further. However, if she did, then I may have to call on you to look at girls born around 29th March in that new area.'

'How will you find out if Helen gave birth somewhere else?'

'Kate's having a DNA test. The pathologist is going to check the result against her parents' post-mortem tissue records. Then she'll know once and for all if either one or both of the Willises were her biological parents. I'll let you know when she gets back to me. It shouldn't take long.'

'OK. I haven't started looking into relatives of Helen and Tony Willis yet but I thought I'd update you with what I had already.'

'Thanks, Pete. I do appreciate it. I wish you'd let me reimburse you for your time, but I know you won't take the money.'

'You can always ditch your new fiancé.'

'Very funny. You know I'm no way sophisticated enough for you.' I'd still not got over showing him up in Hull's most expensive restaurant by catching the hem of my skirt under a chair leg and exposing my sexy underwear to everyone within sight. 'Bye, Pete.'

'Bye.'

It was after nine when Steve got home, so I knew something new must have come in for his department. It went without saying that it was serious. He was in charge of Serious Crimes, after all. He'd texted me before seven to say he'd be late, so I'd eaten already. His tea was plated up, ready for the microwave. As I turned it on, I poured him a glass of wine. We rarely drink except when Steve's not working, but occasionally he'll have just one glass to unwind after a particularly long day, and I could see in his eyes that this was one of those days. He looked pale and exhausted.

'It's not another murder, is it, Steve? You're not up to long days like this. You're supposed to be taking things easy. Your shoulder's not totally mended yet.' I didn't like to fuss, but I was worried.

'Yes, but I'm too tired to go into it now. Don't worry, I won't risk driving with my shoulder just yet.'

Sometimes he talks over his cases, but not always, and I didn't push him. We went to bed early, banishing the horrors of the outside world, and he got up at six and left for work.

Around eight when I surfaced, I turned on the radio and heard there'd been a body discovered at a writer's retreat. I didn't know there was one in the area, but the reporter said it was in a wood near Winestead, just off the Withernsea road to the east of Hull. Apparently the log cabins had been erected recently, the builder hoping to cash in on the current appetite for creative writing courses.

A local author had been running the course. She was interviewed, expressing her horror at the murder and her sympathy for the victim's relatives, and denying that it would be good publicity for her series of crime novels. I'd never heard of her but I bet that secretly she was rubbing her hands in glee. I was tempted myself to rush out and buy one of her books, and I expected many others would be as well.

The reporter went on to say that the victim had so far not been named, but the police were treating the death as suspicious. I expected Steve would fill me in later, so resisted the impulse to look at the online news reports.

I didn't have much to do, and to be honest I was kicking my heels a bit.

Luckily, however, I got a call from one of the solicitors I do legwork for, and I drove to their offices to pick up a large pile of papers to serve on people.

They were mainly orders in connection with debts, notice to quit rented accommodation, or instructions to employers to collect payments from salary. It sounds terribly official and threatening, but mostly I just had to leave the papers at the addresses supplied by the solicitor, and not confront anyone.

It made the hours pass and at least I got to visit a few interesting places I'd not been before, including a tattoo parlour which had a reception desk manned (or should that be "birded"?) by a parrot. It squawked out, 'Busy, please wait'. It was a handsome specimen, sitting in a cage on the counter.

The tattoo artist was busily engaged in a portrait of what might, at a pinch, have been a footballer of note, but he looked up and smiled. I waved the papers at him, put them down on the counter and left. Much as I would have liked to have engaged in conversation, I didn't think the owner would be too happy when

40

he discovered his landlord was evicting him for massive rent arrears, and he might just have set the parrot on me.

CHAPTER 7

'Hi, love. Your dinner's warming in the oven. I'll just turn it up for a few minutes. How's your day been?'

'In a word, busy!'

'I thought as much. I heard on the radio about the body at the writer's retreat, but I haven't turned on the news. I'd rather hear it from you than listen to an endless stream of guesswork and repetition of too few facts. Do you want to talk about it?'

'I don't mind. It's not gruesome. But there's not much to tell yet. We've mainly been taking statements and dealing with the usual preliminaries today.'

'Have you identified the body?'

'Yes. Simon Crawford. It's a start,' Steve answered. 'One of the other writers identified him, but his next of kin is away on holiday and hasn't been informed yet, so we can't release his name.'

'I've never heard of him. Did he write anything I might have heard of?'

'I don't know, but he'd had one novel published and was writing his second.'

'Why was he studying creative writing, then? Surely he didn't need to?'

'It's a retreat. They do run writing courses, and there is one at the moment, which means plenty of interviews, but not everyone there was on the course. Some writers book cabins for the peace and quiet. There's no Wi-Fi, no phone connections, no interruptions. They just meet at mealtimes.'

I was about to ask how they managed to do any research they might need for their books, when I remembered many fruitless hours or so spent trying to find information but getting side-tracked on the internet, and suddenly I wasn't surprised he should choose to get away from it in order to get some writing done. 'So how was he killed?'

'Like I said, it wasn't gruesome. A wound on the back of the head but hardly any blood. No official report from Forensics yet, but David Leadbeater, the pathologist, said the blow to the head wouldn't have killed him. He found signs of suffocation, so thought Simon was knocked out by the blow, then the killer held a pillow or similar over his face to finish him off. No indication as to what he was hit with, even though we searched the cabin and the immediate area outside for anything that could have been used. So, no fingerprints that we can definitely link to the killer.'

'Can't you pick anything up from the actual murder weapon, the pillow?'

'Highly unlikely apparently. As for prints in general, we've not come up with many as the place hasn't been open long. In fact no-one had rented that cabin before, which may be helpful, though there could still be builders' prints, and other writers might have popped in, as well as presumably a cleaner. I'm not holding my breath that we can find a match for any we have on file. In any case, the killer could have been wearing gloves. Despite the daytime sun, it gets pretty cold at night out there at the moment, so it wouldn't be strange for someone to be wandering around with gloves on.'

'Any witnesses?'

'Sadly, no. Everyone we interviewed said that they heard and saw nothing, but it has to be said the cabins are quite well spaced out. There was no sign of a forced entry although we can't find his laptop. The victim was last seen at the communal evening meal. I say "communal", but it's not like they all sit around one big table. Some do. Principally those on the writing course, but the rest generally keep more to themselves, though some do seem to eat their meals together, whether it's just to talk to someone and switch off from their work for a bit, or to give each other a bit of encouragement or even to run through ideas.'

'Do they take turns cooking?'

'No. A woman from a local café in Patrington has a contract to supply meals and she brings them in a small van. There's no kitchen, just a small fridge, microwave and kettle in each cabin.'

As we spoke I'd been getting food on the table. I let Steve eat, before asking, 'Any possible motives or suspects?'

'Well, there seems to be some jealousy washing around under the surface. Only one person actually came out and said it, but it seems some of the unpublished writers cast doubt on Simon's writing talent. Though that could just be sour grapes because he got published and they didn't.'

'Yes, I can imagine. Although I have to say there are some books out there which are not that well-written. You can only assume they got published just because they had an unusual plot, or turned up on the right day - or the author knows someone in publishing.'

'I think you're right there. All these so-called celebrities seem to find it easy to get published.'

'Anyway, back to the murder, Steve. As this place is off the beaten track, then it's likely to be someone at the retreat. Surely that makes your job easier for once?'

'It should do – just like your favourite TV crime series, "Death in Paradise". The trouble is, this is real life and also I can't picture any of them as a murderer. And that sort of professional jealousy - that's not much of a motive. What would they gain by it? The woman leading the course, Jane something, is also a published author, and she seemed a bit aggressive, but I think it was only because we've disrupted her course. No, after reading the interview reports, I'm no further forward. His wife's on her way back from holiday, so she might be able to tell us something that might help.'

'Did she hear about the murder on the news, because that would be dreadful?'

'No. Luckily she was abroad and not reading English papers. Her sister's been looking after the house and going in to feed their cats, and she had the number of the hotel in Malta. As soon as Mrs Crawford officially identifies his body, I can get on with talking to his friends, relatives and associates.' He paused. 'So, Rach, tell me what you've been up to.'

After I'd told him about my encounter with the parrot and provided a bit of light relief, I suggested we went to bed. We'd both been awake early, and I reckoned we needed to make the most of it before Steve's case took over our lives, as his previous murder cases had. We took a long, slow shower together. Getting out in a bit of a daze, I tripped over a towel on the floor and banged the back of my hip. Steve knelt behind me and stroked it better and it took us even longer to actually make it to bed. Eventually we fell asleep in the early hours.

When I woke up, Steve had already left. I must have been so tired, I didn't hear him go. I'd just got in from doing a big shop when the phone rang.

'I'm not theirs', Kate blurted out.

'Oh, Kate, I am sorry.'

'It's just a shock. I mean, I know I was expecting it really, but now it's true. The pathologist has checked my DNA against theirs, so there's no doubt any more. I was even starting to hope that I was Dad's daughter by someone else, and Mam had agreed to bring me up as hers, after you said it was unlikely she'd be able to give birth herself, but my DNA is totally different. I couldn't even be the child of a near relative.'

'It's going take time for you to accept that Helen and Tony Willis were definitely not your biological parents. However, they did love you and bring you up, so they were still your parents in all but name.'

'I know. I'll get over it in time. At least we can get onto adoption agencies now, can't we?'

'I've started initial inquiries on your behalf, as the process is quite long-winded.'

'Thanks for that. Are you sure you don't want any more money? You've done such a lot.'

45

'No, I'm fine. You've had to pay for the DNA test, anyway. I'll chase up the adoption side.'

I rang Pete to relay the DNA test result, but he was out, so I just left a message to let him know. I chased up the adoption authorities, who said I was nearing the top of the list and they hoped to get back to me shortly, then I made a quick call to Mum to tell her about Kate's DNA result.

'It's a sort of breakthrough, even if it means Kate isn't who she thought she was.'

'I know what you mean, but it's such a shame. Poor lamb!'

We said our goodbyes eventually, but not until Mum had brought me up to date with Dad's escapades clearing out the shed and finding a nest of bees. I now knew everything there was to know about getting a beekeeper to come and collect them, then spraying this concoction of soapy water, peppermint oil, cinnamon and cayenne pepper to discourage the ones out foraging from returning to Dad's shed. It would also encourage any new ones attracted by Dad's hebes and other bee-attracting flowers to go elsewhere. Luckily the flowering season was almost over.

My family can wear me out, but at least I know they're mine. I curled up with a book, and was soon deep in the middle of one of those romantic tales involving cupcakes, chocolate and men who seem prickly but turn out to be the perfect one.

A return call from Pete dragged me back to real life. 'Oh. Hi Pete. Sorry to have bothered you. I just thought you'd like to know about Kate's DNA result.'

'It's not a problem. Not good news for Kate, but at least it closes down that line of enquiry.'

'Yes. It's simplified the search, but by no means made it easier.'

'How do you mean, Rach?'

'I chased up the adoption authorities and since I left you that message earlier, they've finally got back to me. There's no trace of any official adoption records for anyone called Kate Willis, and no record of any adoption by Kate's parents. They could only suggest that she'd been adopted unofficially.'

'Did you get anywhere with the address book you mentioned?'

'All the addresses are out-of-date. All I can do is continue working through them, trying to find new addresses from neighbours etc.'

'Yeah, good idea. Someone might know how Kate came to live with the Willis family. I'm afraid missing relatives are really the best bet now though. I'm still looking but I've not come up with any yet.'

'Mm… I'm beginning to wonder if she was abandoned in a carrier bag. Kate said she felt sorry for people abandoned as babies, as they'd grow up never knowing who they were. I hope she's not one of them.'

'I'm pretty sure if someone found a baby, they'd hand it in, and then it would be officially adopted, but you never know. If it is something like that, you stand no chance of finding out who she is, unless her birth mother ever came forward to reclaim her.'

'We'll just have to hope one of us finds something then, Pete.'

'Yeah. Fingers' crossed, eh? Sorry, have to go now, Rach. I'm expecting a call from Shanghai.'

'You high-roller! Bye, then.'

CHAPTER 8

That night Steve wasn't too late, considering the murder enquiry, but I knew from past experience that once his team got a lead, he'd hardly be home.

After I'd told him about Kate's DNA not being a match for the Willises and her not being official adopted either, he commiserated. 'Something'll turn up, Rach, don't worry.'

'Tell me about your case. Are you getting anywhere?'

'The latest theory being tossed around is that someone might have killed Simon to steal his new plot. Personally I find that rather far-fetched, but I have to investigate all angles, so I've had to order the confiscation of all the other writers' laptops for investigation. As you can imagine, that wasn't at all popular. After a lot of discussion with the tutor, the writing course is going to continue with hand-outs from the tutor and reverting to pen and paper for the exercises, but the writers who are using Winestead as a retreat to work on their own projects are up in arms.'

'I bet they are. I can imagine a few bruised egos thinking their work is more important than solving a murder.'

'Yes, but to give them their due, most of the writers are amateurs who have booked themselves in to write in peace during a holiday from work, and they can ill-afford to waste the time. I came up with a compromise of letting them copy the document they're working on from their laptops to some old wiped computers we've got in the storeroom at Central.'

'Any other theories as to motive?'

'Someone said they thought Simon had copied another author's work but I think that was just a rumour floating around.

I suppose we shouldn't be surprised at writers coming up with theoretical motives. That's their job, after all. When asked what they thought about Simon himself, none of the writers could remember having had more than a short conversation with him about generalities connected to the retreat and writing in general. They all say that Simon kept himself to himself, almost to the point of secrecy. His favourite comment, when someone tried to draw him into conversation at mealtimes, was "I can't say anything about that, I'm afraid. I must protect my sources".'

'That sounds intriguing.'

'Yes. It got me wondering if he had any criminal sources, so I'm off to Birmingham tomorrow. It'll give me a chance to look around his home, see if he has an office and interview other family and friends myself. Mrs Crawford popped in to identify the body but wanted to get home, so I have to go there anyway. We can't rule anything out, but I'm beginning to wonder if his murder's connected to the contents of his new book.'

'You're not driving down, are you, Steve?'

'No chance. I can't spare anyone to drive me, so I'm taking the physio's advice and going on the train.'

'Good.' I decided he needed to switch his brain off from murder, so suggested we watch a film.

'Good idea.'

We settled down on the settee but when I asked Steve where we'd seen the lead actor before, he didn't answer. Steve has an encyclopaedic memory for film trivia, so I knew something was bothering him. I pressed "pause". 'Come on. What's up?'

'Something's niggling me.'

'I thought you'd decided to put the murder investigation out of your mind for a few hours?'

'This is something entirely different. A girl came into the station this afternoon and reported her boyfriend hadn't come home the other night.'

'And…' I knew there must be something more. He wouldn't bother too much about a bloke staying out all night, and unless he was considered to be a high risk, they wouldn't prioritise it for up to seventy-two hours.

'Well, she said her boyfriend was Nick Heighway, the young fast-track PC who's assigned to us at the moment, so the desk sergeant rang me to see if I knew anything.'

'And he wasn't in work?'

'He'd booked two weeks off, starting yesterday.'

'So he'd gone away without telling her? Or got drunk to let off steam and stayed out. What's the problem?'

'She said he was working last night. Said she'd been getting a bit sick of all the overtime he'd had to work over the last few weeks whilst he'd been in Serious Crimes.'

'Ouch!'

'Innocent on all counts. He's not worked any overtime at all. I didn't want to drop him in it big-time. He might have another woman, so I told the sergeant to ask her if Nick could have been out with his mates instead and she'd maybe forgotten or got muddled, because he'd not been working at all yesterday. She was quite adamant he'd gone out to work that morning and texted later to say he'd be working overtime again. Eventually she accepted we couldn't do anything at the moment, but she was shaken pretty badly when she heard that he'd booked two weeks' leave. For the time being I omitted to mention that there hadn't been any overtime. That would have only made things worse.'

'But something's still bothering you?'

'Yes. I know he's not been with us long, but he doesn't seem to be the sort who cheats on his girlfriend. Maybe I'm reading too much into it, but I just have a hunch that something's not quite right. If I can find a minute, I'll ring her; check if she's heard from him, or if he's home, nursing a bad head. I'm his inspector at the moment, so it wouldn't be too heavy-handed of me to make a quick enquiry.'

'Seems fair enough, but he has booked two weeks off, Steve. Maybe give him that much grace, eh? Now will you tell me who that it is, please?'

'Ryan Gosling. I thought you knew all the fit-looking

50

blokes?'

'I just couldn't put a name to his face. Though I wouldn't put him in the same league as you.'

'Flattery will get you everywhere. Why don't you fish out some choccie from your hidden hoard and we'll have a glass of wine?'

Steve wasn't back from Birmingham until almost ten the next evening, frustrated by the train delays on a busy Friday evening. 'At least the delay gave me time to type up my notes on a platform bench, so I didn't have to go in to the station. I can email them over to the office.'

'Have you had anything to eat, Steve?'

'Yes, thanks, I got something at the station before I left. I'll just have a drink and maybe a piece of your flapjack, as it smells so delicious.'

'It's got sultanas in it - your favourite. I thought I'd bake some when you texted to say you'd be late.' I'm no cook, but I do make a decent flapjack, if I say so myself. Weigh the ingredients, stir it in a pan then cook for fifteen minutes in the oven and that's it. It's so easy but very yummy, and it has oats, so must be good for you, despite the sugar and syrup. I shouted through to the bedroom where Steve was getting changed into jeans and a t-shirt, 'What's the widow like? Was she any help?'

Steve came in, took a piece of flapjack and ate it in a few bites. 'That was lovely, Rach. I must have been hungrier than I thought.'

'Well, have another and a drink and tell me about this widow. What's her name?'

'Melanie. I wanted to get a feel for their relationship, and also an idea of the plot of his next book, but apparently she knew little about it. That was unusual as he usually discussed his ideas with her. When she asked, he fobbed her off, except for one time when he told her it was about smuggling, but when she started to ask more, apparently he muttered something like "it's better you don't know", and reluctantly she left it at that.'

51

'That sounds intriguing. Did it sound like they got on well?'

'She seemed to be positive everything was fine, apart from this new book. In fact she was quite taken aback when he mentioned going up to Hull to a writers' retreat. It's not something he'd ever done before. She had wondered if he might be having an affair, but dismissed it as ridiculous. I went to see the neighbours and his best friend while I was down there, but even when pushed, they all said they had the impression that Simon was a loving, caring husband, and that an affair was out of the question.'

'People outside of a marriage rarely know what goes on it, though, do they? Presumably she asked him why he was going to a writers' retreat?'

'He told her they could afford it and it should help him get a good chunk of his new book written, being away from the phone and email, which seems reasonable, but interestingly, when she asked him why he was going all the way to Hull, seemed a bit defensive, and muttered something like "that's the only place", so there's probably more to it than meets the eye.'

'Maybe he meant it was close to the coast and a useful background for a book about smuggling.'

'Yes, but smuggling what? Of course, you know the killer took Simon's laptop and all his papers. I asked Mrs Crawford if he'd left anything behind, any early drafts on a home computer, perhaps, or papers in his office, but she said he only used his laptop and he'd not left any papers either.'

'Surely he backed up his work on a memory stick and left that behind safely?'

'He did. I forgot to say. I plugged it in on the train and read it, but there's only two chapters, would you believe, with no mention of Hull, smuggling or anything else useful.'

'That's bad luck. Come on, I think it's time for bed. You've had a hard week so I'll give your shoulder a massage.'

'You won't get away with that. I've got more important places that need massaging.' He pulled me towards him for a kiss. 'Talking about work has made me forget to kiss my fiancée. That won't do.'

We spent most of the following weekend reading, apart from an hour's walk around East Park. Melanie Crawford had reluctantly given Steve the only copy she had of his first novel. 'Unless we get any other victims, then this book doesn't seem to be at all relevant. It's about a serial killer who targets prostitutes.'

'That's a bit of a cliché. How did he get that published?'

'Presumably it was in the period when gratuitous violence was all the rage, before psychological thrillers came into fashion.'

While Steve had been reading that, I'd been skim-reading drafts of novels on the writers' various laptops (temporarily made password-free), to see if any of them related to smuggling, or seemed to have been written in another style. None of their computer logs seemed to show any new works downloaded over the last week or so, which would be the case if anyone had stolen Simon's new book-in-progress, but it was all I could do to help.

The writers' imagination knew no bounds. One story I read concerned a woman who fooled her boyfriend into giving her a thousand pounds a month to look after 'their baby', but it was really a 'synthetic' or A.I. baby, which only needed recharging occasionally. I couldn't see how the rest of the book was going to pan out.

Other books were – a horror story about a monster prowling around underground tunnels beneath a city; what looked set to be a chick-lit book, starting with a girl dumped at the altar who proceeds to open a garden centre to get away from everything and who finds the surly specialist cacti grower is really a lovely man with an unhappy past; and a family saga stretching right through the twentieth century.

There was only one crime novel, but it didn't seem to revolve around smuggling. Five mummified bodies were discovered when contractors were knocking down a factory to build new houses. The first ten thousand words only described the discovery and the lives of the dysfunctional detectives in minute detail.

We ended up thoroughly entertained and convinced we could do better, but no nearer a suspect. 'It was always going to be a long shot, Rach.'

'Well, I did wonder how one of the other writers would have got rid of the weapon or Simon Crawford's laptop if they'd murdered him.'

'We searched everyone's cabins but they could have left the retreat that night and taken them somewhere, buried them, passed them to someone else… There's always that possibility. I admit we always thought it unlikely, though. Unfortunately in a murder case we have to follow every avenue, however implausible, because in the unlikely event it turns out to have been the right one, then it'd be no good looking for evidence or following leads weeks or months down the line. The public would ask why we hadn't checked in the first place. No stone unturned and all that.'

'I don't mind. It was worth a try, and it gave you an excuse for working from home and spending some time with me. Anyway, so who else could have killed him? Something to do with smugglers, do you think? What could that mean, though?'

'It's probably nothing of the sort, but who knows at the moment. I can't rule it out.'

'Didn't anyone see the murderer?'

'Apparently not, but the retreat's in rather an isolated area. We'll have to put more resources into that next week. Come on, Rach. Let's forget about work now. Want to watch more of that box set?'

'You mean "The Detectorists"? Yes, let's. It'll be good to chill out and escape.'

CHAPTER 9

The phone was ringing when I got in from the shops the next morning.

'Hi Rach. I've got news. The family history research has paid off. Helen Willis had a sister.'

'That's brilliant, Pete. Do you have any idea where she lives?'

'I waited to find out before ringing you. Didn't want to raise false hopes. I just hope she knows something about where Kate came from, and how she got to be living as Helen and Tony's daughter.'

'And…?'

'Megan Andrews lives in Sedbergh, Cumbria, with her two teenage children. Have you got a pen?'

Pete gave me the number and address and as soon as I'd put the phone down, I was on the phone to Kate. As expected, she was over the moon to be getting somewhere, even if Megan wasn't her real aunt. I had to tell her that my search of the official adoption records had drawn a blank, but the news about her aunt meant that she didn't take it too badly.

'She might know something about where I came from, Rachel.'

'I do hope so.'

Finding a relative was the priority, and maybe this aunt could solve the riddle of Kate's birth without my taking up any more of Pete's time.

After the first forty-eight hours had passed, Steve's own involvement in the Simon Crawford case had been scaled back to almost normal office hours. Cash for overtime was nearly non-existent, so had to be conserved for more appropriate times when, hopefully, there was a major development in the investigation. At the moment there was a lot of information-gathering by detective constables, and his sergeants filtered it before passing leads to Steve.

After close examination of Simon's head wound, the pathologist had concluded that it had most likely been caused by a large stone, which should have traces of Simon's blood. However, although the police had followed up their initial search with a very detailed fingertip search, they'd still failed to find anything incriminating in any of the cabins or in the surrounding woods, and were beginning to assume that the killer had taken away the stone and dumped it somewhere. After all, whoever it was had also removed all traces of Simon's work.

As Steve said to Rach that night, 'The killer could have simply tossed the stone into the water. The retreat isn't far from the Humber or the North Sea, after all.'

'That's true.'

'There were only two keys to Simon's cabin and both were accounted for. One in Simon's back pocket and the spare locked in the office. The course leader had an alibi as she lived locally and went home every evening, taking the office key with her, so with no sign of a forced entry, we're still looking at the possibility that one of the other writers killed Simon, perhaps for personal reasons, and we're looking into their backgrounds, criminal records etc.'

'Pretty time-consuming, but I'm guessing the lack of a break-in still allows for the possibility that Simon didn't know his killer from the retreat?'

'Exactly. Half the team are exploring the possibility of it being an outside job,' Steve continued. 'Simon could have let someone in whom he knew from elsewhere, say someone he'd met in Hull in connection with his novel, or alternatively the killer could have been someone unknown to him, but with a plausible reason for knocking.'

'It would have to be someone he thought harmless enough to invite into his isolated cabin.'

'Yes. In one of our brain-storming sessions, young Jenni suggested that as Simon wrote crime novels, it wouldn't be too much of a stretch to consider the killer might be someone pretending to be a police officer. I have to say, that lass'll go far. She always comes up with off-the-wall ideas. They may not be probable but they are possible, and one day she might be right. A lot of the other detectives are frightened of being shot down in flames for their suggestions so they keep quiet, and the older ones often just roll out the obvious, so we can get them on the board and eliminate them quickly.'

'If he's a crime writer, surely he would have known to ask to see a warrant card? I would have done.'

'Yes, but not everyone's like you, Rach. It was a new idea anyway, and that's something we've been short of. Maybe Simon didn't invite the killer in - perhaps whoever it was waited near the door and followed him in, even bundling him in through the door - although there were no signs of a struggle, no furniture knocked over and no sounds heard. But as I think I told you, the cabins are detached, so it would have had to be a very loud noise to be heard in the next cabin. And it doesn't help matters that there are few outside lights at the retreat, and no cameras at all.'

'I presume Simon's car was in the car park?'

'Yes. We can't know if he'd been out that night, but if he was, he could have been followed home, hit on the head in the car park and carried into the cabin where he was suffocated. Simon wasn't particularly big or heavy, but we paid particular attention to the car park. However, it's all tarmac and due to the dry weather, there was no chance of muddy footprints. We searched the path from the car park for signs of a scuffle, and took casts of footprints, but they're not much use unless we have something to compare them to, I'm afraid.'

'True.'

'We've dusted Simon's car for prints in case the killer came to the retreat in that. The prints don't match any of the writers, but there's always a chance they belong to the killer. However, they could also belong to anyone he gave a lift to in the months prior to his death, in Birmingham, for example. As we have no suspects, they're not much use.'

'So why did you…?'

'You were going to say, "Waste the time?" Rach? Well, you never know, and it would be no good not taking the prints and then wishing we had in a couple of weeks' time when the car's been returned to his widow.'

'Hmm... Had he been tied up?'

'No signs of any kind of restraint, but if he was killed for information, he might have been too frightened to stay quiet. He wasn't a crook, just a quiet, normal bloke, who happened to be a writer. I wouldn't expect him to sit there bravely if he was being threatened with violence.'

'Was there anything in the car?'

'No - and don't forget, nothing in the cottage either. So, maybe the killer wasn't after information, but looking to recover any evidence of wrongdoing which Simon might have stumbled upon. Presumably the killer took all his notes and his laptop and killed him to shut him up. Simon was a solitary person, so whatever it was that he knew, it probably hadn't gone any further.'

'That's tough for you.'

'Yeah, you know what it's like, Rach. If we don't get anywhere with a murder case in the first few days, it's like wading through treacle.'

'Now you're talking. I almost forgot. I bought some sticky toffee pudding today. Can I tempt you?'

'Don't get me started or you may regret saying that. Serve it up in that cute lacy apron you've got, and you'll be complaining you're too tired to work tomorrow.'

'As if… Though I've got a paying customer to see in the morning.'

'Well, I'll have to restrain myself then.'

'No chance.'

When I got up, I thought of the night before and smiled. We might not get a lot of time together, but I really get on well with Steve. He's reasonably good-looking, tall and strong, but the most important thing about him is that he's kind and thoughtful. Ok, so that's two important things, and of course I love him to bits.

I dressed in smart clothes and, perhaps not bright and early, but in good time at least, I arrived at the house of my new client, Mrs Hanson, not far from Cottingham. A rather severe-looking older lady, she invited me in and offered tea. Once we'd got the niceties out of the way, I got straight to the point. Our phone conversation had been very brief. I'd got the feeling she was concerned we might be overheard.

'Perhaps you can tell me in more detail why you think your husband might be having an affair, Mrs Hanson?'

'He's been doing a course at the university. At least, that's what he told me, but I'm afraid I don't think he's been going there the last month or so.'

'Is that just a hunch, or do you have any proof that he's not been going?'

'It was just a hunch. The way he was behaving. Smiling more. Going out in a new shirt. Not like him at all. And then…'

'Yes?' There was something she wanted to tell me but I could see she was embarrassed and I felt sorry for her. She looked nervous, sad even, leading me to believe she'd only been business-like at first to cope with the situation.

'I'm sorry. This is really difficult for me. I'd follow him myself but I lost confidence driving and Brian, that's my husband's name, said we didn't need two cars any more, and talked me into selling mine to save money. I really miss it though. It gave me independence. Now I have to rely on Brian to take me places and… I just need to know, that's all, so I can decide what to do about it.'

Her words petered out. I've had a lot of clients who want

their husband followed, and I've found most of them talk about wanting their husband back as if he were a possession, someone they needed to carry out practical tasks around the house and garden. That didn't seem to be the case here. 'Janet - do you mind if I call you by your first name?'

'No, it's fine.'

'Well, Janet. I'm guessing you either discovered he wasn't going to the class, or maybe you found something?'

'More like smelt. Perfume on his shirt one night, after he was supposed to be at his night class.'

'I see. Well, if you can give me the details of the class, a rough idea of the time he leaves the house, and which night, I'll follow him.' I didn't tell her not to worry. She seemed too intelligent to be fobbed off. We agreed a fee, and I left, promising to ring.

CHAPTER 10

That evening I followed an overweight Brian as he left the house and drove off towards the university. Could Janet Hanson have been wrong? After fifteen minutes, it seemed unlikely. He turned down a street of terrace houses and stopped. It was too far away from the university to use as a parking slot. Most of the houses were probably shared by students. He knocked on a door and disappeared inside before I could see who answered.

I waited. About half an hour later he emerged from the house and then drove off and pulled up again by the park. And then he sat there. Nothing else happened. He didn't get out. It was like he was killing time until he could go home. I wondered why he'd only spent half an hour with his girlfriend, if that's who she was. When he drove home, I followed him to check he didn't stop off anywhere else, before I returned to the house he'd visited. Maybe the woman was married and only had a small time-slot on her own.

I got out, picking up my folder of notes, to look like one of the canvassers currently doing the pre-election rounds, and knocked at the door. The door opened just a crack. I caught sight of a pale-faced blonde girl in a dressing-gown. 'I'm interested in whether you and your husband will be voting…'

She cut me off. 'Go away, please. I expect someone.' The door slammed in my face. Interesting. I had an address and used my link to the electoral roll to look up the names of the occupants, but no voters were registered at that address. The girl sounded vaguely Eastern European and she was probably renting. I wondered if she was actually waiting for her husband to come home. I waited and a man arrived about ten minutes later. He knocked, which seemed a bit odd. I decided to call on the neighbours. It was only half past nine so not too late to bother people.

'Excuse me, but I wonder if you could help me? It's about your neighbour at number twelve.' I'd not thought much further ahead than that. If anything I suppose I could have waffled on about being a volunteer for a political party, but I didn't need to.

'Are you from the Social? Or the police? I don't know much, but there's something not right next door. Men coming and going at all hours and I've never seen that blonde girl above the odd time at the dustbin and she's always in her dressing-gown. Looks half-starved, and I could swear she had a black eye one time I saw her. The house was empty for about a month after the old lady died and it didn't have a sign up saying 'to let' or 'for sale'. You don't like to interfere but I nearly called the police the other week. There was shouting and banging and then silence. But I thought it wasn't my place to interfere.'

'OK. Thanks. I'll get someone to look into it.'

I went back to my car and rang Steve at home. I told him I thought a woman was being kept against her will as a prostitute, and he said to keep an eye on the house and follow the girl if she left, whether on her own or with someone. He'd have someone round as soon as he could.

His department, Serious Crimes, have a watching brief for such things. He told me all about pop-up brothels once and how the girls applied for jobs in the UK and came here expecting to be nannies. Only they had their passports taken away on arrival and were forced into having sex with a succession of men until they had paid for their ticket from Romania or wherever - mainly Eastern Europe. Only then the organisers added new charges for food, rent, clothes etc. and so they never earned enough to pay their debts, and they never got free. Most of them were hooked on drugs as well, which made them more dependent as well as more in debt.

About twenty minutes later, a police car arrived. A policewoman got out and knocked at the door, while one of

Steve's sergeants, Chris Fieldhouse, waited out of sight to the side of the door. I saw them make their way inside, and wondered if I should leave. A few minutes later another police car arrived with a couple of officers and a woman not in uniform. I guessed she might be from Social Services. Chris came out a few minutes later.

'Thanks for your help, Rach. The blonde girl's not too bad considering. She was terrified at first, but then accepted we're here to help her. There's another girl with jet-black hair, and she's in a right state though. Only looks to be about fifteen, if that.'

'Oh, Chris. That's dreadful.'

'I know. At least you've rescued two of them. It's so hard for us to get a handle on it because the gangs move them around to different empty properties so often, and the neighbours rarely see them, so before they think about getting in touch with someone about their suspicions, the girls are gone.'

'Right then. I'll head off home to Steve and try to decide what to say to my client tomorrow. '

'Can you hold off that until we've spoken to her husband, please? We don't want your Mr Hanson forewarned and scaring off our suspects.'

'Yes, of course.' I wrote down Mr Hanson's contact details for him. 'Will he get arrested?'

'Unlikely, just leaned on a bit to provide any information he knows, such as how he found the girl. Maybe a notice in the gents in a pub, but probably on the internet. We'll stake out this place until someone turns up, but in the meantime we can maybe use the web address to track down other gang members or if we're lucky, other gangs. Shall I give you a ring, Rach, when it's OK for you to report back to Mrs Hanson, or just tell Steve?'

'You can just ring me on the home number, if you don't mind. He's usually very conscientious but he might just forget to tell me if he's had a busy day.'

When I got in, Steve gave me a big hug. 'Quick thinking there, Rach.'

'I always knew I was a big asset to the force.'

One good bit of news happened that week. Kate rang around ten o'clock on the Thursday morning. She sounded really excited. 'I've got three grade A's, Rachel!'

'Oh, that's fantastic! Congratulations! I'm so pleased for you. You deserve it. You must be thrilled.'

'I am. Thanks, Rachel. That means a lot. And I'll be coming to Hull. It's fantastic. I just wish…'

'Don't beat yourself up, Kate. You've worked so hard and you deserve it. It's what you've always wanted and I know you'll have a great time and make a success of your life.'

'Yes. It won't be long now. It's only five weeks or so until Freshers' Week. I've just got to get the accommodation sorted online.'

'I bet you're a bit nervous, but you'll get on just fine. Don't forget to have some fun for a change as well as studying.'

'Will do. Thanks so much. For everything. You're like the big sister I never had.'

'Oh, what a lovely thing to say!'

'I must go now, though. I'd better ring Mrs Charlesworth. Speak soon.'

As I said goodbye, I was touched that she'd chosen to ring me first.

I gave Steve a quick ring. When I told him he said, 'That's great news – and sweet that she said you're like a sister to her. Actually I'm glad you rang. We might have a breakthrough.'

'That's great. Can you tell me anything?'

'We've got a possible lead that someone from outside the retreat might have killed him. The team who initially interviewed people living nearby turned up nothing. But a farmer whose land backs onto the wood came forward today to say his son saw headlights where the track enters the trees. He thought it was a funny place to stop.'

'Why's he only just told you this?'

'The lad's been away on a backpacking holiday with some

mates from university since the murder, and his dad forgot to tell us there'd been anyone else in the house at the time. The lad, Jake, came home at the weekend with his washing, the way lads do every now and again, and his mum just happened to mention about all the extra customers in the village shop where she works. Police in and out all the time buying snacks, she said. It's to be hoped the Super doesn't hear that titbit. He's got a major drive at the moment to get us all fitter.'

'And you were saying…'

'So Jake asked why there were police in the area, she told him about the murder, and he remembered the lights. He's definite it was that night, because he was up late finishing an essay before he went back.'

'Well that puts a completely different light on the murderer's identity, then.'

'Yes, we've got a whole new line of enquiry, which could be good, in that we were getting nowhere fast as things stood. Unfortunately the lead's a bit vague. No number plate or even make for the car. There are no static cameras on that road and not many CCTV cameras on shops or garages in the area either. We're going to have our work cut out to identify any cars around at that time on the night of the murder.'

'Sounds like quite a job.'

'It is. If we don't come up with anything, I might have to consider looking at hours of CCTV, making lists of number plates seen on the A1033 to and from the Hedon roundabout, hoping to find someone we recognise, even though the retreat's about ten miles further east. The proverbial needle in the haystack. And we're going round in circles looking at everything again, in the light of a possible outside job.'

'Seems like you're going to be busy.'

'Yes. I'm afraid I have to consider any little thing they come up with.'

The next morning a new client rang. Carol Stanwick was thinking of expanding her business. She said she'd interviewed several people as prospective managers for her second shop and had almost decided, but would be grateful if I could just run an eye over her two favourite candidates. She wanted me to check out their references in person by talking to ex-clients as well as employers. She had to make up her mind fairly quickly, but she was snowed under sorting out the new premises, and wanted a second opinion as it was a big financial commitment for her.

I pulled a quick favour with Steve, and his sergeant Matt came back with the news that neither had criminal records, which was a start. I knew nothing about beauty salons of any variety, but this was more of a clinic.

Carol's salon offered a range of treatments, and styled itself as a 'face and body clinic', covering a range of anti-ageing treatments such as microdermabrasion, Botox, fillers and thread vein removals as well as massages, tanning, waxing, electrolysis, pedicures and nail extensions. No wonder she'd want to be sure of her new manager's credentials. If things went wrong with some of those treatments, she could be saddled with a big insurance claim, which would at the very least put up her premiums, even supposing she had enough cover. Worse still, her good reputation could be ruined, which might mean the end of her business.

I pulled out all the stops, ringing around, contacting people who'd had similar treatments from each of the candidates as well as checking both sets of qualifications and references from previous employers. I couldn't find any horror stories, just the odd person whose treatment hadn't achieved what she'd expected. As I doubted any of them could reverse time, I reflected that some people were always going to have unrealistic hopes, so dismissed them when I realised they hadn't any real complaint about the standard of work.

No wonder Carol couldn't decide. I couldn't either. My final job was to call on their neighbours, and that tipped the balance marginally. One of the candidates had a habit of boasting about her clients, whilst the other refused to be drawn.

Carol was really pleased with my report, and said that was

the kind of thing that made all the difference to her decision. She insisted on paying me a bonus on top of the sum we'd originally agreed, and said it was worth every penny. It was a profitable week for me, but more importantly, one I'd enjoyed.

CHAPTER 11

I was in the shower when my mobile rang. I saw it was Kate, and rang her back while the kettle was boiling.

'Hi Rach. Guess what? I managed to get hold of my Aunt Megan, up in Cumbria. She and Mam came from there apparently.'

'That's great, Kate. What did she say?'

'She was really pleased to hear from me, but devastated to hear that Mam's dead. I explained about the crash and how the funeral had to go ahead a few days after I recovered consciousness, before I had time to look around to see if there was anyone to call. She was surprised I hadn't known she existed, as she sent birthday cards.'

'Do you remember getting any?'

'No. Not at all. And of course I didn't come across any when I searched the house.'

'That's strange.'

'I know. Anyway, I asked my aunt what she remembered about my birth, and she told me that Mam had had three early miscarriages and was so happy when she rang to say she was pregnant with me, because she was six months' gone. She had the cot, the pram and all the clothes ready, and was really excited. Aunt Megan didn't hear for nearly a year till Mam rang and said she'd had a difficult time but everything was alright and they had a beautiful baby girl. My aunt had been going through a divorce and moving house, so time had just passed. She came to see us when I was about three, and then she only saw Mam again on her own, at funerals, first Grandma's, then Granddad's.'

'Did she say why that was?'

'Mam had gone on her own up to Cumbria, because it was such a long trail and Dad couldn't really leave the animals, and I was in school by then. So she hadn't seen me since I was three.'

'That'll be why you couldn't remember her then.'

'Yes. I told her then that Mam and Dad (I still can't call them anything else) weren't my natural parents; that there'd been four miscarriages. Sounds like the last one must have happened just after she'd rung my aunt Megan to say she was six months' pregnant. I asked if she had any ideas who might be my real mam, but she didn't, and she was so shocked, I don't think she was hiding anything.'

'Did you ask her about other relatives?'

'She said she has two children, a boy and a girl, but that's all. Her husband left her, and she's had a bit of a struggle. That's why she's not had the money to come down to Lincolnshire. It seems she and my mam didn't have any other relatives, and she didn't think Dad had either. Grace is going to drive me up there when we get chance, but in the meantime, I've passed her details on to my solicitor.'

'Oh, Kate. I'm really sorry your aunt doesn't know of any other relatives.'

'Thank you, Rachel, but I'm beginning to think we've gone as far as we can.'

'Don't give up yet, Kate. I've still got some old neighbours I haven't tracked down. Something'll turn up, I'm sure.'

We said our goodbyes. I hoped I'd sounded more optimistic than I felt.

'Anything new, Steve?' I asked that night.

'Funny you should ask. One very interesting thing came to light today. Derek, the desk sergeant, came into our office first thing this morning. He was just back off leave. He'd been in Spain but his neighbour gave him a pile of newspapers to catch up on the local news and he recognised Simon Crawford's photo in the murder report. Apparently Simon had been into the station to ask if he could speak to someone in CID. He'd said he was writing a novel about smuggling and wanted to shadow a police officer who was working on a similar case. It must have been shortly before he was killed, he thought, though he didn't know the exact date.'

'Who did this Derek put him onto?'

'No-one. He gave him short shrift and told him if he wanted any information, he should write to the Press Officer. He never saw him again.'

'And did he write?'

'No. There's no record of it.'

'Well, it's a shame that the lead's a dead end, but it confirms Simon's interest in smuggling.'

'It doesn't get us anywhere, though does it?'

'What about the CCTV?' I didn't think he'd have any new leads on the car driver the student had seen or he would have been bursting to tell me as soon as he got in, but I felt I had to ask.

'Despite all the hours the team are putting in, staring at hours of CCTV, we've had no breakthroughs.' I could see the strain on Steve's face. 'If they don't come up with anything soon, the Super will haul me into his office and insist on scaling the investigation down. There must be something I'm missing.'

'You'll get lucky soon, Steve. And the Super has faith in you.'

'I know. He's not said anything yet despite the lack of progress, but there are some other big cases in the department and I may not be able to hold on to all of my team for much longer. Some'll be called over to lend a hand elsewhere.'

'Come here and sit down. Close your eyes and I'll massage your shoulders.' I hadn't a clue how to give a proper massage, but Steve didn't seem to mind, particularly when he turned the tables on me. We had an early night but we didn't catch up on sleep as we'd hoped. He was gone when I got up, just a scrawled note on the table saying, 'You keep me sane. Love you. Sxx.'

Mum rang just after tea that Friday and asked me if I fancied going to an antique fair at the Floral Hall in Hornsea. It seemed Dad had promised to help their neighbour, Keith, lay his new drive, and she didn't fancy going on her own. I shouted over my shoulder to Steve, 'What are you doing tomorrow morning?'

'If your mum's asking you to go somewhere, just go, Rach. You know I can go into work, and I won't have to feel guilty about it. Plus, I promise I'll take Sunday off.'

'Yes, Mum. Sounds good. What time?'

Arrangements made, I put down the phone and couldn't help saying to Steve, 'You do know that Saturday and Sunday are both your days off, don't you?'

'Yes. I do work a five-day week when we're not up to our ears in a murder investigation as well as other ongoing cases. Come here, you cheeky madam.' Steve chased me round the settee and I let him catch me. I'm hopeless at playing hard-to-get.

In the morning, I picked Mum up and we got there before the fair opened to get the best bargains. There was a mug with mermaids on that we both fancied. 'That's Hornsea. A John Clappison design. They're really collectible now.'

'You're very knowledgeable, Mum.'

'Dad and I have been buying the odd piece of Hornsea Pottery. Reminds us of the days we used to go to the factory and buy things for our bottom drawer. It's a shame you and your sister broke all the mugs. I've only got a few vases and that little biscuit jar left.'

'You mean the one shaped like an owl? I didn't know that was Hornsea Pottery.'

'We've been looking at prices on eBay. Apparently they're rare. It's worth somewhere well over a hundred pounds now. Amazing that survived.'

'Probably because you hid the biscuits from us on a high shelf, and doled them out one at a time. We couldn't break it because we weren't allowed to touch it.'

'Do you mind if I get the mug? Your Dad'll love it.'

'Of course not. You saw it first.'

Then Mum pointed out a pale cream vase with a seventies type girl on the side, with stars in her hair. The shape was unusual, a flattened oval. 'That's an Aphrodite vase. First one I've ever seen. That's by John Clappison as well.'

'That's lovely', I whispered. I didn't want to show too much interest as Mum moved in to negotiate a price, and one thing the antiques programmes have taught me is that sellers don't have to drop their prices if a buyer is swooning over something, because they'll pay the top price anyway. I wandered on and found a stall with jewellery and some old powder compacts. By the time Mum caught up with me, I'd bought a lovely enamel art deco compact. 'I love the vase, Mum, but we haven't much room for pottery apart from mugs in our flat. I'll be able to see it at yours, though. What do you think of this compact? Compacts are something I could collect.'

'It's much nicer than the ones I remember. I think I had one when I was about fifteen, but then everyone went over to liquid foundation and they went out of fashion. I expect your Gran's still got hers. You'll have to ask her when you next see her.'

I was really getting into this antique fair shopping but we didn't spot anything else, and adjourned to the café for a cuppa. 'Let's go to Hornsea Museum now, Rach.'

'A museum? I'm not sure I'd be that interested, to be honest.'

'You will be,' Mum insisted.

It turned out that the museum has an entire annexe devoted to Hornsea Pottery. It was amazing the things they'd made. 'Wow. I can see now why you're so enthusiastic. A lot of the things have that Scandinavian look which is so popular now – or "on trend" as they say on the antiques programmes.'

'I'm going to join the Hornsea Collectors' and Research Society. They have newsletters and meetings. I was hoping you might come with me, Rach. Laura's not interested in anything old. The next meeting near us is at the beginning of December near Barnsley.'

'OK. Count me in.' I could well believe that my sister Laura wouldn't want to be buying retro pottery. She likes everything brand new and quite plain. Minimalist, she calls it. I think it's boring, but you wouldn't expect sisters to be the same and anyway, if she did have some of the Hornsea pieces, not much of it would survive long, the way her twins ran around the house.

Sunday dawned sunny and warm. We were up early and on the road to Whitby by eight. Once past Beverley we made good time. We parked on the west cliff and walked down through the old town to the quaint and lovely Sherlock's café for a drink. Afterwards we decided to saunter over the bridge and along the cobbled street that led to the east cliff.

At the end, by the shop selling Whitby jet, we climbed the 199 steps to the top, urging each other to keep going without stopping. I wasn't as fit as I thought but I made it.

In the shadow of the abbey ruins, we looked at the old worn gravestones battered by the elements in the churchyard, before turning back in search of lunch back down by the harbour. I ran the last half dozen steps and the momentum carried me tripping over the uneven cobbles, and to the far side of the street, where I managed to slow myself down by grabbing hold of an unsuspecting teenage boy, just stopping myself from careering off down a steep narrow ginnel to the beach.

I was totally embarrassed, though obviously not as much as the lad I'd used as a brake. When I turned around, Steve was laughing his socks off. 'Typical! Why didn't you run and save me?'

''No way could I match your speed, Rach – and anyway, it made that young lad's day, being accosted by a sexy woman. I couldn't possibly have interrupted.'

Falling about laughing, we went in search of fish and chips. After we'd eaten, we bought some fresh crab sandwiches to take home for tea, before spending a happy hour or so in the antique shops.

I spent a while browsing the vintage powder compacts. Nothing in particular caught my eye, but we'd had a lovely day and we drove back home down the coast road for a change. The fresh air and exercise did its trick and we both had the best sleep we'd had in a while.

CHAPTER 12

I hadn't any other work waiting for me, so I rang Sarah to catch up on news. Her husband John had booked time off and they were taking Josh on holiday to Centre Parcs. She asked me round for a coffee and to keep an eye on Josh while she packed. He was walking now and into everything. I'm not very maternal, but he's a placid little chap, so I thought I could handle it.

'We thought it'd be fun for him to get a bit of nature. We're going to hire bikes and get some exercise. He can sit in those little trailers they hook on the back. We can take him in the pool as well. He likes swimming.'

I wondered if Steve would want children. Strangely enough, we'd never discussed it, but there again our wedding plans hadn't materialised yet either, so I shouldn't get ahead of myself.

When I got home Steve's sergeant, Chris Fieldhouse, rang to say I could now contact Mrs Hanson. 'As a result of information provided by her husband we managed to make some arrests. It's only the tip of the iceberg, but every little helps and we have some new lines of enquiry. We won't be charging Mr Hanson.'

'Thanks, Chris. I hope you get some more of the bastards.'

I decided to go round to see Mrs Hanson that afternoon. I rang first to check she would be in, and thankfully her husband must have been at work as normal, because she answered. She sounded weary.

'About your husband...'

Before I could say anything else, she interrupted, 'I know everything, Miss Hodges. After the police contacted him, my husband told me all about the girl he'd been seeing. He was scared he'd get a criminal record. He asked me to stand by him. I've asked him to move out for a while. I'm not sure whether I'll have him back.'

'Right. The police aren't going to charge him. His information helped them to make arrests and gave them further leads, and two girls have been rescued.'

I'm glad he's not been charged but he can't take credit for anything. You were the one who saved them. If you send me your bill, I'll get it paid.'

'Thank you. Can I help in any other way?'

'No, thank you. Goodbye, Miss Hodges.'

I felt desperately sorry for her, but I respected her decision to work things out herself. Maybe she could overlook his transgression in time. But it was a hard decision to make, and I didn't envy her.

There's only so much cleaning a girl can do. Maybe some women can vacuum every day, clean windows, scrub floors, polish ornaments, I don't know what else, but not me. I wanted to be working and the office answerphone remained stubbornly silent, so I rang Steve at work, and asked if I could help him.

'That's very kind, Rach, but I can't have you involved in an investigation.'

'That's a bit rich, seeing as how I helped on a couple of your last big cases!' I felt righteously indignant.

'You only got involved because the crimes were linked to your own investigations.'

I was just having a cuppa and a biscuit when the phone rang. It made me jump, caught out sneaking a third choc chip cookie from the tin.

'I'm afraid I might be a bit late tonight for another reason. Something I could well do without, but I should really call and see Karen before I come home.'

'Who's this Karen, when she's at home?'

'Nick Heighway's girlfriend. You remember.'

'He's not turned up then?'

'No. He's due back at work next Monday. I'd put it on the back burner until then, if you remember, though I wish I hadn't now. Anyway, apparently she rang again today, sounding a bit tearful. She's not heard from him in over a week. She could list him as officially missing, but I thought I'd call in and get the feel of the place, meet her face to face. I want to be sure she's not just causing trouble for him because she's cross he's spending a couple of weeks off without her.'

'I could go, if you want. You know me, I'd get more out of her than you would. She'd not mention anything about her love life if you were there anyway.'

'I'm not sure that's a good idea…'

'Oh come on, Steve. Sobbing females, tracing missing people, checking up on people's wives and husbands. It's bread and butter stuff to me and besides, you're busy enough.'

I heard someone shout "Boss" in the background, and knew my boredom was over.

'OK Rach. They live off Beverley Road, so it's not far. I'll text you the address and phone number. You'd better ring before you turn up. She won't know who you are.'

A short while later I rang Karen's number. She sounded really wary, and I realised she might think I was some girl ringing for Nick. I quickly told her I was ringing on behalf of Inspector Steve Rose, and she said, 'Thank goodness.'

'I'm Rachel Hodges. I've worked with the police before, and I want to help.'

'I don't understand.'

'I think the desk sergeant explained that as Nick is an adult, and a police officer at that, with no reason for anyone to think foul play is involved, the police can't use their limited resources to investigate his disappearance while he's still on leave.'

'So who are you and what can you do, if you're not a police officer?'

'I'm Inspector Rose's fiancée, but I'm also a private detective. I expect you've heard about the murder on the news? Well Steve's team's really stretched working on that case, but he cares a lot about his staff and didn't want to let you down, so he suggested I might come round to your flat and see how I might help. And before you say anything about payment, I'd just be calling as a favour to Steve.'

'Mm… well, that's kind of him, I suppose. Can you come round today? I'm getting really worried. I work in a shop five minutes from home, so I could meet you there during my lunch break.'

'Yes, no problem. I've got your address.'

We agreed I'd go round at one. I had something to eat before I drove round. I can't think on an empty stomach. Karen and Nick's flat wasn't hard to find. Parking wasn't easy, but I made it on time.

Karen was slim and blonde. Pretty, too. The thought passed through my head that I couldn't see her boyfriend walking out on her, but I pulled myself together quickly. I was there to work, not to jump to conclusions. She might be a horrid person. We got through the introductions and I showed her my business card.

'I'm glad it's you rather than a policeman, really. They seem to think I'm getting worked up over nothing, and Nick's just gone off with some girl, but he's not like that. If I can convince you, then maybe you can get them to look into it seriously. I know he's not due back at work for a couple more days, but I'm really worried now.'

'OK. I'll see what I can do. It would help if you can tell me a bit about Nick. How long have you known him?'

'I met him at a party in Cottingham when he was a student. We hit it off and we've been together for over two years now. We moved into this flat after he graduated.'

'So he studied law at Hull uni then?'

'Yes.'

'Just like Steve.' I realised I shouldn't go any further into Steve's history, and maybe the "done" thing would be to refer to him as Inspector Rose, but I reasoned that I'd get more out of her if I kept it friendly, rather than coming over all official-sounding.

'I didn't go to uni but Nick doesn't seem to mind.'

I made a mental note that maybe he'd found her a change from girls who were students, but had got bored now. Speculating again, but perhaps with a stronger reason this time?

'And his parents? Where do they live? Have you contacted them since he went missing?'

'They were killed in a car crash a couple of years ago.'

'Oh, I'm sorry to hear that. Any other relatives?'

'Only a brother. I rang him but he lives on another planet, almost literally. He's doing a PhD in astrophysics at Oxford, and doesn't understand what Nick sees in me. He was quite offhand.'

'So I'm guessing he hadn't seen or heard from Nick either?'

'Not since earlier in the year.'

'Does Nick have any close friends?'

'I've rung them all, at least the ones who made it into what passes for his address book. None of us make a note of half the numbers in our mobiles, do we?'

'Can you run me through what happened when you last saw him, please, Karen? That would be the weekend before last, wouldn't it?'

'Nothing much. We went food shopping together on the Saturday morning. He had to work in the afternoon, but then we watched a film in the evening. It was a bit boring, to be honest, and Nick kept looking at his phone. I got annoyed with him, but we didn't have a big row or anything, if that's what you're thinking.'

'And the Sunday?'

'Nick played football on the Sunday morning. I don't know any of his footie mates, I'm afraid. I don't even know where they play but he said it was a big game. He came back really happy, like they'd won a cup or something. I wish I'd taken more notice. After lunch we drove out to Hornsea Freeport and he bought me a dress I liked. He usually hates going there but on Sunday he couldn't have been more loving. That's why I don't think he could possibly have run off with anyone else. He couldn't have just been pretending he cares.'

I suspected that he might have been arranging his fortnight away instead of being at football, and guilt had led him to pay for her frock, but I carried on going through the motions. 'I can't think of anything else at the moment, so I'll let you get back to work. Can I just use your loo first, please?'

On the way to the bathroom, I glanced in the bedroom. It looked fairly tidy, and his side of the wardrobe had some clothes in it, not like he'd done a runner. The bathroom had his shaver, foam and the like, too, but he could always have bought some more somewhere else. His brother seemed to think Nick had made a mistake in settling for a shop girl, after all. The lad had booked leave so maybe he was just staying with someone else while he got his head together and plucked up the courage to leave Karen.

When I got back, I asked Karen if he had a car. 'Yes, but it's parked round the corner on the side street. He always walked to work, because parking's difficult in the centre unless you qualify for a place in the police garage.'

My first thought when she said that, was that he'd left the car to go somewhere with someone else.

As I turned to leave, however, Karen handed me a carrier bag. 'I almost forgot. I suppose you should give these to Nick's sergeant. All his notebooks on that case he was working overtime on. I didn't mention them before, because I thought he might get in trouble for keeping police stuff at home, but I expect Nick would want his sergeant to have them if he can't get in to work. He said he was gathering information to crack a big case. He was quite excited about it. That's another reason why I can't understand why he'd go off on his own. He'd never leave his work stuff behind.'

As I drove home, I revised my opinion. Maybe Nick hadn't left her for someone else, after all. I should have known it doesn't pay to jump to conclusions too early.

When Steve arrived home, I showed him the carrier bag straight away. I'd been gobsmacked when I opened it. 'This is a real puzzle, Steve. In here there's a stack of notebooks. I had a sneaky look and there are times, dates, initials, cash amounts and odd scribbles. Karen thought I should have them as Nick told her he was gathering information to help break a big case. I'm guessing he shouldn't have stuff like this at home, even if he had been working on a case?'

'Correct. I wonder if he's been taking bribes.'

'Could have been, but to be honest, I don't think so. The flat is neat and tidy but apart from the TV, there's nothing that screams extravagance. He could have a gambling habit, but I think she'd have noticed.'

'Unlikely, anyway. I spoke to Tommy Bradfield, his sergeant, about Nick after Karen came into the station.'

'I've not heard you mention him before.'

'Tommy? He transferred in to Serious Crimes about three months ago, but I haven't got to know him that well. He's not been working on any of the cases I've had the most involvement with. Matt's been my sergeant on those, as always. Anyway, Tommy knows Nick a lot better, being his sergeant. He seemed to have a very different impression of young Nick than I did. He said he'd been late on a couple of occasions and was always keen to get away early. He thought he was cheating on his girlfriend, seeing other girls. He thinks he heard the name Sally mentioned once or twice, maybe Diane too. I must have got the wrong end of the stick or Nick behaved differently when I was around, because I thought he was a very earnest lad and hard-working. I try to have a word with the fast-track lads every couple of months and I got the feeling he was keen to get promotion and make Chief Inspector in double-quick time.'

'Are you going to go over the notebooks now?'

'No, love. I'll report him as officially missing and turn the notes over to Tommy in the morning to take a look first, summarise what might need looking into. You did well to get her to give you them. She didn't mention them at all when she came into the station.'

'This Tommy'll be really busy if he's not got Nick. He won't make them a priority. And you're snowed under. Why don't you let me take a look first?'

'They really need logging in, Rach.'

'Well, log them in then. You can't tell me that you'd have lugged them in to work to log them in and then brought them home again if you had time to look at them yourself.'

'Hmm. You're right. Just count up how many notebooks and I'll log them in and out. I'll fetch the evidence stickers home to put on them tonight. But you're not to take them out of the flat, write on them or photocopy them.'

I looked at him as if he'd grown two heads. 'You do know you can trust me with the chain of evidence, Steve. And I won't do anything any differently to you. You'll just be using your resources efficiently.'

'So, you're a resource, now, are you? Does that mean I can make you bend over backwards for me if I want?'

'Maybe, but you'll have to catch me first!'

CHAPTER 13

The next morning I turned on the radio to hear that the unidentified body of a man had been discovered by a couple walking their dog near Cherry Cobb Sands, and I knew Steve's day might be another long one.

The radio presenter went on to say that the area close to the Humber was the site of a World War Two bombing decoy. Apparently these elaborate sites were constructed in an attempt, often successful, to mislead Luftwaffe bomber crews. They were known as 'Starfish' and consisted of lights, fires and artificial buildings, whose purpose was to trick bombardiers into releasing their bombs early - in this case just before they got to Hull.

In the case of Cherry Cobb Sands bombing decoy site, Hull dockyards were reproduced on a small scale, with lights on poles shining down onto pools of water, giving the appearance of a defective blackout. The bomber pilots were tricked by the scale into thinking they were at a higher altitude than they actually were. The body was in one of those pools.

Muttering to myself, 'well, that's something I never knew', I got out of bed, wondering why Dad had never mentioned the place. He must have told me hundreds of facts about local places in the past.

Steve was going to be even busier than ever now, with a second murder to deal with. Which reminded me, I'd promised to go through Nick's notebooks.

I settled down and took my time, making notes as I went along and then put together a summary for Steve. They seemed to be diaries, and from what he'd told me of Nick's service record, they covered the whole period. It was all a bit messy, and

I discounted all but the last couple of months after I realised the earlier part covered meetings, courses and details about the different departments and general work-related information, interspersed with the usual sort of diary entries - birthday reminders, times of football practices and matches, down to 'MILK and 'CHOCOLATE', when presumably his girlfriend Karen had texted him to ask him to bring some in from the corner shop.

I got more interested when, about a month or so before he disappeared, the initial 'S' began to crop up. There were regular short entries of 'meet S in pub', 'see S at lunch break - QGdns'.

Perhaps 'S' was the girlfriend - Sally, was it? - that Nick's sergeant had spoken of? Mention of 'S' continued, but there were also entries with cash amounts, such as 'DH £100', 'DH £200' etc., building up gradually to the days before Nick disappeared, when the amounts increased to £1000 and £1200.

The final week's entries included 'meeting S at The Deep', 'cinema', 'followed D to lock-up' and 'S followed C'. The last entry was underlined heavily - 'car park C met B. Christ!'

The final entry was 'S didn't turn up. It's all over'.

It was too sparse to glean much, but Steve would be grateful for the summary.

When Steve eventually got home, well after nine, he looked dead on his feet.

'Have you eaten, love?'

'Yes, we sent out for something about six, thanks.'

'Well I bet it's all you've had today. Shall I make you a slice of toast with honey to have with your drink while you look over the summary I've done of Nick's notebooks?'

'Could you just give me the gist, please?'

I summed it up, then couldn't resist adding my thoughts. 'He could be having a fling with this S, and the cash figures were gambling debts, or maybe S was married and someone was blackmailing him over his affair, or he could have been looking into a crime. There's just not enough there to work out what he was up to.'

'OK, thanks Rach. It's intriguing but it sounds like there's nothing we can do at the moment. It can wait until he gets back to work and I'll have a word with him then. I could do with clearing my head before bed. Why don't we chill in front of one of those antique programmes you've recorded?'

So Tim Wonnacott and his pals lulled us into a suitable frame of mind for sleep, though I did lie awake for a while wishing I could have found that beautiful art deco perfume bottle that went for so much at auction…

Steve was up and out before I'd properly shaken myself awake. I felt guilty for not making him some breakfast. It wasn't as if I had a hectic life at that moment. My morning was free and I walked into town to shop. The shops were an even greater temptation now that I was living with Steve. I used to live out in east Hull near Mum and Dad. Parking's difficult in the centre, so I used to take the bus usually, but even that didn't make it as easy as walking across through the old town from Steve's flat near the marina.

Wandering around H&M, browsing the jumpers, it dawned on me that I'd better call in at home soon to get clothes for the autumn. Thinking of my old flat as 'home' reminded me of the unresolved state of our accommodation. I still had my flat - mainly because Steve's place was too small to fit all my things into. I'd love a house together, but Steve likes being able to walk to work in five minutes or so. Stalemate. Phone calls to my office - or spare bedroom to you and me - were now being forwarded to an answering machine at Steve's. I won't give that number out to all and sundry, and it's certainly not on my website or business cards, because I want to split off work from the rest of my life and you get some weirdos when you put your name out there as a private detective.

I'd hardly been back to the flat since I got back from Amsterdam. As soon as these murders were cleared up, I'd have to broach the subject of buying a house, particularly as the police headquarters were now set to move out of the town centre, taking the convenience factor for Steve out of the equation. A house and garden was a higher priority to me than a wedding, whatever Gran might think.

At lunchtime, three new jumpers and a pair of ankle boots to the better, I texted Steve to say sorry I'd missed him that morning. He wouldn't have time for a chat but he could read a text over a buttie. I even got a reply. 'Shouldn't be too late tonight.'

True to his word, he wasn't.

'How'd it go today?' I asked.

'Carrying on from last night, mainly. We didn't get that much done at the site last night before it got dark. So it's been the usual, kicking into gear and dealing with Forensics. The lads interviewed the people who found the body and they've been out around the area, nearby cottages, farms and the like, asking if anyone noticed a strange car or van. We're looking at missing persons, but we can't do a great deal until we know who the bloke was, or how long the body has been there. Identification's going to be tough because someone messed his face and fingertips up pretty badly, and it's always harder when a body's been in water anyway.'

'So it's definitely murder?'

'Yes, that's certain at least. He wouldn't get those injuries by slipping into the pool by accident, and anyway it was built with a low concrete wall around it. There's no CCTV, hardly any houses out there, so not a lot of people to ask. That's why it got on the radio sharpish, in the hope it might jog someone's memory.'

'Fascinating stuff about the bomb decoy site. I couldn't believe I'd never heard of it.'

'Yeah. This area never fails to surprise me - these hidden places with their forgotten history, so near to a major city like Hull.' Sitting down to eat, he continued, 'Did you know about the Kilnsea Sound Mirror? Chris Fieldhouse was telling me about it over lunch.'

'No, can't say I do. Surely not another thing Dad's never

mentioned?'

'It's a huge square slice of concrete, standing on its edge in a field near Kilnsea, about a mile from Spurn Point. It's got a dish, almost five metres in diameter, carved out of it on the side facing the sea, and it's an early forerunner of radar. It dates to the early days of aircraft, when aeroplanes and Zeppelins were relatively slow and it could locate them up to twenty-five miles away.'

'Is he sure it's still there? I've never seen it, and Dad took me and Laura out that way to Spurn Point loads of times.'

'Ah, well it's a distance inland to prevent the noise of the waves interfering with the noise of the aircraft. It's next to Eastrington Ponds nature reserve. Chris goes there. He says it's a popular spot for bird-watchers as you get egrets there and rarer birds drop in when they're migrating.'

'Good for Chris. I've never heard of it.'

'He's a mine of information. Once he gets started, you get to know all sorts of historical facts about the East Riding.'

'I get the feeling you're bursting to tell me something else.'

'Yes, I am. How's about this titbit? In the early 1940s the War Office built secret bunkers at Rise where they trained saboteurs in case of invasion. It was so secret, even their families and neighbours didn't know what they were doing and there was no official recognition at all. In fact some were treated as cowards because they didn't join the forces.'

'Fascinating, but not for those poor men. Remind me sometime and we'll certainly go take a look at that radar thing.'

'The Kilnsea Sound Mirror?'

'Yes.' And to show that I paid attention to his work, I added, 'I know this might be a bit off-the-wall, but Nick couldn't be your unidentified body, could he?'

'No chance. Our victim's heavily built. Nick's as thin as a rake.'

CHAPTER 14

Steve gave me a kiss and a hug. 'You look gorgeous. Have you done something to your hair?' He got changed out of his suit while I dished up his tea. 'This looks delicious, Rach. I've hardly had anything to eat today. Have you had a good day? Tell me what you've been up to.'

'Have you got something to tell me?' I cut to the chase. Instead of asking why I might think that, he realised he'd been rumbled. I know Steve well enough to know when he's deflecting me from asking about his day, with too many compliments and questions.

'Well, yes, but... we've identified the body in the pond. We struck lucky. You know the killer did his best to make it hard for us, but he missed a bit of cellophane caught in the zip of the victim's coat pocket. He probably patted the pockets and they felt empty, so he didn't open them. Forensics say it looks like a bit of cellophane they wrap around those little boxes of throat sweets or similar, and it had a partial print. They managed to match it to prints we had on file for a pub landlord. We went to the pub. His barman said he's not been around for a while, so we went upstairs and the room was in a bit of a mess, so it looks like it's him.'

'But that's good news, isn't it?'

'Not exactly. It's Dean Hornby, landlord of The Steam Packet. You know - the pub on Anlaby Road.'

'I know where it is, Steve. Do you think I'd forget?' While trying to track down a missing witness, I'd followed Craig Dobson to that pub, only to be knocked over the head, carted off to an old warehouse and tied up along with his ex-girlfriend. We'd only just escaped when it was set on fire.

'Well I certainly haven't forgotten either, and I'd like you to stay at home for a few days while we track down Dobson.'

'Stay at home! You must be joking. Why?'

'He's dangerous, and we think he might have killed Dean.'

'I thought they were mates? Didn't you say they were both part of the same drug-dealing operation? And anyway, isn't Craig in jail? Wasn't he arrested on the Isle of Man for attacking a customer at the club where he worked?'

'He's out now, so stop trying to change the subject, Rach. I want your word that you'll stay at home, or at least out of the town centre, until we've located him.'

'He won't want anything to do with me, Steve. He said as much when you thought he was behind the fire at my flat and the hit-and-run a few months later. Shame we had no proof he was the one who locked us in that warehouse, so he got away with it. I just got in his way briefly. He'd be more likely to go after his old girlfriend, Lucy Turner. She was the one who could have testified about his drug-dealing.'

'She's disappeared. We haven't heard from her since she was placed in protective custody before Dobson was arrested.'

'Did she get witness protection?'

'No, we didn't need her testimony in the end, so she stayed out of it. Her mum doesn't know where she is, either.'

I doubted that very much. She just wouldn't be telling the police, but I didn't say that to Steve. 'So tell me why you think he might have killed Dean.'

'We don't know for certain he was involved, but he just got parole last week, which seems a bit of a coincidence, added to which, an attempt was made to burn the body to prevent identification, and we know that Dobson likes to set fires, don't we? So we need to question him.'

'And what has that got to do with me, exactly?' I could hear the stroppy tone in my voice and hated it, but I couldn't help myself.

'He might not be our killer, but it doesn't take away from the fact that now I know he could be back in the Hull area, I don't want you getting into trouble with him again.'

'I found Lucy. My involvement with him is over.'

'He might go looking for Lucy again, and if he can't find her, he might come looking for you.'

'Well, I think that's unlikely, and in any case, if he's murdered Dean, I can't see him walking round the town centre.'

'Oh, Rach. Can't you just this once let me look out for you? Can't you just lay low, go to your gran's, stay at home with a book or something? Please.'

I was really annoyed that he didn't want me to make my own decisions, but I knew he meant well, so I decided to stop arguing. 'OK, I promise I'll think about it. Finish your tea and I'll tell you about my day.'

Afterwards we watched TV for an hour until Steve could hardly keep his eyes open. We had a little cuddle and then he fell asleep. I lay there, planning my call to Lucy's mum the next morning. I still had her number in my phone from months ago. Pete had found it for me. If Lucy was in danger, I'd find her and warn her. I might have stopped arguing with Steve, but that didn't mean I agreed with him, and no way was I going to sit at home twiddling my thumbs. What Steve didn't know wouldn't harm him.

The next day I made the call to Lucy's mum but the number had been disconnected. I thought about going down to Lincolnshire, but then decided it would be a lot of hassle, and if I didn't think it was worth it, then it was unlikely Craig Dobson would either. He probably had better things to do, like fleeing the scene of the crime. I hated twiddling my thumbs, but for once, I conceded defeat.

That evening I had a call from Steve. 'We've got a lead, Rach, so I'm going to be late home, I'm afraid.'

'No worries. It's good if you're getting somewhere. What's come up?'

'Simon Crawford's personal effects, clothes etc. were returned to his wife, Melanie, shortly after his body was found but she's only just felt up to looking through them, and she's found a packet of cigarettes in his jacket pocket. '

'OK, so I'm guessing he doesn't smoke, but what relevance does it have? Let me see. He might have been having an affair and the lady in question was a smoker. Her husband finds out and kills Simon?'

'It's a bit more interesting than that. The cigarette packet didn't have a duty stamp on it.'

'What does that mean, exactly?'

'Well, apart from the fact that someone here is in deep shit for not noticing the significance when looking through his belongings, it means that the supplier has somehow avoided paying customs duty on the cigarettes.'

'And?'

'Put together with the only thing Melanie knew about his book, and all the cloak-and-dagger stuff about "protecting his sources", we're now working on the hypothesis that Simon's novel was about cigarette smuggling and he was killed to shut him up.'

'Surely hushing up the smuggling of a few cartons of cigs through the docks wouldn't be enough to make anyone commit murder, Steve?'

'Well, that's where you're wrong. The sums involved in avoiding duty are massive, making it a serious crime. I already knew a bit about it, because sometimes crooks we've arrested have these illegal cigarettes on them. Also, in Serious Crimes we get involved with prosecutions when investigations bear fruit, but most of the work itself - finding and shutting down the smugglers - is carried out by the Border Force. They deal with all forms of smuggling including drugs and weapons as well as immigration and security checks. I'll tell you more about it when I get in, but if you can imagine just one packet of twenty cigarettes costs up to eight pounds in the UK, but you can buy them for only forty pence in Belarus, you'll get the picture.'

'Wow. I didn't realise cigarettes were so expensive. How on earth do people afford to smoke?'

'That's why smuggling's such a big and lucrative business.'

'Hmm… That's about, let's see two hundred cigarettes in a carton, so ten packets… that makes seventy-five pounds a carton more, and those cartons aren't very big. I saw them in the ferry shop on the way back from Rotterdam.'

'Exactly. Anyway, we're liaising with Border Force as of now. I'm meeting a Michelle Rawlinson, who's my counterpart there, and some of her team this afternoon. I'm taking Tommy Bradfield who's now our liaison officer for crimes involving the port. We've already passed over a photo and description of Simon. Right now they should be passing the details to any of their contacts on the docks who might have seen Simon hanging around. Let's hope they can come up with a name for someone he might have been talking to.'

'Go to it. Hope you get a breakthrough.'

'Thanks. They're as keen to follow the lead as we are. It's got increasingly hard for them to stay on top of the smugglers. Such massive sums of money mean there's a big incentive for people just to keep quiet and turn a blind eye, even if they're not otherwise involved in something criminal. Border force may know it's happening but they need to know when, in order to catch them.'

'You've got your work cut out, but at least it's a lead, Steve.'

'Yes, and we're wondering if Hornby's murder might also be linked somehow. He used to sell drugs supplied by Dobson, so why not cheap cigarettes too? I said as much to the Super and he thought with both murders possibly linked by this smuggling angle, he might even be able to give us more manpower to throw at them, rather than scaling it back.'

'Great. I'll heat up a pizza for you when you get in if you haven't eaten.'

'Thanks, love. I'm quite hopeful that we'll crack both cases soon. See you later.'

CHAPTER 15

The week was passing slowly for me, but at least Steve was getting somewhere. When he got home the next day, he told me that they'd had a new development.

'Something from Border Force about the smuggling?'

'No, a different bit of information, but also to do with Simon Crawford's murder.'

'Oh, yes?'

'One of the other writers rang in. He's remembered bumping into Simon in the town centre one day. This was in Paragon Square near the station. This writer, Paul someone-or-other, I forget his name, suggested they have a drink in the Royal Station Hotel but Simon said he couldn't as he was meeting someone.'

'And?'

'Paul didn't think too much of it because Simon always kept himself to himself so he thought it was probably just an excuse, but something came back to him the other day when he was watching a news item on local TV about an incident outside the station. After he'd crossed over to go in the department store opposite, this Paul saw Simon shaking hands with a thin bloke. He saw him hand the bloke a large brown envelope before they turned and walked off together towards the Carr Lane and Anlaby Road lights.'

'Definitely sounds a bit suspicious.'

'Yes, with Hornby's pub just round the corner on Anlaby Road, we're hoping it turns out to be something significant. Time's passed since Paul saw the bloke, so it's a bit of a stretch, but he's going to have a look at what we call our rogues gallery and see if he can come spot the person Simon was meeting. If he can't, we've always got CCTV, but that would take a lot longer, particularly as the writer has no idea of the date.'

We'd been late to bed so I was only just having breakfast when Gran rang, well after nine o'clock.

'I need you to get my pension money. I hurt my big toe at line-dancing last night and I don't want the Post Office people to be holding on to my money. Your mam's not answering her phone, as usual. I don't know why she bothers with one.'

'OK, but don't you have it paid into a bank account, Gran?'

'Why ever would I do that? I'd only have to draw it out again to spend it, and they might not put the money in when they say they will and I wouldn't know. It's not as if they pay you any interest worth having these days.'

'I hope you don't have a lot of cash lying around the house, Gran. You might get robbed.'

'Don't be so daft, our Rachel. I got your Steve to tell me what locks I needed and Wilf fixed them for me. Even got those fiddly window locks. They hurt my fingers with the arthritis, but I'm always careful to make sure they're locked when I go out. I've got a good hiding place too, not that I ever have much in it. It's…'

'Don't tell me, Gran. It's alright. I get the picture. So how do I get the cash?'

'Come round and I'll give you my book and a note to say I've authorised you to get it for me. You can be here in half an hour, can't you? Only I'm going to need it for bingo this afternoon.'

'Can't I just give you a lift to the post office?'

'Well I suppose so. But you'll have to come in with me. I won't be able to manage the steps.'

I was at Gran's by ten, but she still said, 'You took your time!' There's no pleasing her, and by the time I'd helped her on with her sandals, out of her bungalow and into the car, I was beginning to regret not just going to collect it for her. I'd not been sure they'd hand her pension to me though and I didn't want a wasted journey before coming back to take her anyway. Gran looked a mess. Not because the toe had made it difficult for her to dress. She just always does. No dirty or torn clothes. That's not what I meant. She just dresses as if she was a teenager, with lurid colours thrown in.

Today she was wearing a shiny purple blouse and a short bright green and white patterned skirt that finished above her knees. And she had a headband with flowers on it. Not that she has much of her pitch-black dyed hair to need holding back anyway.

I helped her into the post office and got them to give her a chair, as she requested. She supervised my passing her pension book over and was just checking the cash before putting it in her purse when the door was flung open.

'Freeze!' Two young blokes burst in, one holding a gun.

'I've not got much in the till. Just leave now and I'll not call the police,' said the postmaster, which was somewhat foolhardy, I thought.

My second thought was that the taller of the two looked remarkably like Peter Wood, who'd been in my primary school class. Let's be honest - it had to be him. I couldn't imagine anyone else having curly ginger hair, big ears and a strange-shaped scar from where he'd fallen off his bike and his cheek had impaled itself on the handle. I'll never forget the screams. He was only about eight then, and he wasn't full of false bravado like now. I wondered whether to call him by his name and try to talk sense into him, but the small one with the gun might always shoot me to stop me giving evidence.

'It's pension day. Of course you've got cash. You lot, on the floor!' the smaller one shouted viciously, waving the gun in my face. He might have been in my class too, but he had boring brown hair like mine, and no distinguishing features.

Gran interrupted my daydream by saying, 'Don't be so daft lad. I'm not getting down on the floor with my bad foot.'

There was a bit of muttering. 'OK. But the other one better get down or I'll shoot.' They were wearing masks, but not big

95

plastic, face-covering ones, just old-fashioned cardboard ones that just cover the area around your eyes. This was definitely just a botched-together idea they'd thought up on the spur of the moment. Peter - I'm sure it was him - glanced at me and what I could see of his face turned pale in recognition.

I was fairly sure he was regretting he'd ever agreed to rob a post office, and decided that, given the first opportunity, he'd leg it and keep his head down, praying I hadn't recognised him. I turned my attention to the smaller one. I'd seen those sort of guns before and they didn't scare me. I leant down to Gran, as if concerned for her, grabbed her handbag and swung it, knocking the barrel of the gun away from us and towards the window display. I kicked him in the balls and followed up with a kick to the side of his knee for good measure. He went down, rubbing his leg and Gran hit him on the head with her stick.

The postmaster came round from behind his counter with a roll of brown tape and finished the job, trussing the lad up ready for the police. As predicted, Peter had done a runner.

'I'll ring the police.'

'Don't worry, love. They're already on their way.' The postmaster's wife had come through from the back. 'I rang them as soon as I realised what was going on.'

'Thanks. They should get here soon then.' He turned to me. 'You shouldn't have done that. You might have been killed. But, as it was, no harm done, thankfully. I'll see you get a reward from the Post Office.'

'I hit him too. Tell them that. If there's rewards going, I'd like one, too. My pension could do with a boost. Speaking of which, can you pay me now, please. We haven't got all day. I'm off to bingo soon.'

'You've already had your money, Gran.'

She glared at me, then relented. 'Oh, right. How silly of me. Must be the shock. I can't remember putting it in my purse.'

The patrol car came quickly.

'You shouldn't have tackled him. You could have been shot. We were on our way,' were the first words the policeman said while his colleague bundled the would-be thief into the patrol car.

'I really wasn't in any danger, officer. I wouldn't have taken any risks. My fiancé's a police inspector and he wouldn't have me doing anything dangerous.' (Well he doesn't like me to, but I do admit he can't always stop me).

'That means nothing. You couldn't have known he wouldn't shoot at least one of you.'

'But I did.' I kicked the gun over to him. It was light as a feather. 'It's just a plastic kid's toy.' I didn't want to destroy evidence, otherwise I would have crushed it underfoot.

'Well, it's easy to see that in hindsight, young lady, but you shouldn't have taken that risk.'

I'm obviously a firm supporter of the police, but his condescension annoyed me. 'Look, I'm not stupid. He was waving the gun around in my face and I could clearly see the words "not for children under 36 months" on the side of the barrel. It was crooked too. The two halves don't even line up where it's been glued together.'

I'll give him this, he had the good grace to say, 'Apologies. That was very astute of you. I'm sure you wouldn't have intervened unless you were convinced.'

'Of course she wouldn't. You just ask Detective Inspector Rose. They're getting married soon,' my gran piped up.

'Thanks, Gran.' I rolled my eyes and exchanged a small grin with the policewoman, who'd entered the post office in time to hear most of the conversation, having restrained the young lad in the car. The postmaster's wife made us all a cup of tea, and the policewoman took a short statement from Gran and me. I felt a bit sorry for Peter, but I had to pass on my suspicions, all the same. I hoped he'd get off lightly with a timely warning and be put off ever doing anything so stupid in the future.

I was helping Gran into the car when she checked her bag and found she really didn't have her precious pension, but even the thought of having to walk back and go up the steps again couldn't wipe the smile off her face.

'And there was I thinking you were trying to con the postmaster into giving it you twice.'

'As if I'd do something illegal, our Rach. How could you think that of me? I had it on my knee after I'd counted it, but you grabbed my bag to hit that lad, and it must have slid on the floor.'

As it was, she was saved from going back, because the postmaster appeared at the car door with her cash.

Gran was made up with the excitement of knowing she would have everyone's attention at bingo, and line-dancing, and all the other places she went for the next month or more. As I left her bungalow, I could hear her on the phone to Mum, playing up her involvement in the capture of armed robbers.

CHAPTER 16

I was tired after the day's excitement and running round after Gran all morning, so when Steve came in about five, he caught me with my feet up, head in a book.

'Hi Steve. You're early again. That's amazing! I've been dying to tell someone else all about my crime-busting day. Gran already knows. Mum and Dad aren't in, and Sarah's gone to Meadowhall shopping with her mum and little Josh.'

'I thought you might complain that I was interrupting something.'

'Far from it.' I gave him a big hug to show I meant it. I was just about to launch into the whole story, in great detail of course, when he took the wind out of my sails.

'Can it wait until we sit down to eat, please? I have to go out again after we've eaten and you'd be doing me a big favour if you'd come too. If you're up for it, I thought we could eat really early so it doesn't cut too much into our evening and then... I could reward you in some way.'

'Mm... I think I could manage that. Anywhere exciting?' I decided I could just about restrain myself from blurting out my news if I had the prospect of a reward.

'Not exactly, but I could really do with your help. You remember I told you about the writer who saw Simon Crawford handing something to a bloke outside the station?'

'Yes, and?'

'Well he's looked through mugshots and come up blank, so they've had him use an Identikit programme today, and when he was happy with the result, I had a look. I think the identikit picture looks a lot like Nick Heighway. His sergeant Tommy

Bradfield says he can't see it himself though, and he's his boss. Nick should have been back at work today and didn't turn up, so even though it's a long shot, I thought I'd go round to Nick's flat and see if his girlfriend's got a photo that I can show this Paul.'

'I see. You think she'd take it better if I was there as she's met me before?'

'Yes. I don't want her over-reacting if I turn up on my own, thinking something awful's happened to Nick.'

'But surely you must have a photo if he works for you?'

'There's only the one taken when he started. It's not that old, but it's one of those dreadful passport photos. No-one looks like their passport photo, do they? And we could do with a full-length photo to show his build. The writer did say he was thin, and Nick's quite skinny.'

'OK. Sounds good. I'll sling together something quick to eat and I can fill you in on my news...'

'I could nip round the corner for fish and chips if you like? I know they're on your list of things to avoid but once can't hurt?'

I gave in. News of my citizen's arrest would have to wait. 'It'd be great to have an excuse! Stuff the cutting down on bad things for one day. Just put lots of vinegar on mine. I haven't any in.'

Finally, as we ate, I was able to relate the events of the day. Typically, Steve did express some concern that I might have put myself in danger, but I poo-pooed the idea. 'I could tell they weren't dangerous. My dear nephews used to have silvery-grey plastic guns exactly the same. I could see where the two halves were glued together.'

'In that case, you did well, but I wish you didn't get involved in things all the time. You know what I say…'

'Yes I do. "Calamity always seems to follow you around", but nothing bad happened.'

Steve humphed before declaring in a mock solemn tone, 'Well in that case, I shall reward you later on behalf of the city's police force. You should dress appropriately for the ceremony. Perhaps that sexy green silk scrap of a nightie?'

I ate very quickly. I didn't want to waste a minute while Steve was in this mood.

In the car on the way to Karen's, Steve filled me in a bit more.

'I forgot to tell you, Rach. I think this is all coming together now. Ever since we eventually identified the body in the pond as Dean Hornby, something's kept niggling at the back of my mind, but I only twigged what it was when I was writing on the whiteboard in the office today. I put his initials DH instead of his full name, and realised I'd seen them somewhere before – when I finally got around to looking through Nick's notebooks. Going off what Tommy had said, we'd had the DH down as some other girl he might have been seeing, Diane I think he said, although no-one seemed to know who she is. So I had Forensics compare Nick's prints with all those found in Dean's flat and on his van.'

'You had them on record?'

'Oh, yes. It's been policy for a number of years to take fingerprints and DNA of all police officers for cross-checking with our databases before their appointment is confirmed.'

And I'm guessing you got a match?'

'Yes, we found Nick's prints on the inside of the rear door of Dean Hornby's van. I'm afraid it's not looking good at all.'

'So you think Nick was working for Dean Hornby?'

'No. Quite the opposite. It looks like he was working a lead on his own. Foolish lad. Might have been wanting to get all the credit himself. I told you I got the impression he was eager for promotion. I hope he's not got involved in something he can't handle.'

'I thought you said he had some debts?'

'He owes a bit, but it's not a string of debts. He just ran up a few heavy bills on his credit card paying for car repairs and a birthday present or two, for his girlfriend I presume.'

'But Steve, maybe he was snooping around, someone was coming and he hid in the van.'

'Nice try to make me feel better, love, but things like that only happen to you.' I had to agree, remembering my illegal trip to Holland in a mobile home.

It's not far from Steve's to Beverley Road, so it was only about half past six when we knocked at the door of the flat Karen shared with Nick. She was obviously surprised to see us.

'Hello, Karen. Sorry to turn up unannounced. This is my fiancé, Inspector Rose.'

'What's happened? Have you found Nick?' She looked terrified.

'Don't worry, it's not bad news, Karen. We'd just like a full-length photo of Nick,' said Steve in his friendliest unofficial voice.

'You've not found another body, have you? I know you rang me when that other body was found, to reassure me it couldn't be Nick because the bloke was hefty. That was so kind of you, but I've heard nothing since, from the police or Nick.'

'No, Karen.' I interrupted to reassure her. 'There's actually been what might be a sighting of Nick, and the police need to let the witness see a decent picture of him. They only have a grotty little passport photo of his face.'

'I see. Has there been some news, then?'

Steve had told me on our way round that there was nothing to be gained from alarming her too much, but it might help to tell her what he suspected, in case it jogged her memory. 'We think he might have been following a lead without telling us, and that's why he told you he was working.'

'But where is he? It's been ages since I heard from him.'

'I can't say for sure, Karen, but he may have found it necessary to go undercover, and that's why he's not been in touch. Is there anything else you can remember that he might have mentioned at all?'

'No, nothing. There's only one odd thing. I found this photo the other day. It must have slipped out of that carrier bag of stuff I gave you.'

I could tell by the look in Steve's eyes that it was important, but he played it down. 'Thanks very much, Karen. I think that may well be of use to us. Now, if you could just fish out a recent full-length photo of Nick, we won't bother you any longer at the moment.'

As soon as we got outside, I asked Steve, 'What's the other photo of, then?'

He showed me a photo of a packet of cigarettes. 'No duty stamp. This seems to clinch it. It links Nick to Simon as well as to Dean Hornby.'

'But they're both dead. You don't think he…?'

'Killed them? No, I don't. While I can't rule it out, my personal view is, that's highly unlikely, so…'

'Nick might be dead too and you haven't found his body yet. Oh, poor Karen!'

'There is another alternative. Nick could be hiding because he knows who killed them.'

I thought Steve would be dying to get to the station again and get to work dealing with the implications of the photo, but I wasn't going to encourage him. He pulled in by the side of the road, and I thought he was going to say, 'I'm sorry, but…' However, for once I needn't have worried.

'I know what you're thinking but it can wait 'til morning for once. We haven't had any 'us' time for too long.' He ran over to the Sainsbury's Local on the other side of the road, rushed in and then positively jumped back in the car, handing me a bottle of wine and a box of Thornton's chocolates.

'Fantastic'. When we got back to the flat he poured out the wine whilst I got changed.

CHAPTER 17

When I woke the next morning, he'd gone, the empty chocolate box by the bed a sweet reminder of the night before. About ten I got a call out of the blue from Kate.

'Hi Rach. I've had a letter from the solicitor, and he says that, since no-one has come forward in response to their newspaper appeal, and the DNA shows I'm not related to Mam and Dad, who died without making wills - or intestate, as he insists on saying - then my aunt will inherit the estate as their nearest surviving relative.'

'Oh dear.'

'No, it's good. I thought it would drag on for ages longer, but I think he's accepting your research into possible relatives because he doesn't want to do any himself. Now he's got my aunt, and she doesn't know of any other relatives either, he's eager to finish his involvement by drawing up the paperwork.'

'It's still a shame for you to lose your home.'

'It doesn't matter anymore now, Rach. I've accepted they're not my parents and so the farm isn't mine. I'm really lucky that Mrs Charlesworth has given me a home. The farm sale should raise quite a lot of money. It looks like the solicitor will take a chunk of it, but there should be plenty left. Aunt Megan says she's putting me in her will, whoever I am. And she's promised to pay your usual fees, and you're not to say "no".'

'That's very kind of her, but I really don't want any fees. I feel like I've failed you by not finding your real parents.'

'Oh, but you haven't. If not for you, I wouldn't have found Aunt Megan. I tried to talk her out of putting me in her will, but she wouldn't hear of it. Obviously I don't want her to die anyway as she's the only almost-relative I have and she seems nice. And I forgot to say, she's giving me enough cash now to pay my university fees upfront and save all that interest. I'll pay her back when I've graduated and got a job, but still it doesn't seem right.'

'Helen and Tony wouldn't have wanted you to struggle.'

'That's what she said. I suppose Mam and Dad must have loved me very much.'

'I'm sure they did.'

'Right, well, thanks for everything. You'll be getting the cheque from Aunt Megan soon.'

'OK. If she insists, then, but just tell her to make it the fifty pounds we agreed, please.'

'Right, will do then. Bye.'

It was time I caught up with Mum and good job I did. I'd hardly set foot in the door when she started.

'Rachel. Whatever were you thinking of, tackling those armed robbers on your own, and letting Gran tackle the one with the sawn-off shotgun? It was a good job she's been having those karate lessons at the social club or you could both have been killed.'

'You're joking! You know better than to believe anything Gran says, even if she is your mum.'

'Oops! Sorry, Rachel. I've been had again, haven't I? Well, you better come through to the kitchen and tell me what really happened.'

'Gran was just sitting down counting her pension while I tackled the lad with the plastic toy gun, and the other lad just ran off. I recognised him. Do you remember Peter Wood from infant school?'

'Yes. Peter was the one with the scar, wasn't he? Wouldn't say "boo" to a goose, as I remember. Easily led by someone showing him a bit of interest I expect.'

After a cuppa and a scone, and the truth, she'd calmed down.

'How come you fell for Gran saying she had karate lessons?'

'She had that bad toe. I thought she'd been chopping bricks in half, or so she said.'

I couldn't stop laughing. Poor Mum. I brought her up to date with my various cases. I hadn't told her yet that Kate's Aunt Megan had inherited the farm, now the DNA test had ruled out any possibility that Kate was the Willises' daughter.

'Rachel, do you think the Willises found a surrogate mother? You know, paid for someone to give birth?'

'That's a thought, Mum. I'll find out how long those agencies have been going. Not sure if they were around almost twenty years ago.'

I had another mouthful of coffee. 'Just thinking about it, though, I can't see the Willises contacting an agency. After all they had no TV, and definitely no internet. And hardly any money. It would have to be someone local. And the midwife down in Lincolnshire ruled out a baby being unofficially adopted. She said she would've known, and it wouldn't have been allowed. And a proper surrogate would have Helen's eggs or at least Tony's sperm, and then Kate's DNA would match one or other of them, and it didn't.'

'Yes. I forgot that. Then the only way would be if someone gave birth without a midwife and then passed the baby to Helen Willis. But in that case, there'd have been no reason why Helen couldn't register the baby's birth with her and Tony as the parents.'

'I'm not sure about that, Mum. Surely there's some link between official registrations of birth and records of births through GPs, midwives or hospitals, Mum?'

'It could have been a home birth, in private.'

'Mm. But it would be a really risky pregnancy and birth, not having a midwife, and not being able to see a doctor afterwards if there were any problems for either the mother who had given her baby away, or the baby whose 'new' mother hadn't given birth. Too many questions. I know people give birth on their own in extreme situations, but no woman would volunteer for that, particularly if she wasn't even going to keep the baby, unless it was a teenager who kept the pregnancy secret.'

'You're right. It was just a thought, Rachel.'

'In fact, since we know Helen Willis was pregnant just before Kate was born, and had a miscarriage, they couldn't have arranged a surrogate that quickly anyway.'

'Never thought about that. I feel so sorry for the poor lamb.'

'I know what you mean, but it's a blessing her schoolteacher is such a lovely lady, so Kate's managing far better than she might have been.'

I was pretty busy as I'd landed a short term contract, checking up on benefit claimants. They have their own team of people who do it, obviously, but the powers-that-be wanted a massive crackdown with fast results, which meant it was actually worth hiring investigators for a month, me among them, to boost results and show a significant amount of cash saved.

I spent a lot of my time hanging around Hull's many council estates, but also some significantly more affluent areas, showing photos, talking to neighbours and following disabled people and others claiming unemployment benefit.

On the first day alone I spotted a bloke helping out on a building site, and another loading parcels into his van to deliver. I got some satisfaction in taking photos that would prosecute these people as they were taking money that should have gone into paying for doctors and shortening waiting times.

We both had work on Steve's birthday, but he suggested we celebrate with a trip to Beverley Races the next day, a Saturday. On Friday he got away on time and I cooked something special. Well, to be honest, Marks & Spencer did and I just warmed it up, but I did make a chocolate cake with lashings of sticky chocolate icing. Alright, I admit it. The cake was from a packet too, but I had to put in some effort to mix it, and the candle placement on the top was all my own work! The icing was delicious but obviously highly fattening, even to a skinny flat-chested person like me, so extreme exercise was called for. I'd been saving up some new underwear to raise Steve's heart rate among other things, but after a few admiring and lecherous phrases, it was cast aside.

After a leisurely breakfast we drove to Beverley and wandered round the shops, including my favourite antique centre. There were a few pieces of Hornsea Pottery so I treated Mum to a lovely retro black and yellow vase, described as "Imprest vase, John Clappison" on the label. Then we drove to the racecourse and had lunch while we studied the race card. I know nothing about horses, and I suspect Steve doesn't either but it was a chance to dress up and see how the other half live.

On top of the jumper and latest Jack Reacher novel I'd already given him, I gave him a whole five pounds birthday money to squander at will on a bet but he insisted on giving me the same. My choice of horse was easy. There was a white horse, which I reckoned would make it easier to follow when they all galloped off round the far side of the course, and the jockey parading around on it was wearing a green silk shirt, the same colour as my 'scrap' of a nightie that's Steve's favourite. I thought it would bring me luck.

If my life was a novel, I'd have won a hundred pounds or even more (I can dream, can't I?), but sadly it finished second to last. Then Steve blew his fiver on a horse with a lovely swishy tail, but he didn't win either. We consoled ourselves with a cup of coffee. Amazingly neither of us were tempted by the cake, but I must confess there had only been a tiny bit of Steve's birthday cake left in the morning, despite the packet saying 'serves six'.

We then took a walk around the site away from the stands and were just approaching the stables when I saw someone I recognised. It was one of my benefit claimants. He was glancing round, as if to see if anyone was watching him, so I pulled a surprised Steve into a passionate embrace. As quickly as I'd grabbed him, I let go and set off in pursuit of the tubby bloke who was at that moment opening a wooden door about twenty yards away.

It was hard to walk quickly in my favourite red stilettos, but I got to the door in time to watch through a crack as a taller bloke was saying 'You did a good job with the unloading. I'll have some more feed deliveries on Monday. That OK?' They went round a corner so I followed them as quietly as I could. Luckily the straw deadened the sound of my shoes. Not great footwear for surveillance work but I got away with it.

In a small office, the big bloke opened a drawer and handed my benefits cheat a bunch of ten pound notes. I caught it on my phone camera. Job done. I got back outside quickly before they discovered me. 'What have you been up to, Rach? Just look at you're the state of your shoes!'

As I explained to Steve my success, my brain was frantically wondering how I'd get the manure off my shoes, and if it would even come off. Luckily Steve is used to mishaps - after all, he is engaged to me - and he had a carrier bag in the car in which to tightly bundle said shoes. He was even gallant enough to carry me from the car to the flat when we got back, though not without a few sarcastic comments about how I must have eaten more of his birthday cake than he did.

CHAPTER 18

On Sunday morning I woke up to the sound of rain, and lay there listening to it patter on the window. It had been a lovely day yesterday and I decided to bask in the memory. Steve suddenly appeared in the doorway.

'Rach, you haven't forgotten Matt and Alice are coming for lunch have you? The fridge is looking a bit empty.'

'Oh, no. I forgot all about it. I was concentrating on choosing the best birthday cake mix and icing when I went shopping, and it went clean out of my mind!'

'What were we going to have?'

'Er, a casserole I think. I can't do much wrong with that.' My culinary talents are miniscule. I have told Steve in the past that if we ever win the lottery (not that I'd waste money on a ticket), we can employ our own chef. Otherwise he'll either have to find time to do the cooking himself (fat chance!) or get used to basic meals like meat and two veg, fish and two veg, pie and two veg, or if I'm in a rush or forgot to shop or to get said meat or fish out of the freezer, then pizza.

'Tell me what you need and I'll go to the supermarket.'

'You can't.'

'I'm quite capable.'

'No, you really can't. It's only nine o'clock. They don't open until ten so panic over. It'll give me time to think what you should get.'

'I can at least peel the spuds - or are you doing pasta?'

Gone was my quiet lie-in. 'Spuds, Steve, and it's great of you to help.' Thankfully I had got plenty of veg. I'd just forgotten meat and a pudding. Chicken casserole with mushrooms and stuffing to flavour and thicken. That would be fine. I could leave it in the oven until it was time to eat, giving me loads of time to socialise. I can't see the point of inviting people round and then missing half of it because you're messing around in the kitchen.

For pudding I thought I'd do an oat crumble topping on - what? I had a rummage in the cupboard. I had a very large tin of pears. Perfect. I made the crumble mixture - normal but with porridge oats added - tastes yummy, you should try it - while Steve nipped out for four chicken breasts and a tin of custard.

By the time Matt and Alice arrived, everything was under control, and I'd got changed into a decent dress. The casserole tasted delicious and Alice and I got on like a house on fire, which was nice. Suddenly there was an ear-shattering noise. The smoke alarm! I'd put the crumble in the oven when I served up the casserole, but forgotten to set the timer and we'd been talking for maybe a good half hour after we'd finished eating. 'Oops! Sorry! I'll be back in a minute.'

'Shall I?'

'No, it's OK, Steve. I'll just check what's set it off.'

I shouted through to reassure him that the kitchen was in one piece. 'There'll be just a slight delay with dessert. Talk amongst yourselves.'

Lovely Alice popped her head around the door and observed the blackened mess that was to have been a glorious pudding. 'Ouch! Can I help? They'll talk shop for ages so maybe we can rustle something up together?'

I scraped out the pudding into the bin. Even the pears were dried and a bit black under the rock-hard volcanic remains of the topping. 'It's OK. I made enough crumble mix to use another day. It keeps well in the fridge. And the custard's not been opened. All I need is fruit.' We surveyed the store cupboard for other tins of fruit. No joy. 'We can't just have dry topping. I'll have to go out. It'll take ages. Maybe I should…'

'Wait. Here at the back. Ta-da!' With a flourish Alice pulled out a large jar, almost full - of mincemeat.

'That was left over from last Christmas. I had pastry left after making mince pies and rushed to the shops for mincemeat. They only had large jars so there was all that left over. Do you think…?' We inspected the 'best before date' and turned to each other with big smiles and a high five. I really liked Alice.

I grabbed the bigger casserole in my set of three, Alice emptied the mincemeat into it, and I got the topping on. Into the oven, timer set, back to the table - Steve and Matt were still talking. They didn't even ask about the smoke alarm or what we'd been up to. I looked at Alice and we burst out laughing. 'What's so funny?'

'Nothing. Dessert will be about fifteen minutes. Slight delay.'

After they'd gone, Steve offered to wash up. 'This dish is all black.' I'd forgotten to soak it. I told him what had happened. 'Oh, I knew you'd burnt something. You had black bits in your hair, but I didn't like to say.' I hit him with the tea-towel, but I couldn't be cross at him for not telling me. He'd coped admirably once again with my cooking disaster with not one word of criticism. He's a star. Also, I now had a new friend, thanks to him.

Monday was back to work - for Steve at least. After such an eventful weekend I decided to take it easy, apart from cleaning the kitchen, that is. That evening Steve was telling me about his latest meeting with Michelle Rawlinson at Border Force, but admitting they were getting nowhere.

'Unless there's someone crooked in her office, we can't see how the cigarettes get through customs, as containers are randomly scanned to see if there's any secret compartments where things such as guns or cigarettes could be hidden. The smugglers have to know when their lorry might be scanned and avoid it somehow.'

Then he started talking about people-smuggling, and how lorry drivers faced huge fines if illegal immigrants were found in their containers, even if they weren't aware of them. It was deemed their responsibility to check their loads.

I suddenly stopped listening. 'Back up a minute, Steve. Are

you just talking about adults?'

'No. Families too. It's dreadful because they run a risk of dying of thirst or starvation, heat exhaustion or extreme cold, if the container is delayed for any reason.'

'Is there any way that babies can be smuggled in and sold to women who are desperate to have children? Maybe the same happened to Kate? Her mother was desperate for a baby.'

'Bit far-fetched, that, Rach, and I thought you'd already decided that Helen and Tony Willis couldn't afford a surrogate baby and wouldn't be able to get hold of a baby so soon after Helen presumably miscarried? Smuggling would amount to the same thing, only harder to make contact with smugglers than surrogate mothers.'

'True. It was a stupid idea. The Willises didn't even have a computer. I just feel so bad that we seem to have hit a brick wall, looking for Kate's birth parents.'

'I know, Rach, but it was always going to be hard.'

Like Kate, I'd virtually given up on finding her real parents. I'd banked the cheque and then salved my conscience by donating the cash to a children's charity. But things were quiet now, so I went through her file again, and realised there was still a chance I might be able to locate the seven girls Pete had mentioned, the ones not at the same address on the census taken three years after their births. I tried to get hold of Pete a couple of times in the morning, but it was late afternoon before he must have picked up my messages and rang me.

'Sorry I've not been in touch, Rach. I was out in the States, and then I had loads to deal with when I got back.'

'Sorry to have bothered you, then, Pete. I better let you get on.'

'No, it's fine. I'm all caught up now, and I have a bit of news for you, but tell me first why you were ringing.'

I brought him up to date with Kate's meeting with her Aunt Megan, and my thoughts regarding one last ditch effort to track down those girls before closing the case completely.

113

'Good news about the aunt making financial provisions for Kate, but I've already done some work on the census records, even though you said to hold off. In fact, I might have a new lead.'

'What?! I'd given up hope.'

'It wasn't too difficult for me to track down the ones who'd moved house, and were still with their parents at the next census.'

'And…?'

'Six are still with their parents in new homes. They just moved to bigger houses, or a different area. That's the main reason I didn't get back to you as soon as I found out, because they're dead ends. However, that leaves one I can't track down. A Melanie Harper. Her parents, Shirley and Jack, seem to be at the same address and were on the 2001 census, but she was missed off it. I had to check the 2011 census record as well, and to be honest, as you told me to leave it, I've only just realised I never actually followed up on the search I started.'

'Can I do it, Pete?'

'No, it's fine. It was a short job for me. I'd just forgotten to send you the results. Sorry.'

'You don't need to apologise. I told you to leave it, so you've done more than I asked.'

'It could be a simple mistake, and one that was perpetuated as they send the forms and ask you to tick if the details are the same. Maybe because Melanie hadn't reached eighteen, and most people associate the census with the electoral roll somehow, they just haven't been putting her on, but it's worth looking into, I think. If I give you the address of her parents, maybe you could call or ask around at the neighbours and see if you can come up with anything?'

'Of course. That's great, Pete. Maybe we could be getting somewhere at last. I don't want to let Kate down.'

'Maybe, but don't build your hopes up too much, Rach.'

I decided not to tell Kate about Pete's lead until I'd been down to Lincolnshire. I didn't want to raise her hopes for no good reason.

'I'll be out all day tomorrow, Steve.'

'Not up to no good, I hope?'

'As if! I'm going to try to track down the seventh girl born around the time of Kate's presumed birthday. I told Steve how Pete had eliminated all but Melanie Harper. It might just come down to a mistake on the part of the parents, but I feel I have to go and check.'

'I suppose there's a slight chance that they gave their baby to Helen and Tony Willis, so I hope you're lucky, Rach.'

'So do I.'

'But surely a neighbour would know the parents no longer had a baby?'

'It's another farm, middle of the fens. They keep themselves to themselves down there, and who's to say the neighbours wouldn't just keep quiet about it? If no-one asked them any questions, they probably wouldn't tell, even if they knew.'

'Yes, I suppose that might happen. Have you rung the Harpers?'

'No, I thought they could tell me any old thing over the phone if they were set on keeping something quiet, so it means a trip, and it might just turn up the answer, even if I only manage to rule out for definite that Melanie became Kate.'

'It's a long trip on your own. Do you want to wait until the weekend and I could come with you?'

'Nah. Don't worry. It won't be a wasted journey anyway. I've been thinking about looking through local newspapers for the months before and around the time Kate was first seen by Helen's neighbour, and they're not available online. I'll have to look through them at the newspaper offices.'

'Well, if it's late, book in a B&B.'

'OK. I'll take a bag with my toothbrush and clean knickers, "Dad".'

'I should put you over my knee for your cheek, young lady.'

'You'll have to catch me first.'

I got as far as the door before Steve caught me round the waist, kissed me and carried out a more pleasant form of 'punishment'.

CHAPTER 19

For once, I was up and out of the house before Steve the next morning. I made good time after I got past the town centre early morning traffic and over the Humber Bridge. Once off the motorway, the pace slowed as I made my way down roads with supermarket delivery trucks tearing along round blind corners, and tractors emerging from side roads and lanes at a snail's pace. I stopped in Market Rasen for a drink and a wee, before arriving in Frith Bank, a tiny hamlet north of Boston.

All morning I'd been passing fields of cabbages and other crops I couldn't identify. There were enormous machines picking vegetables and I wondered if one of the many migrant workers living in the area could have got pregnant and given up her child to the Willises, but in reality I knew that was just a pipe dream, as the timing would have to have been a million to one chance that a birth coincided with Helen Willis's final miscarriage, never mind how unlikely it would be that they came across someone suitable who wanted to give up her child. I shook the idea out of my head, and concentrated on my one final chance of finding Kate's mother.

I'd already decided for an oblique approach, rather than going straight to the farm, so I stopped at the nearest shop, which sold everything under the sun, including stamps. There was an old small postbox on a post outside. I thought someone here should know everyone.

The woman behind the counter was friendly and not evasive when I asked for directions to Jack Harper's farm. I told her a few white lies, suggesting that my mum had known the family years ago and had asked me to call in when I was passing and see how they were. 'Mum felt very sorry for Maggie, with what happened to the baby,' I added.

I don't know what response I expected - being told to mind my own business, a blank look of ignorance or something else, but I got a sympathetic look. 'Yes, dreadfully sad it was, the baby dying while they were visiting her mother in London.'

I was so taken aback, I muttered a few words of agreement, while she virtually told me that nothing good came to anyone who went to London, then I left as soon as I decently could without actually rushing off. Back in the car, I rang Pete. Luckily he was in his office.

Without wasting words, I asked, 'Are you sure there's no record of Melanie Harper's death? It couldn't have been registered in London, could it?' There was a long pause. I could hear Pete's fingers skimming a keyboard.

'No death registered, Rach. I've just accessed my records, and I'm sure. What have you found out?'

I ran him through my conversation with the postmistress-cum-shop owner. 'Maybe she's not remembering correctly, although it seems strange she would imagine the girl was dead unless someone had told her. I'd better just run it through the official system again to double-check, before you go to the Harpers.' I could hear more typing as he carried on talking. 'Could she have been talking about another child?'

'You mean Melanie Harper had a sister?'

'Or brother, Rach. If you've told me word for word what was said, you both only referred to a baby, not a baby girl, or Melanie by name.'

I tried to recall the conversation exactly but as these things generally go, it was like straining lumpy gravy - only bits still stuck in my head. 'Bugger. Maybe I should go back in the shop and clarify. I could hardly have taken notes, but maybe I should carry a little recorder.'

'In this case it doesn't matter, Rach. The parents didn't have another child, so this woman must have been talking about Melanie. You might have struck gold. Are you going there now?'

'When I've got my head straight and decided what to say. I can't spin the same story I told in the shop. I don't think I can do anything other than come clean and ask them if they know the Willis family, and see what response I get, then take it from there.'

'OK. Just be careful, and if you find out anything, do let me know.'

'Of course. Thanks for checking, Pete. I didn't want to blunder in without being sure.'

As I got nearer to the farm, there were old cars on bricks on some of the drives of the infrequent houses. I saw birds of prey perched on bare branches and an owl swooping down in search of mice or other food. I could imagine that walking home from school down these lanes towards dusk could be frightening in winter. I shivered. The whole area felt eerie somehow.

Then I turned off the main track and drove down a side lane, and then onto an even smaller track until I came to a neat farmhouse. I gave myself a shake and a firm talking to. There was nothing sinister around here, just my fertile imagination. I just wasn't used to these wide empty spaces. All in all, I was probably only ten minutes' drive from that post office.

I knocked on the door, still puzzling about how to gain entry to the house; to prevent the door being slammed in my face. The door was opened by a middle-aged lady in jeans and a t-shirt.

'Mrs Harper? I'm Rachel Hodges. The lady at the shop down the road sent me. She thought you'd be able to help me. I'm looking for someone who used to live around here.'

'Oh, right. Well you'd better come in. I've got some scones in the oven, and I need to keep an eye on them.'

Brilliant. I couldn't believe my luck. I even got offered a cup of tea. I suppose they didn't get many people to talk to out here, but I was surprised she wasn't more wary. 'I'm hoping you might know the Willis family, Helen and Tony. They're from over Boston way.'

She was rather on the thin side for what I imagined a farmer's wife to be, but very pleasant, although I thought I detected a slightly wary note entering her voice when she answered. 'I don't know as I've heard of them. Why are you asking?' I was wondering what to say next, when her husband came in.

'Time for a cuppa, Shirl?' He turned to the table and saw me. 'Hello. We've a visitor. That's nice.'

'She's asking if we know … who did you say? Someone called Williams.'

'Willis. Helen and Tony. Over Boston way.'

'I know Tony Willis. See him at auction in Alford, and down in Boston sometimes. Not seen him in ages though. I can tell you roughly where their farm is, if you want. You've got a bit off track over here.'

'Did you ever meet them, Mrs Harper?'

'No. I can't say as I did. Why are you asking? You said you were looking for someone and Trish at the shop sent you.'

They seemed totally harmless, so I said, 'I'm afraid Helen and Tony died in an accident.'

'Tony's dead? He wasn't that old, only about my age. That's a right shame.'

I looked at them both carefully. 'Did Tony ever mention his daughter?'

'Oh, aye, he was always on the lookout for books for her from the charity shop in the square at Alford. Said she couldn't get enough. Always reading.'

Mrs Harper only seemed as interested as you might be if your husband knew someone and you didn't. I decided to come clean. 'I'm actually a private detective, making enquiries on behalf of their daughter, Kate. It seems that Tony and Helen Willis weren't really her parents, and she wants to know who were.'

'Well, that's a rum do, isn't it, Shirl?'

'It is. Poor lass. What's going to happen to her then?'

'I'm afraid Tony never said anything to me, if that's what you're thinking. We weren't what I'd call close friends. So I don't see how I can help. I can tell you one thing though, he fair doted on that daughter of his. I suppose she must have been adopted?'

'Not officially, no. Actually, I'm trying to find out if Kate was unofficially adopted.' I wasn't getting any reaction of guilt or otherwise, so I decided to press on. 'Helen Willis couldn't have a baby, so we think someone might have helped her.'

'What's that got to do with us? Why exactly are you here?' It was the first time either of them had asked, and Shirley Harper sounded a bit scared.

'I'm afraid there's no easy way to say this, but records show you had a baby girl about the same time as Kate was born and she wasn't living here three years later when the census was taken.'

'That's because she died. I don't know why you came to us. We didn't give our baby to the Willises. We loved her so much. There's no way we'd have given her away.' Shirley Harper started crying. 'I knew someone would come, Jack.'

Jack Harper got up and put his arm around her. 'Hush, Shirl. It wasn't your fault. I knew we shouldn't have kept it a secret. I should have rung.' He turned to me. 'I couldn't think what to do. I was worried about Shirl. She was holding her so tight. I had to prise Melanie out of her arms.'

I was confused. 'There's no need to be frightened. Kate's not angry. She just wants to know who she is. Can you tell me how you came to give your baby to Helen and Tony, please?'

'My wife's telling the truth. Melanie died.'

'I'm terribly sorry, Mr Harper, but there's no official record of her death. That's why I came.' I felt dreadful. Maybe there'd been a mistake in the records, or maybe they'd convinced themselves that she was dead to cope with giving her away. I felt awful asking, but I'd already upset them, so I didn't think it could make it any worse. 'Do you have a copy of the death certificate?'

My question was met with a deep and uneasy silence.

CHAPTER 20

Suddenly Shirley Harper spoke again. 'Our Melanie's dead. She wouldn't stop crying.'

I felt the earth shift under my feet. I looked from one to the other and realised the secret they were hiding wasn't an unofficial adoption. They hadn't reported the death of their baby. 'Mrs Harper…'

'Leave her be, please.' He looked back down at his wife. 'Don't say anything else, Shirl. I'll sort it. Don't worry. I'll ring the police and tell them I did it.'

'He didn't do it. Don't let him take the blame. It was me.'

'Shirl…'

'No, Jack. I have to tell someone at last. She'd been crying on and off all day. I couldn't take it any longer. I was so tired. Jack wasn't here. There was a problem with the tractor. She was so hot. When she started crying again, I thought she was going to explode, or I was. I just couldn't think straight.'

'Shirl…'

She gave him a look and carried on. 'I put her in the cot and closed the door. Went downstairs. Put my shoes on. Walked out the door and down the road. I needed air. I needed quiet. When I got back she'd stopped crying. I got Jack's tea on. After we'd eaten I peeped in the bedroom. She was still. She seemed pale. I was glad she wasn't hot any more. Jack came up the stairs, making a load of noise. I picked her up and rocked her.'

I just sat there. I felt so desperately sad.

'I came in the room when I heard Shirl crying, great big sobs. I couldn't get her to put Melanie down. She was clutching her that tight. Just crying non-stop. I led her into the bedroom and she lay down on the bed with Melanie. I thought she'd suffocated her. I was too scared to call the doctor. I couldn't bear to lose Shirl as well. I didn't know what to do. When Shirl fell asleep, I put Melanie's body in the cot and closed the door. Shirl wouldn't say a word. Not for days. Eventually she told me how she'd gone out and left Melanie alone, and I realised Melanie had had a fever and just died. But it was too late to tell anyone. They would have thought Shirl had killed her and covered it up. I think now the fever might have been a symptom of meningitis or something similar, but there was no information about that or about cot deaths like now.'

Finally I felt I could ask. 'What did you tell people?'

Shirley had calmed down now, glad it was all out in the open. 'You see how it is here. You don't see anyone from one day to the next. We went to my mother's in London about a month after Melanie died. We had to tell her. She understood. She's dead now, rest her soul. When we came back, we told people the baby had died, that we'd had her buried with just the two of us and my mum there, that we couldn't face any fuss.'

'And where is she buried?'

'In the garden where we can sit and talk to her. I dug a really deep hole, buried her in her pram with all her things. I don't regret what I did. I had to save Shirl. She'd never have stood the strain of being questioned, of everyone knowing. I'd better ring the police.'

'I think we all need a cup of tea first. Shall I make it?' Where would we be without tea? I can't say that any of us felt much better, but we slowly came back to the present. I couldn't help saying, 'I wish I'd never come. I'm so, so sorry.'

'No lass. It's not your fault. We've kept it to ourselves for eighteen years but it would've come to light sooner or later. We'll get through it together, won't we, love?'

'Look. I can't tell you not to worry, but like you said, it's better out in the open. Would you like me to get some advice for you, unofficially? My fiancé's a policeman in Hull.'

'No. It's all right, Miss Hodges. I'll call the local police.'

'Alright. I'll stay with you until they come, if I may. I'm a bit worried about your wife.' I was, but I also felt it was my duty to see that the police really came, sad as it was.

When the local bobby arrived in his car, he had a policewoman with him. Jack had already told him the gist of what had happened on the phone. He knew the Harpers well, and was very sympathetic, just gently asking Shirley to repeat what she'd told me.

After she'd finished, he said, 'Now I don't want you to worry, Shirley. It won't be my decision, of course, but unless the post-mortem shows some injury, I expect the coroner to rule that it was a cot death. Although you'd be guilty of "failing to register a death", I doubt very much that the Crown Prosecution Service would think it worth prosecuting in light of your undoubted post-natal depression. And even if they did, I think it's virtually impossible that you'd get a custodial sentence, because it wouldn't serve any purpose.'

Shirley burst into tears. The policewoman gave her some tissues and put her arm around her. Jack said, 'It's OK, Shirl.' I felt dreadful, and my face must have shown it, because Jack turned to me and said, 'Please don't feel bad. It'll just be the relief, that. We've tried to forget over the years, but it's taken its toll. Things seem bad now, but I expect we'll be a lot better once it's over.'

The policeman said pretty much the same. 'Don't worry, miss. It might sound an awful thing to you, but country folk can cope with most things. I'll ring Dan and Carol, who live over the way. They'll see them right, look after them, take them back to theirs for a few nights if necessary or look in on them every day if they need to stay at the farm.'

That made me feel a lot better, and I felt able to say goodbye before driving off. I confess I had to stop a mile or so away from the house and have a good cry myself, but then I pulled myself together and drove into Boston in search of lunch.

I rang Steve and brought him up to date. He must have sensed my mood, and made light of my morning's discovery. 'Only you could go solving crimes the police didn't even know about, Rach. What are you going to do now, come home?'

'No, I'm OK, though I don't feel like looking through newspaper reports this afternoon, but I should do it, now I've reached another dead end. I'm just starving and a bit drained, so I'm going to have a leisurely late lunch and potter around Boston. Then I'll book into that B&B you mentioned, go to the newspaper office in the morning and come home tomorrow afternoon. That's if you can get yourself something to eat?'

'I take it the fridge is empty, so I shall do a bit of work while you're not at home pining for me…'

'Ha!'

'…then visit the canteen and see if they make anything edible these days.'

'Don't work too hard.'

'I thought tonight I'd read through that paperwork again that Nick Heighway kept at home. See if I've overlooked something. I'm afraid I never got around to taking it into the office. I need to get to the bottom of his disappearance. Do you know how many people go missing in the UK every year, Rach?'

'Ten thousand?'

'Wrong. Around a quarter of a million, although most return or are found within a few days, and half are aged between fifteen and twenty-one, so a lot of those will have left of their own accord.'

'And younger children? They're the ones who hit the headlines.'

'Not sure, but I'd say somewhere around fifty thousand aged under fifteen.'

'As many as that?'

'Yes, but that includes a big percentage of runaways from care homes. Well, better get back to work. Look after yourself. Love you.'

'Love you too. See you tomorrow.'

I followed up with a short call to Pete to let him know how

things had gone at the Harpers.

'I'm really sorry it didn't work out how you'd hoped, Rach.'

'Yeah, but it's OK. Better go, sorry but I'm starving.'

I ate a massive lunch followed up by a slice of hot chocolate fudge cake, then felt guilty so tried to walk it off, even climbing the weird-looking church known as the Boston Stump. Halfway up the two hundred and nine steps of St Botolph's I was beginning to regret it, but there was a party of schoolchildren behind, and I didn't fancy squeezing my way back down past them, seeing as how some of the little boys were pretending to be knights fighting with imaginary swords in a castle tower. I made it to the top and had a quick look at the stunning view and a refreshing blast of cool air whilst I got my breath back, before going back down whilst their poor teacher was trying to get them to pay attention and not climb up the railings.

I had to have a cup of tea and a caramel shortbread cake bar in the church café to recover. Later, when I'd booked in at the B&B with just a small sandwich in case I got peckish later, I rang Kate.

I'd been wondering how to break it to her that I'd got nowhere with the one remaining lead. I'd not mentioned to her about Pete's census searches as it seemed like she was getting on with her life, but in the end I thought it only fair to tell her, in case someone ever raised the possibility of such a check and she didn't know it'd already been carried out.

When I'd finished telling her the story of Melanie Harper, and how that meant that, sadly, I seemed to have reached another dead end, she said, 'It's very sad, but it makes me feel glad that I'm alive, Rach. That's what's important, not knowing what my name is. It's who I am inside that counts.'

'Very wise, Kate. You're right.'

'Anyway, I'm glad you rang because I found something while clearing the farmhouse to get it ready for Aunt Megan to put up for sale. You'll probably think it's nothing, but I wanted to tell you, just in case, because it was hidden, so I think maybe it could be important.'

'What was hidden?'

'A carrier bag, pushed down the crack between the sideboard and the wall.'

'What was in it?' The suspense was killing me.

'A pale green babygro, clean but used, not brand new, you can tell. That's it, nothing else.'

'Actually, it might be really important, Kate. Would you mind showing me it when I get back to Hull, please? I'd like to take photos and at least have a think. See if I can come up with something.'

We said our goodbyes after arranging to meet the next day.

CHAPTER 21

The next morning, when I was rooting through the microfiches of old Lincolnshire papers, I came across the report of a baby stolen from a pram outside a row of shops. For a moment I thought the baby could be Kate, until I turned to the next day's paper and saw that the baby had been recovered safe and sound, and reunited with his parents. I tidied up. There'd been nothing else that had caught my eye in the extended period I'd chosen before and after Kate's presumed birthdate. But the story of the baby wouldn't go away, and I rang Steve.

'Hi love, I'm just about to go into a meeting. Can it wait?'

'It won't take a moment. I promise. How many babies go missing every year?'

'Can't be many. They can't run away.'

'I'm not joking, Steve. Babies can be stolen from prams. I've just found a case in the Boston paper, but the baby was found.'

'I don't know how many, but there was a time when there were a few cases of babies being stolen from maternity wards. It led to much more stringent security at hospitals.'

'I can't find any others in these papers, but what if there was a baby, maybe even in an area not covered by the Lincolnshire press, who was never found?'

'Oh, I see where this is going.'

'Helen Willis…'

'… might have taken Kate', we both said in unison.

'OK. I'll look up the records at lunchtime. I'll bring anything I find home with me.'

'That's brilliant, Steve.'

'Don't get your hopes up, but you might actually be onto

something, Rach. Drive safely.'

'Will do. See you tonight.'

It was a long drag back up along the slow Lincolnshire roads, stopping at Tesco in Market Rasen for lunch. After I got on the motorway to the Humber Bridge, it got a lot better and it was only mid-afternoon when I got home.

The lovely café in the marketplace with scones the size of a plate had closed down now, but Kate and I met near Princes Quay shopping centre.

As soon as we'd sat down with our drinks, she opened her bag and took out the babygro wrapped in tissue paper.

'What do you think that says?' Kate straightened out the label on the babygro as best as she could.

'It's very faint. It could be a brand name, but it's too worn to make out.'

She turned it over. 'Look, on the back it says "100% BAU..." something. There were probably more letters, but that's all you can read. I can't help thinking of my mam taking this out and rubbing that green silk label between her fingers, wearing the words away.'

I didn't know what to say, so changed the subject abruptly and asked her how she was enjoying Freshers' Week.

'I've never really been able to socialise until now, and that's a bit scary.'

'You'll soon find your way. Just take it easy and don't get too drunk - at least until you have some friends so you can keep an eye on each other!'

'Thanks for the advice – and for caring about me, Rachel.'

'Now come on, let's hit the shops. I want to treat you to something for your 'A' level results and getting into university.'

'You don't have to, really.'

'I know, but I want to. Students can never have enough clothes. It saves washing. I should know.'

So we had a girly browse round the shops and a good laugh trying things on, and I treated Kate to a pretty top, as well as getting one for myself.

When I got in I put the kettle on and helped myself to a biscuit before typing up my notes. Then I made the mistake of trying to search on the computer for missing babies in 1998. I found some interesting articles about missing babies turning up years later, but most of it related to events outside the UK, and ultimately nothing much looked of any use at all. I would have meandered round the internet for a lot longer if the phone hadn't rung.

As it was, a call from a polite lady somewhere telling me there was a fault on my broadband made me realise I'd wasted a good half hour getting nowhere. I'd checked a previous time with our provider and they'd told me that any such phone calls were bogus, as they never contact customers by phone about a fault. I made a mental note yet again to ask Steve if we could have caller display. I hated answering the same bogus calls. Steve said they can get unsuspecting people to hand over control of their computers to crooks while they supposedly fix faults, and then the innocent victims discover they've had their bank accounts emptied.

I still had time to kill before Steve got in, and found myself back on the computer again, after a frustratingly long wait while it did updates - I hate that word. The system somehow assumes that, when you turn your computer on, you don't actually need to do something on it there and then. And then the damn thing says '60% complete', '88% complete' etc and you think you're almost free to get going, but when it gets to 100% it goes straight into another update. Grrh!

Eventually it behaved itself and this time a different search brought up an article about several instances of children, including small toddlers, who'd been presumed missing at the seaside, only to have been washed up nearby a few days later. It seems that parents thought the children were safe paddling but there was a dangerous undertow. It was totally irrelevant to my case but reminded me of days on holiday in Scarborough, when I'd go down to the sea opposite where Mum and Dad were sitting in deckchairs, then spot shells or get interested in a nearby rock-pool, and before I knew it, I'd have moved twenty or thirty yards along the shore. I'd panic when I looked up and they were 'gone'.

Steve arrived an hour later to find tea on and me switching off with a book. He tossed some printouts on the coffee table. 'There might be something for you in there, Rach. Most babies are found, but there are unsolved cases. In fact there were two in 1998, late spring, early summer - your timescale.' I couldn't restrain myself from picking up the papers. 'Hey, what about my tea? I deserve it unburnt for working through my lunch.'

Reluctantly, I put my excitement on hold. 'OK. Eat first, look later.'

While we ate, I told Steve about my day, ending with the article about children being swept away in the sea. 'It might not be as irrelevant as you think, Rach. The parents reported their children missing at first, didn't they? They thought they'd wandered off, and then when they didn't turn up, they probably thought someone had taken them, not thinking they could drown if they were only in the shallows.'

'Right. But Kate's alive. She didn't get swept away, and she was only a baby. She wouldn't be paddling. I don't see the connection.'

'I suppose it's not much of a connection. It just reminded me that one of the unsolved cases I brought home concerns a baby going missing from its family on a beach.'

'Whereabouts? I didn't notice that in the local Lincolnshire papers.'

'Cornwall.'

'Hmm. I'll read up about the case, but that's a long way off. I can't see a connection to a farm in the depths of Lincolnshire. What was the other case?'

'Now that one's nearer home. A baby snatched from a pram at a car boot sale in a field somewhere near March. That's in Cambridgeshire. Hard to solve, because the mother had no idea how long the baby had been gone. The baby was in one of those pushchairs that's suitable for several ages, not a lie-down old-fashioned pram with the baby's face in front of you. There were things piled on top of the canopy and the mother couldn't see the baby unless she bent down to look. There was a right to-do in the papers at the time, blaming her for being a single mother. Neighbours came out of the woodwork, saying she was always gossiping to her friends and not caring about the baby. I don't expect any of it was true. Single mothers were still totally vilified in those days.'

'I'm presuming you checked the sex of the babies?'

'I am a policeman, Rach. Yes, I only brought home the two that were girls.'

'So, there'd be no CCTV because it was a car boot sale, lots of people, and because the mother couldn't see the baby with a quick glance, it could have been over half an hour before anyone raised the alarm? I know my geography's a bit dodgy at times but Cambridgeshire isn't that far from Lincolnshire, is it?'

'Correct. It's the next county south. Yes. It could be Kate. Unless you have a definite suspicion that links her to the case, I don't think the police can get involved after eighteen years, but maybe you could contact the mother, see what you can find out. If there's any chance at all, you could see if the mother's willing to do a DNA test.'

'I don't want to join in with those people who pre-judged this particular woman, but sometimes I wonder if Kate would really want to find her mother, no matter who she is.'

'Oh, come on, Rach. You know how people can be, eager to find someone to blame. I expect the woman's been distraught all these years. Anyway, Kate could always decide not to have anything to do with her, even if she turns out to be her birth mother. She's eighteen now.'

'True. I'll get onto it tomorrow. It's quite a thing to have a possible lead when only this morning I thought I'd reached a total dead end. What about your day?'

'Simon Crawford's laptop turned up in a council tip today. There are council workers who check electrical goods aren't dumped in with the general waste. No-one can ferret about in the metal containers where electrical goods are thrown - Health and Safety etc. This bloke who found Simon's laptop, he thought it might be worth salvaging, rather than scrapping, so he took it to a mate, who told him it was damaged beyond repair, but he recognised the name scratched on the case as having been in the news. He brought it into the station and we checked that the postcode scratched below 'Simon Crawford', is our Simon's. It's gone down to IT to see if they can succeed where this IT bloke failed. You never know.'

'It'd be a major breakthrough if they can get any of his files or notes. I'll keep my fingers crossed for you.'

CHAPTER 22

After we'd eaten, I read carefully through all the information Steve had downloaded from police files on the missing baby. Amanda Bateman had been taken from a car boot sale near March. Once I'd located it on a map, I could see it was only about an hour south from the Willis family's farm. Kate had told me that her dad often brought books home for her from car boot sales, so it wasn't beyond the realms of possibility that Helen and Tony had gone to them together before they had Kate.

I highlighted all the relevant info and plotted a route to the mother's address. She'd moved a couple of times since her baby was abducted. No doubt she couldn't bear to live in the same house with those unkind neighbours, but she'd kept the police updated each time she moved in case of any news. Claire Bateman was living in Ely at the moment, further south than March. It'd take me well over three hours from Hull, even allowing for only a short break en route, making it a bit far for me to do the trip there and back in a day on my own, particularly once I'd factored in the time and energy spent interviewing.

I'd have to ring first and see how that panned out, but it wasn't as good as seeing someone face-to-face. You could learn a lot by people's expressions and their body language, and seeing them in their own home was important too. There could be photos, and in this case, there might be baby clothes she'd kept with the baby's DNA on them.

Then I had an idea. I changed tack and looked up how long it would take me to go by train. Only two and a half hours and I could rest and snack on the train. Satisfied that I could manage that, I rang the number. 'Is that Claire?'

A cautious voice agreed that it was, and asked my name. I didn't want to get her hopes up, and worse, maybe have it all splashed over social media that her baby might have been found, so I tiptoed around the subject carefully. I'd decided my cover at the beginning would be that I was writing a book about women separated from their babies for life, mainly through adoption, but also death, and that I wanted to round it out with a view of a case such as hers.

'How did you get my number? That was years ago. I'm sorry, I don't want it all dragged up again now. I've got a new life finally, and a little boy, Kieran. He's nearly four. I never let him out of my sight.'

I sensed she was about to put the phone down. 'Please wait, Claire. My fiancé's a police inspector, and you've kept your details up to date in case your daughter's found. That's how I got your number. No-one else will, I promise. Just let me explain a little, please. I want the book to be available to women in the same situation, so they can take some comfort but also practical advice from mothers who've been through the same experience. There's also the very slim chance that your daughter may read it.'

'But Mandy wouldn't know she was mine, would she?'

'Well, I won't be identifying you by name, but stranger things have happened. Please, if you could just spare me an hour one day this week, just to meet me, I'd be so grateful. Think of a woman who might have her baby taken next week or in a month's time. You would be helping.' I knew that it could still go either way, but thankfully she agreed to meet me. 'Just one thing more, Claire. I'd be grateful if you wouldn't mention this to anyone else at the moment, you know, on Facebook or whatever.'

'I don't touch those sites. All this social media stuff wasn't around when I lost my little Mandy, but after the way people were with me…'

'Thank you. There won't be anything put out by me either, I promise.' We arranged that I would go down the following day and see her just after lunch, and I put the phone down. 'Phew!' That'd been hard work, but I was pleased with the positive result.

I caught an early train to Ely. I'd allowed plenty of time as I had to change at Doncaster and Peterborough, and then find Claire's house at the other end, but it went smoothly and I had time to eat lunch and even have a little look around Ely as well, before arriving at Claire Bateman's house.

It could have done with a coat of paint, but there were bright flowers in the tiny front garden, and from a narrow dark hallway, Claire led me into a long, light room, uncluttered apart from the far end where toys had been piled into a corner.

'Kieran's at my mum's. I thought it best so we don't get interrupted, and he picks up bits of conversation now he's four. I'm sorry if I seemed a bit unhelpful when you rang. It's just that I've finally got a home where no-one knows my past. We've been here six years now. Darren comes from Ely and people just accepted me as someone from a different area when we got married. Mum moved down here too, and the neighbours are nice.'

'I'm really glad for you, Claire. It must have been dreadful losing Mandy as it was, but then the publicity as well…'

'It was so long ago. She'd be eighteen. Can you imagine that? Older than I was when it happened. Sometimes, it's awful to say, but I forget for days at a time about her, and then seeing a little brown-haired girl toddling around reminds me. I know she wasn't a toddler when she was taken but that's somehow how I imagine her, certainly not as a teenager. I've very few memories of her. I only had her a couple of months and then she was gone. I wish I knew what I did wrong, how someone managed to get her. Probably someone bending down to look at things for sale under those trestle tables just picked her out of her pram, stood up and walked away while I was looking at baby clothes for her.'

Claire started crying. I felt helpless, glad the little boy wasn't there. I could only give her a hug, then offer to make a cup of tea. I knew I couldn't build her hopes up by telling her Mandy might be Kate.

'I'm all right now. I haven't cried for years. I was due another sobbing session. My mum'd taken me to the car boot because cash was tight. The father was only my age, just a lad really, and we weren't serious or anything. It was over before I knew I was pregnant. He gave us a bit of cash, but that was it. He was never going to be a dad to Mandy. I'll never know if he'd have changed as he got older, but I doubt it. I try to picture people I saw at the car boot, but of course I can't. Now, when I think about her, I just try and imagine her happy. I know she's alive somewhere.'

'I'm sure she is.'

'When there was no news, when they'd checked out the local hospital for mums whose babies were stillborn and might have taken her, and followed all their leads I shut myself down for months. The press eventually left me in peace, but it took a few house moves to shake them off entirely. If my mum hadn't been with me, the police might have thought I'd made it up, that I'd killed Mandy somehow, and gone to the car boot with an empty pram.'

'Have you anything left of Mandy's?'

'I kept her teddy. It was left behind in the pram. It still smells of her.'

'Can I see, please? If you don't mind, that is.'

I hadn't a clue how I was going to handle this, and I doubted the teddy still smelt of anything, but then Claire handed me a lifeline. 'Do you think they can get DNA from the teddy now? Back in 1998 they never tested. I can't remember exactly why, but I think they needed blood or hair, but all that testing's got much more advanced now, hasn't it? Do you think they might be able to track her down now somehow?'

'I'm not sure, but maybe, Claire. You've never washed it, have you?'

'No, it would have taken the smell away. She used to suck its ear when she wanted a bottle. I put it in a freezer bag so I could keep her smell. They said it was no use then, but I thought "you never know" and it was my only real link to her.'

'There might be some traces of saliva. Can I take it to be tested? I'd be so careful. I'd keep it safe.'

'That would be brilliant. I'll go and get it.'

When she came back, I mentioned as if it was an afterthought, 'Maybe I should have a couple of your hairs as a sample of your DNA, to eliminate anything that isn't Mandy's?'

Claire didn't think that was an odd request, answering, 'OK. They didn't test mine at the time either', before yanking out a couple of hairs with roots and putting them in one of those sealable bags that go in the freezer. An hour later I was sitting on the train home, praying that, saliva on the teddy or not, the DNA from Claire's hair would be a match for Kate's DNA.

When I got back to Hull, I called in to the same place where Kate had her DNA tested and left both the teddy and Claire's hairs for testing. Luckily I'd thought to get Kate's approval in writing for me to compare any DNA samples with hers at their lab. I'd told her at the time I took her case that I didn't want her to be too hopeful I'd find her mother, but it would save a lot of time in case I actually did find a likely match. I paid extra for a quick turnaround, a result in two days.

CHAPTER 23

The next day I rang Mum and arranged for her to come round after lunch. I'd been out of the house so much that I had to spend the rest of the morning cleaning and tidying, particularly the bathroom. Mum's always been quite a stickler for cleaning her bathroom every week without fail until it sparkles.

Mum blew in full of energy and full of news. I hadn't seen her for well over a week. Before I got a word in, she was waving a booklet in front of my face. 'Look, Rach, I got the Hornsea newsletter. It's got pictures and a bit about the meetings. There are tables selling pieces of Hornsea and there's lunch too. They put on a lovely spread, by all accounts. And the best bit is they have an auction afterwards. I've never been to an auction, Rach!'

'Neither have I. It sounds great, Mum. Count me in. Tell me the date and I'll put it in my phone and on the calendar.' Phones are great for reminding you on the day, but I forget to look at the coming weeks until it's too late. 'I better join the society too, if I'm going to the meetings. I know it's a nostalgia thing for you, all the old beakers, but it's really fashionable now, all the retro stuff and I know Steve would like the things they made. I wonder if there are any younger people who go. If not, we'll get in at the beginning before everyone catches on.'

'When you get married, and you've got a house, you'll need some nice things to put in it. I don't suppose...'

'No, Mum, no date yet, but even if we don't get married soon, or at all, it would be nice to have a house with a garden, and I'd love to move back out to the suburbs. I know parking's difficult in the centre and it's good Steve's able to walk to work from here and I can walk into town easily, but I could always catch a bus if necessary and Steve, well, the headquarters are moving from the centre anyway, so it won't be a problem for much longer.'

'Don't say you're not going to get married after all? Your gran's done nothing but plan her outfit since Steve bought you that ring.'

'You shouldn't encourage her, Mum. Now let's have a cuppa and a biscuit and I'll bring you up to date on my case.'

'That poor girl Kate who doesn't know who her parents are? Are you getting anywhere?'

'I keep reaching a dead end and then another idea presents itself. This one's quite promising, but then the others have been too.' We settled down and I told her all I'd been up to, before Mum told me the latest events in my sister's household.

'The twins have been round to Gran's to ask about the war. They're doing a project in school about what it was like for children at that time. Apparently there's hundreds of essays in some archive or other that were written by secondary school children in Hull at the time, entitled "What I did in the air raids". Some are really sad, about houses being flattened and next door neighbours being killed, then there are some that say they used to enjoy playing in the rubble, never knowing what they'd find.'

'And Gran - what did she have to say for herself?'

'She said she liked missing school the best, you might know. She's a right fibber, Gran. She's only seventy-six. She can't possibly remember anything herself. She'd only be at most five when the war finished. She was the youngest of six, though, and I do know none of them were evacuated to the countryside. Her dad, my granddad, he wouldn't let any of them go. You see these old newsreels on the TV and forget that a lot of children didn't leave, even though Hull was decimated by the bombing because of the docks.'

'So what do the twins have to do for their project?'

'Write an essay just as if they were in an air raid too. I hope they find out a bit more from someone else or their essay's going to be a bit short.'

Soon the results from the DNA comparison were back and it was bad news. Mandy was confirmed as Claire's baby, but she didn't match Kate at all. I'd been so sure it would work out.

I just had to ring Steve and tell him, even though he was at work. 'It's such a shame. I really warmed to Claire.'

'At least you didn't mention anything about it to Kate. That's a blessing.'

'What am I going to say to Claire now?'

'She didn't know about the possibility that her baby might be Kate either, Rach.'

'But she gave me the teddy and her hairs, hoping they might help track down Mandy, even though she only thought I was writing a book.'

'I think it helped her telling you her story, and she's got a DNA result now. In fact I'll get the details sent to anyone who might possibly have come across a match, Rach. I promise. Police, hospitals, any groups involved with missing persons. Maybe something will come up.'

'Thanks, Steve. I'll let Claire know you're doing that. It'll give her some hope.'

'You're right Rach. Now, come on. Try to cheer up. You did your best.'

That same night I had a call from Kate out of the blue. 'Guess what. When the house clearance people moved the sideboard - you know, the one with the carrier bag stuffed down the back? - they found something else.'

I was just trying to recall the significance of a carrier bag, when I remembered the green babygro. Kate had just showed me the little suit in tissue, so I'd forgotten she'd found it in a carrier bag. 'What?'

'A photo of a beach.'

'Anything on the back of the photo?'

'No, but it was the same small square size as those in our

141

early albums, so I think Mam or Dad must have taken it, which is strange as Mam would never go to the coast. She always insisted that she hated the beach.'

'Can you tell where it is? Anything in the photo to identify it?'

'Not really. Just a view from the promenade or wherever out to the sea across a beach. You can't see anything of the town or wherever it's been taken and there are no cliffs. I don't know if it's any use at all. I feel I've taken up so much of your time as it is. I was going to look up pictures of beaches and see if anything looks similar, or at least eliminate some, but I realised it would take ages and it still wouldn't tell me why she kept the photo hidden in the same place as the babygro. Shall I scan it in and email it to you?'

'Yes, please, Kate. Could you do it today?'

'Of course. Why do you think Mam hid it? I could understand her hiding the babygro, if it was a link with my real mother, but a picture of a beach seems weird. My real mother might have lived by the sea, but surely there'd be a photo of a house, or an address?'

'I'm not sure at the moment, but I've a feeling it may be more important than you think. Thanks for ringing straight away. How are things otherwise?'

'Well, it's the end of Freshers' Week. It's been a bit bewildering, but in a nice way. I'm used to being on my own a lot, so I'm not homesick like some girls.' Her voice changed. 'Sometimes at night I hear that policeman's voice in my head, saying something about Dad deliberately turning the wheel, and I wonder if Dad did crash the car on purpose, now that I know they weren't my real parents. If they were still alive it would probably have come out when I started university that I didn't have a birth certificate. Maybe they didn't want me to find out I wasn't theirs? But surely adopting me, even if it was unofficial, isn't such a dreadful thing to admit, is it?'

'Your mind's just escaping from all the new things going on and worries about your lectures starting soon. It's trying to find something else to think about. I expect that's all, Kate.' I couldn't tell her what I was thinking - that one or both of her parents might have stolen her from her real mother. I brought the conversation to an end as quickly as I could. There was only one thing in my mind. I'd been pinning all my hopes on Claire being Kate's mother, but the photo could lead in a totally different direction…

I told Steve of Kate's find while I searched for the paperwork on the second baby reported missing around the time of Kate's birth, the one taken from a beach. 'I can't believe now that I didn't read the details. I was so sure that Claire was going to turn out to be Kate's mother, the other baby's disappearance just didn't seem important. I could kick myself. I've been wasting time. I could have been investigating both missing babies at once...'

'Don't beat yourself up, Rach. A week won't have made any difference in the grand scheme of things. It's nothing compared to eighteen years, and as you said yourself, that baby went missing hundreds of miles away from the Willis family's farm in Lincolnshire.'

'It might not mean much to us, but to that poor mother it's another week she's been separated from her daughter.' I was moving piles of paper, magazines, books and all sorts of rubbish, but getting nowhere. The table I used as a desk was a tip.

'I can remember some of the details, Rach. The family were on holiday in Cornwall, spending the day on a beach. The baby was taken while their backs were turned. Here's the folder, under the coffee table with last week's TV guide on top of it.'

'Great, can you read it to me please? I've just dropped my glasses.'

'Let's see. The mother went to the café over the road to get takeout drinks, leaving her husband with the baby fast asleep under an umbrella in one of those car seats you can take out and carry, and a three-year old boy digging in the sand. The little boy ran off towards the sea with a bucket to get water, the dad gave chase, had to argue with a toddler stamping his foot and four or

143

five minutes later, when he'd scooped up the boy and turned back, the baby was gone.'

'That's dreadful.'

'Yes. The car seat was empty and the baby had disappeared into thin air. People sitting nearby were either reading, eyes closed sunbathing or whatever, but no-one saw anyone carrying a baby, despite tons of interviews. Even though it was reported within five or ten minutes, by the time a proper search was organised, it was like trying to find a needle in a haystack.'

'What sort of beach was it? Were there cliffs? Only Kate said no cliffs.'

'A wide beach attached to a small village. A couple of large car parks but no CCTV, except inside the shop-cum-off-licence. Police looked at all the footage for that afternoon but there was no baby. The village is down little roads with no CCTV, so no chance of tracing a car. You probably don't remember the appeals on TV. Eighteen years ago you'd be just a kid yourself.'

'I daren't get my hopes up again, but maybe this could be it, Steve. It could be Kate's family. Why didn't I remember? In that diary Kate gave me at the very beginning, she wrote that they never went on holiday, not even to the beach, because her mother hated it. If she'd snatched a baby from a beach, then no wonder she couldn't face going to the coast. It would bring back memories she couldn't bear.'

I'd found my glasses and made a drink while Steve was reading. He passed me the file in exchange for a cup of coffee. When I read it, I groaned.

'What's up?'

'When you said the parents were on holiday in Cornwall, the last thing I expected was to find out they came from abroad. That's going to make a visit a bit hard.'

'Sorry, I don't remember seeing their address. I just glanced down the case details.'

'The parents live in Germany, in a place called Ilmenau, wherever that is.'

'I'll look it up.' A few minutes later Steve announced, 'It's in

Thuringia, which I'm sure you know is in the old East Germany, sort of south of Leipzig. The wall came down in 1989. Hey, it says here that Prince Albert, you know, Queen Victoria's husband, he came from nearby Coburg. It looks really nice in these pictures.'

'I've never heard of Coburg, Ilmenau, or that other place, Thingywhatsit.'

'Thuringia. And Queen Victoria's Prince Albert was the Prince of Saxe-Coburg and Gotha.'

'Oh, really? I'm guessing I can write in English, then?'

'Most East Germans were taught Russian in school but those times are way behind them now. I expect they'll speak English. You can only write and see.'

'I wouldn't want to get their hopes up, but I'm not sure if the same approach as I took to Claire would work. It's much harder to get in touch with people by letter, and I don't know if they'd respond if I just said I was writing a book.'

'If I was you, I'd come clean, but keep the information to the bare minimum. I'd tell them that a girl approached you to find out who her parents were. The man and woman she'd thought were her parents had died, and after a lot of enquiries, you're considering the idea that she was taken from her real parents as a small baby, and the dates could fit with their missing daughter. Say you just want to know if their baby ever turned up. I can't see she did, or I'm sure it'd be on record, but you better check first.'

That reminded me that I hadn't rung Claire to let her know that both her own and her daughter Mandy's DNA samples had been circulated by the police, so I got straight on to it. She was really grateful and I hoped very much that she'd get some good news.

I wrote a letter along the lines Steve had suggested to Renate and Joachim Schneider, putting my return address on the back, which was just as well, as it came back a week later, with the equivalent of 'not known at this address' written on it. I should have been grateful that German efficiency drove them to do that, instead of just throwing it in the bin, but I didn't feel grateful. I felt devastated. I'd all but written the happy ending in my head, particularly when I thought of Kate's aptitude for not just any language, but German itself.

The phone number had been disconnected, so I only had a defunct address, no email and worse, just about the commonest German name there is. In English, it's Taylor, which is quite common, but the German equivalent is even more widespread. I spent the day trying anything I could think of to trace the Schneiders but failed. In the end I had to console myself with the fact that Kate seemed to be getting on with life regardless, and put her mother out of my mind.

CHAPTER 24

'What are you up to today, Rach?'

'I thought I'd see if Sarah wants to go shopping. I need a new winter coat. Mine's looking a bit tatty.'

'Winter coat? But it's sunny outside and it's only the beginning of October.'

'Well, the new ones have been in the shops for over a month now. I know you only think of shopping when you need something to wear right away, but if you browse early you have more choice, rather than dashing out to one shop and getting what's there.'

'But you might find something nicer later.'

I gave him one of those looks that say, "stop talking now and realise you'll just never get it".

He leant down and kissed me. 'See you later then. Enjoy yourself.'

I do love that man.

Sarah couldn't make it. She had her hands full with a sick little Josh. We had a quick natter and I told her not to worry, I'd go round to Mum's and see if she was free for a trip to the Freeport. Dad hates it, trailing round all the clothes outlets, but Mum would jump at the chance. I don't often go shopping with her as she keeps suggesting things I might like, but after a bit she takes the hint and just comments on things I've picked up to consider.

As I had to go down Holderness Road, I asked if Sarah needed anything, and I ended up stopping at the chemist and then dropping off another bottle of liquid paracetamol to save her going out. I had a quick cuppa with her, so it was gone eleven by the time I was back in my car and the traffic on Holderness Road was stop-start.

I was stuck at the lights near Garden Village when I saw a familiar face. My heart nearly skipped a beat. I had to be certain before ringing Steve, but I was ninety-nine percent sure it was Craig Dobson going into that big hardware shop. I turned down Village Road, parked and ran back to the corner. I couldn't imagine he would remember me. We'd never exactly had a long conversation. He'd just hit me on the back of the head and stuck me in a cellar with Lucy, but just in case, I scraped my hair back with a scrunchie to hide my unruly long hair, before crossing over. I walked along, looking in shop windows.

As I passed the hardware shop, he came out carrying a bulky bag. Luckily he must have been buying a few things and that had given me time. Even luckier, he turned back towards town, so we didn't come face to face, but I did get a good look and it was definitely him. I followed him as unobtrusively as I could, whilst fumbling in my bag for my phone.

I swore under my breath when I realised it was out of credit. I know. I should have a contract. Everyone else does. I just hadn't got around to sorting it out. I have a direct debit that pays to load my 'Pay-as-you-go' phone, but I'd been using it a lot lately and it had run out a few days before the next top up. They keep ringing me but I never seem to have the energy to speak to them, or to try to work out if it would really be cheaper or if they're just giving me the hard sell. I decided to keep following him and see if he went down a side street and into a house or something. Maybe then I'd have a reason for asking a complete stranger if I could use their phone to call the police.

He stopped to make a call on his mobile and I pretended to be interested in the cake shop window. I realised I was starving. I needed cake. I could nip in and ask someone to use their phone, and have a cake while the cavalry arrived. The next minute I nearly jumped out of my skin, as there was a tap on my shoulder. 'You're Rachel, Inspector Rose's girlfriend, aren't you?'

To my great relief, it wasn't Craig, but that new sergeant in Steve's department. I'd been introduced when I called in at the station just recently.

'Thank God it's you. Are you tailing Craig Dobson?' I whispered, although Craig had finished his call and was well out of earshot, striding down the road now.

'Yes. I didn't know you knew him. Have you rung the station?'

'No. I know this'll sound stupid but… I must have left my phone on the coffee table.' I couldn't confess to having no credit, now, could I? He'd wonder what sort of idiot his boss was going out with. 'I wasn't exactly planning to run into a fugitive this morning. I've been to a friend's round the corner.'

As we strolled along talking, Craig went into another shop. 'It's OK. I've just called the station and backup's on its way, but it would be less obvious if you could help keep him in sight till they get here. I don't want to lose him.'

'Oh, yes, of course.' I could do something useful at least. Sergeant Bradfield, or Tommy as he asked me to call him, suggested I walk past the shop and take a look and he'd wait in case Craig doubled back. I was just walking past the shop when Craig came out. He went down a side street. I turned back to see what Tommy wanted me to do. He was on the phone, presumably updating his colleagues. He gestured that I should follow Craig, and started moving quickly towards me.

I went to the corner and nonchalantly crossed the street, but Craig was nowhere in sight. Looking down, I saw the street was mainly terraced houses, but there was an alleyway about ten yards from the corner on the opposite side, so I guessed he must have gone down there. I wasn't going to follow him if he had. Tommy hadn't appeared yet and I wondered if he was briefing the occupants of a police car. There was a builder's yard just a bit further down the street on my side, so I walked towards it, thinking it would be full of nice strong builders, a safe place where I could wait and point out the alleyway. And that was my big mistake.

I should have gone back to the main road. I heard a door open and almost in the same instant someone threw a large cloth over my head and dragged me off the street. I cried out but it was too late. My voice went unheard as the door slammed and for good measure I received a punch to the stomach which took my breath away. He pulled off the blanket and looked me up and down.

'Well, if it's not the cow who stopped me getting rid of that bitch of a girlfriend, Lucy Turner. Why are you following me now?'

'I don't know who on earth you think I am, but you've got the wrong person. I don't know you and I don't know any Lucy. Apart from a kid in my class at infant school.' I forced myself to look indignant and not scared. Maybe I could get away with my bluff, get to the safe haven of the builder's yard and ring the police. I thought quickly. 'I was going to the builder's yard down the road to see if they had any odd bricks to build a bookcase with, when you grabbed hold of me. What do you think you're up to?'

The answer was a swift and vicious slap across my face, as I took a step towards the door. He grabbed my bag and threw it in a corner, then kicked my legs from under me. I went down like I'd been on the end of a red card tackle in football. Before I could even think of moving my bruised and aching body, he turned me over and pulled my arms right up my back. I thought my arms would come out of their sockets. He dragged me across the floor and into a small kitchen, kneed me in the kidneys as he used one hand to open a drawer, and then tied my hands behind my back with one of those plastic ties. Then he used my scarf as a blindfold, and jammed a smelly dishcloth in my mouth. Finally he tied my ankles together as well. I wriggled my wrists but it was useless. I was bruised and battered and couldn't move.

I hoped against hope that the sergeant would come to my rescue. Failing that, a back-up car should have arrived by now and they'd station a car in the street while they knocked on doors. What on earth was Steve going to say when I was brought

150

to the station all black and blue to give a statement? That I should have stayed out of trouble, that's what. Ironically, this time I'd tried to do just that.

About five minutes later there was a knock at the door. Craig pushed the kitchen door closed, and I heard faint voices. I banged my feet on the floor as hard as I could, and listened for a response, but all I heard were raised voices, even though I couldn't make out the words through the solid wood door. Good. They had to be arresting him. They'd find me in a minute. Then there was a tremendous crash as if something had been hurled at the door, and I heard a muffled voice say, 'you're an amateur, letting a slip of a girl find you.' Then there was some sort of scuffle. I hoped Craig wasn't getting away. There was more shouting, most of it incomprehensible, apart from what sounded like 'dumping Dean's body without searching his pockets properly.' I could hear an angry 'Get lost!' and then it sounded like all hell broke loose.

Soon it was over. There was silence. I strained my ears to hear if anyone was radioing for back-up. I drummed my feet against the floor again. The door opened a crack, then further. I heard a huge sigh. 'He must be glad he's found me alive', I thought. Then there was a jingle of keys, as though someone was removing them from the front door. I couldn't believe it. What was going on? The back door opened. Why wasn't I being untied?

I heard someone step over me and go out of the back door. It slammed. How was I going to get out of this? Craig must have beaten up a policeman. Was it Sergeant Tommy Whatever-his-name-was? And if so, where were the blokes from the patrol car? Surely someone must have noticed he was missing? I tried to crawl towards the door but it wasn't easy without elbows to propel myself and with my feet tied together. Suddenly I heard the kitchen door open again, and I was unceremoniously rolled up in something dark and smelly, and lifted into the air. I could hear an engine running. I was jerked along in someone's arms for five or six paces, and then dropped onto a hard metal surface.

A door slammed. It wasn't hard to guess that I was in the rear of a van in a back alley.

I waited for the driver to return, praying the police would find me beforehand, but I knew that I was out of sight and incapable of calling for help. I'd already tried to spit the cloth out of my mouth, but Craig had done a thorough job. There was something holding it tight.

Ages passed, or at least it seemed that way. I thought of my bag. The pepper spray. My phone. Granted there was no credit, but you don't need any to dial 999. Would it get thrown into the van with me? Maybe I could get to it later? There was a banging and thumping noise, some clattering, and then footsteps. Craig climbed in, slammed the door and we drove off. I steeled myself for the roar of a siren, but none came. What a bloody mess I was in, yet again.

CHAPTER 25

It was only about six when Steve got back to the flat. It'd been a quiet day. There was no sign of Rach, but she probably hadn't expected him to be back till seven at least. He made a coffee and texted her to say he was home early, in case she was killing time at Sarah's.

He got engrossed in reading some paperwork he'd brought home, and before he knew it, it was seven o'clock with no Rach and no reply to his text. He rang her mobile, but it went straight to voicemail, so he thought he'd give Sarah's home number a ring. It took him ages to find the tatty notebook that passed for Rach's address book, and longer to decipher her writing, but Sarah answered on the third ring.

'Oh, hello, Steve. Long time, no speak. What can I do for you?'

'Nothing much. Just wondering if Rach is having her tea at yours. She's not answering her mobile. Probably buried at the bottom of a bag, under her new coat.'

'Sorry, Steve. She's not here. Change of plan. I had to stay in with Josh, so Rach said she'd take her mum to Freeport instead.'

'Ah! That explains it then.'

'Is everything OK?'

'Yes, don't worry. She can never get away from her mum's when they get talking. She'll have just lost track of time.'

Steve was just weighing up the decision of whether to ring Rach's mum or leave it a while, when he got a call from Michelle, his equivalent at Border Force, to say they'd had a high level tip-off from abroad that a big cigarette consignment was due to arrive in the next week or so. In view of the high

153

stakes involved and the likelihood that anyone in the docks, her department or even the police could be involved, they decided to keep it to themselves for the moment, and only bring in trusted members of the team nearer the time.

By the time he got off the phone it was nearly eight, and he was beginning to worry. He rang Rach's mum's home number. She was usually so startled if anyone actually rang her on her mobile that she either cut them off or dropped the phone. Rach's dad answered. 'Hi Steve. How've you been? We've not seen you in ages.'

'Fine but busy, thanks. You know how it is. I just wanted to talk to Rach and she's not answering her phone.'

'She's not here, lad. Don't tell me she's gone missing again?'

Steve didn't want to worry him.

'Just a bit of miscommunication, I think. Has she been round at all today?'

'No. Her mum spoke to her on the phone the other day, but she's not seen her since the Hornsea Pottery Society booklet came. Should we be worried, Steve? You can tell me. I won't tell her mum. You know that.'

'OK, but I think it'll just be a case of Rach being Rach, if you know what I mean. She was at Sarah's this morning and mentioned she might come round to yours and take her mum to the Freeport.'

'Well I can tell you for certain that she didn't turn up and she didn't ring or her mum would have said she needed some cash to go shopping. I can ask her, but I'd rather not, if you understand me. She's watching TV so she won't have heard what we've been talking about...'

'Thanks. I think that's for the best. I'll get her to ring you when she gets in anyway.'

'Find her, Steve.'

'I will. Try not to worry. You know Rach. She'll be OK. I know she's got in some scrapes in the past but she's not got any cases on at the moment apart from helping Kate find her parents.'

Steve said goodbye and put the phone down, hoping he was right. But where was she? He'd been right when he'd told her dad that Rach wasn't involved in any cases that were at all dangerous. He couldn't see how the one he'd mentioned to her dad could put her in danger. He told himself to calm down but it was hard, given Rach's past history.

He tried Rach's phone again, sent her another text, then wrote a note and put it on the doormat where she couldn't miss it, if she came in without a care in the world, having lost her phone. Then he ran the short quarter of a mile to the station. He popped his head into the IT room, explained the situation and asked Sanjeev if he could do a favour and trace Rach's phone. Then he went downstairs to traffic and asked Rob to put out a request that the patrol cars keep an eye out for her car.

Grabbing a coffee, he went to his office and, not for the first time, trawled through the few home phone numbers that Rach had for friends in her notebook, starting with her sister. He somehow doubted it would achieve anything other than keep his mind off the picture of Rach lying somewhere injured, tied up, or both, but it was worth a try. No joy anywhere. He was beginning to worry.

Sanjeev rang just twenty minutes later. 'Found it, Steve. No calls made at all today, just a couple of missed calls inbound, but it's switched on. I've got the coordinates here. It's off Holderness Road.'

'Thanks a lot, Sanjeev. The missed calls will be from me. I'll take a pool car.'

'Hang on. It's on the move. Shall I come and bring my laptop? I can track it while you drive.'

'That'd be great, thanks.'

They followed the signal, Steve driving fast in the unmarked car, attaching the flashing blue light to its roof until they were half a mile from the signal. 'I'm taking this off now. I don't want to draw the attention of whoever has Rach's phone. I can't understand why she wouldn't answer if it's her.'

The signal left town and meandered along country roads to the coast. It was dark but they were catching up on the slower-moving vehicle in front. By the time they turned down towards Tunstall, they could see a truck up ahead carrying a skip. It stopped, then reversed up to the cliff edge, and the driver got out, walking to the back. Steve got out and showed his warrant card to the startled driver.

'Oh, no! I didn't mean to, but the tip was shut by the time I picked the skip up. The wife said she wasn't going to have it parked outside all weekend smelling. It doesn't smell, but she was having none of it. "Just go and empty it somewhere, Mike", she said. I didn't think it would matter if I dropped these broken bricks and plaster in amongst the rubble from the cliff and then I could park the truck down the side of our house till Monday. I'm ever so sorry, officer.'

'Lower the skip down here where I can look inside.' Steve was no longer paying much attention to the driver. He scrambled up into the small skip and rummaged around, emerging a couple of minutes later with Rach's handbag. 'There's no sign of Rach', he said to Sanjeev, answering his unspoken question. Steve looked through Rach's bag, tipping out the contents onto the front seat of the car, but finding nothing of interest to him in the pile of Rach's belongings, apart from the phone.

'Where is she?' Steve was on the verge of losing it. He could understand how Rach might have put her phone down somewhere and lost it, but not how she would lose her precious handbag.

'Who do you mean? What's all this about?'

'The woman who owns this handbag has gone missing, and you're going to tell me what you know about it!'

'Look, I'm sorry, but I just picked up the skip like I was told to. I never even looked in it. Just backed up, attached the chains and hoisted it up.'

Steve wasn't having any of it. 'Do you expect me to believe that?'

The driver backed up against his truck with his hands up and

Sanjeev got out of the car. 'Inspector…'

'Yeah, I know. He'd have emptied her purse of money and debit card if he was up to no good, as would anyone else who dumped the bag in the skip. I just don't get it.' He calmed down and turned back to the driver. 'I think you'd better give me your name and address and tell me everything you know, including when and where you picked up this skip.'

'My name's Mike Turnbull, but I told you, I don't know anything about the bag or how it got there. It's just my job to drop empty skips at work sites, and collect them when they're full.'

'Just give me the address where you picked it up.'

'A builder's yard.' He gave the name of a street just off Holderness Road.

'That'll be where the phone signal was before it started moving,' said Sanjeev.

'You must have paperwork?'

The driver rummaged in his glove compartment and passed a docket to Steve. 'I dropped it in an alleyway round the back yesterday. This afternoon they rang and asked me to collect it. The boss signed to say I'd collected it, all above board. You ask him.'

'I intend to.' Steve rang the number for the builder's yard. It went unanswered, but then a recorded message gave a mobile number to ring. 'Damn. This is all taking too long.' After about the fifth ring, it was answered. 'Is that Alan White?'

'Who wants him?'

'Detective Inspector Rose. Humberside Police. I'm ringing in connection with the contents of a skip that was collected from your yard.'

'Is there anything wrong, Inspector?'

'We need to look at your premises. Now.'

'What's going on?'

'I can't tell you at the moment, but it could involve a serious crime.'

'OK. I've got nothing to hide. I'll meet you there in ten

157

minutes. You know where it is?'

'Yes. We'll see you there.'

'What about me?' the driver asked.

'Forensics will probably have to give the skip a once over,' unless Rach turns up soon, he added in his head. 'Depending on what they find, we'll be in touch, even if it's just with a demand for a fine for fly tipping. If you drive the skip to the garage at the station, an officer will give you a lift home.'

'Just a moment, please.' Sanjeev turned to Steve. 'Do you need me any longer, Inspector? I hate to bail out on you, but my shift technically finished an hour or so back, and it's just, well, my wife's expecting and it's getting late. I don't like her worrying.'

'Sure, Sanjeev. I wasn't thinking. You've been a great help, but this isn't your job. I'll give Matt a call, drag him out. If you can just drop me back in Hull at this builder's yard, then you can get off home.'

Steve gave Mr Turnbull directions to the police station forensic garage, leaving him in no doubt what would happen if he didn't go straight there. He took his address and phone number.

'Can I ring the wife first, please? I'm sorry I broke the rules. I won't tip things over the cliff again, I promise.'

'That's fine. I'll alert Forensics so they're expecting you, so don't go off on any more wild goose chases, will you?'

Once a chastened Mike Turnbull had driven off, Steve rang Matt and filled him in, before Sanjeev drove him back to Hull.

CHAPTER 26

The van drove quickly but I didn't roll about, so I guessed Craig was just about sticking to the speed limits. At first I tried to count the number of left- and right-hand turns, but I'm not Miss Memory, so I soon gave that up and listened for anything familiar when we stopped. As you might imagine, that was pretty much a waste of time too. I'd tried to rub my head up and down against whatever I was wrapped in, hoping to loosen the scarf covering my eyes, but failed miserably.

The only thing stopping me from giving up hope, was that he hadn't really hurt me that much, and that he'd taken me with him. I tried not to think about the alternative - that he'd hit me so hard that Tommy would be breaking down the door to find my body right about now. Why hadn't I suggested waiting on Holderness Road for police reinforcements, and told Tommy to follow Craig himself? I could have flagged down the patrol car just as easily as him, and I'd have stood somewhere where I could see what happened to Tommy. Call himself a sergeant! Steve'd be sure to have something to say to him when I got out of here.

Craig must have kept me alive as a bargaining tool. That's the only reason I could think of. After all, he tried to kill me once before, even if he got away with it through lack of proof. He was just charged for possession of drugs, and the odd charge of low-level dealing until he got arrested on the Isle of Man for grievous bodily harm and put in jail.

The noise of gravel and the jolting of the van told me we'd pulled into a rough driveway or track. I was betting on us being somewhere in in the countryside east of Hull. Although it could have been the north or the west. Let's be honest, I could only be sure it wouldn't be the south, because we'd be in the Humber by now.

I knew the area to the east well. I'd driven down lots of small lanes at Sunk Island when we'd been looking for a student who'd escaped the clutches of a serial killer. It was deserted and easy to get lost or hide criminal activities. It'd be easy to get rid of a body too... I tried not to think of that but it wasn't easy. Then the van stopped and I heard the handbrake being applied.

The driver got out. A few minutes later I heard voices at a distance. The voices came a bit nearer and I managed to make out someone saying, 'I'll check in tomorrow, and as soon as I can get away from work, I'll be back to deal with the lad.' Then there was the sound of a car, rather than a van, driving off. Next thing, the rear doors were opened and I caught the slightest glimmer of light through the scarf. I tensed, hoping to make a break for it the first chance I got.

Someone picked me up, and I was carried a short distance and put down again, probably on the floor. I wasn't dropped, but the bruises I had already hurt like mad. 'Ouch!' I couldn't help but say the word even though it meant tasting more of the smelly dishcloth. 'Yuk!' I thought, rather than said. I was unrolled from what I took to be a rolled-up rug or bit of lino, and then I was in the air again. I was jolted around and I guessed we were going down some steep stairs. If only I'd managed to dislodge the scarf, but I could see nothing. In fact it was totally dark now and smelled a bit damp, so we were probably in a cellar.

Next thing I heard a key turn, a door open and I was placed, fairly gently, onto the ground. A voice said softly, 'Just so you know - I didn't sign up for this', as I was lifted into a sitting position on a hard surface, back against a wall, with my hands behind me. He went out, but returned about twenty minutes later and I could smell food. 'Behave and you'll be fine. You're not going anywhere with your ankles tied together, so don't try anything. I'm going to take off the blindfold and remove the gag. It's no good shouting. There's no-one can hear you down here. Nod if you understand.'

I did as he asked. The only way I was getting out of here, other than being rescued, was by going along with this bloke until I could come up with a plan. I heard him lock the door. When he took off the blindfold it was hard to see. I blinked and tried to clear my vision. I was sitting on a wooden bench. There was only a dim bulb hanging from the ceiling, but it wouldn't have helped if there'd been a floodlight. My captor was wearing a monster mask - The Incredible Hulk, it looked like.

'You can eat if you agree to behave.' I nodded again. He undid my wrists and pushed a small table next to me. 'You'll have to use your fingers.'

He removed the gag and I said 'Thanks', before taking a gulp of water from the plastic beaker and starting to eat. 'What's your name?'

'No talking or I'll take the food away.'

'Sorry.' I ate the food as slowly as possible, desperately wondering how I might be able to escape, but as soon as I'd finished, he re-tied my hands and left, locking the door after saying he'd be back later with something for me to sleep on. I was grateful that he had left the blindfold and gag off. I considered shouting for help but decided against it as he'd told me no-one would hear me 'down here'.

I was losing track of time, and couldn't see my watch behind my back, but thought it must be getting late when he returned with what looked like the cushion from a sun lounger. He was wearing the mask. 'This'll have to do as a mattress. You'd better get some sleep. The boss'll be back tomorrow and he'll decide what to do with you.'

With the idea of making a friend, in a Stockholm Syndrome-sort of way, I asked him, 'What do you think he'll do with me? I'm scared. I don't know who you are, but please help me.'

'I can't help you. I can't talk to you,' he said. He turned to go.

'I need the toilet.'

'OK, but I have to put the blindfold and gag back on. The toilet's upstairs.'

'Not that dishcloth. Please.'

'I'll get a clean cloth.'

I waited while he locked the door and went, then tried to think how I could best use the toilet break to my advantage. I needed to escape before the boss turned up. Craig Dobson was a cruel, nasty person. I was assuming he was keeping me alive for a reason, but who knew when that reason would cease to exist, and I'd be something to dispose of, nothing more. A shudder ran up my spine and I started to shake. How could I make a plan without getting free, or knowing where I was? I had to take a grip of myself or else I'd not be fit to take my chance when it came.

I'd almost got myself under control by the time 'The Hulk' re-appeared, carrying my scarf and a handkerchief. I hoped it was clean, although getting a sore throat from someone else's germs was hardly the biggest of my worries. Everything annoyingly secure, he hoisted me in his arms and carried me up some stairs. He opened a door, pushed me through it and took off the blindfold. I was in a small room, which only contained a toilet and sink. No window. I tried to speak but couldn't. He shook his head. 'No. Not up here. The gag stays.'

I made a sort of low growling noise and the penny dropped. I could hardly wee with my hands tied behind my back. He untied my wrists, seemingly satisfied I couldn't escape with my ankles tied, and went out, locking the door behind him.

I was desperate so it didn't take long. I sat there, trying to think of an escape plan that would work with my ankles tied together, but couldn't. If I tried to push past him, I'd just fall over. He'd obviously decided I'd had long enough, or had been listening to me wee, as he unlocked the door, before my thoughts got any further.

We went through the reverse procedure. Hands behind back first, then blindfold, carried back downstairs, plonked on mattress, blindfold and gag undone. I just had time to thank him and then he was gone, the door locked and the light turned out. The switch must have been outside, like Steve's bathroom. Sometimes he plays a trick and turns off the light when I'm in there, then he comes in, hoping I'm naked and makes love to me in the dark, talking to me as if he's a mysterious stranger.

I enjoyed the daydream a little while longer as it was so comforting, imagining Steve in the grotty room with me, but then I gave myself a mental shake. If Craig was coming back, I needed a plan and I didn't have one. I was short on ideas. Seducing my guard was about all I had come up with, and although I was desperate enough, he hadn't responded to my attempt to make conversation.

If I didn't get out of this mess, how would I ever manage to reunite Kate with her mother? How angry would Steve be that I'd decided to follow Craig on my own? I didn't want Steve to think badly of me. Maybe he'd think Craig found me by accident? No chance. Things were grim indeed, but I didn't want to focus on the fact I might not survive, so I decided to plan my wedding.

That would make Gran happy at least. Oh, no. What if I never saw my family again? What if Steve didn't want to marry me after all? I had a ring but that didn't mean to say we were actually going to get married. After all, we hadn't set a date. All this thinking was driving me crazy.

CHAPTER 27

Alan White was waiting outside his yard when Sanjeer dropped Steve off, and Matt drew up a couple of minutes later. They asked about the skip and he told them he'd been having a clear-out and had filled it by about eleven that morning.

'Did you toss a handbag in the skip?'

'No. Is that what this is all about? I never noticed any bag, but someone could have buried anything under the rubble, and I wouldn't have seen it.'

'This is a photo showing the bag.' Steve showed him his mobile. He'd managed to find a photo of Rach on holiday with her handbag on her shoulder, whilst he'd been waiting for the manager to arrive. Are you sure you haven't seen it? What about the girl?'

'I haven't seen the bag or the girl, but the skip was down there half the morning, waiting to go to landfill.' He pointed down the alleyway. 'I would have called for collection this morning, but that bloke at number ten had his van blocking the alley, so I didn't ring until I saw he'd moved it.'

'What time was that?'

'I noticed it'd gone at lunchtime, but it could have moved any time this morning, I'm afraid. Fridays are always busy with people coming for supplies to do work over the weekend.'

'Did you see the registration number?'

'No, but he's been driving it around ever since he moved in, so it must be his. It's a white Ford transit. I've seen him going to and fro from his back yard.'

'OK. Can I have a quick look in your yard?'

'Sure. I'll unlock the office too.'

Steve had a good look round but found nothing. He thanked Alan White and let him go, after asking him if he had any idea of the age of the van, or even a partial for the number plate. Unfortunately he'd never paid it that much attention. A white van's a white van, when all's said and done. At least he was sure it was a Ford Transit.

'Lucky for us that the contents of that skip never got to landfill or it would have been like looking for a needle in a haystack and we'd have no idea where it's been.'

'You're right there, Matt. Grab a torch, will you, please.'

Steve knocked at the back door of number 10. There was no reply. It was gone nine and the house was in darkness. He went around to the front and knocked again. No answer. He looked through the window and saw an upturned chair. Then the torchlight caught on a glint in the corner. It looked like a knife. That was all he needed as reason to suspect a crime had been committed. That, and Rach's phone being here before it took a ride in a skip to landfill. He was desperate to get inside.

'We should probably call for back-up, but I think the two of us can handle it - that alright with you, Matt?'

'Let's just do it.'

Matt broke down the door, and Steve went in. He gestured for Matt to stand back. He wanted him outside in case anyone made a run for it.

The door opened straight into a small room. It was sparsely furnished. Steve checked there was no-one in the room before walking cautiously across the threadbare carpet and bending down to look. He'd been right. It was a knife on the floor. As far as he could see by torchlight without picking it up, there was no blood on the blade. Judging from the upturned chair, however, it seemed likely there'd been some sort of a fight. He pushed open the door into the kitchen. It was empty, but another glint caught in the torchlight.

If he'd had any doubts before, they disappeared instantly. He knew Rach had been in this house. A broken silver chain with a gingko biloba leaf was lying on the floor near the fridge, and it was hers. Rach had told him she'd never seen another one like it. Mind you, she'd also said it was lucky and that hardly seemed to be the case.

He didn't want to contaminate the scene further, but he had to check upstairs. Rach could be lying there unconscious. He shouted for Matt to come in and just stand at the bottom of the stairs in case someone was hiding up there, to prevent any suspect from doing a runner. Carefully he went up and into each of the two bedrooms in turn, finishing up in the bathroom, where he got a massive shock.

Lying underwater in the bath was a fully-clothed man. He looked dead, but Steve knew better than to leap to conclusions, because he knew who it was. Craig Dobson. He stood there watching for any tell-tale bubbles until he was satisfied Dobson was dead.

'Matt, there's a body up here. I'm sure it's Dobson. Can you look in the yard for signs of Rach, please? I'll ring Forensics and get the pathologist out here.'

A few minutes later, Matt came back into the house. 'No sign of Rach, boss. No sign of that white Ford Transit you mentioned either.'

'Where the hell was Rach?' Steve wondered desperately. 'Did she escape from her attacker? But if so, why leave Dobson's body in the bath?' She would never have done such a thing. No, it smacked of someone trying to hide the body in a hurry to prevent discovery for some time. The water would mask the smell and moving it from downstairs meant no-one would see it through the window.

Much as he hated to, he had to admit to himself it was unlikely that she'd somehow met Dobson, been recognised, become involved in a fight, killed him, even if accidentally, then left the house of her own free will. Someone had driven away the white transit, and if it was Rach, he'd have heard from her hours ago. No, she'd obviously got caught up in another dangerous situation. How did she manage it? She was only supposed to be going shopping!

It didn't take Forensics long to arrive, followed swiftly by the pathologist, who confirmed that Dobson was dead. 'Most likely a blow to the back of the head. I'll let you the likely cause once I've got him in the lab, but it doesn't look like an accident at the moment.'

'Thanks a lot, David. Can you call the Forensics team up here, please? I need to speak to you all together.'

They gathered in the bathroom before Steve continued, 'I think the killer hoped the body would remain undiscovered. It's the only plausible reason for putting it in the bath. The water would mask any smells. I'm not sure what exactly, but there's something fishy going on here, and with an innocent civilian having been abducted, I want to maintain total silence on the finding of Dobson's body, until we find out more. I'm hoping against hope that my fiancée is still alive. Otherwise we'd have found her body too. That means the murderer must have a reason for keeping her alive and I'm not about to upset his plans until we've found her. Is that understood, everybody?'

There was a chorus of agreement. 'Thanks a lot. Remember, please, not a single word to absolutely anyone - not to your other halves, friends, neighbours, no-one, not even your dog, if you have one - about why you were called out tonight, until either Rachel's found or I say otherwise. Treat this as you would any major secret operation.'

'I'll do the autopsy myself, Steve, and keep it quiet. Don't worry,' David Leadbeater assured him.

'Right, Matt, it's dark now, so we won't achieve too much more tonight. If you wouldn't mind dropping me back at the station, you can get off home.'

'I can't do that, boss. You need me.'

'I'll need a sergeant who's had a good night's sleep more. As soon as it's light, you can get a couple of the lads organised. I want the search for Rach's car to be stepped up in the surrounding area. I want to know if there are any CCTV cameras

167

around here or on the main road. I want to know the reg. number of that van and then I want it traced. I want house-to-house to see if any neighbours have any information at all that might be useful. And I want this house searched top to bottom for any clue as to what Craig Dobson was involved in. Anything to link him to Dean Hornby, his death or his business, including the murder at the writer's retreat. But until we find Rachel, I want a news blackout on Dobson's death. Not a word to the lads. Someone else is involved in this and word travels fast.'

Keeping busy was the only way to cope, and to get the result he wanted - finding Rach. Steve debated whether to ring her dad again, but on the basis of "no news is good news" decided he'd better leave it a while in the hope there'd be something positive to report before nightfall. Reluctantly, Matt dropped him off at the station. 'You should go home and get some sleep too, boss.'

'No, thanks.' Steve needed to be at the nerve centre, ready to go when any useful information turned up. He went to the machine in the canteen for a black coffee and tried to concentrate, but he couldn't get the picture of the body in the bath out of his mind. For a split second, he'd registered a figure and his brain had made it into Rach. He still felt a little bit shaken but he pulled himself together. He was glad he'd let Sanjeev go home earlier. It would have been far too stressful for a member of the IT team.

He'd just got back in his office when there was a call from Forensics at the house. They'd found some blood on the hearth which matched Dobson's. It looked like he'd fallen and hit his head. The death could have been accidental. Steve briefly pondered if Rach could had been the cause after all, but the placement of the body in the bath, her disappearance, her bag in the skip - it just didn't tie up.

Steve put his personal feelings aside and acted like the professional he was, tracking down the owner of the house, a Mr Gallagher. He'd rented it to a bloke for cash about six months ago, he said. Steve emailed him a photo of Craig and got a positive ID. It looked as if Dobson had been living there since he

168

left the Isle of Man. Steve told Mr Gallagher that the house was now a crime scene, so he wouldn't be able to gain access. His only comment was that it was a good job he'd asked for a damage deposit and three months' rent in advance. The place was furnished and he didn't want someone to walk off with the contents, leaving him out of pocket.

Steve was exhausted. Craig Dobson was dead. Dean Hornby was dead. Who, if anyone, was running the smuggling operation now? Had they been replaced by someone working at the docks, cutting out the middlemen? Or, more likely, was there someone higher up the chain? Dobson didn't really have the nous to organise something large scale, and with all the steps taken to silence people, it was looking like it could be a massive operation. He'd have to speak to Tommy in the morning. He was the liaison officer with Border Force. More puzzling, where did the abduction of Rach fit in all this? And how was Steve to find out? The trail was cold. He had no real leads. Just a bog-standard white transit van that had been parked down an alley behind a house rented by Dobson in a back street off Holderness Road.

He knew he should have gone home hours ago. He felt bad, not ringing Rach's dad back, even with no news to report, but reasoned he'd be in bed by now, and hopefully he'd think Rach had turned up and they'd forgotten, or thought it too late to ring him. Thoughts kept whirling through his head. Around one am, he realised he'd be no good to Rach without sleep, and it would be better at home, only five minutes' walk away across Queen's Gardens, than slumped over his desk. When he got there, he left his clothes where they fell and tried to sleep.

CHAPTER 28

I rolled over onto my side to stare round the small cellar room for inspiration and felt something in my pocket. Craig had taken my bag and coat but otherwise not searched me. Presumably he assumed that taking my handbag would remove all useful possessions such as phone, cash, driving licence - and keys.

He probably thought women put everything in their handbags - and I usually do, but when I'd parked the car and run across the road to avoid losing sight of Craig, I just stuffed my car key in the front pocket of my jeans, in among a load of crumpled tissues. I was in such a rush I didn't have time to stop and open my handbag. So it had gone unnoticed. Even I hadn't noticed it until then. I'd forgotten it wasn't sitting in the compartment of my handbag where it always lives.

More importantly, it was on a key fob. I keep my house keys separate as there's three of them (my flat, Steve's and a lobby door too) and I can't stand the rattle of all those keys when I'm driving. And sometimes I go out without the car, with my house keys in my pocket or bag and Steve may need to move the car or something. Or I might lose them - I have a history of that.

Anyway, the key fob was given to me by a client. I'd done a bit of undercover work for him, tracking down a pilferer in the office, and he'd given me the fob when I left, as well as paying my bill. It had his company's logo on - one of those corporate advertising things, but was also a useful present, because it contained a miniature metal toolkit inside the leather fob. You unbuttoned the fob and a tiny screwdriver could be extended from one side, and a small penknife from the other. Now you can see why I was thrilled to have my car key. I wasn't going to gouge my captor in the eye with the key. That would be too difficult, particularly with the mask. No, I...

'Hello', a faint voice came from out of nowhere.

I stopped making my escape plan and curiosity fought with high alert mode.

'Hello back, whoever you are. Where are you? You sound like you're in the wall.'

'I'm locked in another room in the cellar. I don't think you're next door, but maybe in the next-but-one room down the corridor. I heard everything but couldn't speak until he went to bed in case he found out about the air vents and blocked them up. I can't see him hearing through the ceiling or these heavy doors, but we better keep it quiet. It's so good to have someone to talk to. The bloke on guard's not nasty but he keeps talk to a minimum, and I've been here twenty-five days by my reckoning. Who are you and what are you doing here?'

I wasn't sure if it was a trap, so I said, 'You go first. Tell me your story.'

'My name's Nick and I'm a policeman. I stumbled upon a smuggling gang and I've been kept here ever since they caught me following them. They've got this massive job coming up. Enough to make them millionaires by the sound of it. Apparently the boss has said he'll let me go afterwards because he's got a new identity and is going abroad to start a new life, but he's keeping me as a hostage until then.'

'What's your girlfriend's name? And do you have a brother or sister?' I wanted to check it really was Nick Heighway and not someone working for Craig Dobson, possibly testing me to gain my confidence and find out what I knew.

'Why do you want to know that?'

'Just answer, please?'

'OK. My girlfriend's called Karen. She works in a shop. I have one brother. He's at Oxford studying astrophysics.'

'Phew! Fantastic! Hello, Nick. I'm so glad you're alive. Sorry, but I had to check that you were really who you said you were. I've met Karen and she mentioned your brother. I'm

Rachel Hodges, Inspector Rose's girlfriend, I mean fiancée. I'm a private detective and I know quite a bit about the smuggling, the death of the writer, Simon Crawford, and...'

'Oh, no!' Nick interrupted, sounding devastated. 'Surely Simon's not dead. I told him it was too dangerous for him to get involved but he insisted on shadowing me for his book. He was a lovely bloke. I should have stopped him.'

'I'm so sorry. I thought you must know.'

'The last I saw of him was when we'd gone our separate ways after leaving the pub we'd been staking out. The landlord, Dean Hornby, came out of a side alley and before I had chance to react, he'd bundled me into a van. I wish I hadn't been so stupid. I should have taken more care to be sure we weren't being followed. I was too damned cocky, thinking of fast promotion on the back of working a case in my spare time.'

I tried to distract Nick from feeling guilty. 'How did you get to know Simon?'

'It'll be best if I tell it from the beginning, I think. Simon's writing, was writing... a book about smuggling. He'd come up with the idea for his second crime novel. At first he hung around the docks, hoping to get a contact who could help, but then he hit on the idea of shadowing a policeman to make his novel full of real detail.'

'And... '

'He'd been in the station, but couldn't get past Derek, the desk sergeant, so he'd hung around outside instead, hoping to talk to someone who might have time for him. He said he approached me because he heard me say goodbye to Derek, so he knew I was a copper and not a civilian, and I was young, so he thought I might be keen to help. To be honest I couldn't see what I could do, but I said I'd think about it, took his number and said I'd ring if I found anyone who might be able to help him. What happened next was pure coincidence. Just by chance one night I ended up having a pint with some mates after footie in Dean Hornby's pub.'

'The Steam Packet?'

'Yes. Anyway, I was having a laugh with the lads, minding my own business but I couldn't help but notice a couple of blokes come in and be handed small packages from under the counter in exchange for cash. They didn't stay for a drink, so I thought the landlord was dealing drugs. I thought it would do my career no end of good if I could get some information on what I thought was a drug ring, so I started tailing Hornby on my own time. He met with another bloke – he called him Craig - and I followed him too, but I lost him. I thought of Simon, and how if there were two of us, it would be easier to tail him. At the same time it would help him with his book. Why didn't I just talk to the inspector then? I can't believe I got Simon killed.'

'You didn't kill him. He got involved of his own free will. It sounds like Craig Dobson killed him, but go on. How come you ended up here?'

'They must have seen us watching them. I can't forgive myself for being so careless. I thought Simon might end up here too, if they tailed us both, but he never did, so I thought he was OK, still out there somewhere. All I can think is that this Craig - Dobson did you say? - went after him that same night as Hornby got me. Somehow he must have put up more of a fight and wound up dead. I can't get over it.'

'Simon was suffocated. He was back at the writers' retreat. Craig must have followed him there. Maybe he started shouting, and Craig was trying to shut him up. Blaming yourself won't change things. Craig Dobson's a nasty piece of work. He tried to kill me once. My Steve says, instead of letting crimes get to you, you've got to get even, and that means getting the criminals sent to prison.'

'What do you know about the cigarette smuggling?'

'Karen gave me your notebooks after she reported you missing. Your disappearance wasn't a crime - you'd booked two week's leave after all - so Steve - sorry, I mean Inspector Rose - couldn't really spare the time to investigate, but he was worried, and before the time came that you should have been back in work, he sent me round to talk to Karen.'

'What happened to my notebooks? They're the only written proof I've got.'

'Steve logged them into evidence and out again so I could go through them for him, and then I think he must have taken them into the office when your fingerprints were found in Dean's van.'

'I was keeping them at home until I had enough evidence to take them in to the inspector. Even if anything happens to me, at least the inspector's seen them though and he should be able to get the bastard.'

I thought he was being a bit naïve really as they only contained dates, amounts and initials, but I didn't want to depress him further. I also didn't want to tell him that there was no way in hell that Craig would keep him alive when he no longer needed him as a bargaining chip. Craig wouldn't keep him locked up somewhere just to stop this big deal going ahead; he'd just kill him to get him out of the way, like he did Dean Hornby and possibly Simon Crawford. He was only keeping Nick temporarily, in case he got caught. So I kept quiet on that subject. 'Karen's been really worried, but otherwise she's fine.'

'That's a relief. I've been worried about her too. I didn't know what she'd think when I just disappeared like that. But how did you end up here?'

I told him all about my run-in with Craig, the fact that he was top of the police wanted list for Hornby's murder, and about how I'd spotted him on Holderness Road and started following, planning to ring Steve as soon as I knew where he was going.

'Dean Hornby's dead as well?' Nick sounded really shaken.

'Yes. Steve thinks Craig killed him as well as Simon. Perhaps Dean thought Craig was bringing Simon here instead, and was horrified when he heard he'd been killed. Maybe he said he didn't want anything to do with murder.'

'I'm surprised I wasn't killed too, really, hostage or not.'

'Well, there's the none-too-little matter of a massive murder hunt if a policeman's killed. That would have stopped their master plan.'

174

'That Bradfield's got a lot to answer for!'

'You mean that new sergeant of Steve's - Tommy?'

'Yes. He's the one behind all this!'

'What!? You have to be joking! I ran into him when I was following Craig and he asked me to help. I did wonder why he didn't just take over, but he said he'd ring the station for back-up. I saw him on the phone - but now I come to think of it, he must have been tipping off Craig instead. When I turned a corner, Craig grabbed me. That's how I ended up here.'

'I can well believe that.'

I sat there open-mouthed. I was in shock. And absolutely bloody livid with sodding Tommy Bradfield. 'Are you absolutely sure?'

'Definitely. One night we were following Craig from the pub and blow me if he didn't meet with Bradfield. It was a good job it was dark, and I was watching through some trees or he'd have seen me.'

'But how do you know Craig wasn't just passing him information?'

'Because the next day I heard a snippet of one of Bradfield's conversations. He was in the office, but he didn't know I was there. I'd just dropped a folder of loose papers and was down on my knees under the desk when he came in. He was talking to someone about how he'd want a bigger share of the cig profits next time, seeing as how they'd be coming in on both ships. I waited until he'd finished and then five minutes later the inspector called him into his office, so I managed to get out unobserved.'

'So that's how you found out they were smuggling cigs?'

'Yes. As I said, at first I thought it was just small-time drug dealing that he was turning a blind eye to. That's why there's nothing in my notes about cigarettes. When I told Simon I thought it was strange that Bradfield had mentioned cigs, he told me that when he'd been researching for his novel, he'd read an article about the massive difference between the actual cost of cigarettes in Eastern European countries, and the price they get sold here in the UK after duty's been slapped on them.'

'Yeah. Steve told me that.'

'I daren't follow Bradfield, but I kept up our observation of Hornby in the pub, and when Simon was in there on his own once, he got into conversation with a barman and managed to buy a packet of cigs off him with no duty sticker, so we thought we were getting somewhere. Simon kept it but I took a photo with it.'

'Yes. I've seen it.'

'Sometimes we trailed Craig, but he got into a car and it was too difficult then. It looks like he's Bradfield's strong-arm man and like you just told me, he's the one with the links to a network of dealers from his drug days. Bradfield's the one who organised the smuggling through the docks, either turning a blind eye himself or getting others to do it by blackmail or cash incentive. Now he's the liaison officer to Border Force he knows when and where the searches are due.'

'No wonder he didn't follow me round the corner. No wonder there was no back-up. I hadn't a clue. The slimy bastard! How dare he call himself a police sergeant! It makes my blood boil to think I fell for it!'

'Shh! If they hear you, they'll know we've been talking and one of them'll come down and block the ducts.'

I didn't realise I was talking louder, but I must have been. I carried on in a normal, much quieter tone. 'There's more than one?'

'Yes. The bloke in the Hulk mask is here all the time. Another comes sometimes, mainly at night. I've heard him talking and it's not Bradfield. I've not heard him here.'

'Steve'll go ballistic when he finds out about Tommy Bradfield. He's only been in their department a while, but even so. He'll be mad with himself for not sussing him out as a bad apple. We've got to get out of here and let him know.'

'Do you think I haven't tried? But you're right. I've been counting the days and the shipments are taking place eight days from now. We have to tell Inspector Rose what's going on. He has to be told both ferries will be involved. I just don't know how.'

What Nick didn't seem to realise was if we didn't get out of there, then one of us would be dead. Tommy Bradfield didn't need two of us to guarantee him safe passage in case the deal went belly-up. I felt a bit like I was Nick's big sister, looking out for him. Or maybe Nick did know, but he was trying to keep it from himself. Luckily I had the tool that might give us a chance.

'Just a minute. I've got an idea.' I lay on my side, tucked my knees up tight to my body and pulled my hands down my back, forward under my feet and up to the front of my body. Then I pushed my car key up and out of my pocket and grabbed hold of it. I opened the fob and started to saw through the plastic tie binding my hands. As I was doing it, I told Nick what I was doing. He was very encouraging. Then suddenly he was the big brother.

'I'm not sure you should try and take them on.'

'Don't underestimate me. I've had training.' I hadn't, but I wanted to convince myself as well as him that I could do it. 'I'll get us out of here, don't worry.'

'No. If you manage to escape, you mustn't stop for me. You should just run like mad and raise the alarm. Remember the raid will be in eight days.'

'OK. I won't forget, but I can't leave you behind.'

'You have to. If you get your hands and feet free, you can probably get past the bloke who feeds us. He's just a driver. He's not that brainy and there's no way he'll be expecting you to cut yourself free. But you won't have time to do anything but kick or knee him in the balls while he's carrying a tray, and run for it. He's too strong for you to knock him out cold while you free me. If he catches up with you, it'll all have been for nothing. Besides, they won't do anything to me. They'll still have their hostage. And they only need one.'

So he had realised. If I didn't escape, he'd be killed within the next couple of days. The fiancée of a police inspector outdoes a fast-track constable in the hostage stakes any day.

177

'I could lock him in this cell. He's bound to leave the keys in the lock outside. You said yourself, he won't expect me to get free, and there'd be no reason for him to pocket the keys and then have to get them out again.'

'But what if he shouts for help, and the other driver's around?'

'We'll just have to take that chance. With two of us, one's bound to get away, and the worst that can happen is they have to keep that one alive, whichever of us it is.'

'But if I escape, Bradfield'll get away. They'll call off the big job because he knows I can identify him. Listen, please. It's important that you get away. No stopping for me.'

'But…'

'No. If you don't try to help me escape as well, they'll think you don't know I'm here, and Tommy will think he's still safe. It's no good arguing. You have to make sure you get away and tell the inspector when the shipments are due. That way Bradfield will get put away and you'll get your revenge.'

Reluctantly, I had to admit he was right. 'OK. I'm sorry. It makes sense. I just didn't want to leave you here any longer. Just one last thing then, Nick. Have you any clue where we are?'

'No, except we didn't drive for more than ten minutes, so we must be still in Hull somewhere, which gives you a chance.'

'That's good news. I thought we'd be out in the country somewhere. We seemed to be driving for ages. The van must have been going round in circles to disorient me.' Or more likely, I had no sense of time or direction. 'Don't worry. Somehow I'll get to a phone and ring Steve. He'll sort things out from there.'

'OK. You'll need all your wits about you tomorrow, so I suggest you get some sleep.'

'I'm all keyed up, but I'll try. It'll be easier now I've got these plastic ties off.'

'Good. You've done really well, particularly to cut them in the dark. I'll say good luck now. You mustn't talk to me in the morning. I'll see you after Bradfield's been arrested. Just let

Karen know I'm OK please.'

I lay on the make-shift mattress, waiting for sleep to come, but my mind kept racing.

CHAPTER 29

Eventually I must have drifted off but I didn't feel like I'd slept hardly at all. I ached all over from my run-in with Craig. I'd make sure Steve threw the book at him when he caught him. My wrists were sore too. And not just from the ties yesterday. When I felt them, there were several scabs where I'd nicked myself with the penknife. It was very sharp. It had to be, or it wouldn't have cut the ties, so I didn't waste time feeling sorry for myself, although I was relieved I'd not made a really deep cut. I wasn't sure how clean the blade was, but I was fairly sure sepsis wouldn't set in before I got home.

I hadn't a clue what time it was as it was too dark to look at my watch. I hoped I wouldn't have too long to wait. My mind wandered, as it often does. Now, did I use the knife to peel an apple, or… I had a dim recollection of using it to scrape dirt out of the cracks or creases in something, but I had no idea what. Maybe the germs were infiltrating my bloodstream already? Did I feel a bit ill? I shook myself out of the morbid thoughts, stood up and did some light exercises. I could do with the loo, but I'd had nothing to drink since last night, so expected I could hold on for a while longer.

Thankfully it wasn't long before I heard footsteps. I readied myself behind the door, holding the key fob, penknife extended. If I could, I was going to try to slip behind him as he walked in, or at least push him from behind and run for it. I didn't want to have to kick him, elbow him or lash out with the tiny knife unless absolutely necessary, in case he grabbed me.

I was lucky. He stopped partway through the door, presumably because he couldn't see me. I was to his side, so kicked him in the side of his knee, and he stumbled. I pushed him and got outside. He yelled and was up on his feet, pulling at the door as I tried to lock it, but I managed it. That's when my plan fell apart. All of a sudden, another bloke came thundering down the stairs. He shouted, 'what are you doing out here?'

'Damn!' I had no time to think. I just ran at him and kicked up at last minute. He caught hold of my foot but I stabbed him in the hand. It must have taken him by surprise and he instinctively let go and I kicked him on the knee too. He stumbled and somehow I managed to bundle my way past him. It was a close thing as he was heavier and looked more like a fighter than the bloke with the mask. But maybe I could bank on his bulk slowing him down. I ran up the stairs and outside. I was in an old cobbled yard. There were a lot of old pallets and a truck. In the blink of a moment I considered hiding or getting in the truck, but didn't dare linger. There was no lock on the gate. I ran out into the street.

It was still dark and there was no-one around. Behind me I heard the noise of a truck starting. Should I try to outrun it or risk standing still to knock on a door and ask for help? I ran for my life. I ducked down the first side street I saw and among the terrace houses there was a narrow alleyway. The truck couldn't follow me there. Down the alley I turned a corner and found an open gate into a yard. I found a rotten wreck of a shed and hid behind it.

I was far from safe but I needed to catch my breath. I was still covered in bruises from the beating Craig Dobson had given me. I sat on the softest thing I could find, a pile of old curtains, and leant back against the shed wall.

- - - - - - - - - - - - - - - - - - - -

Steve woke with a start, snatches of a dream in his mind. He'd been running, chasing Rach. But every time he almost reached her, she disappeared, only to re-appear in the distance. So he must have slept. It just didn't feel like he had. He had a shower, dressed and put his dirty clothes in the washing machine, catching sight of Rach's favourite shirt. He had to find her. Catching the smugglers was work. She was the rest of his life. At least the two were linked, so he'd have every excuse for making her abduction a priority.

He was in the office by six. Thankfully it was too early to ring Rach's parents. When his men arrived, they knew better than to express the odd word of concern about Rach. He wanted them to work, not express their sympathy. He had someone looking at CCTV in the area, but there was no camera within a mile radius, so the most promising information would be gleaned from contacting all the van hire companies in the city, and he'd already started working on that.

He had a list of places and phone numbers ready. Email addresses were all very well, but people tended to disregard emails or not respond quickly enough, so he split the list with Matt and they started ringing around, asking if a white transit was still on hire to anyone from the Holderness Road address, or failing that, asking for a list with details of all white transits currently on hire to be emailed over for later scrutiny. They'd email out a photo of Dobson anyway. See if that rang any bells. The van may have been hired by someone else, or a false address used. It might have been bought second-hand, or even stolen. Steve didn't like to think of having to go down any of those routes. He was hoping for a quick result.

By nine, he had to concede that wasn't going to happen. He handed over the lists to a couple of detective constables when they arrived, and called a progress meeting for ten am. In the meantime he gathered his sergeants together and briefed them on the previous night's events. He let them believe Rach had probably been taken by Craig Dobson, as the trail led back to his rented house. Tommy had called in to say he wouldn't be in because he'd come down with a bug, which was a pain as he couldn't discuss the Border Force angle with him.

- -

182

I woke to hear a dog barking loudly nearby. At first I hadn't a clue where I was, or what I was doing there, but then it came back to me. I stretched and looked at my watch. I was horrified to find that it was almost two o'clock. I ached all over and was parched and starving, but I realised that not only had the truck driver not found me, but he'd surely given up the search by now. And I'd obviously needed the sleep.

I stood up and cautiously left the shed. There was no-one in sight. I walked to the far end of the alley, rather than leave the way I'd gone in, just in case. There could be someone keeping watch. I'd no idea if the driver had seen me duck into the alley. He or the masked bloke from the house could have been left on watch.

Thinking of our captors, my mind immediately switched to Nick. I drew comfort from the fact that they would keep him alive as a hostage, at least until this big smuggling job had taken place and they'd made their escape to Spain, or wherever it is that criminals hide away in the sun these days. More likely South America. Not Europe any more.

At least Tommy Bradfield wouldn't know he'd been rumbled. As far as they were concerned, I'd never spoken to Nick, and was only aware of Craig as the villain of the piece. I had to get to Steve before the cigarettes were unloaded or whatever was going to happen. Those details were fuzzy in my mind, but I was sure that Steve and the Border Force bods were on top of it. The only thing I did remember about the smuggling operation was that Nick said it was due to happen in eight days' time, which now meant seven.

I was at the end of the alley by now, but the street didn't look familiar. Without my phone, I felt lost. I set off to walk to the first main road I could find. Every corner I turned, just seemed to lead onto another small street. I didn't recognise any of them. Then I heard music, and I knew roughly where I was, because it was the sort of music you only hear in one place - a fairground.

Hull Fair. So I had to be near Walton Street. It's one of Europe's largest travelling funfairs and I'd seen on Look North that it had been opened by the mayor on 6th October. It wouldn't shut until 12 am this coming Saturday, the 14th. I hadn't been for years but I could still recall the excitement and anticipation I'd felt as a small child right up to being a teenager with my mates.

I followed the music and soon turned a corner where a gap in the closely-packed terraced houses allowed a glimpse of the big dipper. Now all I had to do was find a phone.

Of course, when we were kids there were no mobiles, so you had to go to the main road to find a phone box if you needed one. I tried to get the layout in my mind, but the phone box might not be there anymore, and with the site being so big, I couldn't tell whereabouts the main road was. At least it was daylight. It was so easy to get lost at the fair at night.

Some of the smaller, tame rides were already up and running, vying for the youngsters and their parents, and I headed in that direction. I was just wondering if there was a suitable parent I could stop and ask, when I saw him… the bloke who'd chased me from the house. He must have taken up position somewhere where he could keep an eye out for me, knowing I'd probably head this way. He'd seen me, and was running my way, no doubt hoping he could still avoid reporting my escape to Tommy.

No sooner had I caught the quick movement and identified him as the driver I'd stabbed in the hand and kicked, than I was off, weaving and pushing, darting through the gathering crowd of bodies. I risked a glance back. There was now little sign of the limp where I'd kicked him on the knee, but I was still faster. I turned a corner and there was the Ghost Train. I ran past the stunned, spotty teenager on the till and into the tunnel, climbing over the brightly coloured carriages decorated with pictures of skeletons and witches, getting as far from the entrance as I could, and hoping my pursuer hadn't turned the corner until after I'd entered the tunnel.

I was frightened by a loud rumble. One of the carriages came round a corner and was bearing down on me. There was no way I could get out of its path. The tunnel was very narrow at that point. I jumped up on to the front of it, much to the surprise of a couple of girls who looked to be about fourteen. They shouted at me to 'Gerroff!', but I clung on. The ride suddenly stopped. We were in darkness.

My pursuer must have seen me enter and cut the power, or threatened the young attendant and made him do it. The tunnels of the ride echoed with the screams of young girls. Quickly I told the girls that I was on the run from the police, and asked if I could borrow a phone. Eager to help out a fellow troublemaker, the biggest one thrust her phone in my hand. I had to think quickly. I needed to get Steve's help without him letting it be known that I was on the phone.

Luckily, it wasn't my phone I was using, so the number wouldn't mean anything to him. I hoped that meant he was unlikely to blurt out my name when he answered. I prayed I'd remembered his number correctly. When you never have to key them in, you don't know half of the actual numbers you use every day, but I do remember hearing him give it to enough people, that I thought I might have got it right in my head. Thankfully he answered almost immediately.

'Don't talk, Steve, please. It's important. Tommy Bradfield's involved in this smuggling gang.' I raced through the words in my head before he could interrupt or say my name out loud. 'They think I don't know about Tommy, so you can play along and catch him in the act. I don't know if anyone else in your office is involved.' Even if I were to get caught, I knew the message had got through. 'Do you understand?'

I was relieved to hear him say, 'Yes, of course. That's fine.'

I interrupted him before he thought there was all the time in the world for this conversation. 'Great. I'm being chased through Hull Fair. Can you get a patrol car here with a siren to stop this bloke grabbing hold of me?'

I didn't get chance to say any more. I heard someone stumbling on the rails, followed by some cursing. I tossed back the phone, shouted, 'stop him if you can' and ran as fast as I could through the darkness, trying not to turn my ankle.

A couple of minutes later I emerged into bright sunlight and legged it back the way I'd come, thinking it was the least likely direction he'd expect. The rides were mostly for the younger ones at this end. I saw the helter-skelter, which was the highest thing in the immediate vicinity and headed straight for it. I dived into the pay booth and curled up on the floor, trying to catch my breath.

'You hiding from a bloke, love? Don't worry, I'll not let on you're down there.'

'Thank heavens. I'm so scared. This bloke tried to grope me.' Before I could say another word, I heard a siren. 'I rang the police but they won't know where I am. I was in the ghost train when I rang them.'

'It'll be alright. I'll give security a buzz and they'll get the police over here.'

I gave thanks to whoever had seen fit to employ this kind, intelligent bloke and waited for it all to be over.

CHAPTER 30

About ten minutes later I was sitting in the back of a police car, and five minutes after that, Steve was there, holding me in his arms. He sent the driver to get me a cup of hot sweet tea, and had the other bloke scouring the crowd for anyone suspicious, anyone who might be watching me.

'I can't believe one of my sergeants could be involved with a smuggling ring, Rach, even if I've only known him a few months. Are you sure?'

I went on to tell him the whole story in as few words as possible. 'Do you believe me now?'

'Of course I believe you. It's just that Tommy Bradfield came highly recommended by his old inspector. Had an exemplary record and made a lot of decent arrests. Word was he only wanted a move to get higher profile cases than he was dealing with at the East Hull station. Don't worry, I promise I'll make sure he bloody well pays for what he's put us both through.' For once he seemed to realise that I'd not thoughtlessly put myself in danger, but had been deceived by "one of his own".

When the driver returned with the tea, he just said, 'thanks. I'll take it from here. She says the bloke who tried to grope her took off when he heard the siren. She didn't see anything anyway as it was dark in the Ghost Train so she can't give us a description. I'll drop her off at my aunt's house and head back into work.' He kept quiet about Tommy, and I understood he didn't want to take the chance of a rumour starting about one of the sergeants being up to no good, even if he worked in a completely different department.

He led me to his car and drove me home, where I gave him

as much detail as I could remember. He listened without saying a word, just stroking my hair and asking the odd question. He got really excited when I told him that the smuggled cigarettes would be on both ferries. They'd had word from an informer that a shipment would be taking place in a week's time, but it was good to have Nick's confirmation and that extra bit of information.

'That's so important. Good for Nick. Thank God he's OK. I think you're right. He should be fine, at least until this job goes down, and then I'll make it a priority to free him. You do know that I can't risk doing that yet, don't you? I can't risk letting Tommy Bradfield know that we know about him, and he'd know the minute we freed Nick. In fact, much as I'd like to stay here with you, I'm afraid I'd better get back to the station, or else Tommy might get an inkling that I know about him, although he's called in sick today.'

'Why, do you think?'

'Probably wondering what he's going to do now you've escaped. I said I had to go out on an urgent errand, just in case someone else in our office is in on his smuggling schemes, though I really hope not. Everyone else has worked with me for a number of years now, but you can never tell who might get tempted by the lure of extra money, even if it's only in extreme circumstances.'

'Right, but what will you say to Tommy? Surely he should have rung for back-up when I disappeared while I was following Craig?'

'I'll come up with something. At the moment he thinks I don't know he was the one who told you to follow Dobson. Best plan I think, is to say you got knocked on the head and your mind's a blank between walking down that street off Holderness Road and coming to, tied up in the house. I can tell everyone in our section that you've been found, and you think Craig Dobson took you after you followed him, but you don't know where you were kept and you didn't get a good look at the face of the bloke who brought your food.'

188

'Good thinking. But I would surely mention helping Tommy? You can say I've asked after him as I was concerned something might have happened to him as well.'

'It'd be interesting to hear what he says. I could let him tie himself up in knots, but it's more important to make him feel safe and still confident to go ahead with supporting the smugglers.'

'If you don't mention his part, he might get suspicious.'

'I know. I think I might have to prompt him into finding a memory of looking for you and Dobson, but all the doors were shut and he just thought you'd given up and not gone back to tell him, or you couldn't find him or something. He can then act horrified (at my prompting) that you were abducted, and enthusiastic about hunting Dobson down. If he's been ill, that's an excuse for not realising what's been going on.'

'That sounds a good idea.'

'I'll get Matt to try and track down the house where you were kept, just in case they've not moved Nick.'

'Do you think they will have done?'

'I think so. Tommy may be a bad person, but he's good at his job. He'll realise we have to look for the house to see if there are any traces of the gang left - if not the men themselves, then fingerprints or else neighbours who recall seeing the van or the men who held you.'

'Do you want my help to find the house?'

'I don't want you going anywhere near there, love.'

'I'll look on the computer, try to find the most likely streets and look at the street view; see if I can pinpoint the place. I'd be glad to help.'

'Yeah, that's a good idea. Thanks. I'll keep any findings unofficial though. Only Matt will get involved in the real search. You and I know we can trust him not to let anything slip. He's been my loyal sergeant through thick and thin for years. In fact he's the only one at the station who knows that Dobson's dead.'

'He's what?!'

'Sorry. I forgot to say. You thought Dobson kidnapped you,

but it was Bradfield. It looks like our Tommy killed Dobson. I kept it quiet because you were missing. I told Forensics to contact only me or Matt, and no-one else knows, except presumably Bradfield, though unofficially of course. As far as he's concerned, the body's where he left it - in the bath. For what it's worth, I don't see Tommy as a killer. He probably had an argument with Dobson for waltzing round Hull in plain sight, letting you see him, and then taking you and tying you up, instead of laying low in his house, causing Tommy the hassle of kidnapping you.'

'Crikey!'

'It probably turned into a fight, knowing Dobson, and his death might even have been an accident. Forensics thought that a real possibility. He probably took the day off because he's a mess, as much as not knowing what to say or where he stands.'

'So it's not because I escaped.'

'I'm not sure his men will've owned up to it at first, hoping they could recapture you, but they won't be able to keep it from him for long, and he'll hear as soon as he gets to the station because I'll be announcing that you've been found. I only told our office and Sanjeev in IT that you were missing. I'll let it be known you haven't a clue where you were held, as you ran up and down streets, across gardens etc. and just headed for the fair, so it could have been anywhere in that warren of streets. Like I said, I'm only letting Matt look into that, as I trust him not to let on to Bradfield.'

What about Craig's body, though? Won't anyone in his gang who's undercover be spooked by that? Can you really trust the Forensics bods not to ring across to your department?'

'One hundred percent. I shut down that information route good and tight. It helps when you can wave a 'major secret operation' wand in front of their eyes. They're quite good at keeping stumm at the best of times. They can't afford leaks getting out in case it comes out in court.'

'Right, well you better get back to work. As well as looking for the house on a map, I can try to write a description of the bloke without the mask who chased me. I'd be better looking at photos, but I know I can't go anywhere near the station, so I'll just have to do my best. Shame I've always been rubbish at drawing.'

'OK. Best try while he's fresh in your mind, but we'll keep it under wraps until the raid's over.'

'When Tommy speaks to the blokes who were holding me in the house, they'll probably say I wouldn't be able to identify them, hoping it's true, so Tommy will think he's in the clear. I never saw the one in the mask anyway, but he was nice to me.'

'OK, but first you'd better ring your dad. I'm afraid I left him hanging in the air a bit last night. I rang Sarah when you didn't come home and she said you'd gone shopping with your mum.'

'Oops! Good job he has steady nerves, and knowing him, he won't have worried Mum, but I'll ring him before I do anything else.'

'Luckily your face hasn't spread throughout the force. I told the lads in the squad car that you were a relative, rather than my fiancée, and that you'd rung me after the bloke manning the helter-skelter had called them out to say someone had groped you. I don't want the entire Hull force gossiping about you, or word might get out on the grapevine that you were abducted and escaped. My guess is Bradfield will want to keep that little titbit of information away from the ears of the smugglers at the docks. He'll want the plan to go ahead all costs, if he's risked his job on it. In the meantime, I don't want you bumping into Tommy Bradfield any time soon though, in case you let something slip.'

'As if…'

'I know you wouldn't mean to, but your face might give it away. It would be hard for you to treat him just as one of my sergeants, instead of the devil incarnate.'

'I suppose you're right. My blood boils when I think what he put me through.'

'Exactly. Do you think you can lie low for a while until we've wrapped up the case? Maybe go away for a few days with your mum?'

'Good idea. I'll talk to Mum about it. You get back to work. Dad'll pick me up and take me to theirs after I've looked on Google maps a bit. I feel an urge for a trip to Cornwall coming on.'

'Cornwall? That's a long way to go to keep your head down.'

'I know, but while I was cooped up in that cellar, I kept worrying I might not get chance to chase up the lead on the German couple. They might be Kate's real parents and I should do more to try to find where they moved to. They may have kept in touch with someone down there, even if it's not on file.'

'Trust you to be worrying about Kate instead of yourself, but it's a great idea, Rach. I do love you so much. I couldn't live without you, even if I hardly ever tell you that.'

'I know, and I feel the same, but you won't be able to concentrate on anything until you get this all tied up, the bad guys locked up, and Nick released, so just go! I'll leave a note if I find anything.'

We had another hug and a passionate kiss, and then he went out and I went to the kitchen to raid the biscuit tin so I was full of chocolate when I rang Dad.

CHAPTER 31

I phoned Dad and set his mind at rest, without going into detail about where I'd been. I just said I'd ended up spending the night with a friend - it wasn't a total lie; Nick was a friend of sorts - and I'd not been able to get hold of Steve until this morning. I apologised for worrying him, then asked to speak to Mum, who was oblivious to my disappearing act. Bless Dad. He's a star.

As I knew she would be, Mum was all up for going to Cornwall. 'Sounds smashing, Rachel. Your dad won't mind. He can fend for himself for a couple of days and we can spend some time together. We don't often get the chance these days.'

'Right. Do you think Dad can pick me up about eight tonight when I've got myself sorted, please? Steve's on a big case and he won't be home until really late. I might as well sleep at yours so we can get off to an early start.'

Mum agreed and I said goodbye so I could start deciding what to take... The rest of the afternoon flew by as I kept changing my mind as to what weather we might encounter. I couldn't throw everything in. Steve always says I'd take every coat I owned if I could.

After a quick sandwich, I fiddled around on the computer. I had a bit of a disaster there. I'd just got the rough area up on Google Maps, and got myself a drink (orange squash, don't ask me why) and, well… the bottom line is somehow, by accident, I knocked the glass very slightly, and blow me if it didn't go all over my jeans, the table - and the keyboard!

I had to take quick action and save the keyboard first, turning it upside down and unplugging it, and then poking kitchen roll between the keys to dry it off. The jeans got rinsed and ended up in the wash, then I wiped and dried down the table in my underwear, before finding clean jeans. When I plugged it back in it worked, but a few of the keys stuck and I had to hit them hard a couple of times each time I wanted the space key or return. I wondered if Steve knew how to get it unstuck. I had the feeling he once took one of the keys off.

I hadn't time to mess about myself and make it worse, so just got on with the job as best as I could. I was conscious that Dad would be arriving soon. When I was fairly sure I'd pinned it down to the right street, and possibly the right house where I'd been held, I made a note for Steve. I also wrote a description of the driver who chased me through Hull Fair. I saw very little of the one with the mask who brought me food - and I don't think a description of 'brown hair, quite a bit taller than me, with a sore knee' would be much use. I would leave the info on the worktop, as agreed, rather than sending it to Steve at the station.

I texted him to say Dad was picking me up so I could get an early start because I knew he'd not be in until late, and I was leaving a casserole to warm up. He was going to make it clear in the office that I'd been badly frightened and worried about Craig catching up with me again, so I'd gone to Cornwall with my mum on a last minute holiday. I wondered what the two blokes would have told Tommy about my escape. Nick said they were delivery drivers, so I'd expect Tommy wouldn't want to get shut of them so near to the job going down.

 I threw some things in a dish to make a casserole, then packed a small case, discarding half the things I'd mentally packed earlier. Then I looked into train times because I didn't have my car back, and it was a long way to drive anyway. I'd just eaten my half of the casserole when Dad turned up.

Steve rang me at about nine when he got in. I suppose he was early enough that I could have waited for him, but I was glad I hadn't as Steve said he'd had the feeling someone was watching the flat, probably to check that I really had gone and that everything was as Steve had said. I told him not to worry about getting my car back to the flat. I could sort it when I got back. I didn't want anyone to see Steve collecting my Dave and knew he was busy enough anyway. Poor Dave (his number plate has DVE in it). He was my pride and joy, my little Fiesta. I'd get him back soon, and at least I hadn't left him on yellow lines when I'd dashed out to follow Craig.

The next morning I threw caution to the wind and nipped in the phone shop near the station and got a tech-savvy lad to set me up with a smartphone. I needed a new phone anyway and high time I was able to access the internet while I was out and about investigating. I insisted on a smallish one so it fit in my handbag.

Mum and I took the train to Penzance via London as that seemed to be the best route as regards connections. We had to use the tube from King's Cross to Paddington, which was a bit scary, to say the least, trying to get the right tube in the right direction with hordes of people walking in all directions, crossing our path. I've not been to London more than a couple of times and it always bewilders me.

It reminded me of a tale Gran told me the last time I went round. She's never been to London, and says she can't see the point. She said, 'People got on alright in them days without bothering with it, so why should I bother now? There's nowt there except the Queen that we haven't got here.'

I started telling her that there were lots of famous places and there were exhibitions that never came up north, but she interrupted me. 'In our class at school, there was only one boy who'd ever been to London. The furthest anyone else had ever been from Hull was Scarborough or Leeds. In fact us kids were jealous of this one girl whose dad was on Christmas Island. We thought she'd get loads more presents than us. It wasn't until a year or two ago when I saw a bit on the telly about the soldiers having to stand and look at those mushroom clouds on Christmas Island, that I realised what it had all meant and how wrong we'd been to be jealous. She wouldn't have had her dad for much longer, I don't reckon.'

I shook the thought away. 'I'm so glad you're here, Mum. I'm so lucky to have you.'

'Oh, don't be soft, Rachel. I'm having a great time. Just wait 'til I tell Gran.'

It took us a large chunk of the day to get to Penzance and I hired a car to drive the short distance onwards. We headed straight for that beach where the baby had disappeared. It was getting late but we went in the shop and the garage, asking if anyone could remember anything of the abduction. I'm not sure what I expected to achieve, but I just had to be there. I felt guilty for having given up on the search.

We booked into a small bed and breakfast on the edge of the village and ate fish and chips on a bench overlooking the wide empty beach. I'd looked at photos of this place on the tourist website and it'd looked sort of similar to the beach in the photo found down the side of Helen Willis's sideboard, but until I stood in the spot where the photo had been taken, I couldn't be sure that it was. But standing there, I was convinced it was the same place. I felt a shiver of excitement. Kate had to belong to the Schneiders. I was sure of it.

'I'll have to find some way of putting out an appeal on German TV, or in the press, Mum. Maybe even put out a photo of the babygro.'

'Something will turn up, Rach. You're going to see the local police tomorrow. Somebody might remember a detail that wasn't written down, like where the parents worked.'

'Thanks for coming, Mum.'

'An adventure with you. I wouldn't have missed it. And, hard as it is, I can picture myself wandering that beach, having lost sight of you or Laura for just a moment, and panicking, getting more frantic each second. Once a mother, always a mother. You never lose the feeling. Your gran's friend Elsie, she's got terminal cancer, and all she can think about is how her daughter's going to cope with running around after her, and managing when she dies.'

It was October of course, so the sun set early. There was a

chill in the air and after a while we went inside.

I rang Steve and predictably he said, 'Sounds good, but don't get your hopes up too much, will you, love?'

In the morning I left Mum with a romantic paperback in the nearby café and I drove back into Penzance. She was keen to come along but I thought it would look better if I went on my own. I'd rung from the train on the way down and managed to locate the officer who'd been in charge of the search. Bill Trevelyan was retired now, but he met me outside the police station. He greeted the bobbies inside as old friends.

'I got them to look out the paperwork, then sat and read through it all again last night, although it affected me that much at the time, I've never forgotten the case. There's nothing much about the parents, I'm afraid, although there's a photo of them at the press conference. I don't know if you've seen that. We only circulated a photo of Ulrike, the baby.'

There hadn't been a photo in the slim file Steve had handed me, so I asked if I could take a copy. I thought I saw a resemblance to Kate but perhaps I was kidding myself. Bill got someone to photocopy it and told me I could take the file and read through it, so long as I dropped it back before I went home.

'It was a terrible thing, seeing that mother sobbing her heart out when we told her we'd done all we could, and though we'd keep looking, we felt she ought to go home and we'd contact her if anything cropped up.'

'And she never got in touch to tell you she'd moved?'

'No. We were in touch quite a lot at first, but then it tailed off. I think she realised that the more time that passed, the more unlikely it would be that her baby would ever be found.'

I was gutted. Finding out that the photo Helen Willis had hidden matched this place - well I'd got really excited. I'd been sure I'd find out something that would help me contact the Schneiders, but I'd been wrong.

CHAPTER 32

I went back to the village and drove Mum out into the country away from the coast. I couldn't bear to look at it. After lunch we found a pretty village green with seats. Mum read some more and I read the file. 'How could they do it, Mum?'

'The Willises? They might not have gone to steal a baby. Maybe they went on holiday to get away from people asking about their baby, not knowing she'd miscarried again. Then Helen Willis saw this baby unattended and thought she could look after it better. It's such a sad case. I mean, she must have been suffering from severe depression after the final miscarriage. She probably didn't know what she was doing. There are cases of post-natal depression so severe that new mothers have committed suicide, and I expect it was as bad as that for Helen.'

'We'll never know. But if it was an impulse, how did they cope with the baby? The police asked everyone who sold milk formula, nappies and baby seats, and came up with all sorts of info, but in the end it came to nothing. When you've had as many miscarriages as Helen Willis, you wouldn't tempt fate by buying things in advance but they must have at least had a baby seat and milk with them, which they must have bought with that trip in mind.'

'No, Rachel. It might not have been planned. Car seats haven't always been a legal requirement. Helen could have held the baby, maybe sitting in the back of the car until they got to a shopping centre, getting a car seat from Halfords, baby food from a big supermarket. Totally anonymous places.'

'But they went all the way to Cornwall. Surely that was so

no-one would think of looking in the depths of Lincolnshire for the missing baby. I hate to say it, but I think they had to have planned it.'

'You can't be sure. Like I said, maybe they just went to get away from it all - as far away as possible. The baby was probably crying and looked abandoned. Helen probably thought she needed looking after, and grief does terrible things to people's minds. It's a tragedy for all involved, Rach.'

'And there's the car crash. The police had doubts that it was an accident, but Kate couldn't imagine her dad hitting the bridge pillar on purpose to cover up an unofficial adoption, so she accepted that it was an accident. Poor kid. How will she take it, if it turns out that her dad might have had more of a reason than she thought... that he was actually trying to protect her mum because she'd abducted someone else's baby?'

'Let's hope she never realises that her dad might have intended to kill her too.'

'It almost makes me think I should give this up. Maybe this is a case where the truth shouldn't come out.'

'You can't say that, our Rachel. Tony and Helen Willis are dead now so it can't hurt them any more. And what about Kate's real parents? It'd be the best thing in the world for them if you could find them. I know you won't be sure until you meet them and get a DNA test done, but I can tell you think it's likely now.'

'There's no record of the Willises being here, though.'

'But you have that photo. You've seen the beach yourself and I can tell you have a gut feeling. Did the police have a list of people staying in the area?'

'They weren't on it, Mum, but people didn't keep records of number plates or anything then and there was no description of the abductors, so no photos to show round. The night of the abduction, they called all the hotels, B&Bs and campsites in the area, asking for details of anyone who'd checked out that morning or suddenly during the day, and they also asked them to phone if anyone arrived later that day with a baby, but that drew a blank. They might have stopped somewhere on the way down from Lincolnshire and driven on to the village that morning, for all we know. It would make sense that they wouldn't stay that night locally if they'd taken someone's baby.'

'Come on Rachel, let me treat you to a nice meal, then we'll go back to the B&B. If you can't think of anything else, we'll just hand in the file at the police station tomorrow morning and set off home. We could stop at an antique centre on the way. That'd cheer you up.'

At breakfast we told the young woman who ran the B&B that we'd be checking out. 'Oh, that's a shame. You've not stayed long. The weather's changed, I suppose, but there are some nice places to go even if it rains. There's the Tate Gallery at St. Ives, if you were interested.'

'No, thanks. We came down here to see if we could find any information about the family whose baby was abducted, back in 1998.'

'You mean Renate Schneider?'

'Yes. How do you know about her? I'd have thought you were too young to remember that far back.'

'I was only a kid, but I took over the B&B five years ago, and sort of inherited her. Poor woman. She comes every year, hoping against hope that she'll see her daughter and recognise her.'

I couldn't believe it. I was gobsmacked. The B&B was the last place I'd have thought to ask. 'I've been to the police station and they never mentioned her coming back.'

'That's probably because she didn't bother going to see them after the first four or five years, once it got past the time Ulrike would have started school, and they hadn't found her by then. She reckons that it was a holidaymaker who took her, but she can't stop coming here just in case.'

'And you have contact details for her? The ones the police have are out-of-date.'

'I'm not sure I should pass them on. Why are you looking for her? Are you reporters?'

'Just a minute.' I ran upstairs and got the police file and a copy of emails they'd sent to Steve with Humberside Police on them.

I needn't have bothered. By the time I got back downstairs Mum had already told her all about why we were looking, and that Kate might be Ulrike. It was all I could do to stop the pair of them contacting her there and then. I was a bit miffed, but I couldn't really blame Mum. The landlady gave me Renate Schneider's contact details and I promised that once I'd informed the police, I'd email. It would be much easier to contact Renate Schneider in writing, even though she apparently spoke some English.

The landlady accepted that was the best course of action, thankfully. 'Tell her Cath's real pleased for her and I hope she'll still come here again, maybe bring her daughter to see where it all happened.'

I thought that was a bit premature, and I didn't want to get the parents' hopes up until I was one hundred percent sure, but said I'd be sure to pass the message on. I would do, too, just not yet. The police report just stated that the baby was wearing a babygro, with no reference to it being green. Mum said it wasn't such a common colour and that most were pink, blue or white at that time, so I'd already decided on that being the first question I'd ask if I came up with any of my possible parents becoming a probable. Other than that, I planned to keep the email short and to the point.

After agreeing to let Cath know how it turned out, Mum and I took the file back to the police station. The sergeant said he could have kicked himself for not considering that one or both of the Schneiders might still come back and stay at the same B&B. I left my contact details as well as the new ones for the Schneiders. Because it was a cold case for the Cornish police, and I was the one who'd been in contact with Kate, he was happy to leave the rest of the investigation to me, in the knowledge that Humberside Police - aka Steve - would contact them if anything came of it.

I wheedled Bill's phone number and address out of him, and we called in on the way back to the car hire place by Penzance station. The look on his face when I told him was well worth the detour. He had a tear in his eye. 'I never thought to see the day...' I promised him I'd keep him updated, then I sent my pre-planned email to Renate Schneider.

The train had just pulled out of Penzance when my phone beeped to herald the arrival of an email. It almost seemed as if Renate had been sitting by her computer or phone waiting all those years for contact. 'The babygro was green. Why do you ask this, please? Has a body been found?'

'Oh, God, Mum. The poor woman. I didn't think...' I'd only told her that I was a private detective looking into the disappearance of her baby, but not why. I never thought she might think I was getting in touch with bad news. I typed back straightaway. 'No body found. I am helping an eighteen-year old girl to find her real parents. She may be your daughter, but I need to check your DNA with hers before I can tell you more.'

'I am crying. I am so happy. But no DNA was ever taken. What do I do?'

I looked up the details for the laboratory holding Kate's results, with the unique reference number, then I emailed back, 'If you ask the police in Germany I am sure they will arrange a test for you. If not, you can get one done privately. Your DNA test result should be emailed to "…." with reference "…". I will email and tell them to expect it. They will compare the two samples and we should have the result quickly.'

'That is very kind. Thank you so much. May I have your number and telephone you, please?'

Mum looked me in that way she's done since I was a kid. The look that said she really wanted me to do something and it would make her so happy if I did, and so sad if I didn't. 'Go on, Rachel.'

'I can't, Mum. I can't tell her anything about Kate, until we know they are mother and baby, and until Kate says so. It's Kate's choice now.'

'She'd want you to put her mother out of her misery.'

'I know, believe me, I do, but I just can't. At least I've given Renate Schneider hope.'

I typed, 'Sorry. It makes me sad to write this, but I cannot tell you anything more until we get DNA match. Baby may not be yours. Please wait just a little longer. I hope it is good news.'

'Well I suppose you're right, but it seems a bit harsh, Rach.'

'If it turns out she's not Kate's mother, and I'd told her all about Kate, then she'd have got all emotionally attached, only to find out she's back at the beginning again. That would be devastating, never mind harsh. Or she might be the sort to put all about Kate on social media, without so much as a by-your-leave. I've not even met her yet. I don't know what she's like.'

'Oh, I didn't think about that. I couldn't do your job. Always being suspicious of people.'

'Good thing you don't, then. You're too trusting. No-one would think you were Gran's daughter if they didn't know.' Before she could react, I changed the subject quickly, pointing out that the buffet trolley was on its way down the aisle.

By the time we'd changed trains and found seats, I'd had another email from Renate. 'The police in her home town of Eckernförde … where? Oh, yes, she moved. That's why the letter didn't reach her. She's given me her current address. Anyway, they're going to do a DNA test for her this afternoon! I thought they might be prepared to do it to solve their missing baby case, but not so quickly.

I was so excited. I just had to ring Steve. 'I'm so sorry to ring you at work, but I think I've had a breakthrough!'

'So you've tracked down the German woman at last? And you must think there's a strong chance that she's really Kate's mother? That's brilliant news, Rach. I can't wait to hear all about it.'

I'm sure Renate'll be Kate's mother, Steve. Her baby was wearing a green babygro when she was taken. Do you remember the one that was found in the Willis family's farmhouse? That was green too.'

203

'Hmm.' Steve sounded cautiously optimistic. I was convinced, of course, but he was able to be more objective than me, I suppose.

'And we shouldn't have to wait long. I can't bear to have everyone waiting to find out for definite.'

'That's great, but Rach, I've got a meeting. I've got to go now. See you later and you can tell me all about it.'

'Bye.'

Although I was frustrated, I couldn't blame Steve. He was juggling all the balls at work, trying to conceal from Tommy and who knew who else that he'd found Craig's body and knew about the forthcoming shipments, as well as coping with pretending to look for Craig, the chief suspect in the ongoing murder investigations of Dean Hornby and Simon Crawford.

CHAPTER 33

Dad picked us up from the station. I resisted the invitation to go back to theirs for a cuppa, as I wanted to ring Kate's laboratory and let them know Renate Schneider's DNA result would be on its way for them to run a comparison against Kate's. I knew they'd send an online payment request before they did any comparison and I wanted to get that paid as soon as I could so there'd be no delay. I didn't mind paying and I suspected I'd get the money back from Renate anyway.

When Steve got in, I told him about Renate's visits to Cornwall and promised that although I'd found out about the babygro, I'd not mentioned anything else, particularly about Kate, waiting until I was sure. 'That's remarkably restrained for you. I'm impressed. I bet you had to gag your mum though.' He laughed.

'How are things at work?'

He pulled a face. 'I'm a bit tense and stressed with everything, to be honest. However, one good thing while you were away. I managed to nip out one lunchtime to see Karen and let her know Nick had been seen and spoken to and he was well and in good spirits.'

'Oh, that's good of you, love. When we've eaten I'll give you a shoulder and back massage.'

'It'd be a shame to leave the rest of my body neglected...'

'Despite enjoying time with Mum, I've missed you so much, it'd be rude to refuse.'

In the morning I rang Kate. I was really worried about getting her hopes up for nothing, but I had to. The laboratory had insisted that they needed a phone call or email from Kate personally to confirm that she consented to my having the DNA comparison done, as per the signed letter I'd emailed them. It was from the previous test, so was a little out-of-date for them.

'Hello, Kate.' I was determined to take it slowly and sound laid back. 'How are things going?'

'Fine. And you? Is there some news?'

'I've got a strong lead. I've located someone who might, just might, be your birth mother.'

'For real?'

'I wouldn't joke, Kate. I've been down a lot of blind alleys that I couldn't tell you about, but this one seems a real possibility.'

Kate positively squealed with delight. 'I thought you'd given up! Tell me all about it. Go on, please.'

'I'm sorry. I have to respect the woman's privacy in case you're not a match, but I need you to contact the laboratory to give your updated consent to a DNA comparison. I've just sent you an email with the details, but I thought I'd better speak to you first and explain that you shouldn't get your hopes up again until we get the result. Of course I'll get in touch as soon as I know the outcome.'

'How long will it take?'

'A couple of days at the most from receipt of the woman's results. She was having a test yesterday, so not long.'

'Are you sure you can't tell me anything about her, or how you got the lead?'

'No, Kate. I can't. I'm sorry. I wish I could, but I can't. All we can do now is sit back and wait.'

'OK. I suppose you haven't a choice, but call me as soon as you know, either way, won't you?'

'Of course I will. Before you go, tell me what you've been up to since we last spoke.' We chatted for a few more minutes before saying our goodbyes.

I'd just got off the phone when an email arrived from Renate with her full contact details. She lived in a small town on the

Baltic coast of Schleswig-Holstein, which I can only describe as the thin bit at the top of Germany that joins on to Denmark. It seemed that the Germans were living up to their reputation for efficiency, as she said her results would be ready very soon and emailed to the lab in the UK "immediately", so we might only have to wait a few days for the results of the comparison. We exchanged a few emails during the morning and I got to know her quite well.

She was a musician, playing and teaching the violin. I wondered if Kate's love of music and ear for languages made the match more likely. At Ilmenau University, Renate's husband, Joachim, had been employed in the science faculty, doing research into rocket propulsion. After the abduction, recriminations and guilt had almost driven them apart, he'd thrown himself into his work, and said they must try to put it behind them for the sake of their son, Peter, but she couldn't.

However, by the time Peter started secondary school, Renate had accepted that for his sake they needed to move somewhere new where no-one knew them, somewhere where Peter wouldn't be subject to curiosity or bullying. As he'd grown older, he'd suffered badly with the guilt of being the indirect cause of Ulrike's disappearance. Joachim had got a new job at a submarine base on the coast, something to do with torpedoes, and that's where they were living.

Their new home in Eckernförde sounded quiet and idyllic. A small town with a long beach, indoor swimming pool and pleasant pedestrianised shopping centre, close to the Danish border. Their house had a massive garden and Renate had found some solace there, although she had never given up on finding her daughter, hence the annual visits to Cornwall.

Poignantly, she wrote, 'I look every day at the photo of Ulrike and think where she is. I never think that she is dead.' When I read those words, I really hoped she turned out to be Kate's mother.

I filled the rest of my day catching up on housework. With both of us out, you'd think the place would be clean and tidy, but you'd be wrong, of course. Dust just waits for you to turn your back before magically appearing, and when you're rushing in and out, things just get dumped any old where but their proper place.

I'd decided that I needed to get fit. Escaping by running through those streets, I'd become puffed out too quickly. Too many pieces of cake were slowing me down. Even though I rushed round tidying and cleaning energetically, it wasn't going to help much, except the flat looked better. I put on a load of washing and tackled the mountain of ironing. It was as boring as ever, though listening to a 70s compilation CD did improve both my speed and mood considerably, as I sang along.

Late that afternoon I rang Sarah and she told me she'd just started going to the local sports hall where they had badminton for beginners.

'Sounds like fun. Can I come?'

'Course you can. It'll be great. Most people started round about the beginning of the school year so it's been going three weeks already and the others know each other quite well. Although they're friendly, I feel a bit left out. You'd soon get into the swing of it though, and they play doubles all the time, so no-one has to sit out long, if at all. I bet we'd still make a formidable team. You'd soon pick it up again. I didn't find it that hard, apart from serving.'

'They haven't changed all the rules, then, since we played at school?'

'What, you mean like changing the rule on passing back to the goalie in football?'

'Or the rules on hand ball. You should hear my dad going on about that. Mind you, even Gary Lineker and The Match of the Day crew keep moaning, so it's not because Dad's old.'

'Rest assured, the rules are the same. So how about it?'

'When's it on?'

'As luck would have it, tonight. Pick me up at ten to seven? It'd help me not to have to pick you up instead in case John's home a bit late.'

'Can do. I wish I'd not used up all that energy cleaning.'

'It'll have got you warmed up.'

'Knackered, more like. I'm off to see if I've got any shorts that are partway decent. See you later.'

'Will do.'

Steve was suitably complimentary about my housewifely achievements. His offering to send out for pizza to save me cooking after all my hard work wasn't going to lower the calorie intake, but I hadn't the willpower or the energy to turn him down, and I was in a rush to get out to pick up Sarah.

CHAPTER 34

I was a bit tired after my exertions the night before, playing badminton for the first time in years, so I had a lie-in, not even stirring when Steve went out. I had aches and pains everywhere, just like Sarah said. I only hoped she was also right about the fact that I'd be OK after a day or so, and next week, I shouldn't suffer much at all.

I checked my email but there was nothing from the lab other than a brief notification that both samples had been received and submitted for comparison and I would receive the results by post, as such sensitive material cannot be sent by email. As I was paying, the results would come to me first. The email had been sent at 15.30 yesterday, so hopefully they'd be testing today and with a bit of luck, I might get the result tomorrow. Now it was so close, I was worried I'd made a terrible mistake and placed too much faith in the colour of a baby's suit and the photo of a beach.

I was just thinking about going round to Mum's, knowing she'd tell me I was right to do what I'd done, and distract me with her news, when I heard post through the communal letter box. I pulled on my dressing-gown and rushed downstairs, bizarrely hoping the DNA comparison had thrown out a match already, but there were only advertising leaflets. Disappointed, I had two slices of toast and honey. I was going to make porridge, but it seemed a faff just for me.

I rang Mum, but there was no reply, so I sent a text instead. I changed towels and put the dirty ones in the washer with my t-shirt, shorts and towel from the night before as well. I got a text from Mum to say she was in the waiting room at the dentist's "just for a check-up", so no worries, but would be in by eleven if I wanted to pop round.

I made a list of a few things to pick up from the shop, grabbed my bag and ran down the stairs, colliding with Steve's neighbour Mike.

'Hello, lass. Are you alright? You're in a bit of a hurry.'

'Fine thanks.' I didn't want to get caught. Mike can talk for England. Then I felt guilty as he lives on his own. 'Is it dry out?'

'I don't know. I've just been down for the post. Saw the postie coming up the path and wanted a word about those election leaflets. We get so many. They make the place look untidy.'

'The post's been?' I dashed down the rest of the stairs and there waiting for me was - a letter from the laboratory. I told myself not to be daft. Wishing didn't make it true. They couldn't have tested and sent the letter out already. I sat down on the second-to-bottom step and stared at it. I wondered why they'd written otherwise - surely it wasn't to confirm the email from yesterday afternoon? Then I decided it was probably a confirmation of what they were going to do, or a receipt for my online payment. Who knew?

'Are you alright, love? Is it bad news?' I had ripped open the envelope anyway, convincing myself that all my hopes for Kate were resting on this letter. I could hardly breathe.

And there it was - the result of the DNA comparison. They must have fast-tracked the comparison because of the German police connection and got the result in the post about the same time as emailing the night before. I read the letter again. Loads of jargon about 'corresponding points' etc., but at the end, one simple sentence confirming that both DNA samples were conclusively of 'close family members, such as parent and child, or siblings'.

'No, its fine, thanks. Everything's wonderful in fact. Fantastic! Amazing! Wonderful!' I leapt up and did a little jig.

'You look happy. Have you won the pools?'

'Nothing like that, Mike. Just some good news for a friend of mine. She's been waiting a long time, so if you don't mind, I'll have to go.'

I got in the car and sent a text to Kate, asking if I could nip round to see her as I could do with her opinion on something. No immediate reply. She was probably in a lecture. I rang Steve but he was in a meeting. I was so excited, I was fit to burst. I'd just set off for Mum and Dad's, when a text pinged in. I pulled over. Kate asked if I could call round about six. I agreed. I'd gone a bit further when the phone rang. I had trouble finding a place to pull in and all I got was a 'missed call' message. I rang back and Steve picked up. Joy of joys!

'Great news. Renate's DNA is a clear and definite match for Kate's.'

'That's fantastic! Have you told her yet?'

'No. I realised it isn't something that should be done over the phone. I've texted and arranged to go over to her flat at six this evening, so I can tell her face-to-face. I just thought I'd let you know in case I'm still out when you get home. I don't think I'll be long, though.'

'Well, I would have swept you off to bed to celebrate your brilliant detective work when I got home, but it'll wait, I suppose.' Steve made a play at sounding sad, but he knew what this meant to me. 'Enjoy the moment, Rach.' As Gran would say, 'he's a keeper, that lad'.

Of course, when I got to Mum's, I couldn't keep it in. I was crying, she was crying. We were so happy. Mum thought I was cruel making Renate wait, but as I said, Kate was my client, so I had to tell her first, and anyway, Renate didn't know the result would come so quickly, so she could wait until I'd seen Kate. It would only be a few hours.

After I'd got over sharing my joyous news, I caught up with family news. My sister Laura had joined a book group in Doncaster. Something to keep her sane once a month, she'd told Mum. Being the only woman in a house with eight-year old twin boys and a husband did make her crave more female company, and it was a laugh, she said.

'I only read romance but I thought maybe you'd like to join a local book group, Rachel. You did English Literature at the university, after all, though from what Laura said, I think it's more social than intellectual.'

'Might give it a go then. When you've dissected books for three years, you can go off so-called serious books, and I did for a long while, but I've been reading all sorts again lately.'

Driving over to Kate's, I thought back on my university days. They seemed so long ago now. I'd felt almost like a different person ever since I'd taken over the private detective agency from a friend who emigrated to New Zealand. One brilliant thing remained from those days, though - I'd met Steve on a Psychology module we'd both taken.

Kate could tell from my face that the news was good, so I didn't beat about the bush with pleasantries. 'I've found your mother, Kate.' There was a sharp intake of breath. 'And your father. And, wait for it - your brother, too.'

'Really? When? Where? I have a brother as well as parents? What are they like? Did they say why they gave me up?'

'They never gave you up, Kate. They never stopped loving you and wanting you back.'

'I don't understand. How did I...?'

'...come to be with the Willises? This is the hard bit for you. The really sad bit, Kate. I'm afraid you were abducted.'

'You're saying Mam and Dad stole me?'

'I'm afraid it looks like that, yes.'

'Oh, my God. That's awful. I just can't imagine them doing anything like that. Are you sure?'

'It seems like your mum must have been suffering from an extreme version of post-natal depression, Kate, and wouldn't be thinking straight. Women can do all sorts of things that are totally out of character when they're like that. You can't be too angry with her. Think how much she loved you.'

'But Dad?'

213

'We'll never know, but I expect he did everything to try to persuade your mum to put it right, but in the end, if your mum was almost suicidal, he might have felt he didn't have a choice but to go along with what she'd done. I'm so sorry, Kate.'

'And my real parents? How did you find them?'

'I would never have found them if it wasn't for your mother. She's never given up. Never stopped looking for you, even though it was like looking for a needle in a haystack after the police could find no trace of you.'

'What's she like?'

'I haven't met her. We've emailed, but I couldn't tell her anything about you until we were sure. I've only just got the result of the DNA comparison, so she doesn't even know yet that her DNA is a match. I just told her there was a chance. Even I kept thinking it wouldn't be true. It's such an amazing thing after all the false alarms and all these years. Only a few weeks ago there was another possibility, but that mother's DNA wasn't a match.'

'Poor woman. I'm so grateful to you for sticking at it all this time since I first came to you. But my real mother. Do you think she'll be pleased?'

'I think she'll be over the moon, but I wanted to tell you first, in case you wouldn't feel ready or able to meet her. After all, knowing her details is one thing, but wanting to get to know a whole new family is another, and it wasn't my decision to make.'

'Thank you, Rachel, but I've no doubts. I want to talk to my real mother, if that's OK. Where does she live? Can I go round tonight?'

'It's a bit far for that, but you can ring her, if you like. Her English isn't perfect but you speak German.'

'What?'

'You were born in Ilmenau, in Germany. Your family was on holiday in Cornwall when you were taken from your buggy. It happened in an instant, and even though the beach was quite crowded, no-one noticed. While your mum was getting drinks from the kiosk, your brother had a bit of a tantrum and ran off towards the sea, your dad gave chase and when he got back, you were gone. I think you must have been scooped up and wrapped in a shawl, a pashmina, something like that. Your brother blames himself.'

'That's so sad. Where is Ilmenau?'

'It's in Thuringia, the old East Germany, but they live up on the Baltic coast now, not that far from Hamburg, I think. Your mother's been back to Cornwall every year, hoping she might find you. It was a stroke of pure luck that my mum and I stayed at the same B&B. The photo you found was of the beach there, and you were wearing the green babygro when you were taken. Apparently 'Bau...'

'... is the start of "Baumwolle", the German word for cotton', Kate finished. 'I don't know why I never realised that before.'

'Because you couldn't possibly have thought the word would be German.'

'Aside from that, I can't believe you actually went down there. And found out such a lot.'

'Yes, I'm sorry I couldn't tell you at the time, but if it turned out that Renate was nothing to do with you, then I'd have built up your hopes for nothing. I hope you understand. Now, do you want to ring her first, or would you rather I did it for you?'

'Please can I ring? I'm sorry but I'd like to be the one who tells - Renate, I think you said?'

'No need to apologise, Kate. I was only offering to break the ice, but it'll be much better if you ring, particularly as you'll be able to talk to her in German. Though it'd be great if you could give me a ring one day this week and let me know how it went, please.'

'Of course I will. I'll just get a pen for Renate's details.'

'I almost forgot, I've got an old photo of Renate and Joachim here. It was taken at the press conference when you went missing. The police in Cornwall let me take a copy before we had confirmation that they were your parents. I don't expect you'll need it now, though, because you'll be able to get Renate to send you copies of your baby photos and photos of the family in the years since.'

'Yes, I will. It'll be fantastic.'

I knew she was itching to ring, so I just gave her Renate's phone number, and her email address as well, and said goodbye.

I hadn't got to the car before Kate ran after me. 'I'm so excited. I forgot to ask you my real name.'

'It's Ulrike. Ulrike Schneider. And your real birthday is 31st March, not 29th, so you're two days younger than you thought.' I got in the car, still buzzing with excitement. I'd have loved to have been able to listen in to their conversation, but my involvement was over now.

Steve was in when I got home. He'd been fairly busy at work, but a lot of it was for show, keeping busy on minor details to do with the murders, whereas most of his real work was done outside the office - clandestine meetings with Michelle at the Border Force, and her second-in-command, a trusted colleague. The stage was set, in so far as it could be, for a joint operation to break open the smuggling ring and catch as many as possible of the gang, hoping that any who escaped would be fingered by those that didn't. Not long to wait, if all went to plan.

He must have realised I was still on a high and would find it hard to settle. 'Come and get your tea, Rach. When you've calmed down we could walk to that new wine bar and celebrate your success in solving the case. I've got to hand it to you, love, for never giving up.'

CHAPTER 35

We'd just got back when the phone rang. It was a very excited Kate. 'I just had to ring and tell you about the call. I hope it's not too late to be ringing.'

'Not at all. I'm so glad you've found the time to ring me. I thought I'd have to wait to hear all the details.'

She told me that she'd spoken to Renate for over an hour. Renate had insisted on ringing her back so she didn't have to pay, and Kate had been scared for all of a minute that she wouldn't return the call.

'Renate told me that her husband Joachim had never forgiven himself because I was taken when he was in charge. Apparently they'd hit a rocky patch for a while when I couldn't be found, but after about six months, Renate stopped blaming him. She'd come to realise her husband couldn't have done anything else when my brother ran off towards the sea, and it was just the worst luck possible that someone like my mam, Helen I mean, had seen the pram unattended.'

'I'm glad for their sake and yours that your abduction didn't break up their marriage.'

'Thanks, Rachel. I'm really glad about that as well. And I think I can understand how it all happened somehow. My mam wasn't well. Renate realises that too now. Mam probably thought I needed looking after and she so wanted a baby to look after. She must have bundled me up inside her cardigan and taken me back to Dad and the car. I don't blame either of them. Dad would have tried to reason with her but she probably told him that I'd been abandoned and looked neglected. She probably thought that in her own head.'

'I think so too.'

'The saddest thing is that my brother has grown up believing he was to blame for running off. He's never really forgiven himself, despite reassurances from Renate and Joachim. My brother's called Peter, which is also a German boy's name, just pronounced differently. I'm hoping a big hug from me will go some way to helping him realise it wasn't his fault, just a terrible set of circumstances and all's well that ends well. Renate's emailed me loads of photos. Would you like to see them sometime?'

'Yes, that would be great. I'm so happy for you.' I realised I hadn't told Kate her brother's name, nor indeed that of her father, but I didn't want her to think I'd been deliberately keeping things from her, and it was better anyway that Renate was able to tell Kate herself.

'I can't wait to show Mrs Charlesworth as well. She's done such a lot for me, taking me in like that. I've been really lucky. It's strange. I don't feel resentful, even if I should. Mam and Dad really loved me and gave me a happy childhood, even if it wasn't the one I should have had.'

'I think you're amazing, Kate. You're taking it so well.'

'I wouldn't say that. Let's face it, I didn't know what I'd been missing and, although my parents died, I've not been left on my own, and now I've been given a second chance. Up until now it's scarcely affected me, unlike the Schneiders. They've had a terrible time.'

'If you say those exact same words to your brother, I'm sure it will lift the burden of guilt from his shoulders.'

'Well, I haven't told you the best of it - Renate's booked a flight to come and see me. She can't get away for long at the moment but at least it'll be a long weekend.'

'Fantastic! Are all the family coming?'

'No, her husband and Peter can't get away right now, but she's asked me to go over to Germany to spend Christmas with them. And then next year, they'd like me to spend the entire summer there. I'm a bit scared of the thought of flying over there by myself. I've hardly travelled anywhere, except up to here from home in Lincolnshire, and that was with Mrs Charlesworth!'

'It's only like climbing on a coach...'

'I know people tell you that, Rachel, but I'm really not sure I can do it on my own. I thought about getting the ferry and a train but it's a very long way. As it is, Renate said they'd drive or take the train down to Hamburg airport to meet me.'

'But your German would be good enough to cope, I'm sure. It's funny, isn't it, how you've always had an ear for languages?'

'Maybe, but I don't think I subconsciously found learning German easy because I was born a German. It's quite likely that I inherited her aptitude for music, though.'

'Yes, that's possible.'

'Who knows, I may even get a job teaching English in Germany after I get my degree. I think I'd have a good chance of a job, with English as my mother tongue.'

'That's true.'

'Do you think I should call her "Mum" when I see her? It doesn't seem right somehow, but she might be offended if I don't?'

'Did she call you Kate or Ulrike?'

'Kate.'

'Well there you are, then. I expect she doesn't know what to call you either. It may come in time, but don't force it, or else it'll seem false.'

'Thanks for that - and for everything. Anyway, I'd better go. I've not eaten yet and I'm starving. Oh, and get a bill drawn up and I'll pay you when we meet up to look at all the photos I take while she's here. Renate is insisting she pay you the correct amount, however much it is, and I'm sure it's more than the fifty pounds my aunt paid!"

'OK. If it makes her happy, I'll put something together, but it's been a pure joy to me and it doesn't seem right charging either of you. And thanks very much for ringing me and telling me how it all went.'

When I filled Steve in on the bits he missed, he said, 'Maybe we could travel over there with Kate next summer on our honeymoon if she's still not keen on flying, and you can meet the Schneiders.'

Seeing my face, he instantly added, 'leaving Kate with her family, of course! It sounds like a lovely resort and it's near to the Danish border, so we could hire a car and do some touring. What do you think?'

'Sounds brilliant, Steve. Much better than going somewhere roasting and lying on a beach. Neither of us are good at doing nothing. Does that mean you want to set a date, or are we having the honeymoon before the wedding?'

'Yes, we should set a date. Why not? I want you to be my wife, not a long-standing fiancée. What do you say - shall we go for it?'

I gave Steve a tight hug and the sort of kiss that I hope conveyed 'Yes, please!!!!!'

'Right. We better start looking into it then. Not much time to organise a wedding by the end of Kate's summer term at uni, unless you want a quick registry office affair.'

'That might be all we can get, given the time scale, but I'll get right onto it in the morning.'

'I've had another thought, Rach? How do you feel about putting your flat on the market now? I don't want to push you into it. I know you've always held onto it in case things didn't work out...'

'Yes, I will.' The words came straight out, no hesitation. The last six months or so, I'd stopped thinking about the flat in terms of a bolthole, or something that makes me feel I'm still independent. The smell from the fire had long gone, after one of Pete's many exes had pushed burning rags through the door in a fit of jealousy. 'It's just been a case of inertia really. But now's a good time. We could use some of the money to pay for the wedding, have a fantastic honeymoon, and the rest can go towards a house when we're ready for it – that is if you're ready to leave this flat?'

'Yes, I think it's about time. Not only is my office moving so I won't be able to walk to work any longer, but I feel like I've reached the stage where I fancy a garden.'

'OK, so tomorrow do I plan the wedding, put the flat on the market and ask the estate agents to send us details of houses while I'm at it?'

'Probably wait till we've sold your flat and we've got the wedding out of the way, before we look at houses. Sorry! Don't give me that look! Wrong turn of phrase. The wedding is not something to be got out of the way,' Steve added quickly, just saving himself from having a wet dishcloth thrown at him. 'I'm looking forward to our wedding day. It's up to you, but I think you'll have enough on your hands as it is. You've forgotten there's the honeymoon as well. I'll help as much as I can, particularly with the honeymoon planning, but you can do some of the research. You're great at that. It'll give you something to do besides stopping your gran from driving your mum crazy with her ideas for the wedding, not to mention her dress choice.'

'Ha! Ha! Now let's get in some practice at being a proper married couple. I think you need to do some extra work on your seduction technique if we're going to be making love for the next fifty years.'

'Cheeky madam! Although if you insist, we could go to bed early so we can try out something new.'

CHAPTER 36

I woke early the next morning. What with selling my flat, planning a wedding and a holiday, I didn't imagine I'd have time to think about what I was going to do next work-wise, but I couldn't shake off the feeling that I'd left something undone.

And then it came to me. There'd be no happy ending for the girl whose baby was taken from the car boot fair - Claire.

Steve must have taken one look at my crestfallen face when he woke up, and wondered what had happened. 'Is something bothering you, Rach? Is it the thought of Nick still being locked away?'

'No, not that. I understand why, and it'll only be for a few more days, you said, unless he's been moved?'

'Yes. I really hope he's coping, but I think knowing you got away will help. You know we've narrowed the house down to a small cul-de-sac on an estate of old Victorian houses near Spring Bank. Your help was fantastic to select the rough area and then Matt used nearby CCTV to look for the drivers coming and going. If Nick's still there, he should be freed just as soon as the deal goes down, and Michelle at Border Force is convinced it'll be the day after tomorrow.'

'You didn't tell me that!'

'Sorry, love. I've probably got so used to keeping things zipped, that I forgot I could tell you.'

'Well as long as you didn't think I'd blab to anyone. I wouldn't tell a soul. Not friends, not even Mum and Dad. I've totally lost track of the date. Come to think of it, it's been five days since I escaped, and that was on the tenth, so I should have known anyway.'

'So what is it, Rach? What's making you feel down? You're not getting cold feet about making it official, are you? Is it all too much to do in such a short time? We can put the date back if you want. There's no need to postpone the honeymoon. We can just call it a holiday, and go somewhere else when we eventually get married.'

'No. The wedding's under control, Steve. After your brainwave and quick phone call last night, we've got the reception venue sorted, that's the main thing. It was a great idea of yours to ring Ravenspurn Hall.'

'I can't take all the credit. Lee at work had already told me about it.'

'I know, but I can't believe how lucky we are that the owners have just started up this year. Finding a place with a vacant Saturday slot next June, not to mention a cut-price deal so they can generate publicity, was absolutely amazing. We really landed on our feet there. Everything else will just fall into place somehow. No. It's something entirely different.'

'Whatever could it be to make you so down?'

'You'll think I'm silly, too soft-hearted.'

'As if. You wouldn't be you if you weren't, but I love you like that, so just tell me what's on your mind and I'll see if I can help.'

'I wish I could have done more, Steve, but I don't know what.'

'More what?'

'Oh, sorry. I've been lying awake for ages mulling it over. I haven't told you, have I?'

When I told him that I couldn't stop thinking about Claire and her missing baby Mandy, I thought he'd say I couldn't solve everything and I had to accept that, but he didn't. That's how I know he'll be the perfect husband. He tries to understand, put himself in my shoes and thinks about what he can do to help. He doesn't come up with simplistic answers like a lot of blokes. He went in the kitchen to put the kettle on and came back with a nice hot sweet cup of tea.

'I'll read through the file again and have a think, Rach.'

As soon as he'd gone to work, I got out my own notes on Claire's stolen baby. It was so long ago. All I had was a DNA profile. That's when I had the idea. It would be costly, but Renate had insisted on paying me what amounted to a small fortune for reuniting her with Kate - or Ulrike, whichever she was going to call herself.

I rang Pete and had a natter. I hadn't had the chance to give him the good news that I'd found Kate's parents. Needless to say, he was really pleased, even if it didn't come about as a result of any of his computer searches.

We were just like old friends now. There was a bit of well-natured banter, but no flirting any more. With him being in IT, I hoped he might be able to point me in the right direction, even though it wasn't his field, and he said he'd contact a few people and get back to me later in the day.

While I was waiting I made good on my promises to the landlady of the B&B and to Bill, the retired sergeant, in Cornwall and gave them the good news that Renate's DNA was a match for Kate's. I asked Bill to let the police know in Penzance so they could close their case.

Early in the afternoon, true to his word, Pete called back with a phone number and said his computing friend from university, David, would be waiting for my call. When I rang, he quoted me a "mate's rate" that was very reasonable, and outlined what he would need.

'I've decided I'm going to spend the cash Renate paid me on helping Claire,' were my first words to Steve that evening.

'Good idea, love. You've been well paid lately. If it makes you happy, go ahead. Tell me what you have in mind before I tell you my ideas.'

'Are you sure? We might need to spend quite a lot of cash on a house.'

'We've got two places to sell, and an inspector's salary isn't a pittance, Rach. We'll manage. Now spill the beans. I can tell you're dying to.'

'I want to get a photo of Mandy as she would be now. You know the sort of thing? I know she was only a baby, not a small child, but they can go off the mother's face and any cousins. I've spoken to someone and got a price, but it's not cheap.'

'Hundreds or thousands?'

'Hundreds.'

'Well go right ahead. I've had some thoughts about who might have taken Claire.'

'You've got a name?'

'No. Otherwise you wouldn't need the picture. Just an idea of what might have happened. You know the police looked into all the women in the area who had had miscarriages shortly before the baby's abduction? As you know, that drew a blank. But I was thinking. The baby…'

'Mandy.'

'Yes, Mandy. Well, she was taken at a time when not all pregnant women went to their doctor when they got pregnant, or even when they miscarried, particularly among some sections of the community. I'm thinking of the large group of people living in caravans in the area, and more particularly of the workers who pick crops. Some of them are still wary of the police, even now.'

'So you're saying one of those women could have taken the baby and registered the birth in her own name, even if she'd not visited a doctor beforehand?'

'Yes. In those days it was often simply a matter of turning up with your babe in arms at the registry office and getting a birth certificate. There weren't any 'red books' back then.'

'That's what the hospital gives you now with the baby's health record, isn't it?'

'Yes. Also, the police publicised the abduction as well as they could at that time, but that was before social media, and I doubt if all those families spoke enough English to read the papers or listen to the radio, let alone owned a TV. So you see, your picture might well bring some fresh results now; jog a few people's memories.'

'That would be great, Steve. So you think it's worth trying?'

'Yes. I didn't think about a picture though. I just thought of putting the story out there again. Asking if anyone in the area remembers a couple suddenly having a baby, without any sign of a pregnancy.'

'I can do that while I wait for the picture to be produced - that is, if Claire's willing for me to go ahead.'

'If you're sure you've got time…'

'Loads of it. Everyone takes ages to get back to you when you're planning a wedding and there's only so much we can do for our holiday this early. How did work go today, anyway?'

'Bit of news, actually, for once. Sanjeev in IT called to say they'd finally salvaged a few fragments from Simon Crawford's laptop. Unfortunately, it's such a tiny piece and mentions no names, just places and times, so no more use than Nick's notebooks. Sanjeev said he kept trying because he knew it must be important, and that's why it's taken him so long. So, not good news, but at least it's something off the list.'

'True.'

'Otherwise it's the same old, same old. It's hard to concentrate on tying up the loose ends on the murders of Simon Crawford and Dean Hornby when I've come to the conclusion that they were both killed by Craig Dobson. As it is, we're still actively looking for Dobson, because we can't say that he's dead.'

'But at least you'll only have to keep it up for an odd day or so now.'

'Yeah. It won't be long now. Trouble is, Border Force are in charge of planning the searches, not us, so it's hard to gauge how it's going, except at the odd private meeting with Michelle. We only get called in to make arrests.'

'At least that's had its good side with nothing being spoken about in your office.'

'And Bradfield must feel he's still safe. Somehow or other he fell for our story of what happened to you. Mainly because he

226

wanted to convince himself that nothing had come out to affect the smuggling deal, I suspect. You know, you'd like Michelle. She's very approachable once you get to know her, bubbly and friendly.'

'Maybe we should invite her to the wedding?'

'You wouldn't be having a sly dig because I've spent a lot of time with her? Wanting to check her out?'

'No, Steve. I'm way past the jealous stage. If you think she's fun, it'd be nice to meet her, that's all. I haven't many female friends still in Hull.'

'Sounds good. Now let's forget about work and find a film to watch?'

'Or we could see how the other half investigate murders and watch the next episode of that Scandi crime series?'

'Go on then. I get to have a laugh and a moan at the same time, seeing the things they get away with.'

CHAPTER 37

I spoke to Claire the next morning before setting the wheels in motion. She valued her privacy and was worried about the cost, but at the same time I didn't think she'd want to pass up a real chance to be reunited with Mandy.

It took a lot of reassurance and persuasion but I always felt she would agree, and she did. I asked her if I could come down and collect photos of Mandy, Claire herself, and some of her closest relatives, including her son Kieran, and she said she'd root out what she and her mum had, and ring me to arrange it. I rang David and told him I wanted to go ahead with the updated photo, and he said that when he'd got the photos, he'd be able to schedule it into his workload. He was busy, but for a mate of Pete's, it could be done within a couple of days.

Pleased with my progress, I decided it was time I paid a visit to Mum. Dad would be at work, but she only worked a couple of days a week doing the accounts for two small local businesses, and it was one of her days off.

Their house is in East Hull, and as usual I got stuck in the traffic along Holderness Road, but eventually I fought my way through and pulled up outside their pre-war bay-windowed brick semi. Mum was hanging out washing. It wasn't warm, but it was very windy, and she'd washed her summer coat and Dad's, to put away for the winter.

She was really pleased to see me. That always makes me happy and reminds me how lucky I am. I told her about my idea for reuniting Claire with her baby and she was as excited as I was. 'I do hope you can, Rachel. It was fantastic that you managed to give Renate her daughter back and I'm convinced you can do it again. You know I've always had my doubts about your job, with all the scrapes you seem to get into, but I'm so proud of you.'

It was a good thing that Dad vetted the things she heard about my job, or she'd be far more worried than she was already. She'd never heard about my escape from armed thugs in Amsterdam, for one. 'Thanks Mum. That means a lot to me. Now I better get the kettle on and warm us up. We shouldn't be standing around in the cold talking when we could be inside.'

Once I told her that we'd set the date for the wedding - the last Saturday in June - there was no stopping her. 'How are you going to organise it all in just six months though, Rachel?'

'Well, for a start, it's eight and a half months, and we've got a venue booked already.' By the time I'd told her about Ravenspurn Hall and described it as best as I could remember, she was so excited. You'd think I was having a grand affair, marrying into royalty, the way she went on.

'I'm quite excited too, but Steve and I are determined to keep it fairly low key, which means not telling Gran for the time being at least. She'll hardly be booked up on a Saturday that far in advance. We thought it could wait until after Christmas before we told her our plans. Do you think you can manage to keep it a secret from her, Mum? I know it'll be harder for you.'

'It might be, but it'll be worth it. I'll never hear the end of it once she finds out. Me and your dad might have to go away for some peace and quiet. Don't worry. Your secret's safe with us. I'd recommend not telling her until after Easter, never mind Christmas! Now, why don't you stay for lunch, and we could visit a few florists this afternoon, if you want. You might as well make a start while you're waiting to go to this Claire's.'

'OK. Sounds good to me.'

The rest of the day flew by, but by the time I went back to the flat, we'd visited three florists, discussed options and were awaiting quotes. I'd decided to go with a blue and yellow theme when the time came, and Mum agreed. I'm so glad she's not one of those mothers who think they know best when it comes to such things.

In the evening Steve was out at a clandestine rendezvous to prepare for the climax to all their plans - hopefully the arrest of the gang and the crooked officials, including Tommy - so I went scurrying round to Sarah's. After we'd swapped news, she got all excited about the wedding and asked if I'd thought of bridesmaids.

'Steve and I don't want a lot of fuss, but I'd really like you as a whatchamacallit - a maid of honour.'

'Sounds like a cake. But if you mean someone dressed in a nice frock to give you moral support and hold things, then I'd love to.'

'I thought the earlier I arranged things, the better, as people get booked up years in advance it seems, and you know me and formal occasions. I'm prone to panic, so if it's organised early, I might get to enjoy the final bits and bobs. I don't know where to start with picking a photographer, though. Can you recommend the woman who did your wedding photos, if she's still around?'

'Yeah. Her name's Lesley Lomas. She was good. Not bossy and didn't take hundreds of photos either. I've been to some weddings where we had to hang around for ages waiting for every combination of relatives on each side to be captured on film, and most of the guests, including me and John, were bored rigid. You just want a reasonable amount and then get on to the eating and drinking bit.'

'Exactly. I don't suppose you can dig out her number sometime and give it me then, please?'

'Of course. I'm not quite sure where it might be but I'll bring it along to the sports hall next week.'

'Great. See you at badminton then.'

I'd just got in when the phone went. Claire had got the photos and was hoping I'd be able to go down the next day. I told her I'd get the earliest train I could, and went online to buy a ticket to Ely.

Steve was up and out at the crack of dawn, but so was I for once.

I wanted to be able to wish him good luck and give him a big hug before he went.

'So, today's the day.'

'Yes. Must dash. Ferries unload very early. I'll get in touch as soon as I can to let you know how it goes.'

'That would be great but don't worry, I'll hear soon enough. I know you'll be far too preoccupied.'

I didn't mess about sightseeing in Ely like last time. I went straight to Claire's house. She offered me a cup of tea, and I accepted because I was parched. I'm not keen on tea bought on a train, even if there is a trolley, and there hadn't been one this time.

She was nervous. I had to promise again that her address and new name definitely wouldn't get on social media. That seemed to calm her down. 'I don't know why I should be worrying. You were as good as your word last time and you're doing me this enormous favour. It's just…'

'I know, Claire. I can understand, but it'll be alright, honestly. All my request will say is "Missing since 1998. Have you seen this girl? Last seen in the Fens area." It won't mention where exactly she was last seen, or anything about you at all. There's a strong chance that nothing will come of the appeal anyway, but I hope so.'

'I do too. I still don't understand why you're willing to do this for me, but I am grateful, even if it doesn't seem like it.' She handed me the photos in an envelope, and I left as soon as was polite. I wanted to get home and scan in the photos to send to David.

I grabbed a sandwich and a bottle of water at the station and was home by the middle of the afternoon. Half an hour later the digital images were on their way and I gave David a ring to confirm it.

'I'm sorry it's taken so long, but the mother doesn't have access to a computer, so I had to go to Ely to get them myself and she only got the photos together last night.'

'I'll get on to it in the morning. It'll only take a day or so at

231

the most.'

'Thanks so much for dropping everything like this.'

'No worries. I don't often get chance to make a difference to someone's life. I mainly deal with archaeological reconstructions. There's no rush for those and certainly not the same human interest. Anyway, I'd better get on. I'll be in touch.'

I immersed myself once more in matters relating to our wedding. It made the time pass. As you must know by now, I'm not the most patient person in the world. I rang Pete with an update too. He'd put me in touch with David, after all. I realised I'd not mentioned the wedding so I put that right.

He started telling me about his latest girlfriend. 'She's a great girl. Not in your league but…'

'Give over. I bet she's a real looker, with brains to boot.'

'She is actually. Maybe she'll be the one, but I don't think I'm ready to settle down just yet.'

If I hadn't already realised long ago, it was further confirmation that he couldn't have a conversation with a woman without flirting. It didn't mean he was madly attracted to every woman he spoke to. In other words, his brief flirtation with me had been nothing more than that. I was so glad I'd had the sense to realise that in time and not messed things up with Steve. He was worth all the drawbacks of a policeman's long hours.

Talking of long hours, pretty much as I was expecting, I didn't see Steve at all that day. He must have got in during the early hours and got a bit of kip on the settee by the looks of the crumpled cushions, but he wasn't there when I got up. He wouldn't have done even that, if the station wasn't still a mere five minutes' walk away.

CHAPTER 38

I still didn't have a lot on, but I find it hard to relax, so I caught up on some paperwork, balanced my bank account and emptied the bins. The exciting life of a private detective, eh? Actually I found it hard to concentrate, thinking of Steve and hoping the arrests were continuing as expected. You only need the odd little leak and things can go belly-up.

I spent some time getting quotes for suit hire and stuff, but really I was killing time. In the end, I walked into town and mooched around the shops a bit but ended up back at home, waiting for him to call or turn up. I'd bought us a special meal from M&S and a book Sarah had recommended. I gave up trying to keep myself busy and gave in to the lure of the book. Before long, I was hooked and couldn't put it down.

Around six o'clock, David's imagining of how an eighteen-year old Mandy might look now, pinged into my inbox. I could see a lot of Claire in her, and I had sent him a photo of her at that age, but this 'imagined' photo had subtle differences. Claire was adamant she wanted the search kept low key, which for her meant no newspapers or the local TV, which Steve had suggested. I did, however, put it on Facebook, Instagram and various Twitter feeds relating to missing persons, with a link to the photo. All I could do now was sit back and wait.

When Steve arrived home that night, looking a bit worse for wear, I asked him how it'd gone. He gave a wry smile and said, 'Like these things mostly do, I suppose. Not as well as they could have gone, but much better than they might have done.' He gave me the lowdown on the operation in as much detail as he could.

'It was fantastic Nick had found out there would be contraband on the ferry from Zeebrugge as well as the one from Rotterdam. Without that valuable piece of information, even if Border Force had identified one group of containers, the others would have got through. As it was, they caught both. It's never been known for two ferries to be used on the same day before, even if both crossing routes have been used in the past.'

'Good for Nick.'

'Yeah. From the smugglers' points of view, there was double the risk of people talking but double the reward and the safety net that at least the smuggled goods on one ferry would go through. They must have deemed it extremely unlikely that Border Force would have the manpower to keep on searching so intently once they'd found cigarettes concealed on one ship.'

'Where were they hidden?'

'They were smuggling the cigarettes inside shipments of antique furniture. You'd be amazed how many antiques get shipped around. There are vast warehouses full of furniture and the like and they sell online to people all over the country and the world. The UK's a hotspot for importing and exporting antiques. Americans have always loved all that really old stuff they never had over there. Can't get enough of it. And now the Chinese have started buying up antiques like there's no tomorrow. Chairman Mao told them to get rid of all the old imperialist stuff and it was thrown away, burnt mostly, but people today want their heritage back.'

'But if it was destroyed, where's it coming from? Are people reproducing it and selling it as the real stuff?'

'No. They don't have to. In the dim and distant past, China had a thriving trade in making things for the export market, and most of it ended up in Europe.'

'So were the cigarettes hidden behind the furniture?'

'No. Border Force closed down a ring a few years ago that were doing that. They also got another gang who were smuggling cigs in coffee jars. This crew have sort of combined the two, because of the scans and searches. The wardrobes, desks and dressing table drawers, chests and the like were all crammed full of cartons of cigarettes, and locked up. They'd got clearance at the port of origin from some crooked officials, who'd signed documents to indicate that everything had been checked.'

'And Tommy Bradfield?'

'Safely behind bars. Border Force officials shared some of the interviews with us, particularly those with the dock workers. We finally managed to get the name of the person in charge of the smuggling at King George Docks, and he gave us Bradfield's name as the person who tipped them off when searches were to be carried out.'

'Hurray!'

'Border Force are now working with their Belgian and Dutch colleagues to find out his opposite numbers abroad.'

'And Nick?' I asked hopefully, knowing they couldn't have found him or it would have been the first thing Steve'd told me when he stepped through the door.

'We sent a van round to raid the house we'd identified as the one you'd been kept in, but I didn't really expect him to be still there. Even though we laid it on thick about you not knowing how far you'd walked to the fairground and what a lot of turns you'd taken, and not mentioning Nick at all, it was a near certainty that Bradfield would have had him moved.'

'I'm so sorry.'

'It's not your fault, Rach, and we can at least prove Bradfield was involved in Nick's abduction, without dragging you into it. Forensics found evidence that Bradfield had been in the house as well as Nick. We're already hard at work to find out where he is now. We're examining the camera we set up in the shop on the corner of the nearest exit to a main road, although it always was a bit of a slim chance.'

'Do you think he's still alive?'

'Definitely, although Bradfield's refusing to talk at the moment. I think he's hoping we'll soften up if we're not getting anywhere with rounding up everyone involved in the smuggling ring. We're concerned we've missed the person at the top of the chain, and some in the lower echelons. He must know that, so he's holding out to see if he can offer a deal. As he's in the force, he must know we'll be giving him the exact opposite of preferential treatment. His only hope must be that we'll make a trade for Nick's release.'

'And will you?'

'In principle, we wouldn't, but Nick is one of our own, so who knows? We need to get Bradfield to tell us where Nick's being kept, so to let him think he might get a deal, we're still holding back on telling him we've found Dobson's body. He'll think we've not got that much on him. In reality, you can add kidnapping and false imprisonment to his list of crimes anyway – as well as the suspected murder of Craig Dobson, so he's unlikely to see the outside of a prison in the next twenty years.'

When he'd finished telling me his news, I showed Steve the aged photo of Mandy. 'It's going to be hard just sitting back and waiting, Steve.'

'You don't have to. Don't forget that what you've just done will only reach those with smartphones and computers. Your target audience are probably not among those. If you've time, I suggest you put the wedding organising on hold now and go down to the villages near the farms. Talk to people in shops and post offices and farms and put up posters everywhere. It'll cost a bit more, but it's most likely to get a result. Word-of-mouth and posters are your best bets.'

'You're right. And don't worry about the wedding planning being left undone. I've done most of the preparatory legwork, and we can sit and decide some things together this weekend and get things ordered and booked next week. Then we'll be able to put it out of our heads for a while.'

I was keen to get going with the posters, so the next morning I laid out what I wanted, saved it on a memory stick and took it down to our local print shop. I could have done it myself but I don't have the need for a laser printer, only an inkjet one and that would have cost a bomb in colour ink. Also, I could only print up to A4 size anyway, and I wanted the photo to stand out, which meant bigger posters than that.

They said the posters could be ready as a rush job by the end of the day if I paid extra, so I did. I didn't like the wait, but I needed a full day down in Lincolnshire anyway, and it would give me chance to decide how long I would need to get right around the area with posters, and to plan out exactly where I should go. Mandy was taken from a car boot near March in Cambridgeshire, so I was going to have to stay one night at least as it was a long drive.

I did a big shop and some laundry. It was long overdue and took my mind off wanting to get out and start looking for Mandy myself. I still had most of the day to kill before the posters were ready. Steve had come up with a few suggestions the night before, some of which were of a sexual nature and which we acted upon straightaway, but his first idea was one which I thought might be helpful for my investigations.

He'd thought of a way to get contact details for farmers who might know where I should start looking for a lead. Following up Steve's idea, I rang an employment agency in March, and they put me onto an agency in Wisbech.

I asked how farmers went about hiring agricultural workers. I saw no reason to hide my reason for asking and explained about a missing girl and needing to get the photo shown to people in the area who might not normally read the paper or even speak enough English to watch the news on TV. I just didn't say that Mandy had gone missing eighteen years ago, that's all. I was given details of three people who might be able to help. I decided to wait until I met them in person when I could use my powers of persuasion to get them to help me out.

It took me most of the afternoon to work out a route, then I booked myself into what looked like the nicest cheap and cheerful bed and breakfast in Wisbech, as that seemed central for the agricultural Fenland area I wanted to visit. It was also only

237

ten miles from the site of the car boot in March. Then I nipped down to the print shop. Thankfully the posters were ready and they looked good. I packed an overnight bag and was all set to go first thing.

CHAPTER 39

As I drove over the Humber Bridge the following morning I felt a mixture of excitement and nervousness. I'd spent a lot of money but had achieved little so far. There had been quite a lot of emails from people who saw Mandy's 'aged likeness' online, but most asked about a reward before they would say who they thought the girl was, which made me doubt their information. I was so glad I'd not put a phone number on social media, just on the posters I was going to put up locally, or I'd have been fielding unwanted hoax calls or ones from time-wasters for hours on end. A couple had seemed a bit more hopeful and I'd organised my route to take a look at the girls they mentioned as possibilities.

It was a hundred miles or thereabouts, but the time passed fairly quickly with a stop for coffee and cake, a bit of radio and a couple of CDs to sing along to. I booked into the B&B and wandered into the centre to get lunch, taking the opportunity of asking to put up my posters in the post office, a couple of discount stores and charity shops, and the café where I had lunch.

After lunch I drove out to see the only farmer I'd managed to get hold of. One of the two others had an answer machine and I left a message but hadn't heard back. The other just rang and rang with no reply. The farmer I saw, an Adam Sentry, was surprisingly helpful. He wasn't surprised the other two hadn't answered as they'd gone on holiday.

'Both of them?'

In response to my obvious surprise, he told me that although the three of them did use a lot of temporary workers, the harvest

239

was over for this year so the majority had packed up their caravans and moved on. That was a blow I should have been prepared for, it being mid-October.

'So they've all just disappeared or gone home, wherever that is?'

'No, only a few will have done that. The majority will have just signed on to look for other labouring work, because a lot have settled permanently in the local area. You could try asking at the Job Centre in the centre of Wisbech.

That opened up a new avenue of hope. He kindly gave me directions and I drove back into Wisbech. Although it was late in the afternoon by that point, the Job Centre was still quite busy so I had to wait, but a frazzled woman took the poster and waved it in people's faces before coming back to say no-one could recall seeing anyone like Mandy, but she'd been told she could put it on the board by the entrance for seven days.

I was tired and it was getting dark by the time I got back to my car, stopping to put the poster in a couple of newsagents on the way, and buying a local paper. I needed inspiration, if not some leads. I bought a takeaway pizza and rang Steve, who told me not to get down-hearted and that someone was probably looking at my poster that very second. 'I better go, Steve. I need to go to the pub.'

'I presume you mean to ask around and not to drown your sorrows, Rach?'

'Got it in one, Steve. Just remembered how I could extend today's search.'

'Well don't be swayed by an attractive bloke into going home to his place, will you?'

'Fat chance. I'm exhausted. I'm only going to nip in and ask them to put up a poster, then I'm off to bed.'

'OK, sleep well, and give me a quick ring in the morning if you're up early enough to catch me before work.'

Twenty minutes later I was reading the slim local newspaper from cover to cover after calling in the few pubs that Wisbech had to offer. I read a couple of chapters of a crime novel and was fast asleep by ten.

The cooked breakfast was delicious, with my favourite, mushrooms, as well as scrambled egg and bacon. I drove out of Wisbech towards March to visit my Facebook and Instagram offerings. As I suspected, some were in it for a reward, even though none had been offered in my carefully-worded entries, and of the others, a few were less confident of identification and others said 'their' girl had gone missing in the last month or so, completely ignoring the bit about 'since 1998'. Also they all came up with different names. I made notes of their addresses, but wasn't hopeful. This was to be my last day so I drove down to March and handed out most of the rest of my posters. I called at the Antique Centre in Long Sutton to look around and found a couple of blue Hornsea storage jars I liked. At least my trip wouldn't be totally in vain.

I'd just set off back up the A17 when I got a phone call. I couldn't stop and take it and I don't have hands free on the basis that however safe it's supposed to be, I can't drive and carry on a phone call at the same time. I need all my wits about me. I managed to find a café easily enough, and pulled in. The call was from an unknown number. When I rang back, a hesitant voice answered. An older lady with a slightly foreign accent. She said she thought she knew the girl on the poster, but she wasn't missing.

I tried to suppress my rising interest. 'Oh, right. And so you think you've seen this girl recently?' I managed to stop myself from asking her name in case she was frightened off.

'We came over to work on a farm, and stayed here. There was a man and a woman, Sonja, who got a baby where before they didn't have one. It was strange, but they were not a friendly couple and we didn't like to ask. The husband, Karl, was strong and fought when he'd been drinking.'

'I understand. How many years ago was this, please?'

'Like your poster says. It was 1998. I remember because my son left that summer. He went back to Poland. I would not forget

241

such a year.'

'Do you remember what happened to the couple with the new baby, please?'

'They stayed here too. In Spalding. The man would still work for the same farmer as my husband until he died.'

'The baby's father died?'

'No. My husband.'

'I'm very sorry.'

'Don't worry. It was a long time ago. The baby was a girl when my husband died. She must have been about ten.'

'Do you know whereabouts in Spalding they live?'

'No, but the man drank in The Spotted Dog. A lot of them went there but my husband would never go there after work like the others, because he wanted to save money and also there were always arguments and what do you call them - prostitutes.'

'Can I ask your name, please?'

'Ilse. But I do not want them to know it is me that tells you this. Please promise you will not say. But I would like to help the girl if she is missing from someone else. I remember her name now. They called her Saskia. She has not had a good life with a father like that. I would not be surprised at anything he would do.'

'OK', I said quickly before she hung up, although I knew I could find her as she was ringing from a landline. 'Before you go, can you tell me the farm where he works, please? I don't think I should go to the pub to find him if he's as bad as you say.'

'That's a better idea, although they have had the harvest now I think. Ask Mr Shepherd at Low Marsh Farm near Spalding. He will know more. But please, I beg you, do not say anything of me.'

I rang off, after assuring her that I had already been to see one farmer yesterday who didn't ask who had sent me, and I would be able to do the same with Mr Shepherd. I couldn't believe my luck, but tried to stay cautious. This man sounded awful and I had no guarantee that he and his wife had taken

Mandy, and if so, where she might be eight years after Ilse last saw her. Also, it seemed a long way from Spalding to drive to a car boot near March.

I took advantage of the fact that I'd pulled in at a café to have a quick snack. The breakfast had been enormous, and I was only now feeling peckish, even though it was almost three o'clock, but I needed something to keep me going. I located the farm on Google maps. I still carried my old Ordnance Survey maps, but I'd finally made the snap decision and converted to a smartphone on contract, after running out of credit when I spotted Craig Dobson on Holderness Road.

I know I should have done it months ago, perhaps even years, but the thought of choosing which one to have and getting used to using it meant I hadn't been in any hurry. Add to that the fact that my old phone didn't weigh much, only needed charging once a fortnight and I'm not very tech-savvy, and you might understand why I held out so long, but I'd never have been able to email Renate Schneider from the train or do half the stuff I've been able to do since I got it.

The farm wasn't too far away, off the A17 just outside Spalding. I could drive home via Sleaford and Lincoln. The farm looked almost deserted as I drove up the entrance track, but a woman answered the door. I explained about my hunt for the girl on the poster, and when she saw it, she said, 'That looks like Saskia.' I tried not to get excited, but a second positive identification with the same name was promising. Unfortunately, she then threw a spanner in the works. 'I think she went home when her mother died. I've not seen her for about a year.'

'But her father's still in the area?'

'Yes. I don't care for him, but George - he's my husband; he says Karl's a good worker.'

'Do you have an address for him, please?'

'No, love. He lives in a caravan. I think he moves around a lot since his wife died. The caravan used to be here all year round, in a layby just near the end of our lane, but when he was working here on this year's harvest, he came in a van with some of his mates. The caravan could be anywhere now. And even if you were to track it down, to be honest you'd be safer asking the local police to call on him. The mother, she was called Sonja, seemed to dote on Saskia but Karl had no time for her. I even heard some of the men say that he'd only had Saskia so he could claim Child Benefit and stay in England.'

'Can you tell me his surname, please?' If I had to make any phone enquiries, I was going to need it.

'George, what's Karl's second name? I can't remember ever hearing it.'

A voice from the depths of the farmhouse answered - 'Janowski'.

I asked him to spell it, thanked them and drove back towards the main road and Spalding. Time was getting on and I decided to head back home, rather than spend another night in another B&B, but first I needed some cake or chocolate and another cup of tea. I'd only been out of the car, standing on the doorstep of that farmhouse, for ten minutes or so, but the icy wind had cut right through me and I needed warming up.

I stopped in Spalding and ordered a toasted teacake which did the trick. Before I left, I showed the reconstructed photo to the woman behind the counter. She seemed to think the girl looked vaguely familiar, but she only did a couple of afternoons in the café to let her brother get on with other things. I had four posters left, so I left her one and called at the post office, a small supermarket advertising Polish food and a newsagents and asked all of them if I could put one up. Nothing ventured, nothing gained, but I rather felt I'd reached a dead end.

On the long drive back north, I couldn't help feel rather down-hearted. I couldn't help but come to the conclusion that if I did manage to make contact with this Karl Janowski, I was certain he'd tell me nothing, and I would have no way of tracking down his daughter in Poland, even if she was by the remotest chance Claire's daughter, Mandy. I sang along to a cheery 60s compilation CD Dad had lent me, feeling glad I had such a loving family, and would be going to theirs for lunch the next day.

Steve told me not to be down-hearted, but with my best lead on Mandy leading to a girl in Poland, it was hard not to. Even a bar of my favourite chocolate and a glass of wine did little to dispel my low mood.

Despite the actual raids being over, Steve was still really busy, at least during office hours. Overtime had been slashed and Steve was concerned about the lack of hours his team had to search for leads on Nick's whereabouts, but there was nothing he could do about it.

'Good job we're going to your mum and dad's tomorrow. I don't want you brooding all weekend. In fact, I was wondering if maybe I should talk to your dad tomorrow.'

'Yeah. That'd be nice. You can talk about Hull City.' And I fell asleep. An exhausting day and too much wine had done the trick.

CHAPTER 40

On the way to Mum and Dad's, Steve said, 'You never did hear what I was trying to tell you last night. I was going to say that maybe I should ask your dad for your hand in marriage.'

'Are you having me on? I'm not some chattel. This is the twenty-first century.' Luckily I caught his eye and saw he was struggling to keep a straight face or I'd have thumped him on the arm and we might have had an accident, which would have certainly done his reputation as a careful driver no good, never mind causing a major fallout.

When we got there, I got dragged into the kitchen by Mum to discuss yet again what she should wear to our wedding. She wanted to know what colour Steve's mum would be wearing so she didn't pick the same and clash, or worse still, even buy the same dress.

'That's unlikely, Mum, but I'll get Steve to ask Julie when he next speaks to her.'

The phone rang. From what I could hear it was Laura. Knowing Mum would likely be talking to my sister for quite a while, I wandered into the living room where Dad was discussing Hull City's recent run of poor form.

When Mum finally returned, I realised I couldn't keep our good news to ourselves, even though Steve and I had agreed on the way that we should wait because it wasn't absolutely definite and hadn't sunk in properly yet either.

'We're buying a house!'

'Where's that come from? I didn't even know you were looking.'

'It's not definite yet, Mrs Hodges.' Steve turned to me with a laugh and said, 'I didn't really think our plan of keeping it quiet had a chance, you minx!'

I still couldn't believe my luck in finding the house of our dreams on the Garden Village Estate. If I'd not been scouting out a house for a prospective buyer a year ago and then got involved investigating a murder in that same house, I'd never have met the Sandersons who lived next door. Amazingly they'd remembered my desire to live on the quiet estate of solid semis on tree-lined avenues when they decided to downsize to a bungalow by the coast, and they'd actually given me a ring that morning.

They'd not found anywhere yet, but it now seemed as if we might be starting married life in our own home, if the timing worked out well. And of course it came with a large garden, mature trees; the lot. I was so excited. It was no wonder I hadn't been able to keep it a secret.

'They're really lovely people, Mum, so eager to help "a nice couple" like us. I'm still pinching myself.'

Steve and I spent some time with Dad talking about gardens. I was looking forward to Steve and I having a garden and I wanted to learn as much as possible. I was surprised to realise that Steve was really keen as well. 'It'll do us both good to switch off and get out in the fresh air. I really hope it comes off, but I haven't even seen the house yet, so we shouldn't get ahead of ourselves.'

We'd put my flat on the market when we set the date for the wedding, but we wouldn't put Steve's up until the Sandersons had found their new home and things were agreed. 'You'll love it, Steve. I know you will. We can drive past on the way home if you like, check they haven't put a "For Sale" sign up to attract other buyers. I really don't think they will, though.'

'I'm sure you'll have dazzled them with an invitation to visit any time they want.'

He knows me too well, but I didn't give him the satisfaction of knowing he was right. I was saved from answering by Mum calling us all through for lunch. We didn't stay too late because

Steve wanted to call in at the office (inevitably), and Dad was keen to watch football, but it had been a smashing day.

Steve was still apologising as we drove back to the flat. 'Sorry I have to go in, love. I have to get all my i's dotted and t's crossed before tomorrow. Why the Chief Superintendent called this special emergency meeting for a Sunday afternoon, I'm sure I don't know.'

'I do. It's a statement to say, he's behind his men one hundred percent, even to giving up watching sport on the telly after playing golf.'

'You're probably right. I give up enough time at weekends though.'

'But what about Nick? Surely you're keen to have him returned as soon as possible?'

'You know as well as I do, Bradfield's playing a waiting game. The more pressure he puts on, the more likely the Chief will fold and not only drop the charges but let him leave the country. Nick'll be bored to death but he's an intelligent, fit lad. It won't hurt him to be without his freedom a bit longer. He's getting decent food according to you, and his minder is OK. It'll have helped him a lot having had you as a fellow prisoner for a night. Sparkling conversation, wit…'

'Stop it! Be serious.'

'I am. It'll have helped his morale to speak to you, and on top of that he knows he got his message out there so we would be ready to carry out our raids on the right day. Also he'll know we wouldn't let Bradfield slip away like an innocent because we knew all about his money-grabbing scheme.'

'Do you have any sympathy for him - Tommy, I mean?'

'You mean having to pay his mum's fees for the nursing home? Not at all. I feel sorry for his mother, but that's it. We should lock him up and throw away the key. Crooks are bad enough, but bent coppers - I hate them.'

As evidence of his hatred, I noticed that Steve had started referring to Tommy Bradfield more and more by just his surname. 'I know you said you didn't want to charge him with

Craig's murder yet, but what about kidnapping Nick? Surely that can't be dropped even if he were to wriggle out of assisting the smugglers?'

'You mean 'perverting the course of justice', to give the offence its correct title.'

'Don't nit-pick. You knew what I meant.'

'I thought I'd told you. I've not had him charged with anything to do with Nick yet. That's why it's such a delicate balancing act and I have to be very careful how everything is presented. We haven't really got a strong enough case to charge him. Your evidence is only hearsay, based on what Nick told you, added to which, I'd rather not make you testify anyway, and Bradfield's solicitor is saying his client's fingerprints and DNA in the same house as Nick's are just circumstantial.'

'Piffle!'

'Well that's how it goes, I'm afraid. I'm hoping if we hold out a bit longer, Bradfield will be so desperate that he'll agree to giving up Nick's whereabouts in exchange for cancelling out the charge of conspiring with the smugglers and not charging him with keeping Nick against his will. Only we won't include the murder charge, so we should be able to re-arrest him, as long as the Chief hasn't agreed to let him leave the country.'

'Well, if that works, it'll be great, but why would he be desperate to get the deal done so quickly?'

'Because as far as he knows, we still haven't found Dobson's body yet, but that could change at any time. Also, he's on remand and they stuck him in Hedon Road, with the dangerous criminals.'

'Ah! That I can understand.' Mum and Dad didn't live that far from high security Hull Jail, and on the extremely rare occasion, years ago, when a prisoner had escaped, Mum couldn't settle until he'd been caught, despite dad's protestations that he'd be long gone from the town before the news hit the headlines.

He gave me a quick kiss as we parked outside the flat and promised to make it home as quickly as he could.

'I'm sure I can find something to do, don't worry.' I had plans, and they involved browsing home furnishing websites. I should have been ironing or even ringing Julie to ask if she'd found a suitable 'Mother-of-the-Groom' dress, but some things are just that little bit more important.

I'd only just put the kettle on when the phone rang. It was Kate. We had a long chat about her time with Renate, which had gone far too quickly.

'I can't wait for Christmas so I can go and meet my dad and brother. 'Oh, and I've got the money from Renate to pay you.'

We agreed a day to meet up so she could show me her photos, and I got back to making the cuppa.

When I got settled in front of the computer, I found I had a message from the café in Spalding where I'd eaten my teacake the day before. The owner asked if I could ring him as soon as possible as he had some important news about Saskia. I wondered if he really meant for me to call late on a Saturday afternoon, but it did seem urgent. I rang his number but there was no reply. The best I could hope for would be that he somehow had a forwarding address in Poland, but I wasn't going to build my hopes up. It would be too far to travel out there in the hope that this Saskia really was Mandy, all because an artificially aged photo bore some resemblance to her.

I was happily choosing curtain fabric for our new house - saving nice patterns in 'favourites' at least, when the phone rang. We have 'caller display' and although no name registered, I recognised the number, and picked up.

'Hello, is that Rachel Hodges? Your number came up on my phone as a missed call. I'm Harry. Harry Barnes. You were speaking to my sister in the café about Saskia and left a poster?'

'That's right. Have you got any information for me about Miss Janowski?'

'Yes, but she'll be called Janowska. Her father's called Janowski but in Polish the surname changes for a woman.'

'I see. Thanks for that information. It may prove very useful in tracking her down in Poland.'

'You don't need to. Track her down in Poland, I mean. She's living in her father's grotty caravan just outside of Spalding. He moves it around so no-one notices the regular comings-and-goings of course, but I bet it'll be within a ten mile radius of here.'

'Sorry - Harry, did you say? How do you know that, please?'

'She comes into the café now and again, maybe once a week or so, early evening, with several bags of shopping. Though God knows what she buys to eat because she looks so thin. She has long straight hair as well. That's different to the photo on your poster, but I recognised her all the same. And she looks so unhappy, and is always on her own. That's the main reason I noticed her, to be honest.' Harry paused for breath.

'Right.' I tried to encourage him to keep talking.

'I've tried to talk to her but most of the times she comes in, she just clams up, has a cup of tea and waits for her dad to park outside and drive her back to the caravan. But last night she saw your poster, went white as a sheet and started crying. She was really scared. She said her dad would be so angry if he saw it, and that it would be bad for business and she would suffer. I tried to get her to say more, but she only asked me to take the poster down before her dad saw it. So I did.'

'Oh, no. I put up three other posters in Spalding. I don't want to get her in trouble.'

'Tell me where they are and I'll get them taken down.'

'OK. But I'd like to talk to Saskia. Where's the caravan at the moment?'

'I don't know exactly. It was the other week when she said he'd moved it again, but didn't say where.'

'That's a shame. Has she got a job, do you know?'

'She's never said. Look I think I'd better go get those posters, don't you?'

I told him where the other posters were and he said he'd go out straight away and ring me back later.

I didn't know what to think. I was gobsmacked that she was

251

still in England, but worried that I might have frightened her away. I decided to talk it over with Steve when he got in.

CHAPTER 41

While I was waiting for Steve, I thought over what the café owner, Harry, had said. He talked of 'regular comings and goings' at the Janowski's caravan, and he quoted Saskia as saying 'it would be bad for business'. I wondered if her dad was carrying out some illegal work at the caravan and that's why he kept moving.

When he got in, ragged after an hour or so of trying to put his case to the Chief for stalling on a decision about Bradfield, even if it meant Nick wasn't released yet, I filled Steve in on Harry's phone call and asked him what he thought. He said he was concerned that the father might be selling his daughter's services.

'You mean as a prostitute?'

'I hope not, but it sounds a possibility.'

'What can I do?'

'You can't do anything, and she's eighteen, which makes her an adult, and technically able to make her own choices, but if he's coercing her, then that's illegal, and he can be prosecuted if the police can get evidence.'

'So can you help?'

'I can try, love. I'll get on to the police in Spalding in the morning and see if this Karl's known to them first. If we can arrest him on suspicion, then we can interview the girl and ask her for a DNA sample. If, and it's a big if, as we're just going on the statements you've had from a couple of people, she turns out to be Claire's missing Mandy, then she may never have to see her so-called dad again. The police have contact with agencies which can help her start an independent life.'

'Or she can go and live with Claire? Or near her, at least?'

'If she chooses, yes. But remember all her life she's only known this Karl and her mother…'

'Sonja.'

'…yes, her mother Sonja, and she may still cling to him however horrible he is. We just don't know. He won't be allowed to profit from her having sex with others though, so maybe he'll be content to let her go. On the other hand, he might just have her running after him like a slave. There might not be anything sexual.'

'But Harry spoke of comings and goings.'

'Yes, love. But her dad might have all sorts of businesses he carries on, so don't think the worst just yet. Let's wait and see, eh?'

Speaking of the devil, the phone rang just then and it was Harry. He told me he'd recovered all three of the other posters. I told him that my fiancé, a policeman, was standing next to me, and asked if he would be willing to have a quick word with him, and left them to it. I went for a long soak in the bath with lots of bubbles. I needed it.

When I'd finished, I found Steve in high spirits. 'You'll never guess what your new friend Harry's just told me.'

'No, but it seems to be something good. I'm hoping it means Saskia's not being pimped out by her dad?'

'Not only that, at least as far as Harry knows, but he's heard that this Karl is the go-to-person for cheap cigarettes.'

'Interesting!'

'Yes it is, because if the Spalding police haul him in for questioning about possible prostitution, he might well come clean on selling the cigarettes as he wouldn't see that as anywhere near as serious as being accused of pimping his daughter out to local men - and he might just tell us where he's getting them from. It could be off the docks in Grimsby, but I'm betting it's from Hull, on one of those lorries from Rotterdam or Zeebrugge. If he comes originally from Poland, he may even have contacts in Eastern Europe. The Border Force would be

254

very interested in any information we could glean for them from that quarter.'

'Would he know anyone involved in the operation you've just closed down?'

'Possibly. He may know some of the people on the ground in Hull. The ones who escaped the net because they were small fry and we didn't have their names.'

'That'd be good. More arrests means less bad guys out there and more credit for my Steve.'

'I don't want to get your hopes up, but there's always the chance one of them might just know where Nick's now being held, and give up the information to evade jail. I'd rather one of them goes free than Bradfield, wouldn't you?'

'So, it's a win-win tonight. Fancy nipping to the shop for wine and chocolate to celebrate possible good news?'

'You want me to be your slave now, eh?' Steve pulled me down onto his knee.

'Unless you want your fiancé waltzing round the streets wearing a flimsy nightie and dressing-gown, then you'd better do as I ask.'

'And would my mistress like salted caramel or mint in her chocolate this evening?'

'I'll let you choose. I'm feeling generous, now we're almost sure Saskia's not been mistreated quite as badly as we thought.'

'OK. Your wish is my command. I'll be back soon.'

I'd arranged to go looking at wedding dresses with Sarah and was up early the next day so we could get around the shops whilst they were quiet, as she doesn't like to leave Josh with her mum for too long.

We ended up going to three shops, as I couldn't find anything that said "Rach's dream dress". I was tired of fending off the assistants who were coming up with ever more unsuitable choices, and when I realised I was trying to convince myself that the dress I was trying on would be OK, I decided I'd had enough.

'I'm so sorry for dragging you all over and not being able to make up my mind, Sarah.'

'Forgive my saying this, but I get the feeling you're clutching at straws when you say this dress is the nicest we've seen. You don't really like it that much, do you?'

'You're right. It's just the best of the whole mediocre bunch. Oh, Sarah, am I that hard to please?'

'Fashions change, Rach, and this year's wedding dresses are not to your taste, that's all. It's just like shoes, T-shirts or whatever. I'm still looking for a decent cardi, and wishing like mad I'd bought about ten while they were in the shops the other year. These new styles of cardigan have no buttons, and in the winds we get around here, they're useless to keep the draught off.'

'But I need a wedding dress. I can't wait for the fashions to change again.'

'Well, you dragged me into those vintage shops when I was looking for a nice frock for a special night out. Maybe we can come up with either a wedding dress or something stunning that would be suitable?'

'I suppose it's a thought, but my feet are killing me, I've seen too many dresses to know what I want any more, and I can't keep you away from Josh any longer, so let's call it a day.'

'OK, if you're sure you want to give up for today, then it's back to mine for a hot chocolate with some of those nice mini marshmallows I got at that bargain shop on Holderness Road.'

'Hi Rach. How did you get on?' One look at my face told Steve everything he needed to know. 'That bad, eh? Well, I've got a bit of news that might cheer you up. I've managed to wangle it so Karl Janowski gets brought up here for questioning in connection with possible counterfeit cigarette dealing, and the best bit is, he said he wasn't leaving his daughter in Spalding on her own and he might need her to interpret for him anyway. That means she'll be at the station in the morning. Are you free tomorrow?'

'I've nothing that can't wait. Do you think he'll let her out of his sight long enough for me to talk to her?'

'He won't have a choice. He'll be in custody when he gets here until a duty solicitor arrives for the interview, and they can take an hour or so to arrive. I've spoken to Sally, a mate of Matt's who works in Welfare, and she said she'd sit in with you while you talked to Saskia. She's not under arrest, so it would just be a friendly chat about her situation, with no need for a police officer to be present. Sally's often called upon when people from Poland have welfare problems, as she speaks a bit of the language. Her great-grandad flew spitfires during the war, and he settled here, but the family still have links over there.'

'Do you think I can tell Saskia she might have been abducted?'

'Not straight out, Rach, but if she admits to being unhappy with her dad, you might be able to bring the conversation round to why you're interested in her, and see where it goes from there. The very least you can do is explain to her about the poster she saw in the cafe. She must have panicked when she saw a picture of someone who looked like her. She probably didn't look at it closely, but thought it was some kind of "wanted" poster.'

'Yes, Maybe when the punters come she answers the door and hands over the cigarettes, in which case she'll be scared she's in trouble and will be glad to hear she's not. Could I offer a DNA test?'

'I don't see why not, although if she accepts, you'd have to ask Sally to bring in Matt and he'll square it with the police in March. They'll still have the abduction case open, even though it's not been actively investigated for years. It's a cold case like you see on the TV.'

'They didn't take DNA at the time, remember. I got the samples to check against Kate's DNA.'

'OK. You'd need to give Matt the contact details for the company you used.'

'I'll just get them.'

I was so happy. Gone were the negative thoughts from the

257

morning. The perfect dress just isn't important in the grand scheme of things.

CHAPTER 42

The next day went like a dream. Saskia did look quite a lot like the poster I'd had printed, although there were differences. She was scared and confused at first, but having someone there who spoke Polish was fantastic, and when she realised that her dad might go to prison, and so she wouldn't have to live with him any longer, she opened up and told us that her dad had always been cruel and never showed any signs of loving her, but since her mum died, it had been awful.

As a child he'd hit her regularly with a belt, but now he treated her like a skivvy as well, and worse, he hardly let her out of his sight except to go shopping and claim her benefit money. She'd wanted to get some extra qualifications, but he wouldn't let her go to college, and with no money or transport, she couldn't do it without his agreement .She'd tried to run away twice but his mates had helped Karl find her, and then he'd literally chained her up and beaten her until she was bruised and bleeding.

When I heard that, I couldn't help myself. 'What would you say if I told you that you could leave Spalding and live with a nice lady, her husband and young son in Ely?' I shouldn't have said that until she'd had a matching DNA result and she hadn't even had the test yet, but I just couldn't keep the question I was bursting to ask inside my head.

'Is that as a servant or nanny? I have no experience with children, but I could try. I would be happy to be a servant as long as I don't get beaten and if maybe I have a few pounds of my own.'

I took a deep breath and explained why I had put the posters up: that I was looking for a girl her age, who looked a lot like her - a girl who had been taken from her mother as a baby. I told her that someone in Spalding had told me that her mum and dad, Sonja and Karl, had suddenly got a baby the year this baby had been stolen, even though no-one thought Sonja had been pregnant, and there was a chance it might be her.

'I'm hoping you might agree to take a test so we can find out if you are that baby. Do you understand about DNA testing?'

'Yes. I will do it. Even if there is only a tiny chance. Can I do it today?'

I looked at Sally and she nodded, and slipped out of the room to fetch a policewoman with a sterile DNA test kit. After the swab had been taken, Saskia broke down and cried. She kept saying, 'I pray. I pray.' I couldn't help but feel the same. We would both be devastated if it wasn't a match for Claire's DNA.

'I'm sorry but you have to decide if you want to sit in with your dad, I mean Karl Janowski, while he's interviewed. You don't have to. You're eighteen and under no obligation, whether he's your dad or not.' Steve and I had already discussed the possibility that she would decide to refuse, so when I nipped outside to ring him to confirm she was no longer willing, Steve had a Polish translator standing by. I also told him about the abuse.

'I'm absolutely livid that bloody Janowski chained up and beat his own daughter like a dog. I'm not a violent man, but even I feel like putting my hands round his fat throat and squeezing. However, I have to say that it's a great help, Rach. Even though it was horrible for Saskia, it means we can charge Janowski with domestic abuse and keep him in the cells while we push him on the smuggling angle. I'll give Matt a shout before I go into the interview room. If you can give him the details of the laboratory that has Claire's DNA profile, then he'll make a formal request for it to be sent over here as soon as possible. In the meantime our lab can test Saskia's DNA and then they'll compare the two when Claire's arrives. He'll also inform March police that we may have a result on their cold case of Mandy's abduction. I presume Saskia will stay around for the result?'

I asked Saskia if she wanted to go home to Spalding or stay in Hull in a B&B until we got the comparison result, which would hopefully be the next day, although it could take up to forty-eight hours. She wanted to pay but I knew she had very little money and was happy to settle her bill for the B&B myself if it meant I could give her the DNA result in person.

'Thank you so much. I will stay – and when I can, I will repay you. I promise.'

Later that night I found it hard to relax. 'I'm scared it'll all turn out to be my imagination running away with me, thinking Saskia is Mandy.'

'I'm keeping everything crossed, Rach, and I do have to say Saskia does look remarkably like that photo on your poster.'

'Do you think so too? I was wondering if I was seeing the resemblance because I wanted it to be there.'

'But those people in Lincolnshire thought the photo looked like her, didn't they? And look what you've done for Saskia. You've got her away from an abusive man, who'll at the very least get a suspended sentence with probation, and a restraining order to keep him away.'

'Will that work?'

'In this case, yes, I'm fairly sure. It'd be too much hassle for him to track her down and he'd be running the risk of going to jail. He'll find other ways of making money, rather than relying on her benefit payments when he's not working. Gambling, maybe, something like that. Come over here and let's have a cuddle. I'll wash up later.'

I was awake early in the morning so managed to get a word with Steve before his early start.

'I've just looked at the calendar, Steve. I can't believe it's almost the end of October. It's been a fortnight since I left Nick behind in that house. That's on top of the time they had him locked up before then.

'Yes, I know. It's a good job I went round to speak to Nick's girlfriend Karen after you spoke to him in that cellar, and reassured her he was alive and well and working undercover.'

'And what now, Steve?'

'Now he's a vital cog in an extremely sensitive operation. She was very understanding, particularly now she knows for certain he hasn't gone off with anyone else, and that he'll likely get a commendation at the end of it, and a big boost to his career prospects.'

'I hope you get somewhere with Karl today, though.'

'So do I. As it is, I think I only put the Chief off for a couple of days before he capitulates to Bradfield's demands in exchange for Nick's recovery. But I think a night in the cells might well get Karl to name names. He'll have been able to think over what it means to have a criminal record. What are you doing, love?'

'I thought I'd take Saskia shopping. I'm sure she'd like to browse some vintage shops with me. I'm hoping they'll be a better place to find the perfect wedding dress. I just can't see myself in anything I've seen so far in those bridal shops.

'Good hunting, then! I'll try to give you a quick ring if I hear anything, but I can't promise.'

I picked Saskia up from the B&B. As expected, she was a bit on edge waiting to hear if we'd found her real mum, and seized upon the idea of wedding dress shopping as a welcome distraction. We parked up near a place I'd been to before with Sarah, and were soon browsing the rails. There were some nice things and I was tempted by a few, but nothing that yelled 'wedding dress' at me, so we moved on to a charity shop that specialised in wedding and prom dresses. Again no luck. I was flagging and we were about to give up, when a lady behind the counter suggested another shop that hadn't been open long.

We took a break for a cuppa. 'You haven't had a call. They must not be able to match the DNA,' Saskia said sadly.

'It's probably just too early for them to have done it. They had to test yours before comparing it with Claire's and they must have a lot of work on. Don't worry.' To be honest, I was concerned it was taking so long, so I was reassuring myself as much as her. 'Let's go to this other shop. It's not that far away.'

It was more of an antique centre, but some of the dealers had clothes. We'd just gone upstairs and into the first room off the landing and I knew I'd found it. 'Saskia, look. It's perfect!'

'Is it the right size?'

'Yes, it's a 12. Amazing! Can you see how much it costs?'

'The tag's down here. Seventy pounds. That's a very good price I think for a dress like this. Look at the pearls on the bottom!'

'That's what drew my eye to it straightaway. It's gorgeous!' The hem was a series of points, each with a large pearl, natural pearls by the look of them. There were pearls dotted about over the lace overlay on the body of the dress, and the colour was a lovely cream. It was pretty and elaborate enough for a wedding dress, without being a white confection that shouted at you.

'There's nowhere to try it on.'

'Doesn't matter. It should fit. If it doesn't, my Auntie Lesley should be able to adjust it though. See, it's got this little bolero thing made of the same material. I don't even have to think about it. It's mine. Let's go pay for it.'

We had lunch in a little Italian restaurant nearby. I kept pinching myself about how lucky I'd been to find that particular dress. It was a one-off, just waiting for the right person to buy it.

'If you're busy, I can go back to the hotel?'

'No, Saskia, I'm not. Tell you what - we'll have a walk round the lake at East Park. I haven't been for ages. In fact, the last time was probably around Easter when I took my nephews and got drenched on the splash-boat. We ran into a friend just after we got off and I remember how embarrassed I was to be caught with my nipples showing through a wet t-shirt.'

Saskia giggled while I thought back to that day. Pete had certainly been taken by surprise to see so much of me. Funny how I considered choosing him over Steve. How times change… The brisk walk did us both good. It was chilly but fine, with a watery sun. It's a large lake and we watched the ducks and the geese. We'd just spotted a swan when my mobile rang. It was Steve. I walked away a little to take the call.

'Rach, great news! The DNA comparison result's arrived on my desk and it's a match! I thought you'd want to tell her yourself.'

'Oh, Steve, that's fantastic. Can we come into the station to get something in writing? Saskia won't believe it otherwise, I don't think. She keeps saying it won't be true because it would be more than a miracle.'

'Good idea. I can't stay on long, but I was called out of the interview room to be given the news, and I just had to ring you.'

'Why did they call you out? I'm glad they did, but …'

'The importance being, that Karl and his wife stole Mandy and brought her up as Saskia. She's no relative of his, so we can charge him with abduction and false imprisonment, as well as domestic abuse. He was holding out on us, probably because he would have got off on probation at the most on the domestic abuse charge, but the three charges will definitely mean a custodial sentence.'

'Right. So he'll lose his freedom.'

'Yes. I'm going back in there now to tell him, and we'll see what the duty solicitor advises him, but I'm betting it's to come clean about the cigarette suppliers to get at least one of the charges dropped for less jail time or probation.'

'Go, then! I'm off to tell Saskia and then we'll nip in to the station for the official result. Then I'll treat us to cake. Afterwards I'll ring Claire. That's one conversation I've been looking forward to for a very long time.'

As expected, Saskia was over the moon, and soon in tears of happiness. She kept asking, 'Are you sure it's true?' right up until the moment the results were in her hands. Then when it had sunk in, she wanted to know more about Claire. I took her for cake in a nearby café I love, and I told her what little I actually knew about Claire and her family. 'What if she doesn't want to meet me? Maybe her new husband will not allow it. I'm not his daughter, after all…'

It took a while to settle her down. I think it was the fact that she needn't ever see Karl again that finally broke through to her. 'Even if this Claire doesn't like me, I can live on my own. Do you mind if I ring a girl friend I see sometimes, please, and tell her?'

'Go ahead. I'll ring Claire.' We moved out into the marketplace where we could both speak easily.

CHAPTER 43

Claire answered the phone after a couple of rings. I hadn't spoken to her for a week; I'd looked it up on the calendar that morning, but her first words were, 'Did anyone recognise her from the poster? Have you any leads on my Mandy?'

'Yes, and better still, I've found her - and before you ask, she's definitely your daughter. I waited until the DNA comparison result was back before ringing you. I didn't want to get your hopes up if it came to nothing. That's why I've not been in touch for so long.'

Claire started crying. I realised I should probably have gone in person, and I'd been too eager to hear her reaction.

'I'm sorry, Claire. Do you want me to ring you back? I've just this minute heard myself and didn't think things through properly.'

'No, please don't go. I'm just so happy. I want to hear everything.'

'Well, I can bring her down tomorrow if you'd like and you can hear the whole story. I know you're dying to hear how I found her and where she's been, but it'll be better if we can all talk together, I think. She's in Hull at the moment but she's been living in Spalding. Any chance we can meet there, please, then it's not so far for me to drive?'

'That would be fantastic! I'll get my mum to have Kieran.'

'Great. Shall we say about ten o'clock? We can meet at the café whose owner helped me find Saskia. That's the name Mandy was given. I'll text you the address and ring you when we get there.'

'Saskia. That's a pretty name. I can't wait.'

266

We said our goodbyes and then I told Saskia what Claire had said. 'She really wants to meet me? And I'm really called Mandy?'

'Yes, I've arranged to drive you down tomorrow, and don't worry, I'm sure she won't mind whatever you call yourself. Another good thing, you'll finally be able to get proper official documents in the name of Amanda Bateman and then change it if you wish. You can apply for a passport, travel the world.' The tears started again. I couldn't take her back to the B&B in that state, so I decided to take her round to Mum's.

Mum listened to all the story and I think it helped Saskia to listen to it again and for Mum to give her a big hug. It also gave me chance to show Mum the dress I'd chosen for the wedding. She loved it too. 'Oh, that lace is gorgeous! And I bet those pearls are worth a bit. You'll look lovely in it. Are you going to try it on?'

'I'm dying to. I haven't had chance since I bought it this morning.' Five minutes later I was despairing. 'It doesn't fit.'

'Not to worry. They've changed all the sizes. What's now a 12 used to be a 10 when this dress was made. Here's the label. It's a good make, but I could tell that by the pearls. It's by Frank Usher, and it looks to be from the seventies or thereabouts. He's a famous designer. You've bought well, Rachel.'

'Really?'

'Yes. Now you can't see round the back but the bodice fits fine, and with the gathers, the hips are OK too. It's only round the waist there's a problem. I'll ring our Lesley.'

'Thanks. Maybe she can do something with the extra material from the little jacket-thing, because I wasn't planning on wearing that.'

Mum rang and came back to report that Auntie Lesley was free. In fact she was on her way, armed with her sewing box.

'That's fantastic. It'd be great if she could pin it while I'm here, then I could leave it with her to alter. I don't want Steve to see it, and there aren't many places to hide things in the flat. Mine'll be gone soon. I've had an offer on it. Did I tell you?'

My auntie came and everyone mucked in and helped think how best to alter the dress. Before I knew it, it was six o'clock. They were all getting on like a house on fire. Mum decided there and then that Saskia shouldn't have to go back to the B&B, so while she made the tea, Dad drove Saskia to get her things and check out. 'You can call for her early in the morning. She can sleep in your old room tonight.'

'Is that OK, Saskia?'

'It's wonderful. I've never had such fun and your family care like mine never did.'

What more can I say? I know how lucky I am. I drove home to cook Steve his tea, tell him I'd got a wonderful dress and ask him how things had gone with Saskia's so-called father.

Unsurprisingly, Steve wasn't home, but that probably meant he was getting somewhere. I'd had lunch, cake and the odd biscuit at Mum's, so I wasn't hungry yet. To tell the truth, I was so stuffed, even I didn't think I could eat another thing. Steve could have a pizza if he hadn't eaten.

I was worn out. I sat down with a book, and must have fallen asleep because when I woke, Steve was in the kitchen making a drink. 'What time is it?'

'Half eight. Sorry if I woke you.'

'I'm glad you did or I wouldn't have got any sleep later. I must have dropped off reading. It was such a hectic day, but a great one.'

'I've had a great one too. It seems it was none other than Craig Dobson who was the one who'd been down in Lincolnshire touting for business, which told me we were onto the right gang. Karl went on to tell me the names of two delivery blokes who came regularly, and gave us their mobile numbers. We tracked their phones and one came up off Spring Bank, not far from where you were held. The other was off Anlaby Road, so not that far away.'

'Interesting.'

'Yeah. I managed to get a couple of cars out to go and knock on the doors at the same time, and they must have been lying low after their names didn't come up in the raid, because Gary Thorpe was watching TV and Paul Johnson was at his mother's. We searched the houses but didn't come up with anything.'

'Damn!'

'Wait. There's more. When we got them in the station, you could tell one of them hadn't much in the way of brains. This Johnson lad blurted out that he'd had nothing to do with the gang since he'd heard Craig had disappeared. I told him he'd been consorting with a vicious criminal who had murdered two people, and we suspected he must have had help. He went white as a sheet then and said he wasn't involved in any murders.'

'And…'

'To cut a long story short, he told us everything he knew, naming names and places. There were a couple of addresses we didn't know of; storage yards and the like where they met with Craig or someone else to transfer a few boxes of cigs from a lorry to their van for delivery to other areas like Lincolnshire. He didn't know how the cigs got in the lorry. He was obviously just a lowlife who didn't know where the cigs originally came from.'

'Is this the short story, because it seems pretty long to me?'

'Don't be cheeky. I'm giving this the big build-up, just omitting the detail.' He grinned.

'Did you make any significant arrests, that's what I want to know: anyone who might know where Nick is?'

'Yes. Turns out these two were the ones guarding Nick.'

'So who's watching him now? I presume by your grin that he hasn't been killed?'

'He's in the bathroom.'

'Don't be daft. You do know, don't you? I mean, you have sent blokes to free him? If you've given me all this build-up and he's still locked up somewhere and you don't know where…'

At that moment a noise behind startled me and I looked round to see a sheepish young lad wrapped only in a towel. 'I did tell you he was in the bathroom but you wouldn't believe me.'

'Hi, Rachel. Nice to see you. I won't shake hands because…'
He gestured downwards to where he was holding the towel.

'Hello, Nick. So, we meet again. Well, I suppose we never really met properly last time.'

'I'll just get you something to wear and then you'll be presentable for your big reunion with Karen.' Steve disappeared into the bedroom.

'It's so good of you to let me clean up at your flat before I go home. I didn't want Karen to see me looking such a filthy mess, and Inspector Rose was kind enough to suggest I called here to have a shower and get a change of clothes.'

After a bit of drawer-banging, Steve returned with a t-shirt and some tracksuit bottoms. 'Would you believe Johnson only lived two doors down from his mum? And that's where we found Nick, sleeping on a mattress in the locked brick outhouse. They'd been feeding him well and even gave him a duvet when it started to get really cold at the weekend.'

'Yeah. It wasn't that bad. Johnson was the decent one who fed you. It was just incredibly boring and I had to force myself to go through a series of exercises or I wouldn't be able to move now. I'll be so glad to get home.'

'Have you spoken to Karen?'

'Yes. She knows I'm on my way. I told her I had to be de-briefed first.'

'Well, it looks like you have been,' I said, glancing down at the towel. 'Go get dressed, and then I'll heat you both up a pizza - unless you're going home to eat?'

'No, I really need a bit more info from Nick about his meetings with Simon Crawford and how they found out Bradfield was involved. I need a bit of ammunition before I see the Chief tomorrow so he can decide how he's going to deal with him.'

'Right-oh. Will I be in the way?'

'No. It's fine. We can talk in the kitchen while we eat. Nick'll be interviewed in full over the next few days, but we're giving him tomorrow off. You put TV on, read or whatever, if you don't mind. I can warm up the pizza and make notes while it's cooking.'

Nick had re-appeared in the t-shirt and track pants of Steve's. 'It was nice of you to offer to cook, Rachel, and good of the inspector to do it. I'm looking forward to hearing how you got away, if you can bear to re-live it again sometime.'

'Heating a pizza's not really cooking and there's not a lot to tell really, but thanks.'

'What about grabbing some kid's phone in the Ghost Train at Hull Fair?' Steve insisted.

'OK. Speaking of which, I hope you throw the book at that Gary Thorpe. He must be the one who chased me. Anyway, you two get on with it. I'm getting back to my book, otherwise poor Nick'll never get fed or home to Karen.'

Later, after Steve had dropped off Nick to have a long-overdue reunion with Karen, and to ring his brother and anyone else who might have wondered why he'd not been in touch, Steve and I celebrated.

'We're not getting too old, or bored with each other, are we?'

'What do you mean? We're not even married yet!' I protested.

'Well it's chocolate and wine instead of passionate sex.'

'I didn't realise it had to be one or the other, Steve.'

'I've finished my wine and eaten my share of the chocolate, so we could do both. But you've got some left.'

'Very funny, Steve. I'm not leaving my chocolate!'

'I wouldn't dare suggest that! Anyway, it's supposed to be an aphrodisiac, isn't it?'

'It's got caffeine in, I know that. I'm awake and raring to go now. Get your kit off. You've pulled!'

'But you said you had an early start?'

'Are you suggesting I'm past it? I'll show you.' Steve made a run for the bedroom but I got to him first and we ended up in a tangle of limbs on the floor. He started tickling me and then we undressed each other one item of clothing at a time. We took our time and when I peeped at the clock as I went to the loo, I wasn't surprised to see it said half past one.

CHAPTER 44

In the morning, I crawled out of bed and ate my unfinished chocolate for breakfast. It was six thirty.

'Why had I suggested such an early start,' I asked myself?

I picked up Saskia from Mum's and we were on the road by seven o'clock. It was a good two to three hours' drive and we had to get over the Humber Bridge and through work and school traffic. Luckily the bridge was quiet going south to Lincolnshire at that time, though there were big queues heading towards Hull. As I saw the sign for the country park in the shadow of the bridge, I couldn't help but remember one of my first cases, which had led eventually to my being taken prisoner by Craig Dobson. Poor Terry Rogers had died of a heart attack there when Craig tortured him for information. I'd found his body with a stiletto heel in his eye, thankfully inserted after death, to give the false impression a woman had been involved. At least his tormentor had got what he deserved now.

We arrived at the café in plenty of time. The owner was there. 'Today's the first time I've ever seen you looking happy, young lady,' he told Saskia.

'That's because I am, and it's mainly down to you and your phone call to Rachel. Today I am meeting my real mother. I learnt yesterday that Karl Janowski stole me from a car boot sale in March and took me back to Spalding so he could get Sonja, the woman I knew as my mother, to bring me up and they could claim child benefit and be allowed to stay in this country.'

'You're joking? That's awful. Let me get you both a cup of tea. I'm Harry, by the way.'

'It's over now. I can't get back the missing years, and to be

273

honest it's only been since Sonja died that things have been really bad. Sonja stopped him hitting me most of the time. The others on the farm were kind but they were too afraid of Karl to say or do anything. I'm just glad that he's out of my life and I'm going to be reunited with my real mother.'

'That's brilliant. But how did it come about after all this time?'

I told him about my search for Kate's real parents and how it had led to Claire. 'You're a bloody miracle worker, you are, love, if you'll pardon my language.'

'Yes, she is. I'll never be able to thank her enough.'

'Give over. It's my job, but as for you, Harry, not everyone would have got involved. I'm so grateful. I must reward you in some way.'

'Thank you but it really isn't necessary. My reward is seeing you ladies smile. Excuse me though, I must…'

'No problem. Serve your other customers and can you get us a toasted teacake each to go with our tea as well, please?'

It was a good job we'd told Harry the crux of Saskia's story, because otherwise he'd have thought a disaster had occurred when Claire arrived. After she'd hugged Saskia, they were both in floods of tears. Thoughtfully he popped into the back and returned with a box of tissues. I was wondering if I should have chosen a less public place for their first meeting but Claire's home in Ely was a bit of a distance when we'd already come from Hull.

I needn't have worried because the tears soon dried and Claire opened her bag to show Saskia the few photos she had of her as a baby. Then I was able to produce the teddy in the bag that I'd sent for testing. I'd almost forgotten I still had it, but had managed to dig it out that morning. Naturally, Saskia didn't remember it, but I'd learnt by then that she was a very thoughtful girl and she said, 'I don't know why, but I can feel a connection somehow,' which made Claire's face light up.

'Well, I could never have thrown him away, but I didn't in my wildest dreams ever imagine he might one day bring you

274

back.'

I told Claire all about how I'd managed to find Saskia, and she in turn told her mum a little of her life over the last eighteen years. 'I have some photos, just a few, of me as a child, if you would like to see them?'

'Yes, I'd like that.'

'Look, as it's almost lunchtime, why don't we have a bite to eat and then I can run you both to where Saskia's been living and she can show you them. I really ought to get on my way back soon and I'm sure you have plenty more to talk about without me in the way.'

As if he'd read my mind, Harry came over with plates of sandwiches. 'On the house, ladies. I've brought a selection. I didn't know what you'd like.' He waved away our opened purses and protestations, and we turned to the food. I had to admit, toasted teacake or not, I was starving. All this emotion, it takes it out of you.

'But surely you're coming home with me, Mandy, sorry, Saskia?'

'Mandy's lovely, thanks, but I didn't think you'd want me to come to your house until you had spoken with your husband, and I'm not sure what the future will be for me.'

'I don't want to make your mind up for you, love, but Darren and I talked about it last night and he agrees wholeheartedly. We'd both love you to come and live with us and Kieran. I know you must have friends here and work or college, so it's up to you. You can just come to visit. I don't want to overwhelm you and it might be a bit much, meeting the whole family at once, though my mum, your grandma, she's dying to see you. She was with me when you were taken. But it's up to you. I just want you to know I've never stopped loving you and I will always love you.' Saskia started crying again. 'Oh, sorry, I've rambled on and set us off again.'

'It's not that I don't want to come and live with you. I would like nothing better. I haven't really any friends here, only one girl I know. Karl made me stay in the caravan and I had no job or college. I just want to be sure you are not asking me because you feel you have to, because Rachel has suddenly found me.'

'But I only stopped looking because the police told me there was no point and I didn't have any money for a private detective. I never gave up hoping I'd find you. Kieran isn't a substitute for you. He's your brother. I want you both.'

'Then, yes, please. I will certainly come today and meet everyone, maybe stay a day or two, if that is OK? Then I will come back and sort things out here. I could get a place of my own so I'm not in the way, but still see you lots and lots. If there's any way you could help me, I'd be so grateful. I can help you with little Kieran, and maybe train as a nursery nurse. Before my mother, sorry, Sonja, died, I often helped the other mothers in their caravans with their babies and small children.'

'That would be wonderful. Just as long as you know that you wouldn't have to get your own place if you didn't want to. But I can see that now you're grown-up, that's something you should have. It's hard to think of you other than as a little girl.'

'I understand. It will take us both time to work it out.'

'I'm sure you both will. I'm sorry, but I'm going to leave you now. Do please keep in touch, and have a safe drive home. No floods of tears at the wheel, eh, Claire?'

'Don't worry, Rachel. I'll be fine when I get driving. And, by the way, let me know how much the posters were, and I'll pay you for them and for your time.'

'No, Claire. I wouldn't dream of taking your money. This has been the most wonderful early wedding present anyone could wish for. Don't ever mention paying again. Go off, and have happy lives.' And with that, I left them. I just managed to hold it together until I got back in the car before I had to shed a few tears of happiness too.

That day was full of surprises. Faced with the release of Nick and his testimony, the belated release of the news that Craig Dobson's body had been found, and the fact that he was now accused of murder, Tommy Bradfield folded and gave up the name of the very top boss in the smuggling ring - his old inspector at the East Hull police station, Roger Griffiths. Although not in Serious Crimes, he dealt with managers at nearby King George's dock on a regular basis in connection with crimes other than those concerning Border Force, such as theft, criminal damage and disturbances. 'That put the cat among the pigeons, and no mistake!' Steve told me when he rang in the afternoon.

'I had to go and fetch the Superintendent so he could hear the accusation. He got a statement and then left to confront and arrest him. As Inspector Griffiths is the highest-ranking officer at that station, it had to be someone of higher rank outside who officially made the arrest.'

'Wow!'

'Yes. "Wow", indeed. I don't know what went on down there but I can imagine the Super relished rolling his sleeves up and making an arrest for once. Anyway, Michelle and I carried on questioning Bradfield. He said he never expected you to turn up on Holderness Road near Craig Dobson's house, and certainly not to get involved. He said that when he told you he was ringing the station for back-up, he was actually on the phone to Dobson to tell him he was being followed. Instead of doing a runner as Bradfield had expected, Dobson must've taken it into his head to act as impulsively as he usually did, hit you over the head and dragged you into his house.'

'I expect he enjoyed getting his revenge on me for freeing his girlfriend Lucy from that cellar, and making him go on the run, a year or so ago?'

'Maybe. Or maybe it was just because you were following him and he thought you'd ring me. Anyway, when you didn't reappear, Bradfield turned up at Dobson's house, hoping that you'd lost his trail. He couldn't understand where you'd got to, but he presumed Dobson would be laying low out of sight in the house. When he found out what Dobson had done, and that he was insisting that you should be killed, Bradfield started arguing with him. He was angry that things were escalating out of his

277

control again. He'd never intended anyone should get hurt - not Simon Crawford nor Dean Hornby.'

'Well, he would say that.'

'Yes, but I actually believed him. He was only in it for the money. Anyway, Bradfield was adamant he never intended to kill Dobson. Said it was an accident. They argued. He said he was furious Dobson had endangered the whole smuggling operation. Dobson hit him and they ended up fighting. Bradfield pushed him away at one point and Dobson fell against the fireplace, hitting his head.'

'I suppose I can believe that.'

'Bradfield said he had to kidnap you because otherwise you'd tell me what you knew. Of course, he could have pretended that he'd followed you and seen Dobson hit you, then tackled him and he fell and we might have believed him, but he panicked. Who knows, we might have discovered some clue that led us to the smuggling ring in Dobson's house. As it was, he kidnapped you to keep you out of the way for the following ten days, reasoning that you would think Dobson had taken you.'

'Which I did until Nick told me otherwise.'

'Exactly. He was gobsmacked when you got out the very next day, but he didn't know we'd found Dobson's body because Matt and I said you didn't know which of the many terrace houses you were kidnapped from, so we couldn't search for clues. I have to say he was relieved you and Nick were unharmed, though he insisted that was mainly down to him for picking your guards himself.'

'Well one was nice, but the other was a thug. I hope you'll ask for clemency or whatever it's called for the nice one. I think you said his name was Johnson?'

'I'll try, love.'

CHAPTER 45

Steve was as pleased as I was, after I'd told him how the reunion between Claire and her missing daughter had gone. 'I hope I'm correct in assuming you dried your eyes before setting off to drive home?' he asked with a grin.

'Ever the policeman, eh?' I gave him a big hug, particularly for saying I was right not to charge Claire and Saskia anything for my services.

'Do you think Saskia will change her name to Mandy?'

'I'm not sure really. A surname's one thing - although you do know I'm not changing mine when we're married, don't you?'

'Yes, you know I do, and I agree. It's an outdated custom, nothing more, though I don't think we should kick up a fuss if some people send us Christmas cards to Mr and Mrs Rose.'

'Agreed.'

'Good. It seems funny to some people putting both names on an envelope. I don't think they're being awkward, more that they're unsure of the right thing to put.'

'It might be hard for Saskia to start answering to another name at the age of eighteen, even if it is her real name.'

'I expect she'll take a while to decide. You did say Claire didn't sound like she'd be put out if she decided on Saskia rather than Mandy, didn't you?'

'Yes. I'm so glad it worked out well and I was able to reunite them, but it's funny having no new or old cases left to work on. It's so long since I didn't always have that as a case in reserve, so to speak. I better see if there's anything else I can be doing for the wedding. Do you think it's too early to send out invitations? I've been wondering about inviting Kate and Saskia. What do you think?'

'Ah, well, I was going to talk to you about that, and this.' He waved the slim blue folder he'd had in his hand when he'd got home.

'That sounds ominous. Please tell me you've not got transferred abroad like that policeman in "Death in Paradise".'

'No, nothing like that. But you know we joked about having the wedding before Christmas so we could fly over to Germany with Kate because she's bit worried about travelling all that way on her own.'

'Yes. We even talked about going to visit a Christmas market, but it was just a bit of a laugh. There was no way we'd be able to make arrangements at such short notice.'

'That's where you're wrong, Rach. This folder contains all the booking details for a wedding at Ravenspurn Hall, the same place we booked, with catering, a registrar, a disco, hire cars, and even suit hire and flowers, except I think we'd want to keep those that you've picked.'

'Whatever do you mean?'

'Lee, one of my constables, he's had to call his wedding off. He's the one who told me about Ravenspurn Hall starting to do weddings. He was going to lose all his cash, and the entire wedding was going begging. I sort of told him we'd take it over. I hope you don't mind. In fact I hoped you'd be thrilled, actually.'

'I'm stunned. That's what I am. You told him without asking me!!?'

'Sort of. I thought you'd be pleased, Rach.'

'When is this wedding not taking place and why's he called it off? If he's had a tiff with his fiancée, she might change her mind, and it'll be back on again.'

'No, it won't. She's eloped with someone she met on a course from work.'

'Poor Lee.'

'Well, yes. But better he knows now than if she left him standing at the altar.'

'True.'

'But her parents are dead, so Lee took out a loan to pay for the wedding of her dreams, and now he's going to lose it all, and still have to pay it off, on top of being humiliated by Rose-whatever-her-name-is. I know it's short notice, love, but I felt so sorry for him, and not only is it the place we'd booked anyway, but we did talk about marrying before Christmas.'

'Ok then. What the hell. Let's do it! If Lee's had to pay for everything for … when did you say it was?'

'I didn't, but its Saturday November 25th.'

'…OK. Well, we can just pay Lee the lot and I presume it's such a long way off that the hall will refund our deposit for next May.

'I expect they will. We'll be saving them a lost booking with all the drinks sales.'

'And we've not paid anything else apart from the deposit for the registrar. But will they let us change the date that easily, Steve? Don't we have to give so many weeks' notice, like having the Banns read in church?'

'No idea, but I think there's enough time. We've got almost a month. You are taking this remarkably well, Rach. For a minute I thought you were going to blow your top.'

'Come on, Steve. I was just taken aback that you didn't ring me first, but I've been driving all afternoon and I know you wouldn't ring me while I'm driving. Plus, I think it's a marvellous idea!!! All the waiting's just a pain. I've got my dress, well, I will have when Auntie Lesley's waved her magic wand, and I've got no new cases and we can be married ready to move into our new house when it goes ahead.'

'I thought we could try and combine a German Christmas market with a trip to Denmark. Come to think of it, that'll probably be the only difficult part of getting organised in three or four weeks, but it's before the Christmas rush, and after half term, so there might be some free seats. Do you think you can see if Kate could travel with us then? She should have the confidence to come back on her own.'

'I'll manage something. I'll have to do the invitations tomorrow morning, though. Does it matter what sort of paper they're on? And who are we going to invite? It'll be an excuse not to have a big do, I suppose, as not everyone will be able to come at such short notice - how many was Lee having?' I reached out for the blue folder, but Steve couldn't stop laughing. He held it up in the air, out of my reach and gave me a big kiss.

'That can wait until tomorrow. I do love you, Rachel Hodges. You're the only woman I know who would accept her wedding day being moved forward six months or so. You're totally crazy but I don't care. I wouldn't have you any different.'

'So it's sex again tonight then? I'm going to need some more of that magic chocolate first.'

'We're all out of it, Rach, but I'll nip to the shops.'

'Are any open?'

'I'll find one. If necessary I'll knock someone up on some legal pretext and force the owner to hand it over.'

I met Kate for coffee, as arranged, to see the photos she took when Renate had visited. I also had another task in mind, but amazingly I managed to avoid blurting it out the minute we sat down. She took out her phone and proudly showed me what her mum looked like. There was quite a resemblance and I could tell she was happy when I told her so.

Then I decided to take the bull by the horns and tell her about our new wedding date.

'I know you're a bit worried about travelling on your own to Germany the first time, so we were wondering if you could bring the date forward to the end of November and go with us. We fancied flying over, hiring a car and driving up to Denmark. Then we'd come back down to Hamburg for the Christmas markets.'

'That sounds great, Rachel. I'm not sure if I could miss that much of the term though – and I wouldn't want to gate-crash your honeymoon!'

'We thought you could just fly with us and still meet your

parents at the airport. And you'd be getting plenty of German practice. I'm sure they'd let you off a week or two of classes for that.'

'Maybe they would. I'll ask my tutor. It would mean you could meet my family too. Can I think about it, please?'

'No problem. We've decided we're going anyway. Unfortunately I'll have to book the flights soon, but...'

'Oh, why not? It would make it so much easier for me. I'm nervous enough about meeting everyone, never mind flying. I'm sure I can talk the tutor round. I'll talk to him, then Renate, and ring you tomorrow.'

CHAPTER 46

Just over two weeks later, we were almost organised. It's amazing how having little time concentrates the mind and gives you less time to worry or mull over decisions. Steve couldn't take any days off because of the extended honeymoon he was planning, but after the coup he'd pulled off with the recovery of Nick without granting Tommy Bradfield anything in return, resulting in the arrest of a bent Inspector to boot, he was given plenty of leeway and managed to get away at odd times of the day to be measured for a suit and other such essentials.

I did remind him frequently of the part I'd played in bringing about these wondrous results. If I hadn't gone looking for Claire's long-lost daughter, he would never have had Karl to question and things might have turned out very differently. Naturally he granted Matt time off to get his best man's suit too.

You might know, Mum was in a real panic because she'd not got her outfit yet. Dad asked me to take her shopping because he'd stood outside so many waiting rooms, he thought his legs wouldn't work anymore.

'Very funny, Dad. What are you wearing, then?'

'The suit I wore for our Laura and Bob's wedding. I don't know why your mother's making such a fuss about it.'

'He won't get another, our Rachel. The twins are eight now, so that suit's ten years old, if it's a day! He says it still fits him and it's hardly been worn. I don't know what to do with him.'

'It'll be fine, Mum. Don't worry. Steve and Matt are only hiring suits because they wear theirs to work quite a bit and they wanted something that didn't remind them of work, and Steve's dad won't be coming over from Australia.'

'Probably just as well. It wouldn't be nice for his mum to see him with his secretary.'

'Julie wouldn't care, Mum. She's happy on her own, and after ten years, I doubt if that woman's such a bit of eye candy on his arm.'

I'd spoken to the photographer Sarah recommended, Lesley Lomas, and was extremely lucky she could manage our afternoon wedding as well as the one she was booked for in the morning. She had been planning half a day off, because she had a day job as well, and it was quieter in the winter, but Steve said he'd make it worth her while, so that was sorted.

I'd chosen the flowers for next May, and they were spring varieties, so we had to choose new ones. Choosing was harder than the florist finding time to make up the bouquets and arrangements. Seems like late November's a good time for a last-minute wedding.

We'd also got most of the replies to our invitations. I'd used the computer to improvise the wording inside, and bought ready-made folding blue cards and envelopes. I think some of the invitations people have are so elaborate they end up a bit tacky, to be honest, but maybe that's just me justifying my pared-back design! We weren't having as many people as Lee and the evil ex-fiancée were, but the hall didn't mind, and as for the caterers, I think they were just glad it was still going ahead. They'd hardly have bought fresh food in yet, and anything frozen could be used for another wedding.

That left my dress. Which was coming along nicely. I was due for a final fitting at my auntie's that afternoon. There was just the gigantic hurdle of Mum's frock to get over. After going through the long list of places she had tried, I decided to take her to Beverley, where there's a very nice upmarket department store, and if that failed to come up with the goods, some other small exclusive dress shops. After trying on five dresses, Mum ended up with the first one she tried on.

'Are you sure this is the nicest, Rachel?'

'Totally, Mum. It was the first one you were drawn to, and

you'll look lovely.'

'And you're sure Steve's mum…'

'Julie', I prompted.

'You're sure she won't be in blue as well?'

'Definitely. Carly went with her mum last Friday and she picked something in green. The colours will complement each other too. They won't clash. Even better, it fits perfectly, so no last minute alterations.'

We went for a cup of tea to celebrate. All of a sudden Mum sat up and looked horrified. I thought she was about to choke, but I should have known better. 'Oh no, Rachel. I don't think I've got any shoes that'll go with it.'

'I'm sure you have, but we can go look in that shop where I bought my gorgeous red stilettos when I was tailing that woman in Beverley the other year.'

'You're not wearing them to the wedding, are you?'

'Course not. They won't go with my wedding dress, silly. But I might wear them in the evening, even if I have to kick them off when I've been dancing a while. I'm going to wear that luscious black velvet dress Steve bought me. Then later still, I've got a tiny green silk…'

'I don't think I want to know what you'll be wearing on your honeymoon night, Rachel. Some things are best left to the imagination, or not even thought about at all by a bride's mother.'

We got her some new shoes, me protesting the whole time that she'd never wear turquoise blue heels again, and who would notice what shoes she had, to which she replied that they'd be there on the photos for years to come and she didn't want people laughing at her. 'Speaking of which, do you know what your gran's wearing?'

'No, haven't a clue. I can make sure she's not in the same photos as you, or maybe just one, if you'd like?'

'It's not the photos I'm worried about. It's the whole day.'

'Gran's just Gran. She'll never change. People don't get offended. They find her amusing.'

'You see. I said they'd laugh at us.'

'Not us, Mum. They'll laugh at her - and we'll join in. It'll be fine.'

I dropped her off at home and carried on to Auntie Lesley's without her. She wanted to come but I was exhausted as it was. She was much more worried about this wedding than I was. I intended to enjoy it.

The dress was perfect. I loved it more every time I tried it on, particularly as it now fastened down the back. Auntie Lesley had used every one of the pearls from the bolero jacket, sewing them on the dress in appropriate places. I felt like a film star.

'What are you doing with your hair, Rachel?'

'Washing it and putting on a bit of conditioner to make it shiny.'

'That's all?! No veil? No headdress or fascinator? Not even putting it up?'

'Maybe some flowers. Anything else would look daft and not go with the dress - and I love my hair when it's just been washed. It's the rest of the time it looks unruly because it's so thick and curly.'

'Well it's up to you, I suppose.'

And that's what I liked. Just doing things that pleased me and Steve. Having the wedding at such short notice, but still with all the trimmings, was perfect.

The next few days just flew past. Various last minute hitches occurred, but because they happened so near to 'The Day', we either sorted them or plans got changed. Mum got herself in a right state, but I floated along in a haze. As long as we got married and got away, I told myself that was all that mattered.

We even signed the documents to buy the house on Garden Village, as the owners had found somewhere suitable to downsize to. Steve's flat had had a fair share of viewers. It was a good location, walking distance to the town centre in one direction and in the other, the new marina area with its trendy bars and nightclubs. No offers as yet, but that was probably a good thing as we didn't want the pressure of sorting out the paperwork until after we got back.

CHAPTER 47

Ten days later and there were just two days to go. I hated the very idea of a 'Hen Party' so I'd just invited my friends and close female relatives out for a meal. Well, I say 'out' but we were having it at Sarah's so we could relax. We'd ordered food from that party ordering service Sainsbury's have, so neither Sarah nor I had to cook.

It was a perfect evening. I'd invited Sarah (of course), Alice - (Matt's wife), Kate, Steve's mum, Julie, and his sister Carly, who had deserted the heady parties that York's archaeology students frequented, in order to stay in a B&B with her mum until the wedding was over. They were taking in the sights during the day, and they'd been to yet another place on our doorstep that I'd never heard of, let alone visited - St Peter & St Paul's church in Pickering.

They said the medieval wall paintings were not to be missed. Apparently the frescoes cover the entire surface of the nave walls. They date from the fourteenth century but they were whitewashed over in the Reformation, and not uncovered until a hundred years ago. It's on my list for a day trip when I can get Steve away from work.

Mum and Auntie Lesley were there as well of course, and thankfully Mum and Julie were getting on like a house on fire, even though they'd never actually met before. Then there were a couple of girls from the badminton class and some old friends from university who'd left Hull far behind, and whom I hadn't seen for years. We had a smashing time reminiscing. The food was really good, the wine flowed, and I wasn't getting married the following day so I knew we could let our hair down a bit and have time to recover.

Despite my protestations that they weren't getting in the way, Mum, Auntie Lesley and Julie headed off about half past eleven to 'leave the rest of us to it.' I was really enjoying myself.

At midnight there was a knock at the door. I hoped it wasn't the neighbours asking us to be quiet, because we weren't being that noisy (or the alcohol was masking it well). Or Steve? Could his very 'quiet' night at the pub with Matt, Chris and some mates from Hull Uni have developed a fatal flaw, like no-one turning up, or they wanted some female company? Steve hated the thought of a 'traditional' stag night too. He said he'd had to deal with the aftermath enough times as a constable and sergeant, it had totally put him off.

The one person I hadn't expected was Gran. 'Surprise!' It certainly was that, as I'd not invited her or even told her I was having a little do. I love her to bits, but she does have a way of taking over and ends up being the centre of attention. She was dressed in her usual flamboyant disco diva skimpy sequin-bedecked dress, with a feather boa and a face full of make-up. 'Thank God, Mum's gone home,' was my first thought. She presented me with a gift - a fluffy pink mask and fluffy pink handcuffs. I hadn't the heart to remind her Steve could use his own handcuffs, nor that I'd banned people from bringing presents to our get-together because they'd insisted on coughing up for wedding presents.

Speaking of which, we'd asked for people to club together and give Mum the money to buy us some retro Hornsea mugs or a vase for the new house, when she went to the December Collectors' meeting. Shame I wasn't going to be around to make it, particularly as I'd said I would, but I was going to go to the next one now I was a member.

I vaguely wondered how we'd get Gran to go home. I was just debating whether it would be too awful to pass the word to pretend we were packing up and then all turn a few corners and come back here when she was safely in a taxi, when there was another knock on the door.

'Surprise!'

'I think it's for you again, Rach', shouted Sarah.

On the front doorstep was a bloke dressed as a fireman, who proceeded to sing rather badly the well-known tune, 'da da da, da da da da,…' etc, whilst starting to remove his clothes. I swear I didn't know where to look.

'Gran! What on earth do you think you're doing, dragging this poor man out so late?'

'Don't you like it, Rach? I thought you'd appreciate a male stripper at your hen party. It all sounded a bit on the dull side to me when I rang your mam and wheedled it out of her.'

'A male stripper would be bad enough, Gran, but this poor man's your age!'

'He's not. He's eighty-three. I'm only seventy-six, as you well know.'

After that things went rapidly downhill for the next half hour until I could get the old bloke to understand he didn't actually need to take his clothes off, then pile up a plate with leftovers, and get them both in a taxi back to Gran's. Everyone else thought it'd been hilarious, but I was left wondering how I was going to prevent a repeat performance - not the stripper of course, but something equally zany - at our wedding. The party broke up not long after that but it didn't matter. We'd had a great time but I was exhausted.

Our wedding day was bitterly cold - but the sky was blue and the sun shone all day. It was magic. We drove out to the venue late morning and checked that the florist and caterers had done their stuff. We had a room in which to get ready, but I made Steve change first and go into the hall to greet people, before Sarah came to keep me company while I got dressed. The dress looked fantastic, though I say so myself, and when I entered the hall, Steve made my day by saying, 'You look beautiful. I wanted to wolf-whistle when I saw you walk in.'

The wedding was over in a flash. Gran wore the pinkest of pink suits with a matching hat. She was a dead ringer for a fondant fancy. I have to say, even at the reception she behaved impeccably (for her). Apart from forgetting her dentures, all went well.

The next morning we went back to the flat to pack and in the morning Kate came round with her case. Term had almost finished, and she'd finished all her essays and the like, so a couple of missed lectures wouldn't matter in her first year. Her tutor had given her his blessing to go and spend time with her new family for Christmas. He said being immersed in German for three or four weeks would more than make up for anything she missed.

There was only time for a quick cuppa and to see the photos she'd taken on her mobile before we had to get the train to Manchester Airport to catch the flight to Hamburg. That's when we noticed that Gran had grinned on every photo she was in, which meant her gaping gummy mouth was the only thing you noticed. Luckily, Mum didn't know yet.

Mum and Dad had wanted to drive us over to Manchester. I said it was too much of a trek for them. It's a shame there's no budget flights from Leeds – Bradford airport, but that's what you get for living in lovely Hull away from everything. By the fuss they made, you'd have thought we were going to be away for months. After our honeymoon night, I would have been very happy for it to have been true. I couldn't wait for us to be on our own.

Kate's family met us at Hamburg airport and all the introductions were made. We had time for a chat over a coffee before we went our separate ways but it was lovely to actually meet them. Renate wanted us to go back with them but when we said we were on our honeymoon, she smiled and instantly changed her mind, saying we must go and she'd see me another time. They were going by train from Hamburg's airport station to Eckernförde. I had a tear in my eye as I saw the whole family together - mum, dad, son and daughter - chattering away as if they'd never been apart.

We were finally alone, making our way to the exit to find the car hire place. I was so happy. Then it happened. We were going down this moving ramp - like an escalator but without steps, and I was holding the handle of my wheeled suitcase behind me, but it kept catching me up because it was so heavy and the handle was too flimsy for me to keep it at an arm's length. So I started walking but it was catching me up and bumping into my ankles so then I was running, trying not to trip and then I dropped the handle and ran down the ramp so fast I couldn't stop so I had to dodge people walking past the end and stop myself by running at the wall just opposite. Of course, when I turned round, Steve couldn't stop laughing. 'Only you…' he said, folding me in his arms for a hug. 'Are you hurt?'

'Only my pride and the bruises I'll get tomorrow on my ankles. There were all those people watching. It's so embarrassing!'

'Give over, Rach. Airports are so boring normally. They'll have loved it.'

I had to smile. Anyone else might have told me off or pretended he wasn't with me. I do love him.

The flight had arrived in the evening, so when we'd picked up the hire car, Steve drove us north to Lübeck, where we stayed overnight. After all the last-minute planning, it was great to relax. When we woke the next morning after our blissful first night on honeymoon, I didn't think I'd ever felt more loved.

We walked around the old town centre with its cobbled streets, towers and quaint shops, before heading east to Rostock. We spent the day browsing around the harbour and interesting craft shops before catching the ferry to Gedesby in Denmark. In the morning we drove the short distance to Copenhagen, where we stayed for five nights on the outskirts, mainly forsaking the car in favour of exploring the city by public transport, apart from a visit to Roskilde to see the Viking museum and cathedral with amazing tombs of all the Danish kings and queens.

Leaving Copenhagen we turned north-west and drove across the island to Sjaellands Odde and the ferry to Aarhus on Jutland, the Danish mainland. We had lunch there before setting out to drive further north up the coast. The roads were quiet, and although the countryside was mainly flat, the little towns and villages we went through were lovely. The sea sparkled under clear blue skies and the sand was white.

We meandered our way, staying at little B&Bs, impressed by people's friendliness. We stopped in Skagen at the northern tip of the country. On our last night before turning back towards Hamburg and the Christmas markets there was a green glow in the air when we left the restaurant. We walked out of the village to the sea and there, as if performing for us specially, the night sky danced with the Northern Lights.

On 5th June 1984, the Indian army began its attack on the complex at Amritsar which housed the two most sacred shrines of the Sikh community: the Golden Temple and the Akal Takht. Generals who had pledged to minimum force, and on no account to violate the shrines, were not prepared for the fierce and adept resistance they encountered. Having suffered severe casualties, the infantry were driven back, and as a last resort–with approval from Delhi–tanks were ordered in. The Akal Takht was virtually reduced to rubble. It is doubtful if Mrs Gandhi would have initiated Operation Blue Star had she known how bloody and devastating would be the consequences of that 24-hour conflict. Yet up to that point she had resisted any armed intervention in what had literally become a reign of terror in the Punjab. Perhaps, as many, including her son Rajiv, suggested, she waited too long before her attack on the fundamentalist Sikh preacher Sant Jarnail Singh Bhindranwale.

Mark Tully and Satish Jacob, who ran the BBC's bureau in Delhi, here trace the long build-up to the storming of the Sikh stronghold, the shifts of power within the Sikh community and the efforts of central government both to utilize and control them; the rise of Bhindranwale—initially put forward by then President of India Zail Singh and Mrs Gandhi's own son Sanjay—whose extremism placed a wedge between Sikh and Hindu, Sikh and Sikh and the Punjab and India; the indecisiveness of Mrs Gandhi, who paid for the catastrophic aftermath of the operation with her life.

In their vivid and well-documented account of historical and political events, Tully and Jacob bring the Sikh tragedy into focus from many arresting angles. They were the first to film the fortification of the Golden Temple. They met Bhindranwale, his military mastermind Major-General Shahbeg Singh and many of the other central characters in the drama. They gathered eye-witness accounts from every quarter to fill in this remarkable picture of what occurred and present their thought-provoking analysis with eloquence.

Mark Tully, who talked to Bhindranwale the day before the final curfew was clamped on Amritsar and was ordered out of the Punjab by the army on the day Operation Blue Star began, was presented with the 1984 Richard Dimbleby Award given by BAFTA for the Most Important Personal Contribution on Screen to Factual Television and the 1984 Award of the British Television Critics Guild for Outstanding Personal Contribution. In writing this book he and Satish Jacob have extended what began as brilliant news coverage into a work of great historical importance.

Born in Calcutta, educated in England, Mark Tully joined the BBC in 1964 and in 1972 became Chief of the Bureau in Delhi. Among the many major stories he has covered are the Bangladesh War, Mrs Gandhi's Emergency, the execution of Bhutto and the Russian Occupation of Afghanistan. He is now retired from BBC and stays in Delhi.

Satish Jacob was born in Delhi, began his journalistic career with the *Statesman*, worked in Ethiopia for eight years, and joined the BBC to work with Mark Tully in 1978. He recently retired as Deputy Bureau Chief of the BBC in Delhi after having worked for the Corporation for 26 years. During this eventful time, he and Mark Tully made the BBC's Bureau in Delhi a household name in India. Jacob broke the story of Mrs Gandhi's assassination to a stunned nation on 31st October 1984. However, Jacob considers his coverage of the US led war to topple Saddam Hussein to be the most moving assignment he has ever done. He was the only Indian correspondent stationed in Baghdad then. He is currently doing a TV series on the history of Old Delhi.